THE NICK OF TIME

BOOKS 6-10 IN THE CAPITOL CITY MURDERS SERIES

TROY LAMBERT

STUART GUSTAFSON

Published by
CCMbooks
P.O. Box 45091
Boise, ID 83711 USA
www.capitalcitymurders.com

First Printing March 2020

 Created with Vellum

HANGING IN HELENA

BOOK #6 IN THE CAPITAL CITY MURDERS SERIES

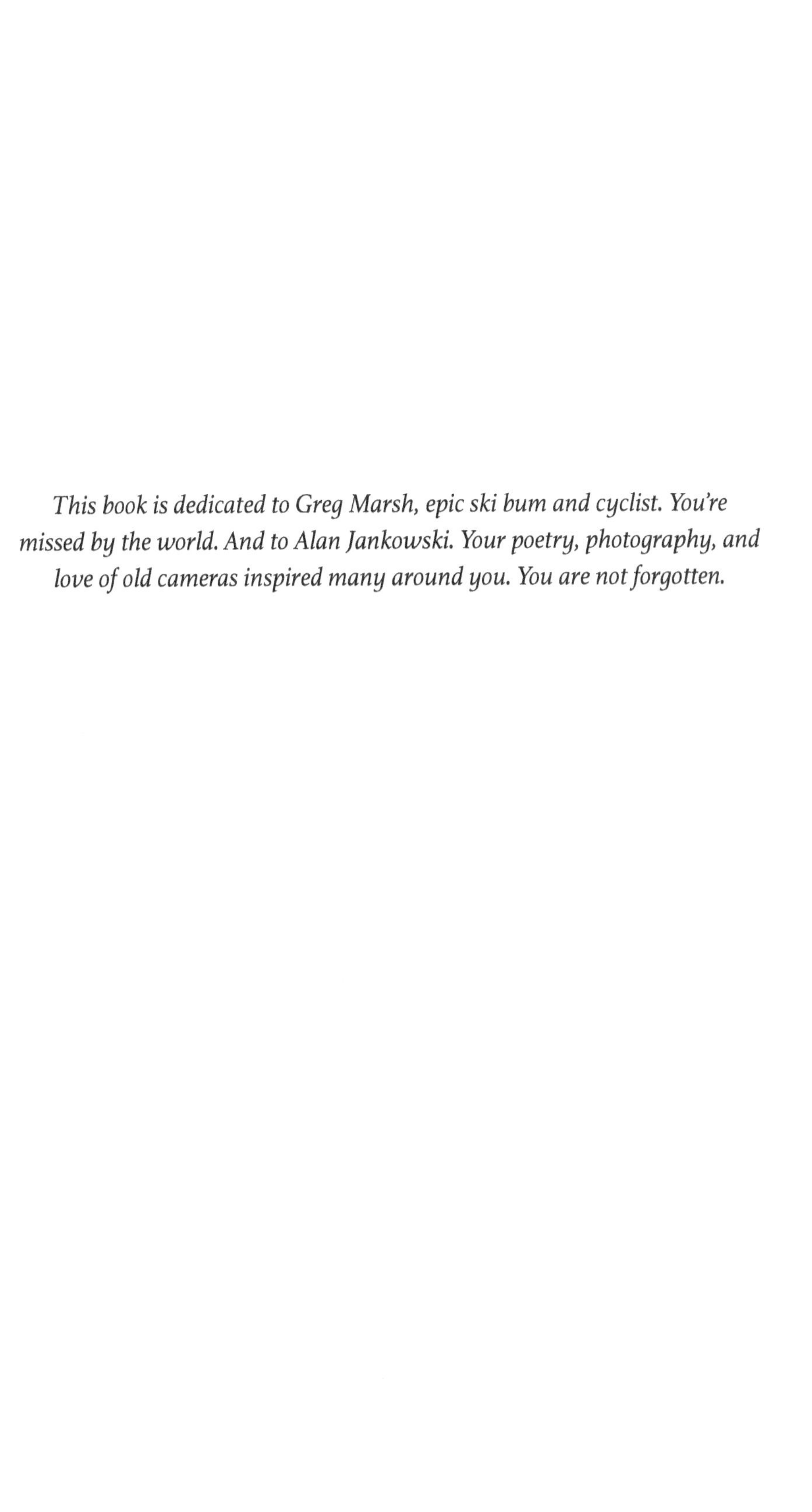

This book is dedicated to Greg Marsh, epic ski bum and cyclist. You're missed by the world. And to Alan Jankowski. Your poetry, photography, and love of old cameras inspired many around you. You are not forgotten.

PROLOGUE: HANGMAN

One cried 'God bless us!' and 'Amen' the other;
As they had seen me with these hangman's hands.
Listening their fear, I could not say 'Amen,'
When they did say 'God bless us!'

—Macbeth

He used the name Harry Hickman, although it was not his.

The hammer felt good in his rope-calloused hands. He performed the task the same way he always had, the way his father had, and his father before that.

Measure twice, cut once.

Create the joint on one end of the board, then the other.

The custom made stool stood below the strongest limb of a tall oak tree at the edge of a meadow. It was just the right height, and a nearly finished set of steps led up one side. The back of it had a handle, the right size of Harry's large hands.

This was not the Hanging Tree, the one of Helena legend. That one had been cut down long ago, and the legends about it were far from true.

Of course, there were other legends and facts around hangings in Helena, Montana, and they made Harry happy to be here. The true Hanging Tree in Helena had been cut down by Methodist ministers in 1875. Most of the time, using a tree limb to execute someone this way ended cruelly, with the victim suffering for long minutes before they died. There were legends of another hanging tree south of town, but he knew them for the lies they were. His great, great grandfather had overseen hangings at the Jefferson County Courthouse in Boulder, albeit for a brief time. Those hangings were legal, but such methods of execution were frowned upon now.

Harry didn't know why. The death he wrought was instant and merciful. An eye for an eye, a crime for a crime, but the Lord never intended for those who violated his laws to suffer on earth. Their suffering would come after death, at the hands of one much crueler than he.

He merely provided a service. Everyone knew the American justice system did not always work. When it failed, certain key people often hired him to make things right.

He balanced the stool carefully. He would burn it after this, for it was the worst of luck to carry around anything used in such work. Once, he'd reused a stool and it had broken under the weight of the criminal before Harry had been able to get the rope just right. He'd been forced to shoot that man to put him out of his misery, something he despised doing. Guns were for hunting, and hunting people was also cruel.

He fingered the sign, the sign that would hang around his charge's neck, written on white cardboard. It, too, would burn.

"MURDER"

A life for a life.

He finished setting the set of steps next to the tall and overly large stool. Grabbing a coil of rope, his swift and practiced hands laid it out on the surface in first a "C" shape and then that of an "S". Pinching it together, he began to wrap, then completed the knot and pulled it tight, studying the eight coils. Perfect. The rope slid through the knot, but not too easily, making the loop easy to adjust while not leaving it loose.

A practiced toss put it in place over the limb. Harry was just over six feet tall, his muscles hard, his aim true, and he had practiced this act dozens of times, not counting the number of times he had assisted his father.

Harry looked at his watch. Just in time. His arms ached, but in a good way, from the work of getting things ready. It had been worth it. The man's last view would at least be a beautiful one.

In the distance, he saw three men making their way up the rocky trail toward the cliffs.

Harry inhaled the scent of wildflowers and pine. He looked around at the soothing landscape, felt the brisk wind on his skin drying the sweat formed by his hard work. The sun was about to set, and no clouds were present in the big blue sky this state was famous for. Maybe when he was done, he could stick around Helena for a few days. It had been a while since he was here, in what had been his home for a brief time, and no one would recognize him anymore. Certainly no one would know who he was or what he did now.

"Jesus," the man in the middle exclaimed when he saw the noose hanging over the limb of the tree.

"I am not Jesus, nor can I absolve you of your sins," Harry answered. "What is your name?"

"I'm Albert. Albert Paulson."

"Welcome, all of you. He is the one?" he asked the man on the right.

The man he'd indicated nodded and grabbed Albert by the elbow. Harry could see the fear in all of their eyes, and that saddened him. He would not kill anyone not deserving of it, not unless he had to. He certainly would not hang them.

"His height is correct," he said. "He is a little heavier than you stated."

"Is that a problem?" The man on the left said. Harry recognized his voice.

"You are Lane, the one who called me. No, it will not be a problem. My calculations allow for a margin of error."

"A problem for what?" Albert asked. "What is that?"

"Do you have the charges?" Harry ignored him. His questions did not matter, not now. He wanted to finish before the sun set and before he had to climb down from this place in the dark, a flaming tree, rope, and man lighting up the sky behind him.

"I do," Lane said. He brought out a folded document, a copy of the form Harry had asked him to fill out.

Harry looked it over, then cleared his throat.

"Will you read them?"

The man on the right interrupted. "I will."

"Fine. Lane, if you would, bind his hands, please."

"O-o-okay," Lane stammered, and from the anxiousness in his voice, Harry was glad he would not be reading the charges. That might take forever.

Albert struggled. "What are you doing to me? What is this about?"

Once the prisoner was bound, Harry led him toward the stool and the tree.

"Wait a minute," Albert said. "Is this some kind of joke?"

"Not at all," Harry said. "I do not joke."

"You're going to—what did I do?"

"The charges," he stated flatly.

"You, Albert Paulson, are charged with the crime of murder. You did, on the night of August 12th of the year of our Lord 2016, beat one Carolyn Paulson, with your fists until she was dead. You did, through trickery and treasonous acts, escape the courts with a minor charge of manslaughter."

"I didn't do it. You got it wrong. I'm not your guy. I just plead so that—" Albert struggled, but Harry held him. He was used to men like this, men who did not want to face the things they had done.

"You, therefore, are sentenced to die on this day by hanging from the neck until you are dead—"

"No! No! I'm innocent!"

They all were, according to them. He'd studied the file before he took the job. Albert was guilty, and this had not been the first time he'd abused poor Carolyn.

Harry forced him up onto the short set of steps on the side of the stool. Men tried to resist, but he had done this many times before. He could make their feet move, make them follow his directions.

"…hanging from the neck until you are dead. May God rest your soul." The man finished. He looked up.

Albert thrashed, but Harry still managed to get first the sign and then the noose over his head and around his neck.

Grabbing the other end of the rope and used it to steady Albert on the broad surface of the stool.

"Stay still," he commanded. "This will go better if you do. Do you have any last words?"

"I'm sorry," he said. "I'm sorry for the things I did, but I didn't do this. Have mercy. Spare me, please."

They were the words of a guilty man, not truly sorry, just trying to prolong his miserable life.

"May God have mercy on your soul," Harry said. He reached up and in one swift motion pushed Albert off the stool and pulled it backwards out of the way.

The drop was perfect. The noose was perfect. He heard a loud snap just as Albert reached the end of his rope.

He twitched, but only twice, and then stilled, swaying in the breeze.

Harry made the sign of the cross, something that had lost any meaning for him years ago, but another thing that was part of The Way.

He then pushed the stool closer, directly beside Albert's swaying feet. He sprayed it down with gasoline, but it would not take much. The wood was dry and ready to burn. He was sure to spray some on Albert's feet and legs, something he loathed doing. Burning the bodies helped him not get caught, but just once he would have loved to show the world his great and merciful skill.

He hoped the grass around the gallows was wet enough that the fire would not spread far, but it shouldn't. Even if it did, small grass fires in this particular area usually burned out quickly by themselves, often barely singeing the trunks of the nearby trees.

He stepped back on to the trail, looking up to see Albert's body swaying in the wind at the end of the rope. His neck was at an odd angle, but one he had seen many times. He pulled a small camera from his pocket and discretely snapped a photo.

He heard retching and turned to see Lane's companion bent over double, puking into the grass.

"Who is he?" Harry asked.

"Carolyn's brother. He's from Colorado but wanted to come see this." Lane was also pale. Harry would bet neither of them had ever seen an execution, let alone a hanging. The sights, the smell, and the look of death could all get to a man if he let them.

"The remainder of my payment?"

"Here you go," Lane said, and tossed him a small bag. Harry glanced inside, seeing the few stacks of hundreds there.

"Thank you," he said. "For your business, and for righting this wrong."

"A-a-anytime," Lane said. "I better get him back to town."

"Good idea," Harry said. "I'll be right behind you."

"We'll be headed out of town right away. T-t-t-hanks for your service, Mr. H-h-h-hickman."

Hickman. It was as good a name as any. He used several. Just never his real one.

While George Maledon IV had a good ring to it, any student of history who glanced at his hands might guess what he did for a living.

A simple toss of a match set the blaze, and he headed back down the trail. The sunset had painted the sky orange in front of him, and the fire painted it yellow behind.

A day or two break, even a week, might be in order. All work and no play did, indeed, make George a dull boy.

1

FIRE IN THE HILLS

Smoke rose in the distance as Nick approached Helena, and if his calculations were correct, that smoke was not far from the capitol building and Main Street, what had once been Last Chance Gulch.

There was a park there somewhere, wasn't there? He couldn't remember. He'd done a little research, but the seven-and-a-half-hour drive had been exhausting. First, he'd been traveling through high dessert, then winding roads, and then I-15, a straight shot that, with mountains far off, told him all he needed to know about how Montana had gotten the name "Big Sky Country".

He knew wildfires were common in this area, but the smoke was black, at least at first. That meant treated wood, if his memory served him correctly.

As he got closer, he saw the smoke first turn to gray, gradually lessen, and then almost disappear. Silencing the music he'd been streaming from his phone to his car stereo, he switched the input to "FM". He hit the seek button and soon found a local news station.

"—still on the scene of a fire in Mt. Helena Park. The cause is as yet unknown, but the thought is that it was human caused, and there may have been some garbage or other wood involved. Firefighters are keeping the media back, but police officers have been seen hiking up one of the trails.

"We'll keep you posted as we have more details available."

Nick hit seek again after that. He'd been streaming music because he thought in Montana, he might find mostly country music, but there was a good mix of rock stations in there, too. He stopped on KZMT 101.1, a station playing some of his favorite classic rock. Glancing at his navigation app, he found he was only seven minutes from his hotel.

His stomach growled. He hoped they had a restaurant or something close. He didn't feel like searching for something to eat, but he needed substantial food to fuel his tall, athletic frame. Road food, including chips, soda, and even trail mix just didn't cut it, and although he had stopped briefly in Butte, the truck stop food just did not seem appetizing enough to justify the time it would take to eat at the sit-down restaurant there. He certainly hadn't wanted to roam too far from the freeway.

He took the exit for Prospect Avenue and found his hotel quickly. There were several in the area, along with several restaurants. When he got out of his car, he could smell the smoke in the air although he could no longer see the fire. The wind nearly slammed the door for him. He gathered his things from the trunk, and another gust shook the car.

He walked up to the front desk carrying his camera bag and rolling his suitcase behind him.

"Hi there," he said.

The clerk looked way up at him even though she was standing.

She must be just over five feet tall, Nick thought as their eyes met. He smiled in what he hoped was an engaging, not intimidating way.

"Can I help you?" She smiled too, and Nick was relieved that she seemed amused.

"I hope so," he said. "Nick O'Flannigan. I have a reservation."

"Oh, you're that photographer guy," she said, blushed, and looked down at her hands. "I follow you on Instagram, so I Googled you when I saw you were coming here. You've had some adventures."

"Here's hoping Helena is a little less adventurous," he said. "It would be nice just to take some photos and relax a little."

"I hope so for your sake," she said. "Sign here. I have you in a third-floor room. The view isn't much, but you can see the mountains if you look to the west."

"I'm sure it will be fine," he said. "Is it always this windy here?"

"Is it windy?" Nick saw a sparkle in her eyes as she said it. "Seriously, it is a lot of the time. You get used to it."

"I saw a fire on my way in. Good thing the wind didn't catch that."

"Yeah. It was in Mt. Helena Park. Luckily, the fire department got there pretty fast, even though the fire started away from the nearest road. Someone called in a tip."

"Really? Any news on how it started?"

"Not yet. But something is up. There were a bunch of police up there along with the fire department."

"Well, I'm glad they got it out, and I hope it's nothing too serious. Is there a good place to eat around here?"

"Other than the usual fast food? There's Bullman's, a pizza joint, but they close soon. You might try the Highway 55 Burgers. They're really good, and the Lewis and Clark Taproom is on the way back. They have a great huckleberry beer available right now."

"Sounds great."

"I'd show you around myself," she said. "But I have to work for a few more hours before the night shift comes on."

"Um, thanks," Nick said. *Was she really flirting with him?*

"Anytime," she said. She took a small card from a holder, flipped it over, and wrote something on the back. "I'm off tomorrow, but if you need anything when you are in town, a local guide or anything, my cell number is on the back."

"Appreciate it," Nick said, taking it. "I'll keep that in mind."

"Helen," she said.

"Nice to meet you," he said, shaking her hand. He headed to his room but could feel her eyes following him.

So much for no drama in Helena. He thought then of Sandra, the gal he'd been talking to and texting since Salem. They weren't really dating, since he was on a year-long assignment traveling the country, but they were...

What? he asked himself. *What are we doing, exactly?*

He'd have to sort out his feelings about it, while at the same time being careful.

He didn't want to hurt Helen's feelings, but he wanted to be careful not to lead her on either.

Nick sighed. Maybe he'd have a week without a mystery, if he was lucky. But it seemed like he'd still have to work through some personal drama. Traveling had been wonderful: Olympia, Salem, Sacramento, Carson City, Boise, and now here. But there were days even this close to the beginning of his trip when he longed for the simplicity of home.

2

BREAKFAST AND BIKES

When Nick headed downstairs the next morning, he found that Helen was not at the front desk. He was both happy and disappointed. It was always good to see a friendly face, even if hers seemed more friendly than he really wanted it to be.

The man behind the counter, rather, the teenager, was friendly enough when he asked about a good Sunday breakfast spot and immediately told him about Steve's Cafe.

"They have huge omelets there," he said. "Even though we have a great, free continental breakfast here." He offered a wink with the final sentence.

Nick had already peeked into their "breakfast room" and found that the offerings of cereal, bagels, and some commercial muffins along with fresh fruit would not be enough to fuel his tall and still relatively athletic frame for long.

"Thanks, man," he said, slinging his camera bag over his shoulder. "They sky seems clearer after the fire yesterday."

"For sure," the clerk replied. "That was something else, even for around here. We have fires all the time, but usually not that close to town, and certainly not set by people."

"So, it was arson?"

"They haven't said officially," the kid said. "But my old man works for the fire department. He says it's human-caused. There was some kind of accelerant."

"Wonder why someone did that?"

The kid shrugged. "Hard to say. Hope it wasn't some bored teens. But he said there was some wood, like something made of a pallet or something. And there's another thing." He motioned for Nick to lean closer.

"What's that?" Nick asked.

"They found a body. The police haven't said a thing yet, but they will, later today."

"Wow," Nick said. Inside, he thought, *Great, another mystery. And the same week I am in town.*

"This is just between us, right?"

"Absolutely," Nick said, making the sign of zipping his lips, locking them, and tossing the key over his shoulder.

He left and headed straight to Steve's. Parking was easy, and hot, strong coffee was served in a ceramic mug with "Steve's Style" on the side.

When looking through the local Sunday paper, Nick saw an ad for bike rentals.

As much as his leg hurt him from walking, let alone running, he'd considered bike riding as an alternative form of exercise and transportation before. Here, it seemed like it might make sense, and with gravel and paved roads nearby, paved trails, and some single-track mountain biking, this week might be a good time to give it a try.

Maybe even in Mt. Helena State Park.

He didn't want to be a part of the mystery here or investigate it in any way, but it wouldn't hurt to see things for himself.

Of course, riding on trails when he had not ridden in quite a few years would be tricky at best. Today was, technically, still his day off. He might just ride around town, take some photos for his website and blog, and get used to being on two wheels.

He could also see how his leg fared with a different kind of exercise. Sure, he would be using new, different muscles than walking, so he was bound to be sore, but there was a difference between sore and the kind of chronic pain he often felt from the broken leg he'd suffered playing college ball.

He could still picture the night of the injury, driving hard, going up for the dunk, and switching to his left hand to lay the ball in instead.

He felt the other player's shoulder as he struck it with his hip, his momentum carrying him up and over, flipping him on to the stadium seats behind the basket. His leg struck first, he heard it snap, and then he landed awkwardly, his lower body out of bounds, his head and shoulders on the court.

Six weeks and one surgery later, he knew his college basketball days were over. His planned path, from Boston College to the NBA had been derailed by a single injury, and a foul to boot.

Ever since, there were times when the weather, walking too much, elevation changes, or nearly anything else would aggravate the pain in his leg, reminding him of the athlete he once was, and how his initial idea of being an accountant had turned into making a career of his photography.

As a freelancer, he'd done a lot of things in a few short years, and the culmination was this year long assignment to photograph every single state capital for *Travel USA* magazine and a book they were creating.

Six cities in, he missed home sometimes, but he had to admit he was really enjoying himself.

He headed to Big Sky Cycling and Fitness, a local bike shop that also had rentals, determined to get fitted and do some simple riding today while he had the chance. Who knew? Maybe it would turn into something he really loved to do.

The sign on the front door said 'Closed', but he tried the knob and it opened. As he approached the counter, a shorter man with white hair, wearing a baseball cap backwards looked up from tightening something Nick did not recognize on a bike tire.

"We're actually closed," he said.

"Sorry, but the door was open," Nick said. "I'll come back."

"Hang on. Since you are here, can I help you?" he asked. He wore a gray shirt with a name tag that read "Greg."

"Sure hope so," Nick said. "I would love to rent a bike, ride around town, and see if I like it."

"Has it been awhile since you rode?"

"Yeah, I suppose it has. Pretty much since high school."

"Were you shorter then?"

Nick thought back. He actually was shorter back then, since he'd really stopped riding his sophomore year, when he'd gotten his first car, started playing ball all the time, and just before his final growth spurt, the one that put him at an even six and a half feet tall.

"Now that you mention it, I was. Why do you ask?"

"Well, I'm not sure we have a rental your size. What are you, about six-five?"

"Close. Six-six."

"You look familiar. Do I know you?"

"Not that I know of," Nick said, but he had a sinking feeling. His crime solving fame had boosted all of his social media, and once you see a six-foot-six red head, it's hard to pretend you don't recognize him, even you just follow him online.

Much like Helen, Greg probably did not know him, but certainly knew of him.

"You are that photographer guy. The one traveling around the country. I follow you on Instagram."

"Well, nice to meet you," Nick said.

"You, too. It really is an honor." Greg stuck out his hand, and Nick shook it.

"You'll probably want a sixty-one to sixty-three-centimeter frame, a double-x. Usually those are special order. I think the biggest we have is a fifty-nine. It would work, but the geometry won't be quite right."

"I'm sure it will work for me, at least to try things out. I'm not a pro or anything."

"Let me go see what we've got."

He disappeared into the back of the shop and Nick decided to look around. There were so many types of bikes, not something he had counted on. His last one had been a Specialized, but a lower end model he was certain, with eighteen speeds and a simple shifter system.

He saw mountain bikes, something called cyclocross, and road bikes, most of which looked much too small for him. Finally, Greg emerged.

"We do have one sixty-two in our rental fleet. It's a pretty simple mountain bike. You can ride it around town no problem and even take it into the hills a little bit if you like. Do you need a helmet, too?"

"Sure do. How much for the day?"

"Well, this one is usually forty dollars a day, but since we're closed, I'll give it to you for twenty. You can even return it tomorrow when we open."

"Thanks."

"You gonna ride up and check out the scene of the fire? Maybe you will see something the police and fire department don't. You could break open another case."

"God, I hope not," Nick said, smiling.

He didn't like this at all. There were some definite minuses to fame, and this was only one.

Greg was very patient. He found a bike rack Nick could borrow, along with a lock. Once he got a rental helmet, and had the bike fitted to him, Nick headed out the door.

"Thanks a bunch, Greg. I appreciate it."

"Yeah! Good luck. See you tomorrow."

Nick waved.

"Let me know what you find," Greg said with a wink.

Nick waved again and decided to take a quick ride and leave his car parked where he was.

He set off at a slow and wobbling pace.

3

NEW FRIENDS

R iding a bike was like, well, riding a bike. After a couple of hours, he was ready to grab a quick lunch.

There were others riding bikes around town too, and Nick waved when they did. Many stared at him.

A six-foot-six redhead, dressed more for a day of walking, wearing sneakers, jeans, and a turquoise polo, on a rather large bike had to be a rare sight in this town. Add a neon-green helmet that did little to hide his hair color, and he imagined what they must be thinking.

The streets were not crowded, and there was little traffic. He found himself grateful for a quiet Sunday morning.

However, while riding he felt rather carefree. The breeze cooled him off, keeping him from sweating too much even though it was warm here, and the sun seemed more intense than in Boise, despite the fact that the elevation was only around 3,800 feet.

He decided to stop for lunch and rolled up to a bike rack in front of what looked to be a friendly place called the Windbag Saloon. He checked his watch, seeing it was right around noon. Fantastic timing.

After locking his bike, he took his helmet off and walked inside. The decor was simple. Wood floors, simple tables, and an nice bar with several taps behind it greeted him.

"Just you today?" an employee approached and asked.

"Yes, Elna," he said, reading her name tag.

"Well, you may want to sit at the bar. It's fixin' to get busy in here."

Elna was both pretty and tall, with light blond hair that was almost white, large brown eyes, and while she was not thin, she wasn't overweight either.

"I'll do that," he said. "Why will it get busy soon?"

"Church will let out," she said. "You're not from around here?"

Her words were both a statement and an question. "Nope," he said. "I'm a freelance photographer, just here for a week. I'm on an assignment traveling around the country."

"What brings you to Helena?"

"The capitol building."

"How exciting! Well, I'm happy to meet ya'. Have a seat anywhere at the bar, and I'll be right with you."

Nick made his way to the bar, hung his camera bag on a hook under it, which was probably designed for purses, and looked over the tap list, selecting a what appeared to be a pretty good porter. He ordered the beer, and then saw a shadow to his right.

A large man, nearly as tall as Nick and much wider, squeezed onto a stool just one over from him. His hair was dark but graying at the temples. Muscular and well-built, his forearms were huge. His large hands looked rough.

His steel-gray eyes met Nick's. "Harry," he said. "What are you drinking?"

"Porter. It's pretty good if that's what you're into. I'm Nick."

"Pleased to meet you, Nick." They shook hands, and Nick felt the calluses on the man's palm. Maybe he was a local rancher.

"What food is good here?" Harry asked.

"I'm not sure actually. I just ordered a burger. I'm passing through."

"Me, too. I'm here on...business."

Nick smiled. "Me, too. I'm a freelance photographer. What do you do?"

"Consulting of sorts," Harry said. "I'm pretty much done with my work but decided to stick around. I grew up nearby. Figured I could take a break for a few days and do some touristy things."

"Here's your burger, hun," Elna interrupted. "Can I get you anything else? Ketchup? Fry sauce?"

"Fry sauce, please," Nick said. "Thanks."

"And for you? Did you have a chance to decide?" she turned to Harry.

"I'll have iced tea to drink for now. I'll take a burger like his," he gestured to Nick's plate. "But with no onion, and onion rings instead of fries."

Nick laughed to himself. That was an unusual order. But to each his own.

He dug in, and a few minutes later, when his food arrived, Harry did too. Nick finished, feeling pretty stuffed and a little bloated for afternoon riding.

"See you around," he said as he paid his bill and grabbed his camera.

"Yep," Harry said. "You, too."

Every table and booth in the restaurant were full, and Elna looked overworked, even though another waitress named Monica had joined her.

Once he was back on the bike, Nick pedaled back towards his car. What he was really in the mood for now was a nap. All the exercise and fresh air, along with the beer and burger, made him perfectly willing to spend the rest of his Sunday relaxing.

When he got back to the hotel, he found they had a bike locker room, and he put his bike inside. Once it was secure, he came out to see Helen was at the front desk. He waved but headed upstairs without talking to her. Maybe he'd see her later, but right now he was too sleepy to trust his reactions.

When he got to the room, his phone rang. It was Sandra.

"Hey, Nick, how is it going?"

"Good," he said. "I rented a bike and rode around a bit. My leg feels pretty good actually, although I'm sure I'll be sore tomorrow."

"Been a while since you pedaled around?"

He laughed. "Yeah, high school. They had a bit of trouble finding a bike that would fit me."

"I bet. The drawbacks of being tall."

"True," he said. "How are you?"

"Nothing new to report. Just working and doing the usual stuff."

"At least, there is no drama, huh?"

"Yeah. I miss you, Nick."

"I know," he said. "I miss you, too. It's going to be a long ten and a half months."

"Yeah," she said flatly. "That's a long time."

"It is," he said. "Are you okay?"

"Sure," she said. "I'm fine. What's on your agenda this afternoon?"

"A nap. Some TV. I took some photos this morning. Maybe I will post them tonight. Tomorrow is another day. I'll get some early shots of the capitol building and go from there."

"Sounds nice," she said.

"What are you doing this afternoon?" he asked.

"I may go to a movie or something. I'm not sure," she said.

"Well, have fun. I'll talk to you later?"

"Count on it," she said, and hung up.

Nick flopped back on the bed and turned on the TV. Soon the droning of the sports announcers lulled him, and his eyes closed.

This bed is really comfortable, he thought to himself. *I feel like I could sleep for hours.*

When he woke, it was dusk, and he found himself really hungry.

4

———

HANGING OUT

The night before had ended with ordering a pizza, a large coke, and some kind of cinnamon sticks with a delicious frosting dip.

Nick had stayed up late editing and uploading photos, and just trolling social media. His nap had left him too rested, so he could not fall asleep until nearly midnight.

His alarm woke him at 6:45 a.m. and he headed for the capitol building. It was time to get some early morning shots with the rising sun. He remembered Emily's admonition. *"Get into that creative mind we hired you for."*

His style mattered, but he wanted different photos of every single place he visited. With the nearby mountains and a zoom lens, he thought Helena was an opportunity for just that.

As he got up, he groaned and stretched. His leg didn't hurt in a bad way, but he'd definitely found some new muscle groups the day before. He decided that the bike would be his primary means of transportation, at least to start the day. He'd stop by and let Greg know how things were going.

His need for speed dictated that after his shower, he dressed in hiking pants and more Montana-appropriate hiking footwear since he didn't really have "cycling gear." He grabbed a bagel from the free breakfast, slathered it with cream cheese, and grabbed a packaged Danish for the road.

As he headed out, he glimpsed Helen down the hall. She seemed occupied talking to another member of the staff, and so he just kept going, wondering why she was still here. *Maybe she left and came back,* he thought.

He grabbed his bike and helmet from the locker, adjusted the strap on his camera bag, and headed to the capitol grounds.

The light was perfect for photos, at least, on one side of the capitol building. The other was in shadow, and Nick determined that he would need midday shots, evening shots, and even some night shots to really make his visit complete. He wanted to wow his editor in every city he visited, and this being number six, he was starting to get a real handle on what she wanted.

This was it, his dream job. The other stuff he did was fine, but this was the thing that mattered more than anything else at the moment. His social media, his macro photography website, and even his freelance photography clients back in Seattle where this all started took a back seat to this.

He had to remember that and keep it in his mind. No matter what mystery came along, what romance, or what other photo opportunities grabbed his attention, this book, this gig was his shot at the big time. Having an entire book of his photos put out by *Travel USA* magazine? What photographer could ask for anything more?

He switched lenses and snapped a series of photos, moving around the capitol building clockwise so he did not miss anything. The dome was extremely prominent. Nick remembered reading that the original design had a smaller dome, more in the Greek style, but the commission in charge asked that the dome be more imposing when the building was already under construction, so the architect agreed and enlarged it.

On top of the dome, Montana's own version of Lady Liberty reached for the sky. Surrounded by an expansive lawn and flower beds, the grounds impressed him, too. Nick snapped a couple of shots of the word "Montana" spelled out in flowers. He also took a photo of a rider on a horse, Thomas Francis Meagher, a statue in front of the capitol, originally created in 1905.

He actually couldn't wait to get inside, where some of the greatest western art was on display, including the Charles M. Russell painting *Lewis and Clark Meet the Flathead Indians at Ross' Hole*. He'd seen pictures when researching for this trip and couldn't wait to see the twenty five-foot-long, twelve-foot-high painting in person.

But as he rounded the last corner, his stomach growled. Nick needed to grab an early lunch before he kept working.

Not wanting to load up his bike again or walk far, he searched the area for lunch spots and saw that Benny's Bistro, a French restaurant, had just opened up, so he headed that direction.

The interior was stylish, if a bit dark after coming from the bright sunlight outside. After looking over the menu, he ordered the Montana Rancher panini and an iced tea. He drank his water first though, knowing the afternoon would be warm and he needed to be hydrated.

As he waited, Nick pulled out his camera and started to go through the pictures he'd taken that morning, deleting the worst of them and any duplicates, and got pretty absorbed. It took him a minute to notice there was a large man standing next to his table.

He looked up to see a smiling Harry.

"Funny to run into you here," Harry said. "Although it used to be a small town, this place has really grown."

"Great minds think alike, I guess," Nick said.

"I suppose you're right. Nice camera, by the way."

"It is," Nick said. "It's the latest thing, really, except for what is new this year. I couldn't be happier with it."

"Good, good. I've always been interested in photography but have only used little point and shoot cameras."

"Those can do a good job with some things," Nick said. "Don't be discouraged."

"I suppose," Harry said. He pulled a little Nikon from his pocket. "This is what I am using at the moment."

"That's cool," Nick said. "May I see it?"

"Sure." Harry handed it over, and Nick pushed the button that turned it on, and looked at the screen. He pushed the menu button and made a few adjustments. He then snapped a photo of the salt and pepper shakers in the center of the table.

"Take a look at that one," he said, actually proud of himself.

"That's good," Harry said. "How did you do that?"

"You have many adjustments on that camera that are on more complicated models. You just have to dig for them. I can show you sometime if you like."

"That would be great. Mind if I join you?"

"Not at all," Nick said, gesturing to the empty chair across from him. Just then Nick's panini arrived.

"Can I get you anything, sir?" The waitress asked Harry.

"I'll have what he is having, but no iced tea. Just water."

"You bet," she said. "I'll have that right out."

Harry smiled as she walked away. "So, what are you up to today?" he asked.

"Capitol building photos," Nick said between bites. "Just the ones that are good in morning light. The rest will have to wait. I may get some evening ones tonight or tomorrow, and I will need some midday and night shots, too. As well as the inside, which I may explore a little this afternoon."

"So, it is true," Harry said, pulling a piece of twine from his pocket. As Nick ate, he tied knot after knot, undoing each one and creating another. Every one of them looked different.

"What is true?" Nick asked.

"A photographer takes dozens of photos to get one good one."

"Usually, that is true unless you get really lucky," Nick said. "Even then, it's probably the experience of taking all of those photos rather than just blind luck."

"I get that," Harry said, and put away the twine as his food arrived.

"So, how did you learn that?" Nick gestured.

"Learn what?"

"To tie all of those knots."

"I sailed for a while, but mostly, my dad taught me. It's in the genes, I guess."

"Have you heard anything more about the fire?" Nick said. "I heard there was a body found."

"Oh?" Harry's interest showed on his face, and Nick continued despite his promise not to share what the hotel clerk had told him. After all, the announcement was supposed to come the night before even though Nick had not yet heard anything.

"My hotel clerk said they thought it might be a murder scene."

"A killing scene, you mean."

"A killing scene, murder scene. What's the difference?"

"Not all killings are murder," Harry said. As he did, he looked down at his hands then pushed his plate away, his sandwich only half gone.

"I suppose that's true. But one caused by a fire that was set certainly seems to be," Nick answered.

"You're probably right."

"You going to finish that?" Nick pointed at the sandwich.

"Nah, I will take it to go," Harry said, turning around and signaling for the check.

"You guys together or separate?" the waitress asked.

"Together, I got this," Harry said before Nick could speak up.

"Thanks. I owe you," Nick said.

"Sure," Harry said. "I'd love to learn more about photography, and have you show me some of those tricks on my camera."

"Anytime," Nick said. He fished a card out of his pocket. "Text or call. I will get back to you if I don't answer. Nice to see you again."

"You, too," Harry said as Nick walked outside and back towards the capitol.

Again, he was full and needed to burn off some calories by taking some photos inside. As he walked, he called the bike shop and told Greg he would keep the bike rental for the week and authorized him to charge his credit card.

5

THE RIDE STUFF

Nick went inside. His legs were sore from riding, and his right leg was giving him a little of the usual trouble from his long healed, but ever present, injury.

That's the one thing, he told himself. *On this trip, I'm not getting enough variety in my exercise routine. Hotel gyms only offer so much.*

Maybe riding a bike was a partial answer, or more stretching like some yoga or something. He might consider finding local studios and gyms and buying week-long passes. Maybe he could even write about it on his website and blog, take some photos. Just a way to drive more traffic and make a little more money. He knew that money would be important when this project was over, even though that was still quite a while from now.

When he entered the front doors, he was immediately impressed by the shiny floors and the view of the dome high above. A railing ran around the central area overlooking the floor below, and he could not wait to get up there and take some photos. Instead, he started with the obligatory shot upward into the dome itself. The crouch needed to frame the shot properly reminded him of how sore his thighs were.

He wandered the inside of the building, taking photos where he could of the various art pieces and the amazing decor. Nick moved around the upper levels, taking a photo of the bell on the second floor, and a shot down the length of the upper level looking toward the well-known Women Build Montana. He also looked forward to visiting the Women's Mural a short distance away from the capitol building.

As he looked down, he thought he saw the now familiar figure of his new friend, Harry, but he couldn't be sure, and it felt wrong to call out in the echoing chamber.

The capitol was quiet on this weekday, much quieter than the one in Sacramento had been with all the children on field trips there. While Helena had grown over the last decade or so, it was still an isolated town nestled up against the eastern side of the Rocky Mountains.

There were few surrounding towns, unlike Sacramento and even Olympia, where the state capitals were centrally located in large population areas. This part of the west was different, quieter, more down to earth. Nick liked that in some ways but having grown up in Boston and lived in Seattle for so long, he missed the bustle of the city, the energy of the crowds, and the constant activity despite all the problems that often came with it.

After a couple of hours, and several unique shots, Nick headed outside, deciding to grab a drink before heading back to his hotel. For him, it was early for dinner and he was still satisfied from his late lunch, but he needed a little pick-me-up before he started editing photos and uploading them.

He got back on his bike and rode to a Starbucks he'd spotted near his hotel. He ordered a small cold brew on nitro and headed for his room and his laptop.

As he left the coffee shop and climbed on his bike, Nick balanced his coffee delicately in one hand and marveled at how quickly he'd picked up riding again. He glimpsed someone walking in the door on the other side of the building, someone who looked a lot like Harry.

Is he following me? Nick wondered. But why would his new acquaintance do that?

Harry did say he was doing the tourist thing, and they were

staying in the same area. It was possible that running into each other was a coincidence.

He probably thinks I'm stalking him, Nick thought, laughing at himself inside.

He managed to make it to his hotel without spilling any of the precious beverage and walked his bike inside to the locker room. After putting it away, he came out to find Helen at the front desk.

"Nick!" she said, waving him over.

He didn't want to go. He felt sweaty and like he might stink a little after the day's ride and exertion. At this point, though, she could not be avoided.

"Hi," he said, walking over. "Sorry for my appearance. I've been biking all day."

"No problem," she said. "You didn't strike me as the biking type."

"I'm not. Or I wasn't. Maybe I am becoming that type. I need more exercise."

"You look fine to me," she said, looking him up and down.

"Thanks," he said, blushing.

"Speaking of exercise, a group of us are hiking in Mt. Helena Park tomorrow morning. You want to come?"

With his bum leg, hiking was not usually his thing, but he did need more exercise, and maybe he could get some shots from there of the town and even the capitol building, although he was not sure it would be visible.

Besides, that was the park where the fire had taken place, the fire and the apparent murder.

I'll go. Just look around. If I get tired, I can always come back down, Nick told himself.

"Sure," he told her out loud. "What time?"

"Eight-thirty."

A bit early, but okay. "I'll meet you there," he told her.

"Great, it's a date!"

A date? Nick, what are you doing?

"Tomorrow then," he said.

He thought of Sandra and how odd she had been the last time

they talked. He had no idea what he was actually happening between them. Was he really going on a date with another woman? He didn't think of it as one, but apparently, she did.

He made his way to his room and opened his laptop. Pretty quickly, he was immersed in his work, and when he reached for this cold brew an hour later, he found that it was empty. He must have drunk it all without really thinking about it.

He stood and stretched, got some water and got back to work. After editing his photos from the day, which he thought were pretty good, he opened his social media sites and his website, adding those photos that did not make it into the file for his publisher, and then posing a question for fun.

"Started riding a bike this trip and am enjoying it. Any advice for a tall guy looking for a good bike?"

He closed the app, and realized he was hungry. Instead of going out, he opened a delivery app and ordered food from one of the local restaurants that way.

He then flipped on the TV and settled in on his bed to wait for his dinner.

The local news started with a story of the predictions for the coming winter, the reporter stating it was supposed to be a rough one, and residents should be prepared for more snow than average.

The next story was about the murder in Mt. Helena State Park. "Local officials still have no solid leads. It could be a few weeks before any autopsy is conclusive, but sources say the cause of death was hanging, and the fire was secondary. We can all be grateful that the fire didn't spread further."

"That was the real danger," a uniformed park ranger said on the screen.

"When asked if this was the work of some kind of serial killer, the police said that is highly unlikely," the reporter said.

"Residents of Helena should not be worried. The killing appears to be targeted at the individual who was killed," an officer with the name "Sheriff's Deputy Nelson" underneath said.

A voice in the background asked, "How do you know that for sure?"

"We can't comment further on an ongoing investigation," he said.

The story ended, and as the sports segment started, Nick heard a knock on the door. He collected his food, tipped the delivery gal, and started eating. He changed the channel to an old movie, one he'd seen before, but didn't mind watching again.

A couple of hours later, food containers gathered and thrown away, he slipped into bed and fell asleep to the droning of the television as background noise.

He never heard the text message alert on his phone.

6

HIKING AND HELEN

The text had been a "Good night" from Sandra, and he'd simply responded with "Good morning," which hadn't gotten him an answer at all. For some reason, the two of them just weren't connecting at the moment, and it bothered him. But he had an appointment to keep.

Not a date, an appointment, he told himself.

"Good morning, Nick!"

Helen greeted him with a great deal of enthusiasm as he locked his bike at the rack near the entrance to the trail. It was funny, but he hadn't even moved his car in the last few days and hadn't missed driving it at all.

He wondered if Greg would sell him this bike, since he was growing to like it.

Then I'd have to lock it up everywhere, and have a bike rack on the car, he thought. *I'll have to consider the long-term issues with carting a bike around for the next ten months.*

Helen broke into his thoughts with a quick side-hug. She left her arm hanging around him though.

"Good morning," he said. He slipped his camera bag over his shoulder but took the camera out and hung it around his neck.

"Everyone, this is Nick. He's a photographer on assignment here."

He waved to the group consisting of six women all close to his age, in their late twenties or early thirties, and only one other guy. He wore thick glasses, a floppy hiking hat, and long, black socks with his hiking boots. An old film camera, probably an Elektra from the look of things, hung around his neck. He looked down at his shoes and mumbled a name Nick did not catch as everyone introduced themselves.

The women all looked to be in good shape, and Nick worried a little bit about keeping up, but he felt good after the last few days. His thighs were a bit sore, but his leg actually felt more flexible, and he'd experienced less pain.

He hadn't felt this good in a long time. He had taken some ibuprofen before leaving the hotel room, just to pre-game a little bit.

"Carol, you lead the way," Helen gestured to a woman who looked to be a little older than the others. "Nick and I will bring up the rear."

They seemed to have a plan for the group hike, and they took off slowly, climbing gently at first. Nick snapped photos of the group hiking ahead and the network of trails. As they climbed higher, the views got even better.

"So, you are just here for a week?" Helen asked.

"Yep. I get a week in each capital city around the country," he said. "That makes this a year-long assignment, pretty much. I'm trying to stay on schedule as closely as possible."

"You've had some adventures so far, according to Google, your Instagram, and website."

"I have. More than my publisher would like me to have. More than I would like. I'd prefer things to be a bit tamer. I am trying to mind my own business, but..."

"Trouble seems to follow you?" Helen said, looking up at him.

"Seems so," he said.

"Who's Sandra?" she asked.

"A friend I met in Salem. She came down to help me in Sacramento when my camera was stolen," he said. "Luckily, I got it back."

"A friend?" she asked quietly.

"Yeah," he said. He remembered his and Sandra's first kiss and the time they had spent together. He wanted to see her again. He liked her. But they had left their relationship at just that. Friends. Even though they'd talked a lot, texted often, called even. She'd seemed a little odd the last couple of weeks, but he was sure they could work things out.

He didn't want to explain that to Helen. Or Gerry, his friend in Seattle who had gotten him this gig in the first place. Or anyone, really. Gerry was rooting for a relationship, but a year apart from someone you'd only really spent a week with? That was bit much to expect of anyone.

He stopped to take a couple of photos, and then looked up the trail. Helen was standing there, staring back down at him.

The light was perfect, and she was smiling. Her brownish-blond hair blew in the breeze, fanning out around her head. He wondered why she hadn't put it up, like many of the other girls had.

Because she was up the trail a little way, they were nearly at eye level. He snapped a couple of shots of her, made a couple of adjustments, and snapped two more. She stood there, letting him do it.

She was confident. Happy. Comfortable. Nick wondered who she really was. A part of him wanted to find out.

Another part knew there were complications to that. The Sandra situation, whatever that might be. There were over ten months left on his current assignment, and that he had no plans, ever, to come back to Helena. At least, not that he knew of.

He let the camera fall to its place around his neck and took a step forward.

"We best catch up with the others," she said quietly, and held out her hand. Nick took it and they walked in silence for a few minutes. Then he let it go under the pretense of taking more photos.

It wasn't much of a pretense. The nature and the views here were amazing. He switched to a macro-lens and started to take close up photos of flowers and plants along the trail, kneeling from time to time.

Helen asked him questions about his trips and his home. He

answered. He asked her about certain plants and flowers, and she seemed to have extensive knowledge of them only a local could.

They crested a hill, his leg aching more than it had been, and he saw something yellow in the distance, blowing in the wind.

"Is that the—"

"Yes, I think so," Helen said. "That's probably where the fire happened."

"Can we go have a look?"

She glanced ahead and saw that Carol was leading the group down a slight incline. She waved and the leader looked at her.

"We're going to go check something out," she shouted. "We'll catch up."

Carol waved and smiled, flashing the okay sign with her fingers.

Nick followed Helen up the hill, snapping only a few photos, and then switching lenses. He wanted to take some wider shots first, and then he might take some closer ones.

He could smell burnt grass and wood as they got closer, the unique smell of a wildfire that seemed pretty universal. Fires did happen in Washington, but mostly on the eastern side of the state. Seattle and the surrounding areas were far too wet, and such fires were not common in Massachusetts, but he'd smelled them elsewhere in his travels.

A wide perimeter around the center of the fire was protected by yellow crime scene tape. Some of it had blown down and some pieces had been broken by the wind. He snapped photo after photo, knowing he would be able to look at them and the scene in more detail once he had them on his computer.

He quickly unslung his camera bag and switched to his long lens, zooming in on the pile of wood. It looked like some kind of a small platform, like a stool of some sort, with some charred steps to one side.

The autopsy might not be officially back yet, and Nick new from his recent experience that the police would not say one way or another until they determined the cause of death for sure. But they had mentioned hanging, and that certainly looked likely.

Asphyxiation to be exact, something he'd learned more about in Sacramento. There hadn't been a lot of details on hanging in the short amount of research he'd done, but he did remember from reading Westerns as a kid that the best hangmen measured the drop and the weight of the subject, making sure their neck broke right away. It made the process faster and much less cruel.

He wondered a bit about the history of Helena. He'd read things about something called the Hanging Tree, but that one seemed to have been debunked. He'd have to look more later. Maybe someone at the museum knew the story. Hell, maybe Helen did.

As he concentrated on the scene and took more photos, he felt someone's eyes on him. He heard Helen gasp from beside him.

He turned, and the thick lens wearing member of their party stood there, holding his camera, which Nick could now see was an old Elektra, in one hand, stood starting at him.

"You're Nick O'Flannigan," he said as Nick's eyes met his.

"I am. You are?"

"My name is Alan. I'm a photographer, too. Film," he said, swinging his old camera up for emphasis. "I don't do digital, at least, not yet."

"That's a nice one. What year is that?" Nick asked. He didn't own any old cameras, but they fascinated him.

"1973," Alan said. "Still works great though. One room in my basement is a darkroom."

"You startled us, Alan. What are you doing away from the group?" Helen asked.

"This is the real reason I came on the hike," he said. "I wanted to get some shots of this."

"Cool," Nick said. "I'd love to have a look at yours when you get them developed."

"I'd love to show you these. And some of the rest of my work," Alan said.

"I'd be happy to share some of mine, too."

"We can compare notes," Alan said. "I also write poetry. Do you write?"

"Very little," Nick said. "I found that my talents were more visual than the written word."

"I think they go hand in hand," Alan said. "How about we get together later tonight?"

"Sure," Nick said, looking at Helen. She looked a little disappointed but smiled anyway. "You're welcome to join us, Helen."

"I'd love to," she said. "I don't have to work later. It's my night off."

Alan scowled, but only for a second, and then nodded.

"We better catch the others," Helen said.

They headed back down the trail. Nick realized he should have brought food along. He was getting hungry, and his watch told him it was past lunchtime already.

As he hiked downward, Nick saw a drone flying over the park. He'd seen some of the photography and videography from them and thought maybe he should look into getting one.

For a photographer, you're sure going through money you don't have yet pretty fast, he told himself. *Bike? Drone? What's next?*

But he did have some money in savings. Maybe he'd have to choose between the two.

He shoved the thought from his mind as he reached the bottom of the trail and climbed on his bike.

"You want to grab lunch?" Helen asked.

"Sure," he said. "I'm starving."

They agreed on a place to meet, and Nick took off pedaling. The ride was mostly downhill, and the wind dried any sweat he'd built up on the hike. His leg was a little stiff, but the ride seemed to help loosen his muscles, at least, a little.

He arrived at the restaurant feeling refreshed, but a little smelly.

It shouldn't matter. He and Helen were just friends having lunch after all. Well, and dinner later, but that would be a threesome. She had to be just as sweaty as he was.

As they ate and shared small talk, all Nick thought of was the photos he'd taken. He couldn't wait to look at them, but he needed to be careful. Only a few would work for his assignment. The rest needed to go in his personal folder. He'd also have to decide what to share with Alan. He seemed like a truly odd duck.

7

WOMAN TROUBLE

Alan sat down to dinner with a portfolio of photos, and a small book of poems. He was clearly excited to have someone to share with.

Nick looked over the poems and realized some of them were really good. Many of Alan's photos were black and white, and striking in their composition.

"You're a talented guy, Alan. What are you doing with these things?"

"They are just for my enjoyment really. I sell a few from time to time, but mostly, I share them with friends and family."

"Well, they are very good, and so are the poems. You should do more."

"I don't know. Maybe someday."

Nick met people like Alan all the time. They had talent, good things to say actually, but they lacked the courage or the motivation to put them out into the world.

Still, if it made Alan happy to do this as a hobby, why not? Why turn it into work for him?

Nick certainly knew firsthand that following one's passions did not mean it wasn't hard work. It just meant if you were cut out for it, you would, at least, enjoy your job.

Helen sat quietly. She interjected from time to time, and even commented on some of the photos. She read a poem Alan had written about 9/11 and teared up a little bit. Overall, she kept pretty much to herself.

They finished dinner, and Alan quickly offered some awkward goodbyes. Nick gave him his card and told him to keep in touch.

He and Helen walked back toward the hotel, in silence at first. Then she turned to him.

"Do you like me, Nick?"

"What do you mean?" Nick said. "Of course I like you."

"No, that's not what I mean." She stopped.

Nick sighed and faced her. "Helen, I do like you. You're very nice. My kind of person, actually. But things are complicated."

"Complicated in what way? Are you seeing someone?"

"That's a good question. Yes, I think so. But it's hard to explain."

"Try."

"We left things as 'just friends'. I like her and, clearly, she likes me. But, Helen, think about it. I'm on the road for a year. Sandra lives closer to where I do than Helena, but we don't even live in the same state."

"So, it's not going to work out?"

"I have no idea how it would," he said. "And it's the same with you. I like you. But I don't know that I ever plan to come back to Helena after this trip."

"I understand," she said. "But we can be friends, right?"

"Yep," he said. "We can be that for sure."

"Good," she said. "See you tomorrow?"

"Sounds good," Nick said. They'd arrived at the lobby, and he gave Helen a quick hug, and then headed for his room. He needed some rest before tomorrow.

～

THE NEXT MORNING, Nick woke early and turned on the news. The top story was that the fire department had declared the fire in the park arson and were actively seeking suspects in that and the apparent murder but had no leads.

"We'll keep you up to date with any new developments," the reporter said. "Now, over to Corey with the weather. Still looking at sun for the rest of the week?"

Nick left the TV on as background noise and hopped in the shower.

Today would be a good day for some inside photos of the capitol building and then maybe some more exploring. When he was dressed, he went down and grabbed his bike, heading downtown where he hoped to find coffee and breakfast before he started working.

His leg felt surprisingly good as he pedaled, and he found coffee and a ham and egg bagel sandwich at a small coffee shop. It was good and filled the empty hole in his stomach. He noticed that not only did his leg feel better, but his core and arms felt stronger after only a couple days of bike riding, too. It seemed to make a huge difference.

And he liked it.

He locked his bike up at a rack across from the capitol and went inside. He wanted a few more photos, and then some more in the afternoon light on the outside of the building.

For much of the rest of the morning, he wandered around the interior of the building again, snapping extra photos and macro photos of several features. A security guard came up to him, a round bellied man with a serious expression wearing a slightly too small uniform and a large cowboy hat.

"How are you doing?" he asked. There was a suspicious tone to his voice.

"Good," Nick answered. He held out his hand. "Nick O'Flannigan, freelance photographer. On assignment here for *Travel USA* magazine."

"Nice. Enjoying your stay?"

"Yes," Nick said. "I really like this town. I never knew some of the things that are here."

"Well, I'll leave you to it. Remember, no flash photography."

Nick simply nodded, and the man moved on. Everyone here was so polite and understanding. He decided to break for a quick lunch and then spend the rest of the day outside. From the look of the sky, it seemed like it would be a beautiful day.

On the way into the restaurant, he noticed a flyer for a community theater play that evening. They were performing *Macbeth*, one of his favorite Shakespeare plays. He wondered idly if Helen was working or had plans. It would be better to go with someone than to go alone.

He fished her card out of his pocket and dialed her cell number.

"This is Helen," she answered.

"Helen, it's Nick," he said. "How is your morning going?"

"Good so far. Just got into work."

"How late are you working?" he asked. "I just saw a flyer for a performance of *Macbeth* tonight and wondered if you might like to tag along with me."

"Sure. What time?"

"Nick squinted at the poster. "Seven, looks like."

"Sure. I can be out of here by then. Want me to meet you at the hotel bar?"

"The lobby is fine," Nick said. The call ended and he took a deep breath. It was just like going to a play with any other friend.

As he finished eating, his phone rang. It was Sandra.

"Hey," he said enthusiastically. "How are you?"

"Good," she said. "What are you up to?"

"The usual," he told her.

"No mysteries this week? How is the bike riding going?"

He laughed. "Mysteries around, yes. But, thankfully, nothing I am involved in."

"That's smart Nick. What are you up to this evening?"

"A local theater is putting on *Macbeth*. We thought we'd go check it out."

"We?"

"Me and a friend I met here," he said. "A gal named Helen."

"Helen, huh?" He detected a note of jealousy in her voice.

"A clerk at the hotel. We're just friends." Nick found himself defensive, and the very idea bothered him.

He and Helen were friends, just like he and Sandra were. Okay, there were differences, like the lack of kissing but he didn't think he should feel guilty or she should feel jealous.

"It's fine, Nick," she told him. "I know you will meet other people along the way. Ten months is a long time."

"Sandra, it isn't like that."

"I get it Nick. Listen, I have to go."

She hung up, and he stared at his phone. Maybe he should call tonight off. He didn't want to lead Helen on, didn't want to anger Sandra, at least, any further, but he felt like a jerk either way.

Women, he thought. *I'll never understand them.*

After paying his check, Nick headed back to the capitol building grounds to get what he hoped would be a large batch of the outside photos he needed, his brain racing in the background the whole time.

He grabbed a quick shower and dinner when he got back to the hotel and dressed in casual clothes for his night at the theater. He was looking forward to, hopefully, some good acting and a quiet evening.

Checking his social media before he left, he was shocked to see that his post about taking up cycling had gotten a lot of attention. There were comments about specific bikes, and even links to some articles about the benefits of riding a bike for exercise and recovery from injuries.

He liked every comment and replied to every response that he could, and then headed downstairs.

8

———

A PLAY ON WORDS

Nick should not have been surprised to see Harry, nor was he really. They made eye contact and waved, but the auditorium was crowded by the time he and Helen arrived.

It felt like a date. Nick had not intended for it to be, but from Helen's outfit and mannerisms to his own nervousness, it felt odd and wrong. He felt like he was cheating on Sandra, even though they had not really established that they were going out or had any kind of exclusive romantic relationship. Especially after the shift he had experienced with her in Boise and early this week, he was not sure what was going on.

But he felt like before anything happened with anyone else, he needed to find out. Nick wasn't promiscuous or the type to hop from woman to woman, so he needed to know.

And that was yet another reason things felt wrong. He didn't want to lead Helen on. No relationship could really be stable with his current assignment, not unless it was with someone who would travel with him the rest of the way around the country. He could hardly expect to meet someone like that. It had been crazy enough for Sandra to come help him in Sacramento. She'd even mentioned coming to meet up with him in a few weeks.

He tried to think of where, exactly, he would be at that point. Wherever it was, it certainly would not be Helena.

He and Helen sat, once they had programs. Nick could see Harry, all the way across the auditorium, but in the second row, watching the still-closed curtain intently.

I'm making friends and even having dates, and then moving on, Nick thought. *This is silly.*

Yet, here he was. Helen smiled at him, and made small talk about work, life in Helena, and other little things. Nick nodded, contributed when he needed to, but his mind remained elsewhere.

Then the house lights went down, and the curtain opened.

Three witches entered. "When shall we three meet again in thunder, lightning, or in rain?" The first line echoed over the audience. He watched, as his favorite of Shakespeare's tragedies began. Tonight, the last line of the first act resonated well with him, because he knew what was coming next.

"Fair is foul, and foul is fair: Hover through the fog and filthy air," the witches said, and then exited.

They were followed by Duncan, Malcom, and the Sergeant in the second scene, but what he really looked forward to was the introduction of Macbeth that would follow.

As the actor entered the stage, Nick held his breath. The other actors had been fairly decent, but none stood out as excellent. But as the first lines dripped from his mouth, Nick was convinced this actor was, at least, for this time on stage, Macbeth.

"So foul and fair a day I have not seen."

Helen squeezed his hand at that moment. He felt himself squeeze her back. Nick thought the actor looked familiar but wasn't sure.

The words matched his mood. It was a fair day because he was doing the things he loved, getting paid to travel to do them.

Yet, it was foul, for he wondered what he was doing, who he was hurting besides himself, and what he needed to do next.

"Come what come may, time and the hour runs through the roughest day."

A tragedy indeed. Nick allowed himself to be carried away, transported into the heart and language of the play itself, following the twists and turns of the plot as *Macbeth* marched inevitably forward.

He listened intently as they broke into another of his favorite moments.

"I have done the deed. Didst thou not hear a noise?" Macbeth said.

"I heard the owl scream and the crickets cry. Did not you speak?" Lady Macbeth answered.

Nick held his breath.

"One cried 'God bless us!' and 'Amen' the other; As they had seen me with these hangman's hands. Listening their fear, I could not say 'Amen,' when they did say 'God bless us!'"

Hangman's hands. Something about those words.

The murder in the park. A hanging.

The killing, Harry had said. *Not all killing is murder.*

"Consider it not so deeply," said Lady Macbeth.

Yeah, Nick, he told himself. *Consider it not so deeply.*

"But wherefore could not I pronounce 'Amen'? I had most need of blessing, and 'Amen' stuck in my throat," Macbeth declared.

Nick looked over toward Harry and could have sworn he saw him wipe his eyes, as if he were crying.

Nick felt Macbeth's guilt, but wanted so badly for him to find redemption, redemption Nick knew he would not discover. Instead, he and his wife would engage in crime after crime and murder after murder to cover up what he had done.

Much like other tragedies, Nick was unable to look away, although he knew every twist and turn of the play. Macbeth and his wife were played so well, that he nearly wept when Macbeth was killed, a scene well set and acted even on such a small stage.

At that moment, he knew what to do about Helen, if not yet what to do about Sandra.

The house lights came on, and Nick looked over to where Harry had been sitting. He was gone.

As they walked out into the cool evening, Helen reached for his hand.

"Would you like to go for a drink?" he asked her, avoiding her grasp by putting his own hands in his pockets.

"Sure," she said.

"Good. I'd like to talk with you about something."

"That sounds ominous."

"It shouldn't. Come on," he said.

She reached out, and he let her take his arm. This certainly wasn't going to be easy.

There was a bar around the corner from the theater, and they stopped there. Being a weeknight, it was pretty quiet. They found a booth in the corner, sat down, and ordered.

Nick asked for an old fashioned, and Helen ordered a gin and tonic.

"Listen, Helen—" he started.

"Nick, stop. I know what you're going to say. "

"And what might that be?" he asked, curious.

"You told me before you just wanted to be friends. Tonight, though, you feel guilty. This—Sandra, is it?"

"Yes, Sandra," he said.

"You're dating her?"

"After the past week or so, I'm not sure."

"But you want to be. Or think you might want to be?"

Nick nodded and swallowed hard. Helen had read him like a book, and she was right. He did want to be friends, but nothing more. He couldn't be.

"That's good, Nick. And I know you're on the road for a year—ten more months, is it?"

"Closer to eleven, but nonetheless..."

"It doesn't matter," she said. "I like you, Nick. I see a lot of guys come in and out of that hotel, traveling through. Some of them like me, but none the way I want them to. I guess you could say I am used to disappointment."

"Helen, I—"

"I know. If things were different. Ya-da-ya-da. I'm happy to be friends, but..." Her voice trailed off.

"But what?" He asked.

"If things don't work out with Sandra, or somewhere down the line you do find yourself back in Helena, look me up, would you?"

"I will," he said.

Helen leaned up, way up, and kissed his cheek. "Thanks for a wonderful evening, Nick. See you tomorrow?"

"Of course," Nick said.

He watched her walk down the street, presumably headed home. He should have offered to walk her, something.

But he did not. He turned the other way and walked back to his hotel, and then decided to go get some exterior night shots of the capitol building. There was no way he could sleep right away, and the night air would do him some good.

For the next couple of hours, he walked around the capitol taking dozens of photos, almost on autopilot. He couldn't tell if any of them were really great, and probably wouldn't know until morning. Once he finally returned to his hotel and fell into bed, he endured a dream filled and restless night's sleep.

9

D-E-R

Hangman's hands. Nick woke from a dream with those words on his lips. He'd dreamed of... what?

A hanging tree, a man, swaying in the breeze, dead.

Harry's hands, making knots with twine as they talked at lunch.

It couldn't be. He was just passing through. What had he said he did for a living? Consulting?

It didn't matter. He needed to get a few more exterior photos today, and then he would almost have everything he needed. He'd return the bike today, and then just relax this afternoon.

Then he thought of the photos he had taken, the ones at the top of the trail, and decided to look at them more closely before he went out this morning just out of curiosity. There had to be something interesting there, other than the scorched tree and the discarded crime scene tape.

He made a cup of coffee in the room with the small coffee maker and opened his laptop.

He started to scroll through the pictures one by one, zooming in here and there. Then he saw it, in a bush about ten yards from the scorched area by the trunk of the tree. There was something white there, like the corner of a piece of paper or something, but larger than letter sized. A sign? It looked partially burned on one side.

Opening the file in his photo editing software, Nick zoomed in and cropped the image. The object might have been made of construction paper, or even a light cardboard, like from the edge of a box.

He could make out what looked like a few letters on the end of it, although at this resolution, they were fuzzy.

"D-E-R," Nick strained to read each letter and said them out loud. The rest of the—whatever it was, had been burned away.

It could be the end of nearly any word. I mean, how many words in the English language ended in D-E-R?

He almost searched the internet for the answer, and then stopped himself.

Murder.

That was the word. He could almost see a curve of ink where the edge of the sign— for that is what he thought it was now, a sign—had been scorched by the fire. The curve of a 'U'?

It's a hunch, nothing more, he told himself. *Of course it was a murder. This sign is not new information.*

Yet he felt like it was. It meant something, not because the killer had labeled the murder scene with a sign, but because...because what?

The one thing the news had not said before was if the body had been identified. He wondered.

Nick grabbed his laptop and rushed downstairs to find a newspaper. As he went, his stomach growled. He'd need breakfast soon. He wasn't going to call the police and share the photo with them yet. He'd made that mistake before, even as recently as Boise. Making a call too soon would make him look like a fool.

Make a fool of myself once, shame on me for not knowing any better. Do it twice? That means I'm not really learning.

Learning what, Nick? he asked himself. *How to be a detective? You should be concentrating on photography.*

As he reached the lobby and grabbed a paper, he nearly ran into a man he recognized, wearing thick glasses, and looking up at him.

"Alan?" he said, recalling the name from their hike.

"Nick," Alan said, and held out his thin hand. "I was just coming to see you."

"To see me?" Nick asked.

"Yeah. I developed my photos and found something that might interest you..." Alan trailed off.

"Interesting. I was just looking at the ones I took."

"I would love to show it to you and see what you think. Maybe compare notes."

"Sure. I was about to grab breakfast. I think I may have found something, too. I was just going to check for some information in the paper."

"What did you want to know?"

"If they released the identity of the victim yet."

"I haven't heard anything. But if there is nothing public yet, I can make some calls."

"Oh, yeah?"

"I've freelanced for both the paper and the Sheriff's department."

"Alan, that's great." Nick didn't want to use his new friend, but if he could keep his own name out of things, that would be fantastic for him, for Emily, and for his current assignment.

Focus, he had told himself over and over. *Focus.*

"Let's head to Steve's," Alan said.

When they arrived, they grabbed a larger table and sat down. Alan pulled out a portfolio case, opened it, and slid out a photo. It was of the same scrap Nick had seen, but closer up and from a different angle. The letters were even clearer.

D-E-R.

"What do you think it means?" Alan asked.

"First, I just found this in my photos this morning, too. Second, your photo is much better than mine. How'd you shoot it?"

"I'm into macro stuff like you. I didn't see the letters at first, just thought the contrast of the white and the scorched edge against the bushes looked cool. When I developed it yesterday, I saw the letters."

"Impressive," Nick said, and he meant it. Traditional film did have advantages from time to time, and his shot had been from much further away. The detail in Alan's was incredible.

"What do you think it means?" Alan asked.

"Murder," Nick said without hesitation. "The question is, did the killer put it there and if so, why? Otherwise, who did, and why?"

"I had the same questions," Alan said.

Nick unfolded the paper. "Let's see if they tell us yet who the victim was."

And there it was, on the front page. A mugshot of a man. "After notifying the next of kin, the Sheriff's department has just released the name of the victim killed in Saturday night's fire. Albert Paulson had just recently gotten out of jail, where he spent two years on the charge of manslaughter for killing his wife, which he said was an accident," Nick read out loud.

"He was in the process of moving back to Helena, where his family was originally from, and sources tell us he was job hunting in the area over the last week or so."

Nick looked up and stared around the restaurant. There were a few people he recognized, probably because they worked downtown or near the capitol building, and he had seen them around or even at other restaurants.

He looked at each table and wondered what each person might be thinking. Had they read the paper? What did they think of this unusual story?

Nick had always focused on photography, *no pun intended*, he told himself. The other aspects of journalism and writing he had pretty much ignored. After all, a picture said a thousand words, right? But sometimes, or so it seemed, pictures were just not enough.

"What do you want to do with this?" he asked Alan.

Alan shrugged. "I don't know. Even now that we know who the victim was, what does this sign mean?"

"Well, we still don't know. I think we should pass along the information to the Sheriff. Your photos are better than mine, so I will let you do that part."

"What are you going to do?"

"Relax this afternoon. I was going to turn my rental bike back in, but I think I'll take a ride after all."

"Want to meet later for dinner? I'd love to learn more about how you do what you do."

"Sure, Alan. I'm always willing to help." A photographer couldn't have a better friend than another photographer.

They parted ways, and Nick headed back to the hotel to get his bike. Maybe he'd take a few more photos in Helena after all. And maybe a quiet bike ride would do him some real good.

10

SUSPECT AT LARGE

Nick trusted that Alan would do the right thing. As for himself, he needed to think. Helen, Sandra, this whole assignment, and his odd obsession with getting involved with crimes and mysteries wherever he went were all things he needed to figure out.

One thing Nick knew about himself was that he was loyal. He wasn't a guy to have a gal in every port, and he really did like Sandra. She was close enough to home that they might be able to make it work, and they had a lot in common. Helen was pretty and fun, but when it came right down to it, she wasn't Sandra.

He found himself pedaling past the capitol building, so he stopped, pulled out his phone, and called Sandra. The call went straight to voicemail. Nick snapped a quick photo of the impressive building, and sent her a text. "Thinking of you."

The word "delivered" appeared under the text, but there was no response.

Nick sighed and moved on. Before long, he found himself riding up a trail in Mt. Helena State Park. His leg ached, but didn't throb, so he hoped in some ways this week had been good. Maybe it was healing a little, or at least building muscle that would help it feel better in the long run. He looked around, finding himself high above the city, near where the murder scene had been. He stopped the bike and hopped off, walking it to where the trail split.

Locking it loosely to the trail signpost, he took out his camera and walked the rest of the way to where he saw the first bits of crime scene tape. He stepped over them, eyes on where he thought the piece of whatever he and Alan had seen should be.

It wasn't there.

So what? he told himself. *Either the police came back and got it, or it blew away. Helena is a windy place, and it is especially windy up here.*

It still bothered him. He and Alan had photos of evidence that had been there but was now gone. But they didn't really tell them or police a thing. You couldn't pull prints off a photo of something.

He looked around again. There was a mark, high up on a thick branch of the tree. Probably where the rope had passed over it.

A hanging tree. Not scarred permanently, as he was sure the bark would heal before long. Just as he was sure the scorch marks would fade with winter, disappear within a spring or two. There would be no evidence left.

Nick remembered Carson City. The smell of decaying flesh. He remembered Boise, and the gruesome discovery of a body there. Sacramento. Salem. Olympia. Wherever he turned, there was death, and not just death. It was death forced upon one human by another before their time.

But was that the case here?

Albert Paulson had been accused of killing his wife. Did he? Was his sentence just, or did he deserve this? Was an eye for an eye even relevant anymore?

He wondered what Harry would think. He hadn't seen him since the night of the play but wondered about him.

"Not all killing is murder," he'd said.

Nick now wondered what he meant by that, and why he'd said it about this particular killing. Did he know something?

As he sat there, his phone rang. Surprised that he had service, he answered.

"Hi, Nick!" It was Gerry, cheery as always.

"Hi, Gerry," he said.

"How are you doing? I saw some of the photos you got in Helena; some great stuff there. Emily says you are getting better and better."

"I hope so," he said. "I'm pretty much done with the photos I need here, so I am just taking some down time. Tomorrow I'll probably relax, pack, and go to bed early before I head out to Bismarck."

"That sounds great. You deserve some rest, Nick. You've been working too hard. How is Sandra?"

"I'm not sure," he said honestly. "We kind of had a tiff, and I'm not sure what to do about it."

"Oh, Nick, I am sure the two of you will figure it out. It seems like she is good for you."

"Yeah. I met someone here, and we went out, just as friends, and I said something to Sandra. She seemed pretty upset. Jealous even."

"What's wrong with that?"

"Well—"

"Nick, if she didn't care about you, she would have no reason to be jealous. The two of you probably just need to talk things out."

"You're right, of course."

"Call her."

"I did. Her phone went straight to voicemail."

"Nick, what time is it there?"

"Getting toward noon," he said, and heard his stomach growl. All this fresh air and exercise had used up his morning fuel.

"She's at work. Not everyone lives a life of leisure like you do."

Nick groaned. "Life of leisure? I wish."

"Well, you have flexible hours. Call her tonight."

"I will."

"Promise?"

"Gerry, yes. I will."

"Good. I just want you to be happy, Nick."

"How are things for you in the romance department, Miss Matchmaker?"

"Well, you know the gal I was seeing?"

"No, not exactly but I knew you were seeing someone."

"We're talking about getting a place together. So, you could say things are going well."

"Good for you," he said. "I really hope it works out."

"Me, too," she said. "Well, I have to go. Deadlines, you know. Keep up the good work and stay in touch."

"Thanks," Nick said, and hung up the phone.

He headed down the hill on his rental bike, and even though the wind was against him, the ride went quickly, and the breeze cooled any sweat that built up.

He went straight to his favorite bistro, thinking a sandwich and some salad would hit the spot.

When he walked in, he saw that everyone was watching the news, and no one even flinched as the bell over the door rang.

"A person of interest has been arrested for suspected murder and arson in the fire in Mt. Helena Park on Saturday. The brother of the victim's wife was seen in Helena that day, and police have tracked him down near his hometown of Durango, Colorado. He was questioned at his home today and is *en route* to Helena to be formally charged.

Sources tell us that when confronted, he confessed to having a part in the crime. Whether that means he acted alone or with others it is hard to say. We'll keep you updated as we learn more."

The news went on with a profile of the victim and his wife, and their tumultuous relationship.

Nick sat down and ordered as conversation around him went back to normal. Now, what he and Alan had discovered didn't make a bit of difference. The culprit was caught, and Nick had nothing to do with it.

He decided that before he had dinner with Alan, he'd go back and take a nap. They could celebrate after all, and then just talk shop about photography. It had been too long since he was able to do that with someone. Since Sandra, at least.

As he fell onto the bed on top of the covers and turned on the television for background noise, his phone chimed for a text message.

"Thinking of you, too," Sandra said. "Busy tonight. Can we talk tomorrow?"

"Sure," he texted back. "I'd love that."

A few moments later, he was fast asleep.

Alan texted while he was sleeping, and Nick got the message when he woke up.

"Rain check on tonight?" it said.

"Of course," Nick replied.

He headed out and found some buffalo wings at a local bar, all you can eat, and got his money's worth.

11

SOLVED?

Nick woke to his phone ringing.

He looked at the screen, and saw it was his mother.

"Hi, Mom," he said, already dreading her inevitable yelling at his father who was often in another room during their conversations.

"Hi, Nick. How are you doing in Helena?"

"Good so far. I actually rented a bike and have been exercising this week. My leg feels pretty good."

"Riding a bike? You haven't ridden since junior high."

"I know, Mom, but I took a chance and I really like it."

"What's going on?" he heard his dad roar from another room.

"He's riding a bike!" his mom yelled. Nick winced.

"What's wrong with his car?" his father asked.

"Your father wants to know—"

"I heard, Mom. Nothing is wrong with the car. It's just easy to ride a bike around this city."

"Nothing's wrong with his car!" she yelled. "He's doing it for fun."

"How are you guys, Mom?"

"Pretty good. Nothing new really."

"That's good, I suppose," he said.

"Well, we're glad you're doing well. You let us know if you need anything at all."

"Of course," he told her. "Thanks for calling, Mom."

He rolled out of bed and headed for the coffee maker. It wasn't the greatest brew, but it would get him through his shower and out into the world. Today should be an easy day.

He turned on the news just as the coffee finished. Then, his phone rang again, and he muted the report. It was Emily, his editor.

"Hey, Nick!"

"Hey there," he said. "How are things back on the home front?"

"Great, great. Everyone likes your photos, and the ones from Helena are your best work yet." She hesitated.

"Why do I sense a 'but' coming?" he asked.

"Well, one of our publishers lived in Helena when he was younger. He'd love for you to get some more shots."

"Of what, in particular?"

"Well, so here's the thing. These are not likely to be shots we use in the book, but of places like his old home, his old school, stuff like that. I have a list of locations and addresses."

"Okay," Nick said. "I can certainly take them."

"Look, I know this isn't really a part of the assignment, but it would make him happy, and earn the project some brownie points."

"No worries. I'll get them today," Nick said. *So much for being lazy.*

"Sounds great. Again, good job, Nick."

"Anytime," he said, and hung up. He checked his email and found a list of roughly a dozen places for him to take photos.

It was time to get moving if he wanted to get any rest at all this afternoon.

He headed for the shower, but the phone in his room rang.

"Hello?" he said.

"Nick, it's Helen at the front desk. There's someone here to see you."

"Who is it?"

"Alan, from the hike."

"I'll be down in a few minutes. Can you tell him I'm grabbing a quick shower, and I'll be there in no time?"

"Sure."

"Thanks, Helen. For more than just the call, and passing along the message. Can you join us for breakfast?"

"Sure. I can have Ann cover for me."

"Great. Be down soon."

Nick rushed through the shower and his morning routine faster than he wanted to. He wondered what Alan could possibly want after he'd rain checked dinner the day before. His last day in Helena was going to prove more eventful than he'd anticipated. At least, he wouldn't be bored.

The elevator seemed to take forever, and he tapped his foot as it descended. Today promised to be a busy one. Over one shoulder he had his laptop bag. Over the other was his camera. At some point, he needed to return the bike, probably before he went to take photos.

When it opened, he saw Helen and Alan in hushed conversation in the corner, pointing to the television from time to time.

Nick looked up, and his heart stopped. "Co-conspirator Sought" the banner under the anchor's face said. And in the corner, over her shoulder, was a sketch of a second suspect in the hanging in Helena. As she spoke, the camera cut from her to a full-screen image of the drawing.

It was his acquaintance, Harry.

For a moment, he just stood there, mouth open, hands sweating. It couldn't be true.

But it must be. How else would they have a sketch of him? Who would have given it to them, except someone who was there when the murder happened?

The killing, he corrected himself.

As he came out of his shock, he could hear the newscaster talking. "—description offered by the initial suspect, the brother of Carolyn Paulson, of a man who was hired to 'deliver justice' as he put it. He says the man was named Harry Hickman, and he got connected to him through another man, Lane Gibbons, who the police are also seeking as a person of interest.

"If you have seen or heard from either of these men, the police are asking that you call the following number—"

An 877-number appeared, but Nick turned away from the screen to face the others.

"Pretty wild, huh?" Helen said. Then she stopped. "You okay, Nick? You look like you've seen a ghost."

"Fine," he said. "Never better. Good morning, Alan. My guess is you want to update me about what happened with the photo."

The whole time in the back of his head, he could hear a small voice talking to him.

You should call, Nick.

Lots of people saw Harry. They will get plenty of tips. There's no need for me to get involved.

You talked to him. You know him.

If he's still in town, he's a fool. They'll find him. If they don't, soon, then I'll call.

"—said they would print it on the front page with the latest update. And look!" Alan held out a paper for him to see, and Nick was glad that although he'd missed the first part of what he said, what he saw was enough for him to understand.

Alan's photo was on the front page on the left side, the drawing of Harry on the right.

D-E-R.

Murder.

Harry had killed a man for murdering his wife, a man who had what? Slipped through the justice system? He was a hired killer, but instead of a hired gun, he was a hired rope?

If Harry knew what was good for him, he was already long gone, especially if he'd seen this article.

"That's great, Alan, and it is a fabulous photo. You deserve the recognition."

"Thanks!"

"Let's go get some breakfast and celebrate," Helen said.

Nick smiled at her. "Sure, let's do it."

She took Alan's arm as they walked out the front door, and Nick knew at that moment that things would be okay.

Sure, he had work to do, but he had time if he worked quickly. The mystery was over, solved with no help or involvement from him, at least not directly.

He followed the other two into the sunlight and let them lead. Helen said she knew just the place to go.

12

THE HANGING TREE

They returned to the hotel after he ate a four-egg omelet and drank the best, and spiciest Bloody Mary he'd had in a long time. Helen went back to work, Alan left, Nick gathered his bike and gear, and headed back to the shop with the bike on the borrowed rack he'd used exactly twice.

Greg greeted him. "How was it?"

"Fantastic. I really liked it. If I wasn't traveling all over for the rest of the year, I'd buy this baby from you," Nick said, patting the seat. "As it is, I'll probably rent wherever I can, and when I get home, I'm buying one for sure."

"That's great. I'm glad to hear it."

"How much do I owe you?"

Greg stroked his chin. "You have a big online following, right? You're blogging about your trip as well as taking pictures for this book thing, right?"

"Of course."

"Tell you what. You do a write up about the shop, and I'll give you 50% off the week."

"That's great. I'll be happy to."

"Awesome. Let me get a picture of you with the bike."

Nick showed him how to use his camera, and Greg snapped the photo. Then Nick took a photo of him behind the counter and settled the bill.

"I appreciate it, Greg," Nick said.

"Me, too," Greg answered. "If you are ever in Helena again…"

Nick looked around. "You never know. I might be."

They shook hands and Greg followed him out to his car, collected the bike rack, and went back inside.

Nick looked at his list of locations, and put them into his phone, letting the navigation app route him to each.

The first was an older coffee shop, one he had not seen before. He snapped some shots of the outside and went in and ordered a latte to go. Might as well have some fuel for the road. The next was what had been an auto shop, now shuttered and closed. Nick got some wide shots, some up close, and a few of a discarded sign laying on the ground behind the building.

The third location was a house on the corner of Highland and Blake streets. He parked down the block, and went to take some pictures, wondering if he should ask permission from the current occupants or at least introduce himself before wandering around outside.

He walked around the corner intending to do just that, and nearly ran into a man on the sidewalk. He was just standing, starting at the house, a baseball cap pulled low over his eyes.

"Sorry," he said.

"It's okay, Nick." The voice belonged to Harry.

"Harry?" he said. "What are you…?" Nick didn't finish the question, unsure of what he really wanted to ask.

"What am I doing here? I assume you've seen the news and the paper?"

"I have," Nick said. "I figured you'd be long gone."

Harry laughed. "I'm done running. By the way, it's not really Harry. It's George."

"George?"

"George Maledon IV, to be exact, although I haven't told anyone my real name in a really long time."

"Why me?"

"I like you, Nick. You're a good guy."

"Thanks, I think."

"You didn't call the tip line." It was a statement, not a question.

"Nope. I figure plenty of people saw you this week. My tip won't make any difference."

"It might. In fact, I want you to call."

"What?"

"Walk with me, Nick."

"Okay."

They walked for a moment in silence. Nick broke it first. "You seem like a decent guy, Har—I mean, George."

"I try to be."

"What happened?"

"I went into the family business. My father, my grandfather, even my great grandfather, were all executioners, hangmen, if you will."

"But did they…"

"No, no. They were all legit, and so was I, at first. Then hanging went out of fashion, even though, if done properly, it's a quite humane means of execution."

"I get that, I suppose. Why go 'freelance', so to speak?"

"Eh. People escape the justice they deserve all the time. One person I knew asked me a favor. The word spread that I would help occasionally, and before I knew it, I was in business for myself. It wasn't like I had a lot of other marketable skills." He gestured to Nick's camera.

"So, you just, kill people for a living?"

"It's not that bad, Nick." George had pulled a length of narrow nylon rope partway out of his pocket, and his hands worked at it quickly and silently as they talked. "Most of them deserve it."

"Most?"

"I've been pretty careful, Nick."

"Why are you still here? Why didn't you run?"

George shrugged. "I'm tired. They have my picture now. Soon, they'll know who I really am. I don't want to live on the run."

"I can't say that I blame you," Nick said, thinking of his own recent travels and homesickness. "So, what will you do?"

George held up the piece of twine he'd been playing with to reveal a small noose.

"How would you want to go, Nick? Given the choice, I mean."

"To go where?"

"Death, Nick. How would you want it to happen? Would you want to see it coming, know what was next? Or would you rather be shocked, and have something happen suddenly?"

"I haven't really thought about it."

"Me, I'd like to see it coming," George said. "I'd want to be somewhere beautiful. Like that park, that mountain up there. I'd like to go in my time, on my terms."

"George—"

"You know where we are?"

Nick looked around and saw they had come full circle and were now standing in front of the house Nick had come to photograph.

"You mean, like Helena, or right here? This spot?"

"Right over behind that house was something called the Hanging Tree. The stuff of legend around here. It was cut down in 1875 by some bishop who thought it was leaning and would fall on his barn, not at all because of what it stood for. Now that spot is in someone's back yard, forgotten by nearly everyone who isn't from around here. Most people have no idea it was ever there and don't understand what it meant."

George removed the hat for a moment, and wiped his eyes, looking slightly upward at Nick.

"That tree represented justice. Sure, some injustice was done there, too, but what hangman hasn't made mistakes?"

"George, what are you going to do?"

"Don't worry, Nick," George said, handing him the small noose. "Everything is going to be okay."

He turned and walked away.

Nick stood there for a moment. Should he call someone? Do something?

Do what? he thought. *Maybe this time, just leave it alone, Nick.*

He turned back to the house and took the last of his photos there, and then moved on to the next location on his list.

But the whole afternoon, he couldn't stop thinking about George, his confession, and the Hanging Tree.

13

THE END OF YOUR ROPE

Nick completed taking the photos. Breakfast had been more than enough to carry him through the day, and he'd lost his appetite after talking to Harry and discovering that he was actually George.

I have to call, he kept telling himself.

Finally, as he got back to his hotel room, he picked up the phone in his room, and thought about what he would say.

"Tip line," a voice said.

"I know the man in the sketch," he said, blurting it out. "His name is George Maledon IV, but he's been going by Harry Hickman."

"How do you know this, sir?" The voice on the other end of the line suddenly sounded really serious.

"He told me," Nick answered simply.

"What's your name?"

"I'd rather not say."

"When's the last time you had contact with Mr. Maledon?"

"A few hours ago," Nick answered.

"Where?"

"Here in Helena," he said, and hung up.

"There," he said, when the call was over, and opened his laptop to upload the final batch of photos before he got packed.

Then he could get out of here before anything else happened, and before anyone connected him to the tip and to Harry, rather, George.

Nick felt like he'd been played, and he was both angry and sad at the same time. Over and over on this trip, he'd been face to face with his own mortality, but never as close as this trip. It was beyond time to go.

He concentrated on his work, and as soon as he was finished, he packed his bag and looked at the clock. It was nearly nine, and he was hungry.

One last supper here, he thought. *Maybe Bismarck will be better.*

He went downstairs and wandered over to the Lewis and Clark Taproom. A little food and beer would do him some good and help him sleep. As he went through the front door, he heard sirens in the distance.

The place was busy, but Nick found a spot at the bar. He ordered the Huckleberry Porter, and a burger and fries. He sat and ate and watched the television mindlessly. Then, the ten o'clock news started.

"Breaking news," the reporter said. "Another body has been found in Mt. Helena State Park on the same site as the hanging victim last week," the reporter said. "Police are not releasing any details, but a source who wished to remain anonymous says this appears to be a suicide."

Me, I'd want to see it coming, Harry/George had said. *I'd want to go on my terms, in my own way.*

Nick took the noose out of his pocket and laid it next to his plate. He downed the rest of his beer and ordered another.

"That's something else, isn't it?" the bartender remarked, gesturing to the news.

"Sure is," Nick said. His beer arrived, and he looked up at the news again, which had moved on to the Friday night high school football scores.

"Goodbye, Harry," he said, toasting the television. "It was nice knowing you."

Nick ate every last bite of both the burger and the fries, suddenly feeling quite thankful for everything he had. He swallowed the last of his beer, left a large tip, and headed back to the hotel for a good night's sleep.

The next morning, he woke early and checked out. He left a note for Helen, one that simply read, "Thanks for everything."

Then he put all of his luggage in his car and programmed in the route to Bismarck. It was going to be a long travel day. Once he was on the road, he called Sandra.

"Hey, Nick," she answered.

"Hey, Sandra," he said. "Can we talk?"

"Sure," she said.

And for the next hour that's exactly what they did.

BRANDED IN BISMARCK

BOOK #7 IN THE CAPITAL CITY MURDERS
SERIES

PROLOGUE: COWBOY GAMES GONE BAD

The golden sun was slowly dipping behind the thin clouds sitting atop Crown Butte, across the Missouri River west of Bismarck, North Dakota. Even though the 260-mile cattle drive from Brandon in Manitoba, Canada, had taken just over a week, the cowboys preferred to do it on horseback rather than in a half-day via train cars. Many of the ways of the "Old West" had gone the way of computers, trucks, and trailers, but the owners of the Lazy S Ranch were holding on to the "old ways" as long as they could.

Fred Stevens inherited the 640 acres from his dad, who'd inherited it from his dad. It was a small ranch, exactly one square mile, but it was a very important ranch in this part of the country. The Stevens name and the Lazy S Ranch were well-respected names in this area of North Dakota. Tens of thousands of cattle had been run through the ranch over the years and the decades, with a significant impact on the local economy. Fred and his wife Norma were humble and generous people, always willing to help anyone in need, even if it was a stranger passing through town who needed a bus ticket or meal. They were good people.

It had become an annual tradition that the Cattle Drive Party would be held at the Lazy S Ranch, and so it was that cowboys from ranches all over the area showed up Friday night to celebrate, to party, and give thanks that the drive had gone off without a hitch. Yes, one of the steers had fallen into a ditch, broken two legs, and had to be left for a butcher to come and take him away. But, for the most part, it was a safe and successful drive.

The sound of Fred ringing the triangle, usually the call for dinner, got everyone's attention.

"Does that mean it's time to eat?" a couple of young newbies asked as they joined the throng making its way toward the large barbecue pit.

"Just about," Timmy Lee answered as he cocked his head slightly to the left. "The ringing of the triangle is more of a way to just get everyone together to raise a toast and offer congratulations for a successful cattle drive." Timmy's eyes rolled as a smirk came across his face. "Rookie," he muttered under his breath as he turned to his life-long friend, Billy Knox.

"Everybody's got to have a first time," Billy responded as his mouth opened widely and yawned. "Long week," he added.

"Yep," Timmy replied. "A week without beer or women. When was the last time we did that? Junior High?"

"That's too long ago for me to remember."

Timmy and Billy grabbed plastic cups and pulled draft beers from two of the many iced kegs near the pit and gathered around as Fred picked up the microphone. He looked out at the crowd, smiled and waved. There was no rush. It was still early evening.

Timmy looked and saw a few of the younger hands drinking their beers. One of the Cattle Drive Party unspoken traditions was that there was no beer drinking until the host said his opening remarks and raised his own glass. "Rookies," he said again as he shook his head.

"They just don't know the traditions, yet," Billy said softly.

The murmur died down once everyone in the group had gotten a beer and settled in. "What a great drive," Fred Stevens said into the microphone as the crowd cheered. Fred smiled as he continued. "I've spoken with all the ranchers, and some are here with us tonight. They all said you guys did a great job."

"And gals," one of the cowgirls shouted.

"You are absolutely correct, young lady. Thank you. Times are changing, and it's not just cowboys anymore. So while your beer is still cold, let's all raise a glass and thank our Lord Almighty for watching over all our cowboys and cowgirls." Fred raised his glass of root beer to the cheers of the crowd. "Cheers!" he added.

"Party time," was yelled by a few of the seasoned cowhands, and the party was officially under way. Lights atop tall poles provided ample illumination as the sun's rays slipped away and the purple and pink clouds lost their color and became gray. Even the gray clouds started to blend with the darkening sky.

The smell and the sizzling of steaks cooking over the open fire surmounted the normal prominent odors of a working cattle ranch. But everyone here knew that "cattle odor" was the smell of money, and this year held a particularly good smell.

People got in fast-moving lines for steaks, beans, salads, and, of course, beer. The annual party was a time for reacquainting, making new friends, bragging about bonuses, and for blowing off steam. That's also what many of the games were about. The steam rising from the barbecue pit as the steaks dripped their juices down into the coals and the flames was really quite symbolic. The ranchers, the cowboys, the cowgirls, the families— they all worked hard, and their hard work and sweat made this all possible. When it was time to let loose, they partied hard, too.

All traces of natural light were gone as everyone ate and the games were underway. Calf roping was going on in one of the smaller brightly lit arenas. It was one of the few games that the younger kids, still too young to be cowhands, could participate in. The game of horseshoes was popular, as was telling jokes and stories. Many of the stories were real, or at least partially true, but many of them were concocted so that the listener thought they were real. And then the punch line revealed the real truth—it was totally made up. And all around laughed. Then it was the next person's turn.

Drinking beer hadn't ever been one of the "games," but it was definitely central to many of the activities at the party. Fred Stevens milled about with his clear plastic cup of root beer. Everyone thought he was drinking from the "special keg" of dark porter that only a few of the cowboys drank from. But Fred didn't partake in alcohol. It wasn't a religious decision, but a personal one. "I've seen too many lives ruined by alcohol," he'd once told a reporter.

"But beer is served at the Cattle Drive Parties. Isn't that a contradiction?" one reporter had inquired.

"Not at all. It's not my place to tell people how to live their lives. And I'm certainly not going to push my ideals on others," he replied. And so it was. Fred Stevens had his own set of morals, but he wasn't going to force his hands to abide by them. After all, these young men and women, worked hard, and Fred's opinion was that it was up to them to decide how they wanted to celebrate.

And celebrating they did. There was one person from the local beer supplier whose full-time job was to monitor and replace empty beer kegs. The cooks had done their job, steaks had been served to everyone, and the coals were now a bright red.

One of the newer games was branding iron tossing, a game where the throwers would see how many times they could flip it in the air and have it land upright. The branding mark would have to land flat on the ground with its handle pointing into the dark sky. After an unknown number of beers, the players decided they should first put the branding irons into the brilliant embers before flipping them.

Billy Knox placed an iron into the coals, pulling it out when it was glowing brightly. He stepped back from the pit and tossed it into the air. Spirals of red were visible as the iron went up and then back down to the ground, landing perfectly flat on the ground, causing it to sizzle. It was the first perfect toss of the night.

Timmy Lee grabbed the perfectly tossed iron and shoved it back into the dying embers. Smoke arose as he stirred it around. He frowned as he saw others congratulating Billy for his excellent toss. Billy was smiling and he raised his beer cup while the others toasted him. All of them cheered Billy, everyone but Timmy.

"That was pretty good," Timmy said to Billy as pulled the iron out of the coals with his left hand. He walked over to Billy and put out his right hand to congratulate him. The two cowboys shook hands, and as Billy lowered his right hand, Timmy lifted the steaming branding iron and thrust it into Billy's chest. His shirt sizzled on impact and the smell of burning flesh permeated the air. Billy took in a deep breath and a slight grin came across his face.

One of the newbies had his phone out and had been capturing the activities on video.

Billy just stood there. He'd consumed enough beer to be at least partially immune to the pain, enough that he could bear it.

"Let's set the brand like we do with the cattle," Timmy said as he reached for a brush that was sitting in a can of liquid. He picked up a small bottle, dumped its contents onto the brush, and wiped it across Billy's chest. Steam rose as Billy breathed in and out rapidly with his mouth wide open. His eyes blinked repeatedly and then he stared straight ahead before he doubled over and fell to the ground.

The newbie continued to video the event.

"Call the paramedics," someone yelled.

1

THE WINDS OF MONTANA

The bright morning sun came directly in through the windshield as Nick headed out of Helena on I-90 East. He looked at his navigation app, and it showed over 650 miles to his next capital city in Bismarck, North Dakota. Even breaking it up into two days, he knew Saturday was going to be a long travel day. Once he was on the road, he called Sandra.

"Hey, Nick," she answered.

"Hey Sandra," he said. "Can we talk?"

"Sure," she said.

And for the next hour or so, that's exactly what they did. Mostly they talked about his trip, and how much they missed each other. She filled him in on her work, and what she'd been up to.

"I'll call again in a few days, okay?" Nick said as he saw a sign that read, "Rest Area 2 Miles," and his body told him he needed to stop soon.

"Sounds good, Nick. Thanks for calling," she said with a lilting emphasis on 'Thanks.'

"Yep. Take care."

"Bye," Sandra said as she ended the call.

Nick flipped on the right blinker and pulled into the rest area.

The bicycling he'd done in Helena felt good, but his long legs were sore from just sitting and driving "I need to do some more biking," he said as he opened the door and held on tight as the strong wind tried to pull it away from him.

He climbed out of the car, stood up, and thrust his arms out wide as he stretched his six-foot six body. Nick twisted his torso first to the left and then to the right and his back popped a couple times. "Ooh, that feels good," he said as he closed his eyes, leaned his head back, and then twisted his head from side to side.

Several drivers stared at Nick as he walked to the covered area where the restrooms were located. He looked at the maps. There was a highway map of Montana and one of the U.S. Interstate Highway System. His eyes were drawn to the Pacific Northwest. "Wow," he said out loud. "Six weeks." That's how long he'd been gone from Seattle. He'd already visited and taken photographs of the capitol buildings in Washington, Oregon, California, Nevada, Idaho, and Montana.

He was now on his way to North Dakota, a state he'd visited once for a college basketball tournament. Nick instinctively reached down and rubbed his right leg. It was during his senior year at Boston College that he broke it during a game in Atlanta, ending his prospects of an NBA career. Nick went inside, relieved himself, and splashed cold water on his face after washing his hands. He rubbed his face and he shook his head side to side a couple times. "That'll help," he said as he headed back outside. The strong wind struck his wet face and instantly cooled him down. He raised his eyebrows as he was now more alert.

Looking at the Montana map on the wall, Nick saw he still had a few more hours to go, most of it running alongside the Yellowstone River. He bought an energy drink and a candy bar from the snack machine and went back to the car. The traffic was light, and the greenery alongside the river made the remainder of the drive more enjoyable. The miles passed quickly. The freeway crossed over the Yellowstone River, and Nick exited in Glendive and followed the navigation app's directions to his hotel, the Yellowstone River Inn.

"Seems fitting, since I followed it for most of the day," Nick said as he got out of the car, retrieved his suitcase from the trunk and the camera bag and laptop bag from the rear seat. The wind was blowing, but not as hard as it had been at the first rest stop.

"May I help you, sir," the desk clerk asked as Nick entered the lobby and approached the counter.

"I have a reservation, the last name is O'Flannigan," Nick replied as he looked around at the rustic Western design.

"Yes, here it is. Just one night sir?"

"Correct."

"How many keys?"

"Just one, please."

"First time here?"

"Yes, on my way to Bismarck."

The clerk—James, his name tag said—looked up, and up at Nick. "You're that photographer guy, right? The one visiting each state capital?"

"That's me," Nick said with a forced grin.

"Well, welcome to Glendive," James said as he handed the key packet to Nick. If there's anything you need, or restaurant recommendations, directions, anything at all, just let me know. We're pleased you chose to stay here."

Thanks," Nick said as he turned to leave, and then turned back. "There is. I've been following the river most of the day. Is there some place to go get some really great photographs of it?"

"Sure," James said as his shoulders lifted, and he took in a big breath. "Have GPS?"

"Yes."

"Go back out the way you came in, go under the freeway and drive along North River Avenue. You'll find plenty of places to park along the road, and it's a two-minute walk from the road to the river."

"Thanks," Nick said as he went to the elevator and then to his room. After unpacking his suitcase and grabbing a light jacket and his camera bag, Nick headed back down to the lobby, taking the stairs.

"It's just about five minutes from here," James said as he saw Nick and the camera bag. "And you should be able to get some great sunset photos," he added.

"I can always use more sunset photos," Nick said as he approached the counter. "What about a place with local flavor for some great western food and drink?"

"The Wagon Wheel Bar is probably the best, plus they have some pretty good evening entertainment if you're into country and western music."

"I like all kinds, especially when it fits with the locale." Nick reached his long right arm across the counter and James eagerly stuck out his hand to shake Nick's. "Thanks again," Nick added as he headed out to the car.

He was able to take some interesting photos up and down the river before the sun began to drop toward the horizon. The clouds changed from white to pinks and purples as Nick snapped shot after shot. "These will be fun to look through tonight," he said as he walked through the tall grasses up to his car. Nick put the camera bag in the trunk, typed 'Wagon Wheel Bar' into his navigation app, and followed the directions. It didn't take long to get there, not that there are too many places to go in a town of five thousand.

The parking lot appeared full as Nick pulled in. He stopped quickly as he saw a car's taillights come on followed by the reverse lights before the car backed out. "Ah, Saturday night," he said as he waited for the car to leave the lot. Nick's car was one of the vehicles that wasn't a pickup truck, the mainstay vehicle for most cowboys and others in the area.

The music spilled out into the lot as the front door opened and a departing couple came through it. "Hi," Nick said to them as he approached the door.

"Howdy," the man said, his girl's arm around his waist.

Nick entered the lively bar. A four-piece band was playing, and several couples were on the dance floor. Nick looked around and saw several empty tables that weren't exactly empty because they had drinks on them. *Probably belong to those on the dance floor,* Nick thought as he continued to look around. His height gave him an advantage of being able to see over everything else in the bar.

"Over here, hon," he heard a female voice holler over the sound of the music. He looked and saw a waitress waving her hand for him to come her direction. Nick nodded and waved his hand. She smiled and started clearing the beer bottles and the plates from the table. Heads turned and followed Nick as he weaved his way through the sea of tables and chairs to one being cleaned for him.

"Thanks," Nick said as he got to the table and the waitress had pulled a chair out for him.

"My pleasure, hon," she said as she looked up at him and smiled. The gap between her two front upper teeth caught Nick's attention. "What can I getcha?"

"Do you have a nice cold porter on tap?"

"Sure do. Anything to eat?"

"Menu, please?"

"Sure. I'll be right over with a menu and your beer," she said as Nick sat down. He looked around, most of the guys were wearing cowboy hats. He was taking in the scenery when the waitress set the frosted glass of porter beer on the table. "Here you go," she said as she handed the menu to him.

Nick looked up at her and smiled. He saw her nametag. "Thanks, Judy."

"My pleasure, hon. You're not from around here are ya?" she asked as she put her hand on his shoulder.

"No, ma'am. Just passing through on my way to Bismarck."

"Where ya comin' from?"

"Came in from Helena today. I'm on a year-long assignment to visit each state capital and take photographs for a travel magazine."

"Sounds like fun," Judy added as she gave his should a slight squeeze while keeping her hand there. "Take a look at the menu, and I'll be right back."

"Thanks," Nick said as he picked up the beer glass and took a long slow drink. "Good," he said to himself as he watched Judy make the rounds to her tables. She returned and Nick ordered a roast beef sandwich and a loaded baked potato, plus a side of fries.

The band took a break, and that seemed to be a signal for many of the patrons to leave. What was originally a packed place was now mostly deserted. Judy brought Nick's food to the table and set it down. "Kind of early for everyone to leave, isn't it?" Nick asked.

"Most of them were here just for happy hour. We'll probably pick up again a little later with the night crowd."

"Got it," Nick said as he looked at the large plate of food in front of him. He picked up the sandwich with beef slices slipping out of the bun. He opened his mouth and took a big bite. He nodded his approval to Judy who still stood there.

She looked around at the now mostly empty tables, then sat down. "Pretty good, isn't it?"

Nick nodded again and tried to smile.

"My shift's over soon," she said in a low voice. "My husband works in the oil fields and he's been gone for three months and won't be back for a couple more."

Nick swallowed a bite of roast beef and took another drink of his beer. "What are you suggesting?"

She pulled her chair closer to his. "You're here for one night. It's been a long time for me."

Nick grabbed a few fries, dipped them in the fry sauce, and put them into his mouth. "Hmm," he muttered after he swallowed. He looked toward the bar and saw the bartender looking at him.

"Don't worry about him," Judy said as she saw where Nick was looking.

"I don't think this is a good idea, Judy."

"Maybe not, but we'd have a good time. I know I certainly would and I'll make sure you do, too."

Nick took a few more bites of his sandwich, staying silent as Judy just sat there awkwardly. He used his napkin to wipe the juice from his cheek and chin.

"I'll be back," she said as she got up and busied herself at other tables.

Nick finished his sandwich, ate most of his fries and half of the baked potato. The beer glass was empty, ad he was still thirsty. He looked and saw Judy headed back to his table.

"How about another beer? This one's on me," she said as she winked and grinned, showing that gap in her smile.

"Better not," Nick said. "I've got more work to do tonight. But thanks."

"What about later on?" she asked as she sat back down and put her hand on his thigh.

Nick reached into his lap and slowly moved her hand away. "Can't do it," he said. "Just the check, please."

"Can't or won't?" she insisted.

"Okay then. Won't. It's not fair to your husband. Check, please."

Judy pushed her chair back and stood up. Her smile turned into a frown "You don't know what you're missing out on, hon. We could've had a good time," she said as she went to the bar.

Nick paid the bill and left. He talked to himself as he walked through the mostly empty parking lot to his car. "What's with gals named Judy? There was that one in Nevada at the gas station, and now this one. Are all Judy's that aggressive?"

2

———

BREAKING NEWS UPDATE

Nick returned to the hotel, had one beer in the bar, went to his room, and spent over two hours sorting the photographs he'd taken along the river earlier in the day. Nick looked at his watch and yawned. After driving for almost seven hours, taking photos along the river, having dinner, sorting and culling the photos, he was tired. "Ten thirty," he muttered as he shut down his laptop and used two black binder clips to hold the room curtains completely shut. He then undressed and took a long, steamy shower.

He crawled into bed, kicking the tucked-in top sheet out from the bottom. His head hit the pillow and a peaceful sigh escaped his mouth. Nick was fast asleep.

"What time is it?" Nick asked as he awoke on Sunday morning. He rolled to his side and reached out and turned the alarm clock to face him. "Ten o'clock?" he blurted out in a surprised voice. The room was mostly dark. He looked toward the window and saw just a thin strip of light along the carpet. He threw off the sheet and blanket, slung his long legs over the side of the bed, and stood up. He walked to the window and saw the two binder clips he'd used to close the curtains and block out all the light. "They sure worked," he said as he unclipped them and pulled the curtains open. The room instantly transformed from black to white.

Nick dressed hurriedly and went downstairs. "Quite a storm last night, wasn't it?" James asked as Nick walked to the breakfast room.

"What storm?" he replied.

"The lightning and thunder. You didn't see or hear it?"

"I was out like a light, and I certainly didn't think I'd sleep in this long," Nick said as he looked toward the breakfast room.

"Well," James said. "You better hurry in there. They shut it down in about ten minutes."

"Thanks," Nick replied. "Oh, and thanks for the Wagon Wheel Bar recommendation. It was good fun and cold beer."

"Glad you liked it," James added, but Nick had already turned and was headed for breakfast before it was too late.

Nick ate quickly and grabbed a banana and a yogurt cup for the drive to Bismarck, and went to his room to pack. Back on the road by noon, Nick looked at his navigation app as he entered I-94. It showed a little under three hours. About thirty minutes later he saw the sign, "Welcome to North Dakota." *Another hour lost*, he thought as he saw the next sign, "Entering Central Time Zone."

Nick's phone rang and he pressed the radio button to answer the call. "This is Nick."

"Hey, Nick," the chipper voice said. "This is Helen, remember me?"

Nick squinted his eyes and pursed his lips as he replied, "Of course I do." *Oh yeah. From the hotel in Helena.* "How are you?"

"Doing fine. I got your note, but I was hoping I could see you before you left."

There was a slight hesitation in Nick's voice as he responded. "I, uh, needed to get on the road. I would've liked to have seen you, too, but I forgot that I was going to lose an hour going into North Dakota."

"Yea, that can be a problem," she replied matter-of-factly before continuing in an upbeat voice. "Did you hear about the second hanging?"

"I did. I saw it on the news Friday night."

BISMARCK 42 the road sign indicated.

"Nick," Helen began in an asking voice. "Would you mind if I met you somewhere and we spent a couple days together? I know you'll be working but I won't get in the way."

Nick's eyes opened wide. *Where'd that come from?* He let out a big sigh.

"Is that a bad idea, Nick?"

"Um, it's not a, a bad idea, Helen," he struggled to reply.

"But it's not a good idea either?" she asked.

"I don't know what it is. Can we talk about it later this week?"

"Sure," Helen replied quickly. "You can call me any time."

"Okay, I'll do that," Nick replied.

"Thanks, Nick. I'll talk to you later."

"Okay, Helen. Bye." The phone beeped as Helen ended the call.

REST STOP 1 MILE, Nick saw the sign. "I definitely need a pit stop now," Nick muttered as he pondered that call with Helen.

Back on the highway after the quick rest stop, Nick entered Bismarck thirty minutes later as the sun behind him slowly worked its way down to the horizon. His app led him right to his hotel, where he parked the car, grabbed his bags, went into the lobby, and checked in. He went to his room, pulled out his camera, and headed back out to get some sunset photos around the capitol building. *They're good,* he thought as he scanned through the digital images on the camera. *A good start anyway.* Nick returned to the hotel, left the camera in his room, and went down to the lobby.

"Sports Inn is your best bet tonight," the hotel clerk replied to Nick's request for a recommendation for a good sports pub.

"Thanks," Nick offered as he nodded his head and entered Sports Inn into his navigational app.

"We have breaking news," the television announcer said as Nick sat down at the pub. "We have just received a report from the Sheriff's Department that Billy Knox, the branding victim at the weekend's annual cowboy party, has died. Several individuals have been questioned, but the Sheriff added that so far, the death appears to have been accidental."

"What's that all about?" Nick asked as a waiter came to his table.

"Some cowboys were drinking beer and tossing branding irons in the air. For some reason, one of the guys stuck Billy in the chest with a red-iron, and he passed out."

"And now he's dead?" Nick asked. "Doesn't sound terribly accidental to me."

"It does sound strange, doesn't it? What can I get for you?"

"Any local dark beers?"

"Let me see; I think we have one. Want a sample?"

"Nah, go ahead and bring me a pint."

"Sure thing," the waiter said as he set a menu on the table and went to the bar.

"Tossing branding irons' in the air," Nick muttered. "Now there's a new sport, and apparently a deadly one." He pulled out his phone and did a search for 'branding iron tossing.' "Wow, there actually is such a thing. Crazy," he added as he shook his head back and forth. He noticed an article titled, 'Accidental or Not?' "Hmm, maybe it was murder instead of an accident," Nick said as he saw the waiter approaching with his beer.

3

WHERE'S MY PHONE?

The screeching sound of the old radio/alarm clock blared as Nick forced his eyes open to locate the source of the noise. He reached out with his left arm and slapped the top of the radio. The blaring continued. He turned onto his left side and found the culprit with his right hand. He felt along the top until he found a button to press down. He did and the sound went away.

"What a way to wake up," Nick muttered as he tossed the bedding aside and sat on the side of the bed. He got up and put on his workout clothes and headed toward the door as the alarm came on again. "That could probably wake the dead it's so obnoxious," he said as he went to turn it off. *Maybe I'll just use my phone from now on,* he thought as he headed out the door. He took the steps down to the first floor where he'd seen a sign for the Gym. He stuck his card key into the lock and heard a click.

He stepped inside and looked around. "Three pieces of equipment. Wow," he said. "I need to find a real gym with more than just these machines," he added as he looked at the treadmill, the stair stepper, and a weights machine. *This will have to do for now,* he thought as he stepped on the treadmill. Nick finished his morning workout on the third machine about an hour later. He wiped his face, neck, and arms with a clean towel, tossed it into the empty bin, and headed back up to his room.

After showering, shaving, and getting dressed, Nick grabbed his camera bag and headed downstairs, taking the elevator this time. Monday morning traffic was congested as he neared the capitol building. He continued to North Seventh Street where he found the Farm House Inn, known locally for its great breakfast. He pulled into the parking lot and had to go around the back of the building to find an open spot.

"The reviews were spot on," he told the waitress as she brought the check to Nick. "That was one of the best meals I've had in a long time," he added.

"I'm glad you liked it, sir. Is there anything else I can get for you?"

"Actually, Mary," he began as he looked at her name tag. Nick pulled a card from his shirt pocket and handed it to her. "I'm on a year-long assignment to visit each state capital and take photographs for a magazine based out of Washington. Would it be possible for me to leave my car in the lot for a couple hours while I walk back up to the capitol building rather than trying to find a closer place to park?"

"I don't see why not but let me go check with the manager."

"Thanks," Nick said as she turned around and walked back to the cash register. He picked up the bill and stood up. He smiled and nodded as Mary talked to the manager who looked in Nick's direction.

He swore they were both checking him out, and he felt really uncomfortable. When he wasn't dating anyone, he never got this kind of attention. Now with Sandra, and possibly Helen interested, he'd suddenly become a chick magnet.

Nick started walking toward the register when Mary met him halfway. Her eyes were mid-chest level on Nick, and she leaned her head back as he looked at her. "The manager says that of course, you can leave your car here."

"Thanks," Nick said as he handed her a ten-dollar bill. "Working the lunch shift?"

"Sure am."

"Save a table for me, I'll be back," he said in a soft voice. It never hurt to flirt a little, since they were doing him a favor.

"I'll be here," Mary said as a smile came across her face and her cheeks turned slightly pink.

Nick paid the bill and thanked the manager who pointed out a place for him to move his car. He moved the car, grabbed his camera bag, looked back inside the restaurant, and saw the two women staring at him. He waved to them with his free hand, turned and walked the three blocks to the capitol building.

He reached into his pants pocket for his phone, but it wasn't there. He went back to the car, but didn't find it there either. He checked the restaurant, but they hadn't seen it, and it wasn't near where he'd been sitting.

"Oh, well," he said as he resumed his walk to the capitol. "I'm sure I just left it at the hotel."

Nick easily saw the top several stories of the capitol building several blocks away. The bright sun reflecting off the tall Art Deco building, reported to be the tallest in the state, made it look like a giant slab of white marble.

Nick spent several hours taking photographs of the inside and outside of the twenty-one story building. He'd walked up over a dozen flights of stairs before he took the elevator to the top. *At least it's slightly downhill,* he thought as he left the capitol and headed back to the Farm House Inn. "With the shots I got last night, I'm pretty much done here," Nick said as he approached the restaurant. He put the camera bag in the car, re-locked the car, and took the camera inside with him.

"Walk off that breakfast?" the manager said as Nick entered.

"Pretty much," Nick said. "That's the second capitol building I've seen that doesn't have the typical dome on top. The top of the one in Salem, Oregon, was a bit weird, looking almost like a geared shaft sitting atop the office buildings. The one here is definitely quite interesting."

"So you're traveling to each state capital taking photographs for a full year?"

"Yes, I am."

"You know," the manager said. "We could use some new pictures of the restaurant for our website and advertising. Do you think you'd have time to take some for us?"

"I'm sure I would, but I'd have to charge you."

"Of course. Maybe we can talk after lunch?"

"Sure," Nick said as he saw Mary coming through the swinging double doors. Her lipstick looked fresh and her hair appeared to have been recently brushed. "Hi."

"Hi," Mary replied. "Get all your pictures taken?"

"I think so," he answered. "You have a table for me?"

"Sure do," Mary said as she led Nick to a booth in the corner. "What did she want?" Mary asked in a quiet voice as Nick was sliding into the booth.

"Oh, she just wanted to know if I could take some photographs of the restaurant."

"That's all?"

"That's all. I told her I'd have to charge her, and she seemed fine with that. I can always use a little extra work and money on the side."

"I'd get the check up front and take it to the bank right away. She has a way of stalling people who do things for her." Mary winked and set the menu on the table. "I'll get you some water," she said as she turned and left.

Nick saw the manager looking in his direction and he nodded and smiled at her.

The manager came to Nick's booth after he'd eaten lunch. "Mind if I sit down?"

"Not at all," he replied. "It's your restaurant."

"When do you think you could come by and take some photos?"

"Well," he began. "First I'd need to have a list of what type of photographs you're looking for. Breakfast time, etc. Full house, empty place. Inside, outside, kitchen. I'd need to know exactly what you're looking for. I'd then write up a quick agreement. For small jobs like this, I ask for payment up front. Once I get payment, then I'll take the photos and deliver them to you, in digital format. If you want actual prints that will take loger and cost a little more. Does that all sound okay?"

"I didn't think it would be that complicated."

"Well, without knowing what you want, I don't know what to charge. And it needs to be in writing so we each know that I've done what you've asked me to do." Nick paused. "Is that a problem?"

"No, not really. I was just thinking we could do this just between two friends." Her voice got softer and she stared straight into Nick's eyes.

"You have a business and I have a business, and I need to have a contract for everything I do, even small jobs. I know it's a hassle, but it's really the best for both of us so that things are clear from the start."

"I see."

"I leave on Saturday, and so I'd want to get started as soon as possible." He pulled a card from his shirt pocket and handed it to her. "Give me a call when you have things figured out, and it will take me about an hour to come up with my price and the short agreement. Is that okay?"

The manager swallowed hard, closed her eyes, and then opened them. "Sure. I should have it done later tonight."

"I'm hoping my phone's at the hotel, but just in case, shoot me an email. That's on the card too."

"I'll call you tonight, and don't worry. Lunch is on me."

Nick smiled. "Thanks, but the contract I have with the magazine says I can't accept goods or merchandise without paying for it. It just keeps everything on the up and up."

"That's fine. Mary will bring you the bill," the manager said as she started to make her way out of the booth.

Mary brought the bill and Nick gave her a twenty-dollar bill, more than enough to cover the lunch and a nice tip.

"See you again?" she asked as she handed him a slip of paper that he stuck in his pocket.

"Yes," Nick replied. He returned to his hotel room, and his phone was right there on the desk. The red voicemail light was flashing. He looked at the number, it was his parents' house. He listened to the message. It was marked urgent. "Hello, Nick. It's your mom. Your dad had a heart attack, but the doctor said it wasn't too bad and he should be home in a couple of days. I'm going back to the hospital so I won't be home for a few hours. Bye, Nick."

"I wish they had cell phones," Nick said as he sat down on the bed. He closed his eyes and nodded his head slightly. *A few days of peace and quiet in the hospital might do dad some good,* he thought as he leaned back on the bed. The busy days of driving and doing a lot of walking had sapped much of his normal energy. Taking the stairs most of the way up the capitol building hadn't helped either.

His minded drifted to childhood images and he fell asleep. He didn't hear his phone ring as he slept.

4

WHAT'S IN A BRAND?

Nick awoke the next morning to the screaming sound of that same alarm clock. "Enough of that," he said as he ran his fingers along the length of the cord until his hand hit the wall. He grabbed the plug and pulled it from the receptacle. He took a quick shower, got dressed and felt something in his pants pocket. He pulled out the slip of paper that he'd put in there yesterday. 'Mary' was written in beautifully stroked cursive handwriting along with a phone number. *Oh, yeah. Mary.*

He reached for his phone and saw that he had a message. *"That's right I need to call and see how Dad is."* He started to call home, and then thought, *"I'd better check the message first in case Mom called again."* He started the message and hit the speaker button. "Hi, Nick. This is Roberta, the manager at the Farm House Inn. It's Monday evening, and I have the list of photos I'd like taken while you're in town this week. Can you come by the restaurant so we can discuss it? I'm here all day, every day, so just stop by when you can. Thanks, Nick."

Nick let out a big breath of relief that it wasn't his Mom calling with bad news. "Ah, Roberta," he said out loud as he sat down in the desk chair. "I was wondering what her name was." He took in a deep breath and slowly exhaled. "Call Mom," he said into the phone and he put it to his ear. The phone rang three times before it was answered.

"Hello?" It was always a question when she answered the phone.

"Hi, Mom. It's Nick. How's Dad?"

"Hi, Nick. He's doing better. I was up there this morning, and the nurse had him up and walking slowly around in the hall. She said the doctor wants him to be able to walk for fifteen minutes without getting winded before he can come home.

"How'd he look?"

"He looked good, and the nurse said she would have him walking every four hours. Nothing too strenuous, but enough to make sure he's healthy enough to come home. Maybe even in a couple days."

"That's great news, Mom." Nicks voice went from excited to somber and he spoke slower. "How are you doing, Mom? Are you okay?"

"Of course, I'm fine, Nick. Why wouldn't I be?"

Nick hesitated before answering. "We both know that Dad hasn't done much since he retired. He's not as young as he used to be, and I'm concerned about his health. And I'm also concerned about you since you have to do almost everything around the house."

"Nick, I did everything around the house when your dad was working, so it's not different now. I'm fine, I just wish you were back in the area so we could see you more often."

"I know, Mom. It won't be too many more months until I'm there. In the meantime, we can still talk anytime you want."

"That sounds good, Nick. Thanks."

"You're welcome, Mom. I love you, and tell Dad I love him, too. Let me know when he comes home."

"I will, Nick. Thanks for calling. I love you"

"Love you, too, Mom. Bye now."

"Bye, Nick."

"Might as well get two things done at once," Nick said as he grabbed his camera bag and notebook and headed down to his car. He pulled into the parking lot at the Farm House Inn ten minutes later.

"Are you a basketball player," a young boy asked as he and his mom were walking out of the restaurant.

"Not anymore," Nick replied. "But I used to be. Do you like basketball?" he asked as he knelt down so the two were at eye level.

"I liked it when I was younger when I had my own basket at home, but now the basket at school is too high for me."

"Don't worry about that, you'll keep growing."

"Will I be big like you?"

"Maybe not, but you'll still be big enough to shoot the ball into the basket."

"Come on, Timmy," the Mom said. "We have to get you to the doctor's office."

Nick looked up at the Mom and smiled. His right knee popped as he stood up. "From the injury that took me out of the game," he said as she watched his long body arise. Looking down to the young boy, Nick continued. "You be brave and strong at the doctor's Timmy. Tell him you want to be big and strong and play basketball when you get older. Okay?"

"Okay. Thanks, mister," Timmy said with a big smile on his face.

"Thank you very much," the mom said as she grabbed Timmy's hand and headed to the car.

"My pleasure," Nick replied.

Mary approached Nick as he entered the restaurant. "Hi," she said as her eyes widened.

"Hi," Nick answered. "Breakfast for one?"

"Sure," Mary replied. "Roberta said she had something to talk with you about, so is that corner booth okay?"

"Sounds good." *Her hair is in a tighter ponytail and her dress seems more form fitting today,* he thought as he followed her to the farthest table in the restaurant.

"Coffee and orange juice?"

"Good memory. Yes, thanks." Nick said as he slid into the booth, stopping halfway around on the quarter circle vinyl bench.

Mary left and Roberta approached with a pad of paper in her left hand. "May I?" she asked.

"Of course," Nick answered.

"Thanks for coming in so soon. Here's what I was thinking of," she said as she slid the pad of paper to Nick.

His head moved side to side slightly as he read each item, each shot and angle for updating the restaurant's website, menu, and other materials. "Nice and thorough," he said after going through the long list. May I take this sheet with me? I'll need to run some figures on my laptop and prepare an agreement once I have a final number." He paused. "Um, I have to stop in at the Sheriff's Department this morning, but I can be back here this afternoon to discuss it with you if that's okay." He slid the pad back to Roberta.

"Sure," she said as she tore the top sheet of paper off, handed it to Nick, and he folded it and put it into his shirt pocket.

It was like they had a tag team act underway. First it was Mary leaving and Roberta approaching. Now Roberta was leaving Nick's table and Mary was approaching. He saw the steam rising from the silverish colored coffee pot and the large glass of orange juice she had on her tray. She reached forward and set the glass in front of him, and then poured the coffee. "Any time to look at the menu?" she asked with raised eyebrows.

"Not yet," Nick said as he shook his head sideways.

"Not a problem, I'll be back." Mary turned and walked away. Nick looked around the restaurant and saw that most of the men were watching her. A slight smile came across his face. *I bet they're all married*, he thought.

"Ready now?" Mary asked as she returned a couple minutes later.

"How about a four-egg omelet, with everything in it," Nick replied.

"You got it," Mary said as she took the order to the kitchen.

Nick pulled Roberta's sheet out of his pocket. He nodded his head up and down as he scanned the list. "Quite a few different settings," he said softly. "My time, her money. That's okay," he added as he returned the sheet to his pocket.

"Wow," he said as Mary approached and set his plate on the table.

"Pretty big, huh?" she said.

"It's a good thing I'm hungry. Thanks."

Mary smiled as she turned and left.

Nick let out a big sigh a few minutes later as he ate the last bite of the omelet. He took the last sip of the juice finished his third cup of coffee.

"Any more coffee or juice?" Mary asked as she approached.

"No room for it," he answered, and then with a slight grin he added, "I know that's hard to believe, but I am full."

"Here's your check, but no rush."

"Actually, I've got to head down to the Sheriff's Department." He looked at the check, pulled out his wallet, and handed Mary fifteen dollars. "Thanks, I might be back later this afternoon with some paperwork for Roberta."

"I've got the afternoon off if you want a local guide to show you around the city."

"Sounds good. I've got, uh, a few errands to do, but I'll give you a call once I know what my timing is."

"Okay," Mary said with a weak smile. She picked up the check and went to the register.

Out in his car, Nick entered Bismarck Sheriff's Department into his phone, pressing the Directions button when the address appeared on the screen. "Turn right on North Seventh Street," the instructions began.

"You have reached your destination," the app announced as Nick pulled into the Sheriff's Department parking lot ten minutes later.

"May I help you, sir?" the uniformed officer asked as Nick entered and approached the counter.

"Yes, sir," Nick replied as he displayed his media badge. "I'm a freelance photographer passing through the area, and I'd like to speak with the person leading the investigation into that young cowboy's death, the one that was branded."

"Your name, sir?"

"Nick O'Flannigan," he said as he pulled a card out of his wallet and handed it to the officer.

"Have a seat, sir, and I'll see if he's available."

"Thank you." Nick said as he sat down on one of the wooden benches.

A stocky man dressed in a suit that probably fit him several years ago came through a door and approached Nick as he stood up. "I'm Deputy Reynolds. Is there something I can help you with?"

"Yes, Deputy," Nick said. I was hoping to see some of the photos of that branding victim."

The man chuckled slightly. "Sorry, we can't do that. Privacy and all that kind of stuff."

Nick pulled out his wallet and showed him his media badge. "I'm in town for only a few more days. I'm a professional, and I won't reveal anything to anyone, and nothing you share with me will be made public."

"Sorry," Reynolds repeated.

"Oh," Nick replied. He then continued in a lowered voice with his eyes intently focused on the deputy. "Here's the deal. I'm a photographer on a year-long assignment to visit each state capital and took photographs for a big magazine. My own specialty is macrophotography, and sometimes I see details that others miss."

"Let's step outside."

"Sure," Nick responded as he followed the deputy back outside.

"If you sign a Confidentiality Agreement and promise not to reveal anything, I can put a few of the photographs on a thumb drive if you have one."

"That would be great," Nick said "Let me get one from the car." He got a thumb drive from his camera bag and handed it to Reynolds.

"Come back in and give me five minutes."

"Thanks," Nick said.

Five minutes turned into ten. But the deputy came back out front, handed Nick a form to sign, which he did, and then handed him the thumb drive.

"Thank you, sir," Nick said as he left the building and returned to his hotel room to research cattle brands and the branding process.

5

BUT WHAT ABOUT . . . ?

Back in his hotel room, Nick opened his laptop and searched for "Bismarck cowboy feuds." "I didn't think there'd be this many articles," Nick said as the results filled pages of pages on his screen. "As far back as the mid-1880s," one article began as it detailed the generations of bad blood between several prominent families in Burleigh County, of which Bismarck had always been the main town.

"Wow," Nick said as he continued to read the articles. He picked up his phone and called the Sheriff's Department.

"Sheriff's Department," the female voice said.

"Deputy Reynolds, please," Nick said.

"Just a moment, please."

"Deputy Reynolds."

"Deputy, this is Nick O'Flannigan. We spoke a little while ago."

"Oh, yes."

"Well, I've done some research, and I think that the cowboy's death was payback for some steer rustling a while back. From what I read ..." Nick said before he was interrupted.

"You're not from around here, right?" the deputy asked.

"Right."

"That was resolved several years. The cowboys involved in that all moved away, and the ones around here now are either all new ones, or they were too young back then."

"But what about ...?"

Reynolds didn't let Nick finish. "I think you should stick to taking photographs or studying them and let us deal with the investigations and whatever you can find in them. Anyone in this office can do a Google search. That's not what you told me your area of expertise was."

"But..."

"Please, sir," the deputy interrupted once again, his voice getting sharper with each response. "You do your job, and we'll do ours. Okay?" The last word was more of a statement than a question.

"Yeah," Nick replied, his voice deflated as much as his ego. "Mind if I ask if there's been any cause of death reported?"

"Well," Reynold began hesitatingly. "I probably shouldn't tell you this as it's not public yet."

"I won't tell anyone," Nick said.

"Okay. We just got word from the coroner that he thinks the young man had a heart attack."

"Hmmm," Nick uttered. Thanks."

"Yep," Deputy Reynolds said and the line went dead.

Nick set the phone on the desk. "Focus, Nick," he said to himself. "You're here to take photographs, not get involved in something that is either way over your head or you'll find that it's best if you didn't get involved."

He pushed the phone aside and went through the photos he'd taken here in Bismarck. Some went into the *Magazine* folder and some went into the *Personal* folder on his laptop. Some of the duplicates or just not great photos he deleted. He went back through the ones for the magazine and selected the best ones to upload.

Emily's going to love the ones from the top of the capitol, he mused as he slowly nodded his head while watching the uploading progress.

After all the process completed, Nick picked up his phone and commanded "Call Sandra."

"Hello," came the female voice after only two rings.

"Hey, there," Nick said. "How ya doing?"

"Oh, hi, Nick. Everything's good here. How's Bismarck?"

"It's a pretty nice town. People are friendly, most of them anyway, and the Missouri River runs along the edge of town. I was thinking of going kayaking."

"That sounds like fun," the perky voice said. "Are we still on for Denver in a few weeks?"

"Sure," Nick replied without hesitation. I've got my car, so I can pick you up at the airport. Let me know when you've got your ticket."

"Okay. Are you involved with anything yet?"

"You mean ...?" Nick let it trail off.

"You know what I mean," Sandra interjected. "A murder case, for example?"

There was a slight pause before Nick answered. "Well," he stammered. "Not involved, per se, but there was this one mysterious death, and from an article I read, most deaths like that are murder and not accidents. I was able to talk the deputy into letting me have a copy of some of the photographs, and they didn't look pretty." He went on to describe how the victim had a cattle brand imprinted on his chest.

"That's horrible," Sandra said.

"Yes, it is, and the coroner is calling it a heart attack. But the victim was my age, and while it's certainly possible for someone young to have a heart attack, the odds against it are really high. I think there's more to it than that."

"Uh, does that mean you are getting involved in the investigation?" Sandra emphasized the word 'are.'

Nick didn't respond, not sure what to say.

"You are, aren't you?" Sandra asked.

6

———

KAYAKING THE MISSOURI RIVER

Nick awoke on Wednesday morning to a gentle "good morning" wake up call from his phone. The hotel alarm clock he'd unplugged the day before had been plugged back in while he was out, but he made sure that annoying alarm wasn't set to go off. After showering and dressing, he took the stairs down to the breakfast room. He tucked a copy of *The Bismarck Tribune* under his arm as he passed through the lobby, ate a quick breakfast, and then returned to his room.

"Call Mom," he said into his phone.

"Hello?" the familiar voice answered on the other end.

"Hi, Mom. Just calling to see how Dad's doing, and if he's still coming home today."

"Hi, Nick. He seems to be doing well, even though he still complains about them making him exercise and walk around. I was there for about an hour this morning, and the nurse said she thinks the doctor will send him home for sure tomorrow."

"Well, that's good news. I'm glad he's feeling better. You know how to call me if you need to at any time."

"I know, Nick. Thanks for calling. I love you."

"Love you, too, Mom. Bye." And the call ended. He then sent a text to Mary. 'Got super busy yesterday afternoon. Sorry. Rain check?'

Nick opened his laptop and checked his email. There was one from Boston College about an upcoming reunion. As he scrolled through the message, the mention of the annual Alumni versus Varsity basketball game brought back painful memories. He reached down and rubbed his right leg. It hadn't been hurting him until he read that part about the game.

"Darn it," he muttered as he massaged his knee. Maybe with some biking and increased exercise on this trip, he'd be able to play at least a little bit. He could hope anyway.

He scanned through the remaining emails and found nothing he had to attend to right away. He pushed the chair back and picked up the morning's paper.

"What's going in the area today?" he questioned as he unfolded it and perused the articles. "Hmm, not much, is there?" he said as he got to the last page, the ads. One of the advertisements stood out with its headline in all caps: FORENSIC ACCOUNTANT. "Looking for that special person who can look at P&Ls, Balance Sheets, and spreadsheets, and see more than just numbers," the ad read along with the contact information.

"Forensic Accounting," Nick mused. "I remember that class. What was it that the prof kept drilling into us? Oh yeah. He'd say, *'The details behind the details are what are important.'* That's probably why these cases, especially the murder cases, intrigue me so much."

His phone began to vibrate on the desk, and then the ringing started. Nick looked at the display.

"Hey, Gerry," he said into the phone after he pressed the green button.

"Hey, Nick. How's it going?"

"Good, a bit early for you, isn't it?"

"Yeah, my alarm went off early for some reason. No big deal," and she paused. Then, "Anything new with Sandra?"

"We spoke yesterday, and she's probably coming to Denver in a few weeks to spend a few days with me."

"Hmmm, sounds serious."

"I don't know about that," Nick replied. "I did the married thing for a few years, and that didn't work out. I'm not sure if I want to get serious again."

"You don't have to make a long-term commitment right away. Just enjoy being with each other. If it's meant to be something more, it'll work out that way. Just don't try to force it either way."

"Damn," Nick said. "You always know the right thing to say."

"Experience. I've tried both ways, and I'm pretty happy now. So, have you two discussed having separate rooms or at least separate beds?"

"Hadn't thought of that. We did have separate rooms in Salem, so that might not be a bad idea."

"Well think about it, and make sure she is one hundred percent comfortable with whatever arrangements you decide on."

Nick's phone started ringing again and he looked at the display, Editor Emily it showed. "It's Emily, gotta go. Call you later."

"Bye," Gerry said and ended the call.

"Good morning, Emily," Nick said cheerfully into the phone.

"Hey, Nick. How's Bismarck?"

"It's nice, another small friendly town that happens to be a capital city."

"I bet it's quite a change from the larger cities like Sacramento or Olympia."

"Definitely," Nick responded.

"Those photos from the top of the capitol building were quite spectacular. How tall is that building?"

"Twenty-one stories, the tallest in the state if you can believe that. And it's not even half the height of the Space Needle."

"I guess it's nice that there are some places that haven't been overrun with growth and progress, not that they're even the same thing at times."

The two continued with small talk for a few minutes.

"Well, I just wanted to touch base with you," Emily said, "and to make sure everything is going well."

"It's all great, no more car problems or anything else to get in the way."

"No more murder mysteries?"

"Nope," Nick replied.

"That's good. Keep up the great work, the team is loving your photos. Any more coming from Bismarck?"

"Thanks, Emily. Yeah, I'll be getting a few more shots later today and possibly tomorrow. It's supposed to be cloudy so I might be able to get some artistic ones."

"Good job, Nick. Thanks. Stay in touch."

"I will, Emily. Bye now," he said and ended the call.

Nick re-opened his laptop and opened up the agreement he'd created for Roberta for photos she wanted him to take at the Farm House Inn. He calculated it would take him about eight hours given the different times of day and evening he'd have to be there. "She might balk at four hundred and eighty dollars, but that's still forty percent off my normal rate, and the extra cash wouldn't be bad." He copied the file to a thumb drive, grabbed his camera bag, and went downstairs to the Business Center.

He printed two copies of the three-page agreement, and drove to the restaurant.

He didn't recognize any of the employees as he went inside. "Hi, is Roberta here?" he asked the one at the register.

"No, she had some errands to run, so she's gone for the rest of the day."

"Well, how about Mary?"

"Her day off."

"Okay, um, do you have an envelope you can put this in for Roberta? She asked me to bring it to her," Nick said as he tri-folded one copy of the agreement.

"Sure, just a minute," the waitress said as she turned and went through the door marked PRIVATE. She was back out in less than a minute and handed an envelope to Nick.

He put the folded agreement and one of his cards inside, closed the flap, and wrote ROBERTA on the front. "Give it to her when she comes back or put it on her desk?"

"Yep," the waitress said as Nick handed the envelope to her.

"Thanks," he said as he turned and left the restaurant.

Nick spent the next three hours at the Dakota Zoo, since photos of animals were always popular. *Maybe none for the magazine, but I can certainly use them for my website and social media,* he thought as he sat at a table and ate lunch. The cloth umbrella was lowered and tied. *The wind doesn't seem that strong, but I'm not from here,* he thought as he watched the tall trees sway back and forth and the fallen leaves skitter across the pavement.

He finished his lunch, got up and went back out to his car. He'd already gotten the name and phone number for a kayaking center along the river, and he called them.

"Bismarck Kayaks, how may I help you?" the voice answered.

"Hi, I'm just visiting here, and I was wondering how much to rent a kayak for a couple hours this afternoon?" Nick asked.

"Oh, I'm sorry, sir. The waves are too high for us to allow anyone to go out onto the river today."

"Really? The wind doesn't seem that strong here at the zoo," Nick countered.

"The steep banks along the river create quite the wind tunnel effect, and it's much stronger here than at the zoo. The winds are expected to die down tomorrow if you want to give us a call again."

"Yeah, I'll do that," Nick said. "Well, maybe I can go rent a bike instead," he said as he headed back to the hotel. "Or, ..., I can call Mary and see if the offer to show me around town is still open."

7

WHAT'S IN THE CAN?

Back in his hotel room, Nick opened his laptop and went to YouTube. He did a search on "steer branding parties," finding about a dozen videos. He watched several, and there was never any dangerous play with the branding irons. They served one purpose, and that was to brand the cattle. Several of the videos did have a large open container, *a five-gallon can?*, with a broom handle sticking out of it. He did more searching, but he didn't find any answers as to what was in the container, and why there would be a broom handle sticking out of it.

The walking through the zoo had tired Nick out some. He ordered a pizza and a large bottle of Pepsi since they didn't have Coke products from a local pizza joint and asked for them to be delivered to the room. He went down the hall and filled the bucket with ice and returned to his room to hear his phone ringing.

"Hello," he said.

"Oh, hi, Nick. This is Roberta from the Farm House Inn. Sorry I missed you earlier today, but I had a few things I had to take care of."

"No problem," Nick replied.

"I looked at your agreement, and I don't have any problems with the terms, but four hundred and eighty dollars seems a bit high for just taking some pictures."

Nick closed his eyes and smiled. *She wants a professional to shoot the best possible photographs, but she doesn't want to pay for the experience.* "Well," he began. "That is already a discounted price off my normal rate. With all the different shots and times of day you want, I figure it's at least eight hours of my time. And it's not all at once either. I'll have to make several trips. My standard rate is a hundred dollars an hour, and I've already given you a forty percent discount. Maybe you can find someone here in town willing to work for less, but I know what my time and expertise are worth. So, if you're asking me if I would lower it, I'm sorry I can't."

"Hmmm," she replied, and then continued in a lowered voice. "Well, I know you said something about not accepting free meals, but could we include some as part of the deal, and cut the price down that way?"

"I appreciate what you're suggesting, and it is creative, but I need to stick to the price."

"Having your name with the photographs could be good for your business," Roberta replied.

"If I were going to be around here, yes." Nick paused. "Thanks, Roberta, but I don't think it'll work out. My price is four eighty. If you can't do it, that's fine."

There was a knock at the door. "There's my food for the evening, so I've got to go. If you change your mind, give me a call tomorrow."

"Okay, thanks. Sorry we couldn't work something out."

"I agree, Roberta," he said as he hit the red button to end the call.

"Coming," Nick yelled toward the door as he got up and grabbed his wallet.

"Thanks," he said to the delivery person as he paid. including a nice tip. "Smells great."

"Hope you enjoy it, sir," the pimple-faced teen who delivered his food said.

"I'm sure I will," Nick replied as he closed the door. He set the box and the Pepsi bottle on the table, turned on the television, and looked for a sports station. He watched a re-run of one of the Final Four basketball games as he ate the Meat Lover's Delight. "I wish I'd remembered to have them toss in some red pepper flakes," Nick muttered as he took the last slice out of the box. He shook his head as he watched a blatant foul go uncalled. "They called that one on me every time," he said. He put the empty box in the waste basket and the half-empty Pepsi bottle in the mini-fridge.

"Sports, pizza, and Pepsi, not a bad evening," he said as he finally turned off the television and got ready for bed.

8

BREAKFAST WITH LOCALS

The aroma emanating from the empty pizza box was still present as Nick awoke the next morning. He burped, "Definitely some sausage and garlic," he said as he headed to the shower. The smells from last-night's dinner made him think of breakfast.

"I'm definitely not going back to the Farm House Inn," he said as he got out of the shower and got dressed. "Let's see what Yelp says," he added as he opened his phone and search for a top-rated breakfast place.

The Little Cottage Café caught his attention as the list appeared on his screen. His stomach growled as he looked at the pictures of the Caramel Roll and the Rancher Special.

"Oh, my," he mouthed as he licked his lips in anticipation. He typed the address on East Main Avenue into his navigation app and headed out, notebook in pocket and the ever-present camera bag slung over his left shoulder.

"Definitely a popular spot," Nick said as he pulled into the almost-full parking lot. "That typically means really good food," he added as he parked, left the camera bag in the car, and went inside.

Heads turned as he walked in. Six-foot-six and bushy orangish hair was probably not a common sight around town. Wanting to fit in as best as possible, Nick took the open stool at the five-seat counter. "Good morning," he said to the men on either side as he sat down.

"Mornin'," the one on the right replied. "New to the area?"

"Yes and no," Nick answered. "I'm on assignment from a magazine to spend a week in each state capital and take photographs for an upcoming book. This is my week to be in Bismarck."

"Mornin', hon," the waitress said as she set a menu down. "Coffee?"

"Yes, please, and a large orange juice," Nick replied.

"More coffee, Sam?" she asked the man on Nick's right after she filled Nick's cup.

"Just a half cup, Sal," he replied.

Nick looked at her name tag. 'Sal' was Sally.

She poured Sam's coffee, and then went to Nick's left. "How 'bout you, Jim? Refill?"

"No thanks, gotta get goin'," he answered.

"Be right back with your juice," she said to Nick as she left.

"So how's it going?" Sam asked.

Nick turned slightly to his right. "It's going well," he said with raised eyebrows. "Everyone in town seems quite friendly."

"Well," Sam began in a slow drawl. "Most of us have lived here our entire lives, so everybody knows everybody. Now, that's not always a good thing," he added with a sly smile on his face.

Sally reappeared with a large glass of orange juice and set it in front of Nick. "Ready to order?"

"Yes, I am. I'd like the Rancher Special and a caramel roll, please."

"How do you want your eggs?"

"Sunny side up."

"Thanks, dear." Then looking at Sam. "Anything else?"

"That's it for today, Sal."

As she left, Nick took a sip of the juice, and turned back to Sam. "Mind if I ask you a question about something's that caught my curiosity?"

"Go right ahead, son."

"It's about the cattle branding."

"That's pretty big around here. Almost everyone is involved one way or another, either their ranch, or supplies, or something else to keep the business going."

"Yeah. Well, I saw a video online where there was can with what looked like a broom handle sticking out of it nearby where they did the branding. What's that about?"

"It's a liquid that they brush on right away to set the brand and stop any bleeding. By stopping the bleeding, there's not much of a scar, and it helps prevent infection. You know, each head of cattle is worth a lot of money, and they don't want anything to take down even one of 'em."

Nick leaned in a little closer toward the older gentleman. "So, what's in the can?"

"It's typically a mixture of water, some rubbing alcohol, and then some liquid vitamin K. It seems that everyone's got their own particular recipe, but they're all pretty much the same, and it's that liquid vitamin K that's the important thing. It's what stops the bleeding by coagulating it."

"Interesting," Nick said as he nodded his head slightly. "Very interesting. That cowboy that died, what's his name?"

"Yeah, that was sad. Billy Knox, nice young man."

"Any family around here?"

"His dad, William, is just about a mile outside of town. You at a nearby hotel?"

"Yes."

"Everyone knows the Knox family, so I'm sure the clerk at the hotel can draw out a map for you. It's easy to get to, just a few turns on unmarked roads. Well, I've gotta get goin'. Good luck taking those pictures."

Photographs, Nick thought as he shook the man's hand. Sally brought Nick's food, and it smelled as good as he thought it would from the photos on Yelp. Jim had already left so it was just Nick with an empty stool on cither side of him as he enjoyed his breakfast. There was hardly a drop of anything left on his plate after he finished. He let out a big sigh and pushed the plate back a bit. He lifted his coffee cup, but it was empty. *That's okay, I don't really need any more.*

Nick paid the bill, left the café, and drove to the capitol building for his last round of interior photos. He'd already taken the main ones. Now was the time to focus on some artistic shots, some for the magazine and some for himself.

9

FAMILY HISTORY

In addition to interior photos, Nick walked around the twenty-one story capitol building capturing shots of the Art Deco as a framing object with trees, sky, and even a flock of birds as the main focus. He returned to the hotel, downloaded the photos to his computer, sorting them along the way. Some were perfect for the magazine, and others he chose to keep for himself.

His conversation with Sam at the restaurant came back to him. *What did he say?* "It's a liquid that they brush on right away to set the brand and stop any bleeding. By stopping the bleeding, there's not much of a scar, and it helps to prevent infection." And then, "It's typically a mixture of water, some rubbing alcohol, and then some liquid vitamin K. It seems that everyone's got their own particular recipe, but they're all pretty much the same, and it's that liquid vitamin K that's the important thing. It's what stops the bleeding by coagulating it."

"Wow," Nick thought as he did some online research. One article said, The vitamin K (K from the German word *Koagulation*) is used as a blood clotting agent, which then helps set the brand faster and cleaner.' Nick did more reading. "What?" he exclaimed as he saw an article titled, 'Too Much Vitamin K Can Cause Hypercoagulation.'

He clicked on that link:

'Hypercoagulation is the name for excessive blood clotting. A blood clot is the mass that stops the bleeding when you get a cut or other injury to the skin that ruptures a blood vessel. It is the proteins in your blood that help to form the clot. This is called coagulation, which helps when you are injured because it slows the loss of blood. However, if there is too much clotting, aka, hypercoagulation, this can be very dangerous. Blood clots can form, or be transmitted to vital organs, such as the heart and the brain. This can cause serious health problems, even leading to death.'

Nick continued to read, this time out loud. "A blood clot in the heart or lungs can cause a heart attack."

"That's what the coroner said it was, a heart attack," Nick blurted out. "Maybe that heart attack was caused by this hypercoagulation." He shut down his laptop, grabbed his notebook, and headed down to the lobby.

"Everyone in town knows the Knox family," the hotel desk clerk said. He drew a map to the Knox ranch while Nick stood patiently by.

"Thank you very much," Nick said as he picked up the map and went to his car. There was nothing he could actually enter into his navigational app, so he just followed the directions written on the hand-drawn map. Thirty minutes later, after a trip that might have taken only twenty if he hadn't turned right instead of left, Nick arrived at the Knox ranch.

He walked up the three steps to the porch and rang the doorbell even though the front door was open but covered by a screen door. Knowing that his height could be intimidating to some, Nick stepped back as he saw the gentleman approach the door.

"Yes?" the man asked.

"Hello, Mr. Knox. My name is Nick O'Flannigan, and I'm not from around here, and I'm not an investigative reporter. I'm a professional photographer passing through, but I was hoping you'd be willing to talk with me about your son and his recent death."

The gentleman on the other side of the screen just stood there.

"I'm sorry, sir. I know it must be tough" Nick paused. "I'll leave," Nick said as he turned to leave."

"No, that's okay," the man said. "Come on in."

Nick turned around, entered through the opened screen door, and the two men shook hands.

"William Knox," the rancher said.

"Nick O'Flannigan, Mr. Knox. I know this is difficult, and all you'll have to do is say the word and I'll leave."

"Come on," Mr. Knox said as he led Nick into the living room. "Have a seat, please."

The men sat down, and Mr. Knox was the first to speak. "So, what brings you here to Bismarck?"

"I'm on a photography assignment to visit each state capital and take photographs. It's not glamorous, but it's not a bad way to make a living."

"Where do you live?"

"Originally, I'm from Boston, now in Seattle. But actually, right now my home is whatever hotel I'm in for the next forty-some states."

"It sounds sort of interesting," Knox replied. "But why are you interested in Billy's death since you're just passing through?"

Nick shrugged his shoulders. "Honestly, I don't know. But someone having a heart attack at my same age seems a bit odd. Is there any history of blood clots in your family?"

Mr. Knox leaned back in his chair. "Why, yes," he responded. His right hand stroked the back of his neck and the down the front before he continued. "Actually, Billy had blood clots removed from his legs years ago. They called it Deep Vein Thrombosis, or DVT, but it was all taken care of with a simple surgery."

Nick continued the questioning. "And the rest of the family?"

"You're just a photographer?" Mr. Knox asked.

"That's all," Nick replied. "But my penchant for macrophotography seems to lead me into discovering or noticing details others don't."

"I've been diagnosed with the same thing," Mr. Knox began, "and

I've been on Warfarin for years. It seems that I had passed it on to my son."

"I see," Nick said as he sat back and breathed out through his nose.

The men sat in silence for a couple minutes. "Were you aware," Nick began, "that Warfarin was originally used commercially as a rodent killer?"

"You're kidding," Mr. Knox said.

"Not at all," Nick replied. "And vitamin K was used as an antidote to that poison."

"Really?" Knox asked.

Nick explained what he'd read online, and then the two men, one old enough to be his father, chatted about cattle, ranching, and even a little about photography.

"Thank you for your time, Mr. Knox," Nick said as he stood.

Mr. Knox stood and the two men shook hands.

"Everyone in town I've talked to said Billy was a really nice young man. I'm sorry for your loss, sir," Nick said as he handed a card to the man.

"Thank you for your kind words, young man. Safe travels on your journeys," Mr. Knox said as he opened the screen door and Nick left.

10

BEST STEAK IN THE STATE

Finding his way back into town from the Knox ranch was much easier than finding the ranch itself. Nick got cleaned up in his room and headed back down to the lobby.

"Good evening, Mr. O'Flannigan," the desk clerk said. "How's your stay?"

"It's been good, thanks. With all the cattle ranches around here, there's got to be some good steak places. Any recommendations?"

"Personally," the clerk began. "I like Peacock Alley. It's not the highest rated in town, but I've always gotten a good meal, really good service, and cold beer. Plus it's a place where the locals like to hang out."

"Sounds good to me," Nick said as he typed 'Peacock Alley' into his phone. "Thanks," he added as he nodded his head and extended his hand to shake hands with the clerk.

"Have a good evening."

"You bet," Nick said as he went to his car and let his navigation app lead him to the restaurant. "Might not be the best in the area, but it looks pretty busy," he said as he pulled into the nearly full parking lot.

"Dinner or bar?" the restaurant hostess asked as Nick entered.

"Dinner, for one."

"Is the bar okay? There are tables as well as seats at the bar itself," she said.

"The bar's fine," Nick replied.

"Just right through here," she said as she pointed to her left. "Any place you want is fine," she added.

"Thanks," Nick said as he turned and entered the noisy bar area. He looked around, most of the tables were occupied, so he went to one of the many open seats at the bar.

"Good evening, sir," the bartender said as he approached. "Cocktail? Beer? Glass of water while you decide?"

"A porter or a stout, please," Nick replied.

"Regular or tall?"

"Tall."

"Certainly." The bartender got a chilled glass, and slowly filled it with a nutty brown beer. The frothy foam looked like a one-inch flat ceiling as it extended above the rim of the glass. The bartender—his name tag said 'Bob'— gently set the glass in front of Nick. "Don't get a lot of customers asking for the porter," Bob said. "Most of the locals drink Bud or Coors."

Nick took a drink and smiled. "I grew up in Boston, and those were considered cow piss when I was in college. I got introduced to the darker beers at the frat parties. They seem to have a little more body, plus I like the flavor."

"That's like most things. If it's what you like, then that's great.." Bob looked around, no one seemed to need anything. "New in town or just passing through?"

"Passing through, although I'm here for a week."

"Business?"

"Kind of. Taking photographs in each state capital for a national magazine." Nick took another sip of the beer. "That cowboy who died at that party last weekend. How often does that sort of thing happen?"

"It's an annual party to celebrate the end of the cattle drive."

"But being branded with a branding iron. That seems a bit over the top," Nick added.

Bob leaned forward, glanced to his left and then to his right. "There's a video of that. It shows the other cowboy deliberately jabbing him in the chest," he said in a soft voice.

"A video? I hadn't heard of that. I was out at the Knox ranch today, and Mr. Knox didn't say anything about it."

"Not many people know it exists."

"And how do you know?"

"I've got my sources," the bartender winked. "If you don't confess to a priest, you come to me around here."

"Do you have a copy?"

"No, but I've got the link to it on my phone."

"Wow," Nick said as he sat upright in the bar stool. He pulled his wallet out his back pocket, and then pulled a card and a twenty out of it. "Send it to me?" Nick asked as he handed the card and the tip to Bob.

"I will as soon as I have a break."

"Thanks. May I see a menu, please?"

"Of course," Bob said as he went to the end of the bar to get a menu and check on his other customers.

The evening went by quickly as Nick ordered a Porterhouse steak and "whatever the chef thinks goes best with it." He ordered another beer as Bob brought out two large plates out to him. "Wow," he said as his wide-open eyes took in the feast before him. He sliced into the steak and smiled. "Perfect."

Nick went back to his hotel room after a filling dinner of the most tender steak he'd had in a long time, a fully loaded baked potato, mixed vegetables, and buffalo fries. He opened his email and there was the link from Bob. He watched the video, and it was apparent that the other cowboy intentionally poked Billy in the chest with the hot branding iron. That didn't seem to faze Billy, but then the other cowboy did something else, and that's when Billy reacted. Nick downloaded the video to his laptop and turned on the television.

Just then his phone rang. *Who'd be calling this late?*, he wondered. "Hello."

"Hey, Nick. It's Helen. I thought you were going to call me about getting together."

"Yeah, hi. Sorry, but I got a little involved here," he replied.

"What's her name?"

"Nothing like that, although there is one gal who wanted me to take some photographs of her restaurant, but she wanted me to do it for almost nothing No, there was this cowboy who was burned with a branding iron. you know the kind they use to brand cattle? Well, he died a couple days later, and the coroner is calling it a natural death from a heart attack. As if getting burned by a branding iron is natural. I think it was something else, and I just saw a video of the incident. I think it was a murder."

"I figured you get involved if there was something to get involved with. But what about us?"

Nick cleared his throat. "Things are a little complicated right now, Helen. "

"So that means ...?"

"Um," he began slowly. "I don't think us will work right now."

"Because of Sandra, or is it me?"

"Definitely not you. I'm going to be seeing Sandra in a few weeks. So maybe after that, we can talk about it again."

Silence. Then a soft, "I just want to be friends, Nick."

"Look," Nick continued. "I'm not trying to string you along. I'm just being honest. I don't know what's going to happen, and I certainly don't want a girl in every town. I'm not that kind of a guy."

Sniffles. Then, "I like you, Nick. I think we could be good together, or at the very least good friends."

Nick nodded his head and let out a big sigh. "Let's talk in a couple weeks. Maybe we can get together for a weekend or something. Perhaps I'll know more how it's going with Sandra. Or not going with her. Is that okay?"

"Sure, Nick."

"I'll put a reminder in my phone to call you.

"Okay. Thanks."

"I will call, Helen."

"Sure, Nick. Bye." The line went dead.

"Oh boy," Nick uttered as he scanned through the television programs, saw nothing that interested him, and turned it off. The video replayed in his mind as he got ready for bed.

11

THERE'S MORE TO THE STORY

After a long, hot shower to clear his head from last night's call with Helen, Nick went downstairs for the hotel breakfast. *I'm going to get tired of these pretty soon,* he thought as he went back to his room. He grabbed his laptop and his camera bag and headed back downstairs.

"How was the dinner last night, Mr. O'Flannigan?" the clerk said as Nick passed through the lobby.

"It was really good. Thanks, but I'm in a bit of a hurry." Nick continued out to his car, and then drove to the Sheriff's Department.

"Good morning," the deputy at the desk said as Nick entered. "How's it going for taking the pictures?" It was the same officer Nick had spoken to the last time he was there.

"Going great," Nick said. "Just about all done. Um, is Deputy Reynolds in? I've got something he's really going to want to see."

"I think so, let me check," the officer said as he picked up the phone and punched in a few numbers. "Yeah, that photographer guy is here again and asked to speak with you. He said he's got something you'll want to see."

The deputy nodded his head as he listened.

"Okay, I'll let him know."

He hung up the phone and looked at Nick. "He said it would be a few minutes, but he'd like you to go to one of the waiting rooms. I'll show you where."

"Sure," Nick said as he stood up and followed the officer.

Reynolds opened the door about ten minutes later, and walked in. "You have something for me to see?"

"I do. Good morning, Deputy," Nick said as he stood up and shook his hand.

"I hope it's good."

"It is," Nick replied. "Let me show you a video," he said as he motioned for the deputy to sit on the same side of the table.

Reynolds sat down, and Nick started the video on his laptop. The deputy's eyes widened as he watched and listened. "Where'd you get that?" he asked when the video ended.

"I can't reveal my sources," Nick answered. "But see how he's branded on the chest and then the area is brushed with liquid from that can? I talked with his dad yesterday, and he said that Billy had blood clots in his veins removed as a youngster. And his dad is on Warfarin. So it's highly likely there is a family history of excessive blood clotting."

"So? The coroner said it was a heart attack."

"Right," Nick said. "But Timmy said, 'Let's set the brand like we do with the cattle,' and then brushed the liquid onto Billy's chest. But before he did that, he squeezed more liquid out of that other bottle. And Billy's dad said that the branders usually had some extra vitamin K nearby in case the brand wasn't setting immediately. So it's certainly possible, and also quite likely, that the extra amount of the vitamin K created an immediate clotting effect. Notice how after Timmy brushed the liquid on that Billy was taking short breaths and put his hands to his chest as if he was in pain?"

"Yeah, the pain from the branding iron," Reynolds replied.

"Or," and Nick paused. "The chest pain because of the immediate blood clot that went to his heart. If he was already at risk for blood clotting, as his Dad is, and Billy had already had surgery for removing clots, then the high concentration of vitamin K could cause hypercoagulation. And when that happens, a blood clot in the heart can cause shortness of breath, chest pain, and trigger a heart attack."

"Are you a photographer or a medical student?" the deputy asked.

"Photographer, but I've, uh, learned a little more about the human body as I've traveled around."

"Let me watch that video again."

Nick replayed the video, and Deputy Reynolds leaned forward to focus on the action. "It's possible," he said as the video ended. "So the other cowboy is Timmy Lee, and he and Billy Knox went to school together and were best friends. That was until Timmy's girlfriend dumped him and started going out with Billy. Let me call the coroner and see what he's found in the formal autopsy."

"Good," Nick said. "And have him check the blood for an elevated level of vitamin K."

"Yep," Reynolds said as Nick arose and left the waiting room and the building.

Nick went to the hotel and uploaded his final set of photos to the Cloud. Several minutes later his phone rang.

"Hi, Emily," he said as he answered.

"Hi, Nick. Great photos. I like the artistic touch you added to the latest set."

"Thanks. That tall capitol building seemed like the perfect prop for some of them."

"Well, they looked great. Good job and keep up the good work."

"Thanks, Emily. I'll do my best."

"Great. Take care, Nick," the editor said as she ended the call.

12

HEADLINE NEWS

Nick let out a big sigh as he plopped down on the bed. It had been a busy week, but a productive one. He was glad that he and Sandra were going to have some time together in Denver in a few weeks. *She's great professionally and she's nice personally,* he thought as he closed his eyes. *But is that what it takes for a long-term relationship?*

He didn't expect to fall asleep, but he did

Upon waking, Nick splashed water on his face and changed shirts. He picked up his phone and searched Yelp for sports bars. "Nope," he said as the list appeared. "Been there already," he added. "Here we go. Good reviews," he said as he exited the app and entered 'Elbow Room' into his phone and headed downstairs.

"Ever been to the Elbow Room?" Nick asked. "Seems to have decent reviews on Yelp."

"Yeah, I like it," the clerk responded. "It's not fancy, but the drinks are good and reasonably priced. The food's okay, and it's filled with TVs."

"Thanks."

"Oh," the clerk added as Nick was leaving. "The action really gets going in a couple hours, although it should be happy hour right now."

"Thanks, an early night for me as I'm heading out in the morning." Nick continued out to his car and was at the Elbow Room in less than five minutes. The noise level was high as Nick entered, some from the televisions with different stations, and some from the patrons.

"Table, booth, or at the bar?" the hostess asked.

"Any of the TVs have local news?"

"One over in that corner by that empty booth," she said as she motioned with her right hand. "It might be hard to hear, but I can turn it up for you if you want."

"Thanks," Nick said as he followed her. Heads turned and watched Nick as the former basketball player made his way across the room. As he slid into the booth and looked at the TV, he remarked, "The sound's fine. Thanks." He stretched his long legs out under the table, straddling the center post.

A waitress appeared immediately, "Hi, there. Don't recall seeing you in here before."

Nick smiled as he looked up from the menu. "No, ma'am. In town for about a week and heading out tomorrow."

"What can I getcha?"

"A tall, dark beer, please."

"Sure thing."

Nick pored over the menu, eyeing the nice selection of burgers. The sound from the TV overhead was just noise, noise like everything else that was going on.

That changed when he heard, "Coming up on the early evening news in just ten minutes, we have exclusive new developments in the death of the local cowboy who'd been branded and died." His ears heard that clearly. *New developments? I wonder what they are,* he thought.

"Here's that tall, dark beer for you, sir," the waitress said as she placed a coaster on the table and then set the glass on it. "Have you decided?"

"How about the Cowboy Burger and a side of Mac and Cheese?"

"That's a lot of food, but I think you'll be fine," she said with a wink and a smile.

"Thanks," Nick said as he reached for the frosted glass. "Ooh, that's good," he said to himself as he tasted the beer.

His food arrived just as the news story began at the top of the hour. Nick looked over and up at the set. The text at the bottom of the screen said, **Cowboy Arrested for Friend's Murder**. "Good evening and welcome to the early evening news here in the capital city. We start tonight with the exclusive story of how the Sheriff's Department has arrested a man in connection with the branding death of another cowboy at last weekend's annual cattle drive party. We had reported earlier in the week that the coroner had said that Billy Knox had a heart attack, and that his death was initially ruled as natural. The Sheriff's Department said that a tip from an anonymous source led to further investigation. Here's a clip from an interview we had with the Sheriff's Department just a few hours ago."

The screen changed from the news anchor to an already running film clip. " ... and his death had initially been ruled as natural from a heart attack. But upon further investigation, that appears to have been triggered by a clotting agent that had been applied to the area where he was branded." Deputy Reynolds continued. "I saw a video of the incident where it appeared the suspect added some extra liquid to the brush before applying it to the victim's chest. That liquid has been confirmed to be liquid vitamin K, which can cause hypercoagulation. I spoke with Mr. Knox just about an hour ago, and he told me of the family history of clotting.

"When I passed this news on to the coroner, he did some additional work and found that a blood clot, likely from the wound, had moved into the heart, causing the heart attack. We then got an arrest warrant and went to Mr. Lee's house where he surrendered without incident. He said that his girlfriend left him for Billy Knox, and he confessed to spiking the solution with the additional vitamin K after they'd been drinking, knowing that it might cause serious harm to the victim. Mr. Lee is currently in the county jail awaiting his arraignment on Monday morning."

Nick nodded his head and smiled. *The bad guy was caught, and my name stayed out of the story. Whew!* He ordered another beer as he ate his meal. *She was right, it was a lot of food.* The local news continued above as just noise as his eyes roamed to other televisions around the area. As he finished everything, he looked at his watch. He'd been there for a little over an hour. About half the people had left the area.

"Anything else, sir?" the waitress asked as she approached.

"No, thanks," Nick said. "Guessing that happy hour is over?"

"Easy to tell, right?" she said with a smile as she set the check and the tray on the table.

Nick had his credit card ready, and he took a quick glance at the bill and put his card in the tray. "Thanks," he said as he handed the tray to her.

"I'll be right back."

Nick's phone rang. "Hello, this is Nick."

"Hi, Nick. It's Mary from the Farm House Inn. Is it too late for dinner?"

He chuckled. "I'm sorry. I just finished and was heading back to the hotel to pack. I was hoping to have you show me around own as you offered, but I got sort of tied up in things around here. Um, if you're not working in the morning, maybe we could have breakfast somewhere before I leave?"

"Well," Mary said as her pitch increased. "I do have the early shift, but I can take an hour between nine and ten. Is that too late?"

"Not at all," Nick said warmly. "I'll pick you up at the restaurant at nine and we'll go somewhere else if that's okay."

"That sounds perfect, Nick. Thanks. See you tomorrow."

"Yes, Mary. Good night," he said just as the waitress brought the receipt for Nick to sign. Nick signed the bill, returned to his hotel room, and plopped down on the bed. "I can pack in the morning," he said as he got up and took a shower before going to bed.

THE END

SOME FACTS ABOUT BISMARCK AND THE STATE OF NORTH DAKOTA

- The population of Bismarck (about 61,700) is smaller than Fargo (about 105,500), while Fargo accounts for about one-sixth of the state's overall population.
- Speaking of Fargo, the movie *Fargo* wasn't shot there. Neither was the TV series.
- As mentioned in the story, the capitol building is the state's tallest building at 241 feet. It is also the only non-symmetric capitol building in the fifty U.S. states.
- The people of North Dakota set a [still-standing] Guinness World record in 2007 with 8,962 people for "Most people making snow angels simultaneously."
- The capital city was originally named Edwinton in 1872 after Edwin Johnson, a supporter of the transcontinental railroad. The name was changed a year later to honor German Chancellor Otto von Bismarck. The idea was to attract German settlers to the area, and it worked! About 60% of today's population is of German descent.
- North Dakota is one of seven states with only one member in the U.S. House of Representatives.
- In some parts of Canada and the United States, a round

jelly-filled doughnut is often referred to as a "bismark" or "bismarck." The consensus is that since jelly doughnuts were invented in Germany, an appropriate nickname for them was after the Chancellor, Otto von Bismarck.

- North Dakota is the most rural of all the states, with farms covering more than 90% of the land. The state ranks first in the nation's production of spring and durum wheat.
- Milk is the official state beverage of North Dakota (as it is for most states that admit that they even have an official state beverage).
- State law requires most pharmacies in North Dakota to be owned by local pharmacists, meaning that national chains can't operate pharmacies there.

PARRICIDE IN PIERRE

BOOK #8 IN THE CAPITAL CITY MURDERS
SERIES

PROLOGUE: HAPPY BIRTHDAY

The fact that the window was open was unusual, but it was a cool and calm night. Nathaniel Tatanka, known affectionately as "Tank" by his friends, sat at the dining room table with a large cake in front of him.

Two wax numbers, a six and a three, were in the center, and the few friends who had come over were singing, most slightly off-key:

"Happy birthday to you! Happy birthday to you!' the notes slid joyfully into the night air.

Tank shivered a little bit, but not from the cold. Something felt wrong tonight, something in his spirit. It should be a celebration, but he felt a sense of dread instead.

He looked around the living room at the walls, the fireplace, the furniture. Something was missing. His sons were not here, not that he expected either of them to be, but it wasn't a someone, but a something.

Tank struggled to identify it in the crowded room.

What isn't here? he wondered.

It's a tough question for anyone of a certain age to answer, he thought.

There might be a space on the mantle, a picture taken down to be dusted, and he'd have forgotten that he even took it down, let alone where he put it. This was his life now, one of routine. If he put his keys down in the wrong place, he might spend hours looking for them, or even have to call his best friend, Forrest, over to help him.

"Blow out the candles!" unified voices told him, waking him from his reverie.

"Don't forget to make a wish," one said loudly.

He closed his eyes and did just that.

Then the cutting of the cake began. Tank took the first piece offered to him even though he had requested a small one. Diabetes, once a specter talked about by older friends, had become a part of his own conversations with his physician including the words, "pre-diabetic" and "risk of heart attack." Once a big eater of breads, carbs, and a lover of dark beers, Tank had become a carb-conscious eater and a drinker of pilsners, and not many of those.

He wandered the room, shaking hands with new arrivals who dropped in, and looking at the growing pile of gifts, something he wondered if a man of his age needed or deserved. He knew his friends. Most of the gifts would contain coffee, alcohol, or even some of his favorite foods.

Forrest appeared by his side. "The boys didn't show, eh?" The mountain of a man wore his dark hair in a long braid down his back with beads woven in. He was well-muscled for a man in his sixties, but if you were tall enough to look him straight in his deep brown eyes, you could see the kindness there.

Even if you weren't tall enough, there was something about Forrest that always seemed to be on your level. He'd been Tank's best friend for as long as he could remember.

"Didn't expect them to," Tank answered. "Haven't seen Nate Junior in ages."

"I'm sorry man," Forrest said. "I wish those boys could see past your split with their mom. How long has it been since David..."

"Two years," Tank said. "How long has it been for you since Jack ran off?"

"About the same time your David disappeared."

"You haven't heard anything?"

"Not a word. That one was my fault. I was too hard on him, expected too much of the boy."

"And I own my mistakes with David's mom. We all make mistakes with our kids. But I was hoping for at least a birthday wish from those I have left."

"Speaking of wishes, what did you wish for?"

"As if I'd tell you. You've been asking that every year since before you were tall enough to reach the top shelf in the fridge."

"Will this help?" Forrest pulled a brown paper bag from behind his back and handed it over.

Tank slid the bottle out of the inglorious gift bag and whistled.

"A twenty-one-year-old scotch? You went all out."

"How could I not? Happy birthday, my friend."

"Thank you. Stick around after the party and we'll crack this thing open," Tank said.

"Of course." Forrest shook his hand and then Tank retreated to the kitchen where he put the new bottle on the table.

As the night went on, people wandered out into the night and to their own homes. Pierre, South Dakota is a small town, but one with a surprisingly high property crime rate, so people still retire early and lock their doors.

The cake was decimated. Most of the other snacks were gone, and there were empty cups and bottles scattered throughout the living and dining room areas. The gift from Forrest now sat on the dining room table, open.

Tank and Forrest retired to the back porch, each with a tumbler in their hands, the bottom of each decorated with a golden shot of scotch.

"That was some party," Tank said.

"Yeah, people around here love you, man."

"No, really, come on."

"Look, you've done a lot for this community. When you retired from the police force, you stayed. A lotta folks would have left."

"You stayed, too, Forrest."

"Yeah, but I'm just a lousy barber," he grinned. "Not the badge wearing law man."

"Some would say that means you changed more lives than I ever did."

"Well, they'd be wrong," Forrest said. My legacy will be an empty chair and some random hair clippings that drifted under a cabinet when I was sweeping up."

"Not true," Tank said, taking another sip of his scotch. "No one would believe you missed any hair sweeping up. That shop of yours is immaculate."

Forrest took a small sip of his drink, lowered it, and then took a larger one. "That may be true, but it ain't much of a legacy. At least, you got your kids, even if they don't come around as often as you like."

"True," Tank said. He thought again of his children and their absence tonight.

"And speaking of my legacy of cutting hair, I know tomorrow is Saturday, but I have to work the morning, at least. The price of taking Mondays off."

"Aw, hell. No one would know if you opened half an hour late on a Saturday."

"Not true," Forrest said. "I would."

He downed the last of the amber liquid and stood. "I love you, buddy. I'll stop by tomorrow afternoon when I close up. Unless you have other plans."

Tank snorted laughter. "I'll check my schedule."

He walked his friend to the door, and then turned around to look at the mess in the living room once Forrest was gone.

"I'll clean up in the morning," he said to the empty room. "Not like anyone will be stopping by early."

He downed the last of his drink and set the empty tumbler on one of the low side tables, careful to slide a coaster under the glass just in case. Then he headed upstairs to bed.

He wasn't sure if it was an hour or three hours later, but Tank woke to a thump from the floor below.

Quietly, he rolled out of bed, sliding his feet into the slippers there. He looked at the clock. 1:15.

Tank slid the drawer open on the bedside table, looking for the pistol he usually kept there, but the drawer was empty.

He'd taken it out to the shop to clean it.

Damn it, he thought.

He moved down the stairs quietly. He'd lived in this same house for over thirty years, and knew every step and every sound it made, even if his hearing wasn't what it used to be.

Someone was there.

He considered calling out, considered calling the police even, but he'd left his cell phone upstairs. He hadn't had a land line in over five years.

One step at a time, he made his way downward. Every now and then, he would hear a sound, but there were no lights.

Good, he thought. *I'll have an advantage.*

Tank reached the bottom level and stopped to listen.

There. To the right. An ex-cop, he wasn't nervous about facing someone down. All the crime around here was committed by punks anyway. They'd spook and run as soon as he confronted them.

He saw a shadow move quickly across the doorway.

"Hey!" he yelled. "Get out of here!"

There was no answer.

"Hey!" he said loudly. "The cops are on their way. Get out while you can!"

It was a small lie but should be an effective one. Still, no answer came.

Tank looked over by the fireplace and then realized what was missing. The fireplace poker. It hadn't been their earlier. He looked around for a weapon of any kind.

He saw the tumbler sitting on the table and grabbed it, felt its weight in his hand. It would have to do.

He reached the corner where he'd seen the shadow, and waited, slowing his breathing the best he could.

A second later, a head appeared around the corner.

Tank swung the tumbler at the burglar's head, and then stopped just before it struck.

"You?" he said. "What are you doing here?"

The shadow swung an object, striking him in the ribs and sending him crashing into the wall.

He sucked in a breath, a painful exercise, and pushed himself to stand, and defend himself. But his attacker struck again, this time at his knee.

Tank folded with a curse, but turned onto his back, bringing his arms up.

"Why?" he asked. "What are you doing?"

The shadow didn't respond, but the object it was wielding crashed into his head and it was the last thing Tank ever saw.

1

—————

ARRIVAL IN PIERRE

Nick looked carefully at the map in front of him. Sure, he had an app for that (who didn't?) but he liked to scout his route ahead of time, and he saw that with a simple change and adding a little more than an hour, his drive from Bismarck, North Dakota to Pierre, South Dakota could be a bit more scenic.

Now, eight weeks into his year-long assignment to photograph all of the state capitals for *Travel USA* magazine, some aspects of travel were starting to get a little bit old, but the one thing that seemed to last was that he loved the drive from city to city. It was an opportunity to be on the road, see some new territory, and, most of all, take some more great photos.

Nick checked out of his hotel and folded his six-foot six frame into the driver's seat. He'd selected his car for both legroom and headroom, since, when he was at home in Seattle, he had little reason to drive it other than long distances or, at times, when he was almost sure he would be stuck in traffic.

He'd been glad to leave each city already on this trip, and he'd never missed home quite so much as he did right now. At least, he'd avoided the news when his anonymous tip had led to the arrest of a suspect in the intentional branding and murder of a local cowboy.

Mystery and murder seemed to be following him on this trip. If he was a superstitious guy, Nick would have wondered if he was causing the phenomena, but he didn't think like that.

What he did know was that he was good at this 'spotting clues' stuff. Photography was his passion, sure, but catching bad guys was fun, too. Well, maybe not all fun. He thought back to Helena and the hangman there. That one had been a little too personal.

He fired up the car and turned on the radio. If mysteries and murder were the only issues with this trip, he would be doing great. This was a dream assignment after all, but added to the mix were two women, Helen and Sandra.

He'd met Sandra in Salem, then she'd helped him out in Sacramento, and they'd been talking ever since, including a plan for her to join him in Denver soon.

Helen had come along in Helena, Montana.

Sure, the alliteration of their names, both Helen's and Sandra's was one odd thing, but the other was how opposite they were. Sandra was tall and Helen was short, over a foot shorter than Nick, and while they had much less in common than he and Sandra, he liked Helen, too.

His parents were another issue with this much traveling. His dad's recent heart attack had him wishing he was closer to Boston.

At times, he looked forward to the end of this journey. Travel was great, but being home was also great.

All these things rushed through his head as he headed south, choosing the route that most closely followed the Missouri River, hoping to take some photos that, while not for his current assignment, would keep the fans of his social media and his website, macrophotogrphy4u.com, coming back for more.

Just as he cleared the outskirts of town, his phone rang. The screen said 'Ben', the young software engineer subletting his apartment in Seattle while he was on the road. Nick answered using his car's hands-free device.

"Hey, Ben. What's up?"

"I'm not sure how to tell you this," Ben said.

Uh-oh, Nick thought. *I hope he didn't get that promotion he talked about and has to move.*

"Shoot," Nick told him. "It can't be that bad."

"Well, you got some mail. And I opened it."

"You opened it?"

"It was from the State of Oregon and said 'Urgent'. I thought it might be important, but I wasn't going to disturb you if it wasn't."

"And?"

"Well, um, did you get a speeding ticket in Oregon a while back?"

"I did!" Nick said. "I don't think I actually paid it."

"Seems like you didn't. This letter threatens to suspend your license and a bench warrant has been issued for your arrest."

"A bench warrant?"

"Don't worry. It wouldn't matter much unless you are in Oregon at the moment, but it isn't good either."

"Can you take a picture of that and send it to me?"

"Yep, and I'll scan and email it to you. Everything else going okay?"

"Yeah, as good as can be expected. Thanks for the 'heads up', Ben. Everything good with you and the apartment?"

"Oh, yeah. No worries. So far, no word on the promotion, so I should be good to go here unless something unexpected happens."

"Sorry to hear about the promotion but can't say I'm sorry you're staying. Things will work out for you."

"I'm sure they will," Ben said. "I'll get this to you right away."

"Thanks, man." Nick hung up and looked for the next exit and spotted a sign for a rest area up ahead.

"I can't believe I forgot that," he said to himself. He thought back to the trip from Olympia to Salem, and how he'd taken the long way that time to see some scenery. Running later than he'd thought, he'd been stopped by an Oregon State trooper and issued a speeding ticket. He hadn't thought about it since, even though the officer had told him to pay it when he got into Salem.

He pulled into a parking spot and opened the glove box to his car, fishing out the offending ticket. There was a phone number on it, but it was Saturday. He might be out of luck until Monday.

He checked his email and looked over the court document from the State of Oregon. At least, his license wasn't suspended. Not yet.

He tried the phone number on both pieces of paper, but with no luck. Nick opened his phone and set a reminder for Monday morning to call them back. He hoped it would be pretty easy to settle over the phone.

Looking out of the window, he saw a great view of the river beyond the restrooms and few scraggly trees in the rest area. There were even a few people lining the shore with binoculars and cameras.

Nick grabbed his camera bag from behind the seat, then opened the door and stood, slinging the bag over one shoulder. As he straightened and stretched, he turned.

Right beside him was a South Dakota state patrol car. The officer got out of the car and stood as well. He couldn't be much shorter than Nick, although the brown trooper hat perched on his head could be adding a couple of inches. He looked like a linebacker and Nick noticed that on his finger he wore a gold ring that looked like some kind of award.

"How you doing?" the officer said.

"Good," Nick answered. "Just starting my trek down to Pierre and decided to grab some photos."

"It's a good spot for it. Nice camera. You a pro?"

"I am," Nick said, feeling a bit uncomfortable. He'd never felt like a fugitive before.

"Cool. I only dabble myself. You look like you played basketball."

"I did. College. A broken leg took me out of my NBA dreams."

The cop flashed the ring at him. "One Super Bowl for me. My two-season NFL career ended up with a crossing route across the middle. Compound fracture, and a spiral one at that. I was lucky to pass the physical for this job."

"Yeah, it's a bummer," Nick said. "But you always know when the weather will change, right?"

"True that," the officer said. "Richard Fletcher. All my friends call me Fletch."

"Nick O'Flannigan. Nice to meet you." They shook hands. "I'm going to go grab those photos."

"Sure, sure." The officer smiled. "Have a good day and travel safe."

Nick waved and then breathed a sigh of relief as he walked away.

First thing Monday, he'd get the ticket taken care of and he'd no longer be a criminal himself.

He took several photos along the river, and when he came back to his car, the officer was already gone.

Nick made a few more stops along the way, stopping for photos and stretching his leg along the Oahe Reservoir, which a nearby sign declared was the fourth largest reservoir in the United States. Another sign told him the power the dam produced supplied electricity to a large part of the North Central United States.

Despite all the stops to take photos and sightsee, he arrived in Pierre early in the afternoon and drove straight to his hotel.

The hotel clerk looked up at him and then stood, whether to try to feel like he was on a more level playing field or just so he didn't feel looked down on.

"Can I help you?" he asked.

"Yes, I have a reservation," Nick said. His height and his red hair made him hard to miss, but also made it hard to blend in.

"Sure, gotcha. You're that photographer guy."

"Yes, I am."

"Carol down at Prairie Pages, our local bookstore, would be delighted to meet you. She says she'd love to talk to you about Pierre."

"Does everyone know I am coming?"

"Oh yeah. This is a small town. Your visit is big news. It would be headlines, except for the murder."

"Murder?"

"Last night. First one in, like, five years. They think it's a burglary gone wrong, but still."

"Fantastic," Nick said, thinking it was anything but. He'd be the number two news story except for a rare murder. At least it might keep any small-town reporters away from them.

What did he expect, though? As the second least populous state capital, only bested by Montpelier in Vermont, Pierre was bound to be a little dull, or so he thought. A murder made things exciting, but even a visit from a not-so-famous photographer made a difference.

It made sense though. How many books featured a small town like Pierre?

"You're in room 215, end of the hall. There aren't a lot of places for dinner, but they're all good."

"I'll come get some recommendations in a little bit," Nick said.

The room was clean and neat, nothing fancy, but it would do nicely. On the desk was a local newspaper, flipped to the headline.

"Ex-Cop, Tank, Found Dead After Birthday Party," the headline read.

Horrible, Nick thought.

He sat down on the end of his bed to read the article before he unpacked.

2

———

THE BOY

Pierre, South Dakota was just what Nick would expect from a small town, but not what he would expect for a state capital. Sunday morning was, well, quiet would probably be the best word. A number of businesses were closed and church parking lots were full. The capitol building itself was closed for the day but he could walk around outside.

It was beautiful, a regal building dominating the downtown area, and understandably so. It had a high dome like many of the other capitol buildings with the exception of Bismarck, but it was dark rather than the typical light stone. It was similar in design to the one in Helena, and he read that a huge renovation had been completed in 2013.

Closer to the Missouri River that ran through town, some buildings were run down, and there were signs that this was not the best of neighborhoods. Nick didn't exactly feel uncomfortable, but he did remember his camera being stolen in Sacramento, something he had been lucky to recover. He stayed alert as he walked around.

He saw one Hughes County Sheriff's Deputy roll by in an SUV and Nick raised a hand in a wave.

The weather was cloudy, a little cool, but that made for good light, and he got some great shots of the river, even zooming in on a discarded can and getting a great shot; the can clear in the foreground, the river a blur behind it.

As he stood, he felt like he was being watched. He turned around quickly and saw a boy, probably a teenager, duck behind a concrete abutment. He raised his camera and held perfectly still. When the boy poked his head up again, Nick snapped a picture.

The boy turned and ran. Nick got a couple shots of him fleeing.

As he lowered the camera, his stomach growled. He pulled out his phone and saw that the Branding Iron Bistro had decent reviews, great coffee, and most importantly, good breakfast. The Grilled Loaded Burrito looked good, but so did several of the other dishes. He headed that way, snapping photos of the town as he went.

The name of the restaurant, of course, brought back thoughts of his last adventure in Bismarck and he smiled to himself. These towns might not be so different after all.

The smell was the first thing that he noticed upon entering Branding Iron Bistro, and he knew it was going to be a great day. The coffee was amazing, the food spectacular, and it was quiet mid-morning. He had a feeling there might be an after-church rush, and Nick thought of his parents back in Boston who would be getting out of mass about now. They always went out to Sunday brunch themselves, so he could call them in a couple of hours.

As he sat drinking his coffee and eating his breakfast, a sheriff's deputy walked in followed closely by another man wearing a suit. They ordered and sat down not far from him.

"Who'd want to hurt Tank?" the man in the suit asked the deputy.

"I have no idea, Chuck," the deputy answered. "Forrest is understandably broken up about it. We found Tank's older boy and shared the news. He's pretty devastated."

Nick didn't want to listen in, but it was hard not to. The first murder in a town in four years was the talk of the town, and the context did make him curious.

"Yeah. I'm sure even his step kids are upset. Tank was a good father, even if he wasn't a great husband." The deputy paused.

"So, it's not a burglary then?"

"Nope. Not likely, although keep that under your hat. We haven't made an official announcement yet, but there wasn't anything of significant value missing. All Tank's stuff, including that autographed baseball he is so proud of was still there. It appears to be a homicide. He had a glass in his hand, but there was nothing in it. Seems likely he was using that as a weapon."

"Where was his pistol?"

"Out in the shed. He must have had it out there to clean and never brought it back inside."

"Damn. It's a shame. You think it was maybe one of the guys he put away?"

"Tank? Nah. He was a gentle giant and a good talker. When he took someone to jail around here, the rare times he had to, they would be more likely to thank him for the ride."

Chuck snorted. "You're probably right about that. You have any ideas at all?"

"No good ones. We're still looking at evidence. Waiting on prints to come back—we don't have a lab locally since we never need one. Tank was well liked. We'll find out who did it."

Nick put down his fork, realizing that during their conversation, he'd eaten his entire breakfast and his coffee cup was empty. He got up to get a refill.

As he turned around, he found the deputy right behind him.

"I saw you earlier," he said simply. "Taking photos down by the water."

"Yes, I'm a freelance photo—"

"No need to tell me who you are, O'Flannigan. Everyone in town knows you're coming in to take photos for some book or something. We're happy to have Pierre featured."

Nick sensed a "but" in the statement, but simply said, "Thanks. I'll do my best."

"I also know you've been involved in some mysteries through your travels, and I know about your involvement in Bismarck."

Nick paused. His name wasn't even in any of the papers there. How did this deputy know he was the anonymous tipster?

"I have," Nick replied out loud. "Not intentionally, at least, for the most part. I guess this kind of stuff just follows me around."

"Hmm. Well, I was actually going to ask you for your help."

"My help?"

"Just a simple thing. The best photographers we have work for the local paper—the editor wants to interview you, by the way—but we don't really have a police photographer. We usually don't need one around here."

"I see. I'm not a police photographer though."

"I know that. But you have a pretty nice camera there," he said, indicating Nick's camera bag on the table. "And you can follow directions, right?"

"Of course."

"Well, if you could follow one of my officers around and take some photos of the scene tomorrow, that would be great."

"Sure," Nick said. "I'm happy to help."

"We'll pay you, of course. Maybe not what you're used to, but there will be something in it for you."

"Sounds good," Nick said. "Here's my card."

"Thanks," the deputy said. "Here's one of mine in case you have any questions. I'll call you tomorrow." He turned and walked out and Nick saw that Chuck, the man in the suit was gone.

"Great," he said aloud. "I guess I'm involved now."

But how could he expect to remain anonymous here? There was no way. For this week, at least, he'd have to live with the fact that he was locally famous.

He walked back toward his hotel. He'd call his parents and then get some rest. Maybe this week, in this small town, it wasn't going to be so peaceful after all.

He also wanted to give Emily, the editor at *Travel USA* magazine, a 'heads up' about the potential publicity. He sighed as he walked up the stairs to his room.

Once inside, he called and left Emily a message and settled in for an evening of sports and pizza, if he could find a place to order one.

A few hours later, he was asleep.

3

THE SCENE OF THE CRIME

Early Monday morning, his phone rang. It was Emily, calling him back.

"Hi, Emily," Nick said, answering the phone on the first ring.

"Nick, how is the bustling metropolis of Pierre?"

"Well, I wish I could say that things are nice and dull, but it doesn't seem like things are going to turn out that way."

"Oh, no, Nick. Don't tell me—"

"Wait," he stopped her. "Let me explain. Turns out that Pierre doesn't get a lot of media coverage, being a small town and all, so even in coming to town I am somewhat of a local celebrity."

"And it's hard for a tall red head like you to hide."

"I'd like to think it's my stunning personality that makes me stand out," Nick said. Emily laughed.

"On top of that, there has been a rare murder in town."

"Murder? Now, Nick. We talked about this."

"The locals don't have a good police photographer. They asked me to take some photos of the crime scene and I told them I would help. That's all. They're even paying me. I'll keep that as low-key as possible. Nothing printed locally should get any national exposure. I'll be careful, I promise."

Emily sighed. "Okay, Nick."

"The good news is the local bookstore, Prairie Pages, wants me to stop by for an interview. I'll talk up the coming book and the magazine and get us some great exposure here."

"That's great, Nick. Positive publicity like that we can handle."

"Emily, I would love to keep a low profile, but that is getting harder as I travel along, and much of the time, people know I am coming. Big cities let me blend in a little more. But Helena, Bismarck, and here? Not a chance."

"Okay, Nick. Just try to keep things upbeat and positive, and don't tick off any locals with your sleuthing."

"Got it. Talk to you later."

Nick ended the call, and it was followed by another from his Mom.

"Hey, Mom. How's Dad today?"

"He's in better spirits. The best since his heart attack, but he's still a little tired."

"How about you? Are you getting any more rest?"

"Nick, I'm fine." His mother would have told him she was fine if she had a gaping hole in her chest, but because of his assignment and being thousands of miles away from where his parents lived in Boston, he couldn't really control the situation.

"If you need a nurse to help out or anything, let me know. I can even take a break and come visit if you need me to."

"Nick, your father was helpless when I married him. This is no different."

Nick could hear the weariness in her voice and he knew she wasn't telling him everything. He decided to, at least, send flowers and made a note on the hotel stationary by his bed as a reminder.

"Okay, Mom. I have to go."

He looked at his list. The sheriff's deputy said he would call, so he had to wait for that, but in the meantime, he needed to call the Oregon State Police and clear his name.

He dialed the number in the photo Ben had sent to him, then put the call on speaker. He kept the photo open in case he needed the numbers on the ticket or the case number.

An automated menu directed him to press 5 for tickets and citations and, from there, he went through the secondary menu to actually speak to a person.

"This is Jules," a voice said. "How can I help you?"

"Hi. I need to pay a speeding ticket. I was traveling through a few weeks back and I forgot to show up to pay the fine."

"Do you have the case number?"

"Sure." Nick read it to her.

"Uh-oh," the voice said. "Seems like your payment is a bit overdue."

"That's what I understand, but I'm on the road for the next year, and I'm currently in South Dakota."

"Okay. Hold for a moment. Let me see how we can resolve this."

Hold music started and an odd instrumental version of "I Shot the Sheriff" played as he waited.

Very funny, he thought.

"Mr. O'Flannigan?"

"Just Nick," he said.

"Yes, okay. We usually don't do this once something gets to the warrant stage, but you can pay the fine over the phone if you like, and the warrant will be dropped within twenty-four hours."

"Sounds good. Can I give you my debit card number now?"

"Go ahead," Jules said.

Nick gave it to her.

"All set," she said a moment later. "You're clear. Let me give you this confirmation number though."

"Sure," he said and wrote it down.

"If, for some reason, you get pulled over in the next twenty-four hours before this is cleared, that number should get you out of trouble."

"Thanks," Nick said. "Have a good day."

"Of course," she said. "You, too."

Nick entered the number into the notes on his phone, just in case.

After all, he would be working with the police today. It never hurt to be careful.

His stomach growled and he knew he needed breakfast.

His phone rang with the thought, and he answered, "Hello?"

"Deputy Christina Fabbri," a female voice said on the other end of the line.

"Oh, hi. I'm Nick O'Flannigan—" he started.

"You're the photographer guy!" she said. "I'm so excited to work with you. You're kinda famous around here."

"So I've been told," he answered.

"Can you meet me at this address at ten?" She gave him a street name and number.

He glanced at the time. Nine-fifteen. Ten seemed reasonable. No place here could be more than a few minutes from another.

"Sure, I'll grab some breakfast and coffee here at the hotel and meet you there."

"Oh, no. Don't do that," Officer Fabbri said. "Meet me over at the Perkins. I know it's a chain, but the chef there is fabulous and they have great coffee from Mighty Missouri Roasters in Bismarck."

"I was just there and never heard of them."

"Shame on you. See you in a few minutes."

Feeling he had no choice, Nick grabbed his camera bag, packed his laptop, and headed downstairs.

In all of this other local excitement, he still needed to get the capitol photos. Somehow, this week felt like it was starting out a lot busier than some of his other trips and he was in the smallest town yet.

4

———

TAKING THE SHOT

Officer Fabbri, who insisted that Nick call her 'Christina', was right. Perkins had better coffee than he expected and the food was pretty good for a chain.

Even hidden in her uniform, the officer was an attractive woman. Slightly stocky, what Nick could see of her arms revealed well-toned muscles. Her smile was subtle and infectious, her eyes blue and merry. Her blond hair was tied up in a tight bun, but he would have bet it was actually pretty long.

She ate with precision, not rushing, but not slowing either, and conversation was minimal as they ate.

"I told you so," she said, gesturing at his empty plate with her coffee cup. "You can't beat the steak and eggs here."

"You were right," Nick said, wiping the corners of his mouth with his napkin and tossing it onto his empty plate. "That was some great fuel for working."

"Agreed," Christina said. "Let's get going. Any questions before we head out?"

"I'm sure we'll figure it out. I'm here to take whatever photos you need." Nick patted the side of his camera bag. For him, this side job produced both excitement and anxiety. He loved helping the police solve crimes, but he did have a job to do. That job had to take priority.

"Okay. Why don't you follow me over?"

They paid the check and then exited the restaurant. Nick slid behind the wheel of his car and followed the police cruiser through the streets into a small neighborhood.

Most of the houses were a little run down. He could tell that many of them used to be nice, but had suffered from neglect, probably over the last decade or so judging by the chipping paint, occasional cracked or boarded up window, and the tall weeds decorating many former well-maintained yards. Steps, leading to leaning porches, sagged. Trees and bushes were overgrown and untrimmed.

He wondered what had happened here. A few of the houses were an exception to the run-down rule. Fresh paint, manicured lawns, and newly replaced roofs set them apart. They pulled up in front of one of these well-kept houses, the front door of this one was decorated with yellow crime scene tape.

Nick got out of the car, stood, and stretched, hearing his back pop and then his shoulder. He needed more exercise while he was here, and to describe the hotel gym as 'inadequate' would be to pay it a compliment.

Christina exited her police cruiser and opened the trunk. She came out with gloves and booties as Nick approached. After glancing at his hands, she put the first pair of latex gloves back and came out with a larger pair.

"When we go inside, you put these booties on," she told him. "When you come out, take them off. If you go back inside, put on a fresh pair. Don't take the gloves off, and if you find something, don't touch it. Take photos, and then let me know. We aren't the FBI here, and we don't have a great crime lab. I think our last murder was four years ago. But I did go take a course in Virginia, so we still need to keep the scene intact just in case we call in other authorities."

"Haven't you already gathered evidence from the scene?" Nick asked.

"Everything obvious at first glance. This is the more thorough, and quite honestly, boring part of the investigation. We need to look at everything. Mostly, I will ask you to follow me and take photos of every item no matter how insignificant it might seem. We'll then have a reference to where everything was, even if we take it with us."

"Got it," Nick said.

With that, they ascended the porch steps, Nick following closely behind the deputy. She looked around the porch area, and directed him to take photos facing both directions, a close up of windowsills, and even the door and doormat.

When he was done, she pulled the crime scene tape on the door to one side and ducked underneath. She gestured for him to follow and Nick did so with some difficulty.

"Booties, please," she said as soon as they were inside, and Nick complied.

The house was neat, but not overly so. A matching loveseat and couch set sat at right angles to each other, a table topped with a gold lamp completing the corner between them. On that table, and a small coffee table in the center of the room, there were a few red plastic cups and a couple of plates holding, what appeared to be dried frosting, and plastic forks. A few empty beer bottles stood like sentinels guarding the mess.

"Tank's birthday party was the night he got killed. It appears he straightened up a little or someone did, but didn't clean up every-thing. He was a bachelor after all, so he must've left some things for morning."

Nick took photos of the leftover plates and forks, then the cups, noting a smear of lipstick on the rim of one of them. He even crouched as low as he could and got a shot of one of the cups with the couch in the background. It looked good, a rather artistic shot if he said so himself.

They moved around the living room first, him taking photos of the fireplace and the tools there, the floor, and the bloodstain where the victim was found.

He turned around in the room, taking as many photos as he could of the door and windows from the inside.

"No sign of forced entry?" he asked.

"Nope," Christina said. "Tank usually locked his door, but the thought was that maybe he didn't that night. His best friend left shortly before he went to bed. The victim was killed a couple of hours later, at least, that is the ME's first impression. We'll have to wait for an official report that will come from the state lab. We don't have a local one for cases like this."

"Who's your ME then?"

"A local funeral director and embalmer. He has some formal training, but most of his conclusions are based on experience. Like I said, our last murder was four years ago, and the killer confessed on the spot. We don't get a lot of call for CSI type stuff. That's where you come in."

"Right place at the right time," Nick said, and then realized how that sounded. "I mean—"

"Don't apologize. I get it. You didn't know him, and if you can help us catch the killer, then you are absolutely in the right place at the right time."

Nick shut his mouth after that and made few comments and a lot less conversation as they went about their work. He simply snapped photos as requested.

When they were done to the deputy's satisfaction inside, they went out in the back yard. As instructed, Nick took the booties off and stashed them in his front pocket.

They moved, first, around the house and then, outward. As they got beyond the sidewalk attached to the back steps, Christina's arm shot out.

"Stop!" she told him.

Nick did.

"See those footprints? Get some close ups of them."

Nick complied, feeling more like a true detective now. Crouching, he captured the imprints the shoes had made.

Tennis shoes, he thought. *Not running shoes, more like skate shoes. And small feet.*

He took a photo of his hand next to one of the prints for perspective, and then his own shoe next to it. He was a size fifteen, so the shoes that made the impressions had to be an eight or nine at most.

They followed the footprints to the edge of the back yard. A row of bushes marked where the property ended. Nick stretched his neck and looked over the top of one of them.

There was something there. Something red.

"Officer Fabbri?" he said. "I've found something."

Without stepping into the bushes, Nick raised his camera as far as he could, and snapped some photos of what appeared to be a backpack there.

"Good job," she said, stepping up next to him. Even though she was nearly five-nine, Nick stood almost a foot taller than her at six foot six. Still, when he pointed, she could see what he was talking about.

"Did you get it?" she asked.

"Yep. All set."

The officer stepped into the bushes and carefully lifted the pack by one of the straps. Her blue gloves contrasted sharply with the dirty red bag. Nick took a quick shot of it dangling from her grasp and noticed an odd patch on the back. *Probably from a scout troop or something,* he thought.

He looked over the bush again.

"Um, Christina?" he said hesitantly.

"Yes?"

"There's something else there."

Under the bag, in the mud, was a fireplace poker, one that he bet would match the set of tools inside.

"Oh my god," she said. "I'm glad you spotted that."

Nick smiled, and then the radio at her shoulder crackled to life.

"Dispatch to Deputy Fabbri," the voice said.

"Go for Fabbri," she answered.

"We need you back here as soon as possible. We have a suspect in custody and some new evidence."

"I'll be headed your way in five," she answered, and swore after she released the mic.

"Can you run back to the car and get me a large plastic bag from the trunk?" she asked Nick, tossing him her keys.

He caught them. "Sure."

Nick jogged around the house and back out front to the car, opened the trunk, and got a large plastic bag, he assumed, to put the fireplace poker in.

When he returned to where she was, he found that he was right. She held the poker up with a gloved hand gripping the handle and lowered it into the bag.

"Alright, let's go," she said. "I need to you follow me to the station so we can get those photos off your camera."

"It's okay. I can process them for you in my hotel room—"

"No, you can't. This new suspect might solve things. But they might not. And that's evidence you have there. Any processing will be done at the police station, on our computers. If we have to use it, there can't be any doubt about its validity."

"Okay, right behind you," Nick said.

As he got into his car, he thought about how thorough she was being. This was the side of the police work he hadn't seen before, because he had not worked as closely with law enforcement along the way as he was now.

He discovered that he liked it. The rigidity and routine suited his personality just fine. Maybe he'd found another avenue for his career as a photographer.

The thought evaporated as Christina accelerated through the streets toward the police department and Nick struggled to keep up.

5

RUNNING INTERFERENCE

Nick reached the station only a moment behind Christina, but she was already headed inside. A couple of Hughes County Sheriff vehicles were parked outside along with a black SUV with government plates. He hopped out of his car and headed into the low, white building called the Solem Public Safety Center. White walls and gleaming tile defined the space, which broke off into a couple hallways. A receptionist who looked a little overwhelmed pointed to the left and Nick went that way.

Christina stood in front of a small doorway talking to a man wearing what appeared to be a cheap suit. Nick hung back for a moment until she gestured him forward.

"Agent Mather, this is Nick O'Flannigan. He's a photographer who's spending the week here, and he was kind enough to help us take some photos of the crime scene today."

Nick nodded and held out his hand. "Pleased to meet you."

"Agent Mather is with the FBI," Christina added. "Apparently, the Governor called them in to consult on this case and he only arrived a few moments ago."

"Perks of being in the state capital," the agent said, shaking Nick's hand. "Now that we have a suspect, I probably won't be here long."

"I guess that's good," Nick said. "We did find some evidence at the scene of the crime, but I'm not sure how relevant it is now."

"Let us worry about relevance. Can we bother you to take a few more photos for us?"

"Sure," Nick said. "What do you need?"

"Right this way," the agent told him. "We recovered some evidence, too."

"Who's the suspect?" Christina asked.

"Tatanka's younger son from his second marriage. He was found trying to take a bus out of town. Poor sap already has warrants out for his arrest for possession and failure to appear. He had a baseball bat with him, business end stuffed in his backpack. There's blood on it."

"Blood?" Officer Fabbri asked.

"He says it isn't his old man's, but we'll have to test to make sure. It fits with the victim's wounds though."

"How about a fireplace poker?" Nick interrupted and both of them stared at him.

"I guess we'd have to look at it," the agent said slowly. "Aren't you just a photographer?"

"Um, yeah," Nick said.

"Then stick to taking photos. We'll determine what fits and does not fit the crime, okay?"

"Sure," he said. A moment before, he'd been excited to be part of the investigation. Now he just wanted to be done and out of here. "Where did you want me to take the other photos?"

"Deputy, can you show Nick to the evidence room. Just a few quick ones of the alleged murder weapon. We won't take up much of your time."

Nick followed Christina quietly.

"You can't butt in with the FBI here," she told him. "Us even having you help is bending a bunch of rules. In fact, we should run a background check on you and make you a temporary deputy to make things on the up and up."

"That's fine," Nick said. "Why not?"

He snapped a few photos of the bat, some overall, some close ups on the blood on the end, and some closeups of the handle, where white dust still revealed the whorls and swoops of fingerprints.

It took only a few moments.

"Alright, let me get some information from you," Christina said, flipping open a notebook. "Then I'll show you the computer where you can upload your photos. Be sure to delete them when you are done."

"Of course," Nick said. She took his social security number, date of birth, and his home address, then led him to an older monitor connected to a large tower computer system. In the front, there was a slot for a memory card.

"Here you are," she said. "Create a folder with today's date on the main drive and put the photos in it. We'll take it from there."

Nick sat down and did as he was told, first plugging in his memory card, creating a new folder, and transferring the photos. It didn't take long, and as the last of them were loading, he heard Christina enter the room again. He turned around and saw that she was a little pale.

"Uh, Nick, is there something you want to tell me?"

Then it hit him. The ticket.

"Oh, yes. I can explain. I got a speeding ticket outside of Salem, but I forgot to pay it. They sent me a letter and I took care of it this morning. They said it might take a day or so for things to clear the system, but I have a document on my phone that should clear things up."

"Okay. I sure hope so."

Nick showed her the document, and he sent it to her official email.

"Let me print this and take both to the boss," she said. "In the meantime, stay right here. Don't go anywhere."

Nick obeyed, scrolling through his phone as he waited.

A few minutes later she returned. "You're clear, Nick, at least we won't be arresting you."

"That's a relief."

"But until this is officially cleared, a day or two, I can't have you helping us anymore."

He was actually pretty happy. He should be concentrating on his assignment and enjoying the positive publicity he had opportunity for. The local paper and the bookstore, both could be a bonus for him and the magazine.

"One other thing," Christina said. "You need to go out the back."

"How come?" he asked.

"The press is out front. A lot of them. Seems our little story got some media attention when the FBI came to town. You don't want any part of that."

"No, I don't," Nick said. "Thanks for the 'heads up'. Which way?"

She showed him a back way and he ended up walking around the building and to his car, trying to remain as inconspicuous as possible.

For a tall redhead, this was nearly impossible, but Nick put his chin down, hunched a little, and looked down at his feet while he walked quickly and with purpose.

Miraculously, it worked. The reporters were all focused on the front door, apparently waiting for someone to come out there, and none of them even looked his way.

Two strokes of luck in under an hour, Nick thought. *Better go for three.*

He decided to get some lunch and then take some photos at the capitol building before stopping by the local bookstore.

For once, he understood why people hated Mondays.

6

PRESSING MATTERS

The capitol building was only a few blocks away, and it wouldn't have been a long walk, but remaining anonymous during the walk might have been tough. His car provided him with some cover, at least, until someone noticed the Washington plates. He'd just have to hope none of them were that observant.

Maybe he could remain anonymous, at least, when it came to his police work this week. The ticket had gotten him shoved out of the police investigation, and now working his way back in might be nearly impossible, and a blessing in disguise.

He decided to eat at Wonderful House, a highly rated local Chinese place for lunch. As he drove along Capitol Avenue intending to take a left onto Pierre Street and find parking, he noticed there were news vans all along the street and a huge number of reporters crowded the small sidewalk and steps leading to the capitol building.

Great, he thought. *Maybe they will be gone by the time I am done with lunch.*

But he wasn't hopeful. Maybe he wouldn't get his initial photos until tomorrow.

He sighed, parked, and headed for lunch, hoping the Kung Pao Chicken lived up to the reviews online.

He could see through the restaurant window that it was busy inside. As he entered the door, the hostess looked up at him. "Just one?" she asked.

"Yes," he said. "Anywhere is fine."

She looked around, appearing to be a bit frazzled.

"How about that small booth in the corner?" she asked.

"Sure," he replied.

She showed him to his seat, and he ordered an Asahi Lager, the Kung Pao Chicken, and a couple of spring rolls.

The food came quickly and was delicious. Not more than fifteen minutes later, he found himself done eating.

He tipped back the last of his beer and debated about what to do. After paying the check, he went out to his car.

As he did, his phone rang.

"Hey, Gerry," he answered.

"Hey, Nick. How are things?"

Gerry was one of his best friends from Seattle, and the person who had gotten him this gig in the first place.

"Good," he said. "A little more exciting than I expected in a town like Pierre. How about you?"

"Well, we've decided that Catherine won't move into my place, and I won't move into hers. We're looking for a new place we can share and call 'Ours'."

"Sounds like things are getting serious," he said.

"They are. She's a wonderful gal. I'd love for the two of you to meet."

"That would be great."

I was actually thinking the two of us might fly out to see you when you're in Denver."

"In Denver?" Nick answered. "That's when Sandra —"

"I know, Nick. We hate to crash your party, but it might take some of the pressure off the two of you."

"Pressure?"

"You know. The pressure of that first meeting after you both admit you are interested in each other."

"You assume that's already happened."

"Well?" Nick could hear the impatience in Gerry's voice.

"Well, what?"

"Have you actually talked to her yet about what your relationship will look like?"

"I'm hoping to do that in Denver."

"That's good. Look, we'll come, stay out of your way, and just be a part of the scenery. We'll meet for drinks and dinner, but there are plenty of things for us to do on our own while you take photos."

Nick sighed. He couldn't tell her 'no' and he did want to meet the woman she was dating.

"Okay," he said out loud. "I'm sure we can make it work."

"Me, too. I'm so excited to see you, Nick."

"I can't wait," he said. "Talk to you soon."

"You, too, Nick. Stay out of trouble."

"I will," he said, not even convincing himself.

He headed back toward the capitol and found a parking spot on the street behind one of the media vans. He would have to take the photos he could without them in the way and come back later for the rest.

There had to be a back entrance or a side one, so Nick grabbed his camera and went around the back of the building looking at the ground and where he was stepping rather than at the mass of reporters focused on the front door. He stopped and took photos of the side of the building from the grassy area there, careful not to get any of the media or their vehicles in the photo. He looked at the shots, and even on the tiny screen, he hated them.

As he rounded the back of the building, he saw a large man with a video camera and a woman with a microphone trying the back door. It was locked.

He'd seen all he needed to for today. Maybe they'd give up after dark, and he could get some night shots, and if he got here early enough in the morning, some daylight ones before the media frenzy showed up.

The news would have to die off in a day or two At least, he hoped so. It was only a small-town murder. How long could that stick in the news cycle?

As he headed back to his car, he glimpsed a young boy wearing a hoodie, the same teen he's spotted before he was sure, trotting down the street away from him. Nick watched him glance back from time to time, and then turn down one of the side streets. He wondered if the kid was following him.

The Prairie Pages bookstore was not far, and Nick decided to walk there. He might as well talk to the owner and maybe set up a time to chat more later this week.

He walked that way, and as he did, his phone rang again. It was Emily, his editor, so he answered.

"Hey, Emily."

"Hey, Nick. How goes the battle? Your little capital is making the news."

"Yes, it is. That, actually, is kind of frustrating. The media has the capitol building surrounded so I couldn't get any good photos at all."

"That's understandable. The hype will die down before you have to leave. How did the photo session go with the police?"

Nick explained about the photos and his ticket, the reason he wasn't part of the investigation, even taking photos, from here on out.

"That's one less thing on your plate. Be thankful. You'll get your photos. I believe in you. When that's done, you can even move on early if you want to."

"Not sure how possible that will be," he answered. "I am going to try to photograph Capitol Lake and a couple of the memorials around the building tomorrow. I'll go for some early morning shots before the press arrives, and maybe some evening shots over the next couple of days.

"Fantastic," she said. "Don't worry, Nick."

He arrived at the bookshop, an older building with a second story that had a red brick facade that clashed with the lighter brick of the lower level. A simple sign announced the name of the store. Next to it was Second Edition Family Clothing, and Nick idly wondered if the businesses were related somehow. As he opened the door, a bell dinged overhead.

"Can I help—?" the bookseller stopped and looked up at him. "Oh, my. You're the photographer fella."

"I am. Nick O'Flannigan."

"Carol," the woman said. She was short, pleasantly plump, and wore her gray hair in a short cut spiked on top. She wore a knit sweater and a dark skirt that reached nearly to the floor.

"Nice to meet you," he said, glancing around the small store. The store was nice and well-organized for such a small space. Art decorated the walls, and local jewelry and other items were also displayed for sale near the small cash register.

"I heard you wanted to talk with me about the work I am doing?"

"I did," she replied. "When will this book you are working on come out?"

"Well, I'll finish the photos in a little over ten months. With production, I imagine sometime six to nine months after that."

"Oh," she said, looking disappointed. "I was hoping it would be sooner."

"That's the publishing business. It only works so fast."

"I understand," she said. "And Pierre will be featured?"

"It will be one of the state capitals in the book. We'll have all fifty, with their capitol buildings and other photos."

"I see," she said. "Any chance you'll be releasing smaller books featuring some capitals with more detailed photos and information?"

"Honestly, none that I know of. The magazine I am working for may have some features before the book is complete, but I don't control that. My contract is just to take the photos they ask for."

"Could you ask them? It would mean a lot to our community to have something that just focuses on us and our state."

"I can," he said. "I don't know that it will change anything."

"A book like that would do really well here."

Nick thought about the small town they were in, and what a difference even a small article might make to them and their community.

"I will ask," he said. "And I'll let you know."

"I appreciate it," she said. "It's nice to meet a professional photographer of your renown around here.

Are you still helping the police?"

"No, that didn't work out," he told her.

"Too bad," she said. "Come by later this week. Let me know what your editor says. Maybe we can talk about an event at some point."

"Sure," he said.

The bell dinged as he walked out into the light of the afternoon. He looked across the street, seeing the tattoo shop and the hardware store down the block. A few cars were parked in the diagonal spaces, and a little further down the street, four kids, probably around twelve or thirteen, talked and played.

Nick turned left and walked back toward where his car was parked. He needed to find some dinner soon. He could take more photos tomorrow.

The media vans still filled the street, although it looked like a few had left for the day. Nick got into his car quickly and drove back toward his hotel. Maybe he could order in, something like a sub sandwich or a burger, and gather his thoughts.

Suddenly, he was very tired and even a little discouraged.

CAPITOL CONFUSION

"My father was a good man," the man on the local morning news said. "He wasn't the warmest of guys and kinda kept his emotions under wraps. That's probably why Mom left him, or one of the reasons. But for the most part, all of us kids and step kids liked him."

The view switched to a reporter in the studio. "Nathaniel Tatanka, known as "Tank" by his friends, was killed in an apparent burglary, but some suspicious activity and the fact that not much, if anything, was missing caused the sheriff's office to suspect homicide. A person of interest, one of Tank's stepchildren, was detained on suspicion of the crime, but has since been released pending further investigation."

"Tank was a great guy," a giant of a man said. Behind him was a barber shop. "We were best friends forever. I can't imagine anyone killing him. I hope they find who did this so the community will feel safe again and we can offer closure to his family."

"Of course, this is an ongoing story and we'll give you updates as we have them. Now, on to the weather. Can we expect more rain, Evan?"

The weatherman droned on and Nick turned to his breakfast, a four-egg omelet with an English muffin on the side and some loaded hash browns. Maybe this was a simple burglary after all and the cops he'd overheard in the restaurant were wrong. If he had prescription drugs or cash, maybe the burglars left the physical possessions alone. His mind kept turning to the kid he'd spotted, the backpack, and fireplace poker. Was that the real murder weapon? And why would anyone but the killer drop those things in the field behind Tank's house?

They were questions Nick was unlikely to answer. From outside the investigation, he had no clue how, or even if, his photographs would help.

At least, the media storm might be quieted by the capitol building and he would be able to get some good photos taken today.

He finished up and paid his bill, then drove toward Broadway, behind Capitol Lake. He could park in one of the spaces on the street and start there, working his way around to the Fighting Stallions Memorial. As he stepped out of the car, he turned and saw a near perfect shot overlooking the lake with the capitol in the background. The angle and the light were perfect.

He grabbed his camera before the sun could move and spoil the light, and quickly started taking photos, walking around the edge of the lake farthest from the capitol building. Once he'd gone most of the way around, he stopped at the Fighting Stallions Memorial, taking his time and taking both wide and close up shots.

The sculpture of the horses locked in combat offered some great opportunities. From one side, Capitol Lake was in the background, creating a great backdrop. From his height, Nick framed it right in the center of the shot and snapped several photos. Then he stood on a bench, giving him an even higher vantage point. Following those, he went around the other side and took several photos from a crouched position looking upward.

He stood, and his knee popped, letting him know he'd been abusing it a bit this morning. That was okay, the photos he was getting would be totally worth it.

He made his way parallel to Broadway Avenue, coming at the building from behind like he had before, but this time, there were no reporters in the parking lot, although it was crowded. The legislature must be in session, or there was something else going on, but most of the cars had South Dakota plates, so he assumed they belonged to locals.

Before going inside, Nick walked to the west side of the capitol building and took some photos there, capturing the black dome rising above the white building, the sun still a little to the south, meaning there were few shadows for him to deal with.

His morning was going great.

As he rounded the front of the building, he was glad to see there were only two small news crews and one of those seemed to be packing up. The news this morning about the stalled investigation must have killed the sensationalism of the story or, at least directed it away from the governor's office.

Emily had been right. The hype wouldn't last beyond the local news for long.

Nick walked up the front steps, not looking at any of the reporters there, opened the front door and walked inside.

He hadn't taken two steps into the interior of the building before a sheriff's deputy he vaguely recognized stepped in front of him.

"Hi there," he said. "What are you doing inside? We said no press."

Nick looked down at him and the deputy, not much shy of six feet tall himself, looked up.

"I'm not press, exactly," Nick said.

"Oh, yeah. I recognize you now. The traveling photographer. Sorry. We've had so much media around the last few days, we just can't be too careful."

"I understand," Nick told him. "Alright if I take some interior photos? I promise to stay out of the way and getting some pictures for my assignment is my only motive."

"Sure," the deputy said. "Let me get you a visitor's badge. We usually don't bother much with them since this is such a quiet town, but we will today."

Nick followed him to what appeared to be a hastily set up table and took the badge, clipping it to the lapel of his shirt.

"Thanks," he said. "You won't even know I am here."

"As tall as you are, I would doubt that," he said. "We're really happy to have you."

Nick nodded.

He turned and looked around the foyer. A polished floor led to the bottom of a marble staircase ascending to the next level. Yellow light came through panels in the ceiling in an elongated rectangle-shaped dome.

He raised his camera and got several photos from that angle.

He, then, headed up the stairs, wincing as he went, his knee reminding him he needed to exercise and stretch more.

As he neared the top of the staircase, a woman walked toward him. She was brunette, brown eyed, average height, and she wore a smart blue blazer and a skirt that matched.

"Good morning," he said.

"Morning? It's closer to afternoon," she answered with a smile.

"I stand corrected," Nick said. "That must be why I'm feeling hungry."

"A tall guy like you probably needs a lot of fuel. You must be the photographer?" she said, indicating the camera around his neck.

"Guilty," Nick said.

"Governor Norman," she said, holding out her hand.

Nick shook it. "Pleased to meet you, ma'am."

"The pleasure is mine," she said. "We appreciate what you are doing."

"Thanks," Nick said. "I am enjoying your town." He thought about adding the word "small" but didn't want to offend her.

She laughed. "I'm glad. With all the hullabaloo about the murder, I hope you haven't had too much trouble?"

"Not today. Seems the excitement is dying down."

"We hope so," she said. "I have a meeting, so I have to go. Maybe I will see you later this week. Talk to my assistant, third door to the left, if you want to set up a time to have lunch. I'm not sure what my schedule looks like, but she can tell you better than I can."

"Definitely. Thank you." Nick said, and the governor offered him a little wave as she walked away.

Nick shook his head. Small town, small state, and friendly. He walked toward the office, thinking that it would be great to have lunch with the governor and get some photos at the same time.

After he made an appointment for Thursday, Nick looked at his watch. It was getting close to one-thirty. He could get some food, go sort through his photos, and come back to capture this gorgeous upper floor tomorrow.

As he walked out the door into the now warm afternoon sun and made his way back to his car, he debated about where to grab something to eat. The Branding Iron Bistro had been a good choice and it wasn't far. His leg was letting him know he needed to be done walking for the afternoon, at least.

As he approached his car, he saw a teenager leaning over it, putting something under his windshield wiper. It was the boy he'd seen a couple of times now.

"Hey!" he yelled.

The kid looked up, made eye contact, and ran. Nick started after him, but his leg immediately protested. Instead, he snapped a couple quick photos with his phone, hoping maybe he got a face, something someone would recognize.

When he pulled the piece of paper from under the wiper blade, he unfolded it and read it.

"It wasn't a burglary," the paper said. Under that was scrawled a phone number.

"The police pretty much said that, at least at first. What does that even mean?" he said out loud. "And why tell me?"

Nick set the piece of paper on the passenger seat and headed for lunch, glancing at it from time to time, puzzling over it and what to do the entire way.

It seemed he was being dragged back into the investigation, but not by the authorities. He'd have to tell someone, but who?

8

TAKE NOTE

Lunch went quickly and Nick went back to his hotel room, the paper from his windshield stuffed in his pocket. He made his way to his hotel room and set his computer up at the little desk provided. He popped the memory card out of his camera and into the slot on his laptop.

There were a lot of photos to go through, so he started by sorting them, oldest to newest.

Then he stopped. For some reason, he hadn't deleted all of the crime scene photos. In fact, he hadn't deleted any of them. The news of the ticket issue had distracted him. The memory card from his camera was nearly full.

He switched to a list format instead of thumbnails and highlighted those photos and his finger hovered over the delete button.

It wouldn't hurt to take a quick look, he told himself. *I might see something the police don't. I can pass the information along anonymously.*

Nick clicked away from the photos removing the highlights then switched back to a thumbnail view. He opened the first photo. It showed the outside of the house. Following those, there was a series of the front porch and the interior. There was the large bloodstain and the fireplace, with two tools in the holder instead of three.

He knew where the third had ended up, the fireplace poker under the backpack.

Something was off about the living room though, and Nick looked again, clicking back and forth between the photos.

The problem wasn't what was missing. It's what wasn't.

Next to the television, still in place, was a stereo system and a turntable, one that could not have been cheap. Two speakers across the room on the fireplace mantle were still there along with the baseball the one cop had talked about. Yes, a lamp was knocked over, drawers were rifled through but little, if nothing, appeared to be missing.

Excited that he may have discovered something, he clicked ahead through the photos. The pictures in the kitchen yielded the same results. There was a set of knives, kitchen appliances, and even what looked like a barely opened bottle of liquor, and not the cheap stuff. He zoomed in to see the brand and age of the Scotch.

He opened a browser and looked it up online.

"Whew!" he said out loud. "300 bucks?"

It just made no sense as a burglary. Maybe they took some cash, and maybe he even had a look around, but the thieves, whoever they were, left a lot of valuable property sitting there. What was it the news had said? Prescription meds? Nick fast forwarded to the photos in the master bathroom and noted that the medicine cabinet was not even opened, let alone raided.

So what? he thought. *What are you going to do? Tell the cops that a bunch of stuff is still there, and risk getting in trouble yourself?*

No. He had the 'all clear'. He wouldn't get in trouble, except that they had warned him off the investigation.

But he had something else. He looked down on the table and saw the folded piece of paper he'd found on his windshield.

He took a deep breath and read the message again. "It wasn't a burglary."

He certainly had photographic proof of that. So, he dialed the number starting with the 605 area code.

"Rawlins Municipal Library," the voice on the other end of the line said. "How may I direct your call?"

"Uh, the library?"

"That's right, sir. Can I help you?"

"I'm not sure. I think I have the wrong number. I'll check and try again."

"Okay, have a nice day."

The call ended. The library. Why the library? How could they possibly help? The kid certainly hadn't answered the phone.

Nick looked at the time. It was past three, and he hadn't uploaded a single photo to the magazine cloud folder. Every bit of his time since lunch had been spent going through crime scene photos he wasn't even supposed to have.

Damn.

He looked up the library and saw they were open until nine. He would need to eat later anyway, so it wouldn't hurt to stop by. Maybe the kid he kept seeing was hiding nearby or something?

Then why give me the phone number?

The whole thing made no sense.

I'll check out the library first, and call the sheriff after that if I have something concrete.

Unable to bring himself to delete the crime scene photos, he loaded them into a folder on his desktop titled "Pierre Crime Scene", then transferred the raw capitol photos to a different folder he created titled "Pierre Capitol Photos".

For the next hour and a half, he worked on sorting and editing those, realizing he had some really great shots. Emily would be impressed.

His phone beeped and he saw a text from Sandra.

"How goes it?" he read.

"Good," he typed back, and sent a quick selfie.

He got one back of her smirking.

"Good to see you. Call you soon?"

"You bet," Nick typed back. "Can't wait."

A couple of silly emojis followed and Nick sent some back. He really did like Sandra and how much she checked on him. He could talk to Gerry, and to Emily even, but Sandra was different.

With half his brain focused on the phone and text conversation, he selected a folder from his computer, and uploaded it to the magazine cloud drive, closed his laptop, left the hotel, and headed for the library.

He parked and walked inside. A long desk faced the front door, backed by a tallish woman in a light tan sweater made of leather, and a long black skirt. She wore the obligatory tortoise shell rimmed reading glasses around her neck. Her sparkling green eyes and smallish nose decorated her well-tanned face, topped by a tuft of straight black hair.

"Hi there," Nick said, and she looked up at him.

"Oh, hi!" she said. "You're the photographer guy!"

"I am," he said, wondering if someone had circulated some kind of flyer with his photo on it around town before his arrival. Of course, his appearance was distinctive, but everyone seemed to recognize him on sight.

"Someone left something here for you this afternoon," she said. "Here it is."

From under the counter, she pulled an envelope. Written on the outside, in neat handwriting, was his full name. "Nick O'Flannigan."

"Who left it?"

"A local teenager, a kid in a hoodie. He looked vaguely familiar, but I don't know his name. He kinda looked like Tank, the man who was killed last week."

"I have heard about that," Nick said. He turned the envelope over in his hands, seeing that it had been sealed rather than the flap tucked inside.

While he was insanely curious about what could be inside, and why it would have been left for him, he didn't want to open it here in front of the librarian. His instinct told him that would be a very bad idea.

How did he even know I would come here? Nick wondered. Then it came to him. If he had identified himself earlier when he called, he would have been told there was something waiting for him. Instead, he'd come out of curiosity. Whoever was leading him down this path, wherever it was going, was smart. Probably clever too, but someone who, for whatever reason, didn't want to talk to him in person.

Looking up he saw an expectant look on the face of the librarian as she looked from his face to the envelope and back again.

Nick waved the envelope in one hand and then slapped his other hand with it.

"Thanks for passing this along," he told her. "I appreciate it."

The woman looked a little disappointed, but said, "Anytime. Thanks for stopping by."

Nick exited the building and sat in the driver's seat of his car. He carefully tore the envelope open.

The piece of paper inside contained a list of eight names. Five of them had been crossed out and three remained. One of them was circled.

David Tatanka.

Nick had never heard of him. But he knew between this and the photos he had, but was not supposed to, he needed to talk to someone inside the investigation that now seemed all but closed.

He took out his phone to dial Deputy Fabbri's number when his phone rang. It was Emily, his editor.

"Hello," he said.

"Nick?" Emily answered. "I know it is late, but did you upload the wrong photos to our shared drive?"

Nick blanched.

"I hope not," he answered.

"I hope so," she countered. "The ones you did upload are not of the capitol and a few of them are quite disturbing."

"Sorry, Emily. I'll get back to my hotel and fix it right away."

"Back to your hotel?"

"Yeah. I'm at the library."

"The library?"

"Long story. I'll fix this within the next few minutes."

"Okay, Nick. I hope you aren't getting off track."

"Not at all. You'll like what you see once you see the right photos."

"Good," Emily said, and hung up.

Nick put off his call to the deputy and rushed back to the hotel. He needed to make this right and then really delete those photos.

At least once he pointed out what he'd found to the right people.

9

DEAD BOY WALKING

"This is Deputy Fabbri."

"Hi, this is Ni—"

"I can't answer your call right now. Either I'm off duty or out on a call. If this is not an emergency, please leave a message. If it is, please hang up and dial 9-1-1. Thank you."

There was a pause followed by a beep. Nick hung up. He'd just have to call in the morning. The photos were sorted now—the actual crime photos were only on his desktop, and the capitol building ones were loaded in the cloud folder the magazine had provided him with.

It was only the second time during this entire trip he'd mixed up photos and uploaded the wrong ones, but he could tell they had upset Emily.

That wasn't a surprise either. As he looked back through them, Nick realized how ugly they could be to someone who was not used to viewing a crime scene.

"Wait a minute," he said out loud. "Am I someone who is used to seeing crime scenes?"

The answer a few short months ago would have been a resounding "no" but since the start of this trip, all that had changed. He had changed.

One glance at the clock told him it was time to get to sleep. All of this would make more sense in the morning.

He laid down and closed his eyes, and a matter of seconds later, he was sound asleep.

His alarm woke him at 7:15, his usual time. A second later, his phone followed, and he saw a local number, but one he was not familiar with, on the screen.

"This is Nick," he answered.

"Hi, Nick. This is Christina."

"Christina?"

"Deputy Fabbri, from the other day? You called me last night."

It was a statement rather than a question, so Nick answered appropriately. "Yes, I did."

"But you didn't leave a message."

"I didn't," he paused for a second. "I have some information related to the murder investigation that I think you should see."

"Nick, I thought the sheriff told you to stay out of it."

"He did. But this information just...well, it came to me without me asking for it. Can we meet, off the record, and then you can do whatever you want with what I have."

On the other end of the phone, she sighed. "Okay. A girl has to eat breakfast anyway. Same place as before?"

"Sure," Nick said. "Give me half an hour."

"See you soon."

The call ended and Nick headed straight for the shower, making it a quick one, rapidly put on some clothes, and ran a comb through his bushy red hair. It would have to do. He grabbed both his laptop and his camera bag and headed for the door.

This was a risk. Once he showed her the note and the photos he was supposed to have deleted, he would find himself intimately involved in a case, again. He still had night and early morning photos to take, lunch with the governor on Thursday, and an interview with the local paper that, understandably, had not happened yet.

Thus were the joys of a busy news cycle. The interview, yes, he wanted that in the paper for the publicity. But, if possible, he wanted to hide his involvement in the case.

What was it he had told Emily? "I'll keep things as low key as possible. Nothing printed locally should get any national exposure. I'll be careful, I promise."

That promise sounded empty as he pulled into the Perkins parking lot, where a patrol car was already sitting.

Nick walked inside and the deputy waved him over to a booth.

He shook her hand and slid into the seat opposite her.

"I want to say something to start out," she said.

"Go ahead," Nick said, curious.

"I hope you aren't using this as an excuse to have breakfast with me. You're handsome and all, but I'm not really…"

Nick held up his hand, but she ignored it and kept going.

"…into you that way. It's just that you're traveling, and I am not into the whole short-term thing, you know. I mean we could have a drink or something, but nothing beyond—"

"It's not like that," Nick interrupted. "First, you are nice, and I do like you, but I am actually seeing someone." It wasn't a complete lie, and Nick needed something to set her mind at ease. "Second, I really do have information for you. I'm hesitant to share some of it, but I feel like I have to."

The deputy breathed a sigh of relief. "Good. I was worried there for a few minutes. You didn't seem like that type, but I had to be clear. What do you have?"

Nick sighed himself, and pulled out his laptop, waiting a few moments while it woke up.

"I just want to say that I kept these photos accidentally. I honestly thought I deleted them, but when I opened the memory card to load the others, they were still on it."

"They didn't check that when you were on the computer at the public safety building?"

"I guess not," he said. "The distraction of my Oregon ticket situation probably. But that isn't all. Maybe we should start with this."

Nick pulled out the note that had been put under his wiper blade and showed it to her. "I've been seeing a kid around town, always wearing a hoodie, and every time I try to approach or get close to him, he runs. He left this on my windshield."

"Interesting," she said. "That's the phone number to the library."

"I know that now. I called and went down there to find this." He handed the second envelope over.

"There's a list inside, with a name circled, one I haven't heard before."

As she looked at it, she went pale.

"In the photos, I saw—"

"I have to go," she cut him off. "I will let you know if this goes anywhere."

"But I haven't shown you—"

"I have to go." She stood abruptly and sprinted for the door without another word.

Nick looked around and a waitress approached. "I guess Christina had to leave," she said with a wink.

"I guess so," Nick said, still in shock.

"You still want breakfast?"

"I do, actually," he said. "I'm starving."

She took his order and brought coffee, and while he waited, he opened the personal file on his laptop, and scrolled to the photo he'd captured of the boy following him the first day he'd arrived. He cropped and enhanced it the best he could.

The boy was about fourteen he would guess. Long, black hair framed dark eyes and a flat nose. The logo on his hoodie was blurred even with the high resolution he'd used.

"Who are you?" he said aloud.

"Who is who?" the waitress asked, a pot of coffee in her hand.

"Do you know this kid?" he asked, turning the screen toward her.

Her mouth opened in a giant 'O'.

"Um, no. Never seen him before," she stammered.

"Are you sure?" he pushed.

The waitress shook her head. "No. Nope. I mean, yes. I'm sure I haven't seen him."

"Okay," he said, and shut the laptop. "Just curious."

He thought of the list of names, whishing he'd kept a copy for himself, but he did remember the circled name. "David Tatanka."

"You sure it isn't David?" he said to her back, and she stopped mid-stride and turned around.

"It can't be," she said simply.

"Why not?"

"David Tatanka disappeared two years ago when he was twelve. His body was found in a fire at an abandoned cabin out by the reservoir a month later. He's dead."

Nick stared at her, stunned. He hadn't said the last name on the list, but the waitress had known. And the boy, who was supposed to be dead, clearly was not.

Either that, or Nick had the first verified photo of a ghost he had ever seen.

10

THE MISSING PIECE

Nick had heard that a criminal always returns to the scene of the crime. It was some kind of compulsion that often compelled them to see what they had done. Suspects also often inserted themselves in the investigation, wanting to know what the police knew, and to show off their cleverness.

It amused him that he, as a would-be investigator, did the same thing, but he had no choice. If he was going to get to the investigators, get them to listen to what he said beyond a simple clue but with real facts, he needed to go get some.

To do that, he needed to go back to the scene of the crime, back to where he'd found the backpack, and hope he found something else. Something he could use.

He also secretly hoped to see the boy again. The 'dead' boy, the one he had taken photos of. Because he was real and Nick knew it.

And he had questions.

Who did the red backpack belong to? Why had it been placed over the murder weapon? It certainly did not look like it had been dropped there. Was the boy the killer? Why give Nick, of all people, any notes or clues at all?

So, after he finished breakfast, full enough to take a nap, he drove to the home where the deputy had taken him instead.

He could see that the crime scene tape was still over the door, but he wasn't worried about that. What he wanted to see was outside, not inside. He had all the evidence he needed from indoors to prove, as far as he was concerned, that this was indeed a homicide, just as the police had suspected at first.

But there was something on the note he had possibly missed, something in the yard, a clue that would tell him what direction to point the police, and even that FBI agent, if he was still around.

He got out of the car and grabbed his camera. Nick shoved his phone in his back pocket and circled the house, looking around the back yard more carefully this time. It was large, there was a small fence to one side, but with no rear fence it offered no privacy or defense.

Then he remembered the footprints. Small feet. Tennis shoes. Those had been his first thoughts, but he looked down at them now.

They led away from the house, not toward it. Whoever had made them came from the house, and ran...where?

And more importantly, how did this person get to the house? he thought. *Were they at the party? Who was there?*

He didn't have a list, so there was no way he could know.

That's because you aren't an investigator, Nick, he told himself. *You're a photographer, and you need to stay out of it.*

There was something about the kid, though. Something desperate.

He's not the killer, Nick thought. *He saw something that night. And he's trying to tell me about it. Think.*

So Nick turned around and faced the house. If the kid did see something, where would he have been in order to see it?

There were windows. A high one toward the rear of the house looked in on the kitchen. Nick could almost see in it on his tip toes, but a kid wouldn't have been able to. Not unless he was back a long way, and besides, the murder had happened in the living room.

Nick moved toward those windows, and as he came to the first one and looked at the ground next to it, he froze.

There were two clear footprints in the dirt there, small tennis shoe prints. Ahead of those were two round impressions with only the front of the shoe prints in them. Like those that would be left by someone on their tip toes straining to see into the window in front of them.

At this window, Nick did not have to strain to look in. He looked straight across the living room to the exact spot where he had photographed the bloodstain.

The cause of death had been revealed as blunt force trauma. Not something a kid could do, at least not easily. "Tank" was described as a large man.

The boy had been right here, seen something, and then?

Along the side of the house, there was a flower bed and bordering it were several paver stones. Nick took photos of the shoe impressions that followed the pavers in the flower garden, one that was currently sans flowers, around the back of the house. They ended right next to the porch, and right where the other footprints started.

He backtracked slightly, and photographed bits of mud that might have come from a pair of tennis shoes, bits that sat on top of the pavers he suspected the boy had used to get to the back of the house and split.

Why run? What was he afraid of?

Everyone assumes he's dead, but why did his disappear? And if he is not dead, whose body was found in the cabin?

He followed the footprints, careful not to disturb them and pausing to take photos from time to time. Then he noticed something. As the prints approached the back of the yard, they got deeper and farther apart.

The boy, or whoever had made them, had started running.

Nick's breath sped up with his heart rate. Suddenly, he felt as if he was reenacting that night. The boy had fled and started running. Why? Had he seen someone or had someone seen him? There was no evidence of another set of footprints.

What Nick did know is that ghosts usually didn't leave footprints either.

He went around the bushes this time. Last time, they had stopped where he found the backpack, but he wanted to look beyond them, for...

And there it was. A second set of footprints had approached the spot where they'd found the fireplace poker. They were larger prints. Boots, they looked like.

Nick snapped several photos of them. They came, from the direction of the house, but from the side not the back. He could backtrack them in few minutes, but first he wanted photos of the scene here.

He started to piece it together. The boy had been on one side of the house and seen the murder. The killer exited the other side, ran, and dropped the fireplace poker before making the footprints he found heading toward the side street. The boy had followed, chasing him, and dropped his pack on top of the poker so the police would find it.

For some reason, the boy wanted to stay disappeared. He didn't want anyone to know he was alive, let alone around town.

Nick was sure that's what had happened. What he didn't know was why the boy had picked him, of all people, to tell.

Nick decided to head to the place where he'd first spotted the boy and see if he could find him again. The boy was David Tatanka. He was sure of that.

It was just past noon when he arrived down by the river. There was no one around. Nick took some quick photos, something to justify his time there, and got back in his car. It was time for lunch, and another visit with Deputy Christina Fabbri, whether she wanted to hear what he had to say or not.

It was time to get this off his plate and on to someone else's. Someone who could do something with the information he had.

He decided to try a Mexican place not far from the Solem Public Safety building. He'd get dinner, go tell the deputy what he had found and get some rest before tomorrow, when he could pretty much finish taking photos, meet the governor for lunch, and try to finish his assignment with no more drama.

The smell of fresh salsa, spices, and refried beans cooking assaulted him, and he smiled as his stomach growled.

He had things all figured out, and once the cops thanked him, he could be on his way.

PUZZLED IN PIERRE

Lunch was great, if a bit filling, and once he paid, Nick headed for the public safety building again. There was no press outside so, he went right in.

"Is Deputy Fabbri in?" he asked the person behind the desk.

"I think so. Let me check. Can I have your name, please?"

"Nick O'Flannigan."

"Do you have an appointment?"

"No but let her know I have more information for her."

"Okay, sir. Hang on a few moments."

Nick was almost disappointed. Although he had seen her the first time he was here, the receptionist treated him like anyone else. She didn't recognize him as the famous photographer in town or just didn't acknowledge it.

He'd almost gotten used to the celebrity thing around here. Annoying, yes, but flattering, too.

So he waited.

A few minutes passed before the deputy appeared.

"Can I help you?" she asked, almost coldly.

"Yes, I have some more information for you about the murder last week."

"You mean the burglary, since that's what we've decided it is?"

"No, I mean, yes, but it wasn't just a burglary."

"How do you know?"

"Because almost nothing was taken. I can show you in the crime scene photos—"

"The ones you aren't supposed to have, related to the investigation we told you to stay out of."

"Yes, but—"

"What else, Mr. O'Flannigan?"

Things had gotten suddenly formal. Nick felt like he was talking to a different person than the deputy he had first taken photos for.

"It's also about David Tatanka and the crime scene. I went back and took additional photos."

"Let me get this straight," the deputy said. "You kept crime scene photos you were instructed to delete—"

"Not on purpose."

"You kept them," she continued. "Then you went back and took more."

"Yes, but you don't understand. There are footprints. Evidence."

"Evidence gathered by you?"

"Yes. I have it right—"

"So how did you gather this evidence? Did it follow the proper channels and protocol so we can actually use it?"

"I didn't disturb evidence. I just took photos. You can go document it for yourself once you see what I have."

"Okay. But you say it's regarding a boy who has been dead for two years."

"But he's not. I saw him. I have a photo of him."

"You have a photo of someone who resembles him."

"How sure are you it was his body in that fire?"

"So now you are questioning our police work from two years ago? You're a photographer, here for a week, taking photos of our town for a magazine. You're not a detective, not law enforcement, and you're going to tell us how to do our jobs?"

"It's not like that. I'm just trying to help!" Nick found his voice rising, his temper starting to flare. He knew, in his head, he should keep it under control, but he found himself getting angrier.

"You know, I am regretting the fact that we ever enlisted your help with crime scene photos. We would have been fine without you."

"I regret helping you, too. I would have been gone by now, photos done."

"Well, here's an idea for you. Finish up. Leave. This was a burglary, nothing more. An odd one for sure, but it was not an elaborate homicide. Even if it was, none of this concerns you."

"It does involve me," Nick said quietly. "The kid. The note. And you know this is far from a simple crime. If you want to leave it that way, you got it. But you know I'm right."

"That's how I want it," the deputy said. "Goodbye, Nick. Good luck with your photos."

She turned her back and stormed off. Nick stood there, his breath coming in hard gasps.

This was not the response he had anticipated, in fact, not even close. Sure, she might have been reluctant to listen at first, but he had done their work for them.

Just leave it, Nick, he thought to himself. *Take your photos, have your lunch with the governor, and move on. They don't want to solve their own crime, what's that to you?*

But there was something else wrong. Why would the police not want to solve a crime? Why would it be so bad if the boy was alive?

Unless they knew it wasn't him in the cabin a couple years ago. Why cover that up? Again, whose body was there if it wasn't David Tatanka?

Was that the only reason they didn't want the solution to the crime? Did they think the teen had done it, and they didn't want to charge a kid they had declared dead two years before with a crime?

What he did know was that he'd stepped in some local issues, ones he had no idea existed, and as a result they didn't want to hear at all what he had to say. He headed back to his car, ready to do as he had been told. Leave things alone. Then he remembered something else.

There was one person. Maybe only one who he could talk to in order to find out more information. A local who the police might listen to if he pressured them instead of Nick.

Nick had seen him on the news. Big guy, long black braid, standing in a barber shop. Fred, Frank? Something with an "F" but less common. Forrest, that was it. How many barber shops could there be in Pierre?

A quick search on his phone, and a listing for Smart Style Hair salon came up, not one that he thought would look at all like the one the man had been standing in. There was Dakota Barber, The Gentleman's Barber Shop, and one more downtown.

Forrest Cuts, the listing said, and showed him an address and a phone number.

Hours on Wednesday, 7 a.m. to 5 p.m.

He looked at his watch. If he hurried, he could catch Forrest before he closed shop.

Nick brushed his hands through his hair. He could use a cut anyway, and what better spot than a legit barber shop in a small town?

Nick drove that direction, even though he could have walked.

This was his last straw. If Tank's friend and local icon believed the burglary story and didn't want to help, he really would leave things alone.

As he pulled up out front, his phone rang, the now familiar area code in front of a number he didn't know.

"This is Nick," he answered.

"Hi, Mr. O'Flannigan?"

"Yes?"

"This is Delta Cartel, with the Capital Journal. As you can understand, it's been a busy news cycle, but I'd love to interview you before you leave about your time here, what you are doing next, and the project you are involved in."

"I'd love to," Nick answered, thinking he would like anything but that. Interviews weren't bad, but in this town? He didn't want to be honest about his visit and how things had gone. What he wanted to tell her was that he had a sensational story, complete with photos, about a dead boy who came back to life to tell him about a crime that was more than a burglary.

He might have thought that was an answer to his problems, but he was afraid he might run into the same local bias with the paper that he had experienced with the police.

That probably wasn't fair to the paper or the police but, at that moment, that's how he felt.

"Okay," he heard the response. "How about Friday morning?"

"Sure," he said. "Around 10?"

"How about 9? I'll buy your breakfast at the Branding Iron Bistro. It's a great local place."

"I've been there, but I will certainly go again," Nick said.

"Great," Delta answered. "See you then."

Ah, well. Nick thought. *So much for leaving town early.*

As he ended the call, Nick checked his watch and looked up. Forrest was locking the front door, about an hour early by his guess.

He quickly got out of his car and waved.

"Hi, there," he said.

"If you need a cut, which you definitely do, come see me tomorrow," Forrest said. "I'm closing up early." He didn't have to look up at Nick too much, being a tall man himself. He was built much broader than Nick in the shoulders, more likely a football player in his day rather than a basketball player.

"Yeah I do need a cut," Nick said. "But I also have some questions for you."

"Aren't you that photographer guy, the one taking photos of the capitol building or something?"

"That's me."

"*Travel USA* magazine, right? I keep that one in the shop. I've probably seen your photos."

"Probably. But I only did a little work for them before this assignment."

"Well, I've lived here my whole life. I can probably answer questions about the town for you if you want, although I'm not sure how that will help you any."

"The questions aren't about the town," Nick said. "They're about your friend, Tank. I saw on the news—"

"Are you a reporter now as well as a photographer?"

"No. I was helping the police with the investigation—"

"Some investigation," Forrest snorted. "They even have any suspects yet?"

"I don't know," Nick said. "The point is, I think it's more complicated than it seems at first. In fact, I don't think it's a burglary at all."

Forrest took a step toward him. "What do you think it is, then?"

"I think it's a murder, plain and simple."

"You have proof of that? What do the cops say?"

"They don't believe me, but I'm not sure why. I told them that I had seen a boy, who I think is David—"

"David Tatanka? Tank's son?"

"Yep."

"He's been dead for two years."

"I know that, now. But maybe—"

"Listen. I don't know your angle, or what you get from this, but David is dead. My son...my son went missing around then too. Tank and I were both broken up around the same time even though we lost our kids different ways, and that's one of the reasons we became even better friends. You digging up ghosts and making these claims—"

"Almost nothing seemed to be missing from the house. What burglars would rob a place, kill the owner, and leave everything behind?"

"Did you check his medicine cabinet?"

"Yeah, I did. It was closed."

"Tank was on some pretty good meds. One for depression, others for pain when he needed them. That's what junkies look for. How many pawn shops you think we have in town that wouldn't recognize his stuff if some punk tried to sell it? But pills? Those are easy."

"I guess I should have opened it, but listen—"

"No, you listen. There's no murderer here in town. This is a burglary gone bad, that's all. David is dead. I haven't seen my kid in over two years, either. He ran off to the big city, sick of this little spot in the road. And who could blame him? If I was seventeen, I might have done the same."

"I'm just trying to help."

"You're not the first outsider to try to help like this. Let it be."

"Okay," Nick said quietly. "Seems that is what everyone wants me to do."

"You can still stop by for that cut if you want, tomorrow morning. You got quite the look going there, and I'd be happy to get you cleaned up. In fact, no charge for you. Just mention my shop in your little article or book or whatever. Might be good for business to say I was the guy that cut the photographer's hair."

"Deal," Nick said. "See you tomorrow."

He left, heading back to his hotel. Later tonight, he could grab some night shots of the capitol building. Until that point, he could grab take out from somewhere even if he had to settle for fast food, and plan his final photo shoots. Late night tonight, sunrise on Friday, and he should have it nailed.

He tried as hard as he could to put the mystery out of his head, but the image of the boy kept swimming back into his head.He ended up taking a short nap after eating, and after he woke spent about two hours circling the capitol building taking the night shots that his editor Emily seemed to love so much. He then dropped into bed, exhausted.

12

A CUT AND A CLUE

A pastry breakfast and coffee were all Nick grabbed, because he didn't want to be too hungry for his lunch with the governor. There was nothing like making a pig out of yourself in front of an elected official.

The bell dinged over his head as he entered the barber shop, a bell that seemed to be a common feature of many of these small-town shops.

"You did show," Forrest said. "Have a seat."

"Of course," Nick said. "Who doesn't want a free haircut?"

"I do want to apologize," Forrest said. "I hope I wasn't rude. Tank's passing is hard on all of us. Crimes like that are rare around here."

"I get that."

"Last murder was like four years ago and the guy confessed on the spot."

"So I have been told. What about two years ago though? The fire and the cabin?"

"That was no murder. Accident. David trying to keep warm, or so the fire department figured. He fell asleep, the fire in the fireplace got out of control, and that's that. It's sad, really. He was one of the best of Tank's kids and step kids. Nate Junior, the one named after him, didn't even show for his old man's birthday party, and the younger one they picked up on suspicion of the crime early this week. He's one of those junkies we were talking about earlier."

"Shame," Nick said. "I couldn't imagine that. I miss my parents like crazy."

"Oh, yeah?"

"They're in Boston. I live in Seattle now, and with my own freelance work, usually I have a lot of chances to go see them, but with this assignment they are more limited for sure."

"That's a tough one. I'm sure they miss you, too."

"They do. So, how many kids did Tank have?"

"Well, technically he had four but he also had three step kids. Of his own, he had three boys and a girl. Nate Junior, Matthew, the one that got arrested, David, and Sara. Then he had his step kids, two boys and another girl. He doesn't see much of any of them since his last divorce even though one of them, Christina, lives right here in town."

"Christina?"

"Yeah. You might have met her. She works for the Sheriff's office like Tank did. Deputy Fabbri. Sound familiar?"

"Yes," Nick said, the sound of scissors clipping overhead reminded him he actually was getting a haircut, and he hadn't told Forrest a thing about what he wanted for a hairstyle. "She's been my contact at the department."

The scissors stopped. "She has?"

"Yeah. I wonder why no one said anything. Isn't she a little close to be working the case?"

"Hell, everyone was close to Tank. It's a small department. Still, I'm surprised she didn't say something herself."

Nick thought of the footprints. Large boots.

Christina's feet weren't small.

She hadn't found the fireplace poker until Nick found the backpack, the red one.

Had the boy left it there to give its location away? What if she'd 'missed it' on purpose?

That would explain her reaction to his new evidence. Because her reaction was hers, not that of the entire police department.

"Did Tank get along with Christina?"

"Until she decided to go to the academy and join the sheriff's department. He didn't want her to be a cop like him for sure, and they argued about it. I think she just wanted his approval. But when she applied, he recommended the department turn her down."

"And they didn't."

"Nope. He was retiring from the local police force. The sheriff needed new deputies and fresh faces. She was top of her class. They had to hire her."

"So, I take it she wasn't at the party either?"

"Nope. He might not have let her stay even if she showed up."

'Wow," Nick said.

Their conversation paused due to the buzz of clippers, and then Forrest spun him around.

"What do you think?" he asked.

The cut was a little shorter than what Nick usually got, but he had to admit the shorter sides did look good, and the top blended nicely.

"That's great," he said.

Forrest took the time to shave his neck, and they talked about Pierre, the revitalizing economy due to the natural gas industry, and the high hopes the town had.

"Thanks," Nick said, passing Forrest a generous tip. "For everything, the cut and the conversation."

He glanced at his watch as he left the shop. It was just after ten. He didn't have time to do much before his lunch, but after that, he intended to head back to the crime scene one more time.

Maybe Christina knew something she wasn't saying, and if he could get past her to someone else in the sheriff's department, he could put this to rest once and for all.

He wanted to have as much evidence with him as he could when he made that call.

He headed to the capitol, intending to take a couple more photos of the interior in case he'd missed anything, and then join the governor for lunch.

As he pulled up outside the building, his phone rang.

"Hi, Emily," he answered. "How are things?"

"Good, Nick. We love your photos you got this time, once we got the right ones."

"You'll be happy to know I'm headed to lunch with the governor."

"Good! We love those kinds of photos."

"A few locals have asked about a feature on the town. Have you thought about doing some of those as we go along, kind of teasers for the book?"

"We have. We wanted a few in the can in case we needed extra material, or you got delayed in one city or another."

"Oh good. That sounds great."

"If they do well, especially the online editions, you'll get a bonus from those. We really want this to work for all of us, Nick."

"That's great," he told her. "I know the folks here would love it. Maybe we can even let the local paper run a few photos?"

"Sure. Just be selective."

"I will. I have an interview scheduled with them on Friday morning. I'm going to try to get some sunrise shots of the capitol that day. I got several late-night ones last night. I'll upload them this afternoon."

"Good. Looking forward to them."

Nick ended the call. He grabbed his bag and headed into the capitol.

With a little over an hour left, he made his way around the lower floor, capturing closeups of art, sculptures, and more before heading up the stairs. He made his way around up there, too, and then arrived at the governor's office a few moments early.

When he ducked inside, he saw that she was waiting for him.

"Hi there, Mr. O'Flannigan. I've been looking forward to our appointment all morning."

"Me, too," Nick said. "It's my pleasure."

"Let's go down to Richie Z's for some BBQ. Sound good?"

"Sure," Nick said, and his stomach growled. "I haven't tried there yet."

The governor laughed. "Seems your stomach agrees."

They walked over, talking as they walked, the governor pointing out the different parts of the city, much like Forrest had, about hope for the future.

When they arrived, they were shown to a table right away, and the place definitely lived up to the hype.

When they were done, they walked back toward the capitol building and where Nick's car was parked.

"How did your interaction with our law enforcement community go?" she asked.

"I, uh, wasn't able to help as much as I would have liked," Nick said simply. He didn't want to add more, certainly nothing negative.

"That's too bad," she said. "I'm sure they're grateful for what you did and could do."

"For sure," he said. "May we stop for a few photos here?"

"Sure," the governor said.

Nick set up his tripod and got some shots of her on the capitol steps, and then further out, with the entire building in the background.

He used the timer on his camera and got a couple of them together, taking care to set the right angles since he was much taller than she was.

"Thank you for your time and conversation," he said, when they were done. "I appreciate it, and I am sure the readers of our book will, too."

"You're welcome," she said, and walked up the steps and into the building.

Nick turned and walked back to his car. One more visit to the crime scene and a phone call.

That's all the involvement he would have in any mystery.

"I couldn't be as much help as I would have liked," he said out loud. "What a stupid thing to say."

He got in his car and drove toward the now familiar neighborhood where Tank had been killed.

When he arrived at the house, he saw a familiar patrol SUV already there.

It seemed he was not the only one taking another look.

13

CONFESSION

Nick stopped his car and took a deep breath.

All he wanted to do was share what he'd learned. If Deputy Fabbri let him do that, he'd leave and not look back.

If not, he wasn't sure what he'd do. Maybe the paper would be the answer after that.

He got out, taking his camera and bag with him. He had an idea where she might be headed, whether she felt guilty or was just curious.

Nick headed around the back of the house. She could be inside, but he doubted that.

She'd be where he told her he'd found more evidence unless he totally missed his bet.

As to her timing? She probably knew he had a lunch with the governor, and she'd warned him off the case. From her perspective, what reasons would he possibly have for being here?

And what is your reason for being here, Nick? What will you do even if she is here? Citizen's arrest a deputy?

He had no idea, but he kept going anyway.

As he neared the back of the yard, he saw Deputy Fabbri from behind. Her shoulders appeared to be shaking.

"Christina?" he said.

She spun. "What are you doing here?"

"Just wanted to look around one last time."

"Don't you think you've done enough?" Her eyes were red and puffy.

"I'm not sure what you mean by that."

"You bring up ghosts. David. Poor David. And Tank. You think someone killed him. Everyone loved him."

"Look, I'm sorry," Nick said, holding his hands out from his side. "I don't mean to cause any pain. It's just that things don't make sense."

"Life often doesn't."

"That's not what I mean. Don't you want to know what really happened to Tank? To your stepdad?"

"I know what happened to him. He was killed, for nothing. Maybe a few pills, the little cash he might have had around."

"Doesn't it seem like there was more passion behind this crime? More motive than a robbery? I mean, it was brutal."

"Yeah, it was. Glad you noticed, Sherlock."

"I'm not a detective, but doesn't that indicate some anger? Some emotion beyond wanting a few pills?"

"You never know with these junkies."

"What if—?" Nick stopped.

Coming from between two houses, he saw the boy, the teenager he'd seen and photographed.

"David," he said, and pointed.

Christina's eyes darted the direction he pointed.

"David!" she said. Then more quietly, "David."

The boy, still dressed in the same hoodie he'd been wearing the first day Nick saw him, came forward slowly, and Christina backed up. "But...you're dead."

The boy simply shook his head. He didn't speak at all.

"How...? Where...?"

Still David stayed silent. He pointed at Nick, and then at Christina.

"Nice to meet you, finally," Nick said to him. He tried to keep his voice gentle and non-threatening, but he couldn't change his size or completely hide his aggravation.

The boy simply nodded.

Christina looked right at her brother. "Where have you been for two years? What happened? What about the cabin and the body? I have so many quest—"

"I'll tell you about the cabin," a deep male voice said, one Nick recognized right away. "David didn't die in that cabin, but someone he was with did."

"Hi, Forrest," Nick said, and turned around. "How did you know?"

"Oh, I knew right from the start. I knew those boys were together, running off. I thought it might have been David in the fire, like they said at first, but I started to have other suspicions. It was my boy, Jack. You knew, didn't you, Christina?"

Nick looked at her face, and she stared at the ground.

"Tank did, too. But you had more than a hunch. That's the reason the two of you had a falling out."

David shook his head.

"When did you know for sure?" Forrest asked.

Nick stayed still, confused. Christina stared at Forrest. David glanced between the two.

"Wait a minute," Nick said. "The boy who died in the cabin was your son?"

"Jack," Forrest answered. "His name was Jack."

"So, who...?" he stopped and faced David. "Jack died in the fire. So where have you been?"

David shrugged and made a circle with his finger that seemed to say, "Around."

"Did you come back for your dad's birthday?"

David nodded. From his pocket he pulled a notebook and started scribbling.

Christina just stared.

"What are you doing here, Forrest?" Nick asked, still watching the boy.

"I followed her. When you told me she was your contact at the department, I knew she had something to do with this."

"Killers often insert themselves in the investigation," Nick said aloud. "They also often return to the scene of the crime."

"I didn't mean to. He wouldn't let me see David, even though I knew he was still alive. David, I—"

She reached for the boy, and he brushed her hand away.

"I just wanted to see you," she said. "I knew you wouldn't miss his birthday."

As she talked, Nick read the scribbled notes, the printing neat and straight like the other notes he'd received.

"I was in the fire," it said. "I escaped. Jack didn't."

"You can't talk, can you David?" Nick said. He turned to the others. "He was there the night of the fire, in the cabin."

Christina paled, and stepped back.

In his pocket, Nick felt for his phone and held the side button, set up as a panic button that dialed 9-1-1 and sent help to his location. He had set up the same thing for his mom and dad, but they always forgot to use it. Nick hadn't thought he would ever need it.

David sighed, a silent, breathy sound. He pushed back his hood and unzipped his hoodie.

His throat was covered with burn scars from one side to the other.

Christina gasped.

"Who started the fire, David?" Forrest asked.

His hand pointed to Christina.

"Why?"

"He was always dad's favorite. Him and Nate Junior. Us girls were always second in his mind."

"So you tried to kill David?"

"No. I didn't have to. He and Jack left a fire in the fireplace when they went to sleep. I just helped it spread. I wanted to scare them, not kill anyone."

David pointed to his eyes, and then to her. He repeated the motion.

"I saw you," Nick interpreted. "He saw you then. And he saw you now."

Christina sagged. Her eyes dropped to the ground. "I'm sorry," she said. "So sorry. I never meant for it to happen like this."

Out front, two SUV's screeched to a halt, lights flashing. One bore the Pierre Police logo, the other had a Hughes County Sheriff's badge on the door.

Nick stared at them, distracted, until he heard David scream. The boy, not yet a man, rushed his sister, bowling her over. Her pistol flew from her hand and landed on the grass.

"No," she said, struggling against him as he sat on her chest. "Let me end it."

David held her down, and she went limp. He pointed at himself, crossed his arms over his chest, and pointed to her.

Christina sobbed and looked up at him. "I love you too, David."

Two officers sprinted across the lawn and the boy stood.

"Put her under arrest," Forrest told them, pointing at Christina. "For the murder of Nathaniel Tatanka. She confessed."

The other officers looked puzzled, but Nick nodded, and they did as they were told.

"We're going to need your statement," one told Nick. "And any evidence you have."

Nick nodded. "I'll meet you at the department in a few moments."

He turned to David. "Why me? Can I ask?"

The boy shrugged, took out his notebook and wrote something down.

"You're not from here. And you looked like you cared."

Nick nodded. The boy wasn't wrong.

"You've been healing the last couple years, haven't you?"

The boy wrote a word, and showed it to him. "Surgeries," the paper said.

Nick nodded. He held out his hand. The boy shook it.

He mouthed the words, "Thank you," and then walked behind the city police officer, getting into the second SUV.

Nick snapped a photo of the cuffed deputy being loaded into the sheriff's SUV, and then made his way to his own car.

At least, the mystery part of things was over.

14

AN EXIT INTERVIEW

Nick woke to his alarm, set for five in the morning. He still had to get those sunrise shots, and he wanted to leave at a reasonable time the next day. The desk contained three or four Chinese takeout containers from his dinner the night before.

Most of his afternoon and well into the evening had been spent at the police station. This time he really had deleted the crime scene photos after handing them over. He'd double checked.

He'd kept one photo, that of Christina being cuffed and put into the SUV. He sent that to an email address at the local paper, one he thought probably belonged to Delta, who appeared to be the editor in chief.

She was the same person who would be interviewing him this morning.

First things first. He dressed quickly and made a cup of coffee to go using the small pot in his hotel room. It wasn't great coffee, but it was better than no coffee at all.

As the sun rose, he moved around the capitol building, the dark dome standing out in stark contrast to the pink and purple in the sky, created by the perfect amount of cloud cover.

Emily would love these. He'd save a couple to give the paper, along with a few of his other photos. He already had a folder started.

This was something he should do in every city when he could. They were great for the magazine and he hoped for his own career after this assignment was over.

By the time he was done, it was nearing nine, and his stomach told him loudly that it was ready for breakfast.

He headed for the Branding Iron Bistro, thinking of the mystery in Bismarck with the cowboys branding each other and now here, David, a young man who had lost his father and his friend two years before, who'd now lost his sister. There was a lot of tragedy and pain here.

Maybe Wyoming would be a little less eventful.

Delta was already waiting for him, and he recognized her from her photos online.

"Hello there," he said. "Nice to see you."

"Nice to be seen," she said. "This isn't too early for you, is it?"

"Nope. I've been up for a few hours. Had to get some early light photos of the capitol building."

"I bet those are great," she said.

"I've got a folder of some my editor told me I could share with you for your article if you like."

"That would be wonderful. I got your shot last night. It's in the paper today."

"Glad you could use it," Nick said.

"So I guess that is where we'll start the interview," she said once he'd ordered. "What was your involvement with the murder case here?"

"The police needed a photographer to help out, so I jumped in."

"Why were you at the house yesterday?"

"There were some lose ends," Nick said. "I'd prefer you ask the police about that."

"Sure," Delta said. "I'd rather have your side though."

"I can't say much. I took some photos that showed evidence that led to the killer's confession."

"And they also led to the revelation that David Tatanka is still alive, and that another boy died in the incident at the cabin two years ago."

"Not intentionally, but yes."

"How do you feel about that?"

Nick sighed. "I think murder is pretty senseless. Nearly every city I've been to on my assignment, there's been one killing or another. I'll never understand all the reasons people can find to hurt one another. Remember that movie, *Mockingjay*? Did you ever read the book?"

"I did," she said.

"Do you remember what Peeta said? 'Oh, no. It costs much more than your life to murder innocent people. It costs everything you are.'"

"I don't remember that quote."

"It sums it up for me. I want no part of murder. If I never hear of another one, let alone help solve one in my life, I'll be a happy man. But that's pretty unlikely the way things have been going."

"Perhaps so," she said. "On a happier side, let's talk about your assignment. You're visiting every single state capitol building over an entire year?"

"Yes, ma'am," he said.

"And you're driving to each of them? What has that been like?"

The conversation flowed from there, away from murder and mystery, and to the photos he was taking and what he thought of the various capitol buildings and their designs.

The interview passed quickly, and he finished his breakfast as she wrapped things up, asking about his social media and his website.

"Thanks, Nick," she said. "For meeting with me and for the interview."

"My pleasure," he said.

Once they were done, Nick made a decision. His capitol photos were done. He could upload them tonight.

He drove out to the Oahe Reservoir, north of town, to an area called the East Shore Recreation Area, and sat looking out at the water. Tomorrow, he would be headed for capital city number nine of his fifty-state journey.

He hoped this time, things would be a little more peaceful.

As he sat there, his phone rang. Surprised he had service at all, he answered.

"Hi, Nick," Sandra's voice said. "How has your week been?"

"You won't believe it," Nick said, and proceeded to tell her everything that had happened, grateful to hear a familiar voice and have someone he could talk to.

THE END

SOME FACTS ABOUT PIERRE, SOUTH DAKOTA

Pierre, South Dakota is the second least populated state capital, only second to Montpelier, Vermont. For a small town, in a small state, there are still some amazing there.

This includes the Oahe Dam on the Missouri river. The damn creates a tremendous amount of power, supplying most of the North Central United States. This dam creates Lake Oahe, the fourth largest man-made reservoir in the United States.

Understandably, such a small city has a low crime rate. Murders are rare, so making a believable story required some research. There are some crimes in Pierre, and the most common are personal property crimes. Thus the premise of a burglary and an incidental murder came into being.

While in this text she is fictionalized, the current governor of South Dakota is the first woman governor in the state's history. She is from a small town of 637 on the eastern side of the state. The state faces many challenges, including revenue generation for public education. The primary industries in the state are agriculture, mining, manufacturing, tourism, and a now thriving casino industry.

If you do plan to visit Pierre, don't miss Prairie Pages, the local indie bookstore, the great places to eat, and of course the lake and the recreation it offers.

CARNAGE IN CHEYENNE

BOOK #9 IN THE CAPITAL CITY MURDERS SERIES

PROLOGUE: HALLOWEEN HORRORS

"Remember to say 'Thank you,'" Janice reminded the children as they ran to the door.

"Trick or Treat," the costumed children yelled in unison as they climbed the steps and stood on the front porch of the old brick house. Lights were on in the front yard and on the porch itself, along with plenty of interior lights. The front door was open but the screen door let the interior lights flow out onto the porch to help illuminate the trick-or-treaters on the typically cool Cheyenne evening.

"Well, who do we have here?" the kindly old man said as he approached the screen door, a bowl of wrapped candies in his good left hand. He used the back of his sore right wrist to gently push open the screen.

"I'm Batman," the littlest one said as he held out his plastic pumpkin, and the old man obligingly dropped a few candies into it.

"You look familiar," the old man said to another youngster.

"No, I've never been here before," the young boy said. "We just moved in this year."

"Didn't I see you in the movies?" the man asked as he looked out toward the adults and flashed a big smile.

"I'm Spider-Man," the youngster replied, holding out a pillow case.

As the man dropped some candy into Spider-Man's pillow case, he turned his attention to the young girl. "And who are you, my dear?"

"I'm Elsa," she said proudly. "I'm the Snow Queen from *Frozen*. Do you like my gown?"

"It looks absolutely lovely on you. Here you go," he added as he held out the bowl for her to take some candy.

"Thank you, mister," the children yelled as they turned around and headed back down the steps and ran toward the waiting adults at the street.

"Thank you," Janice and the other adults yelled as they waved to the old man, and pointed their flashlights down the dark street. That routine was mostly the same throughout Cheyenne, Wyoming's capital city, as children dressed up as their favorite characters and went out trick-or-treating. Most parents were either at home to hand out candy, or were accompanying their children as they didn't want them out on their own. Though rated as a relatively livable city, Cheyenne's crime statistics placed it rather low on the charts.

"Do you mind going with them the rest of the way?" Janice asked her adult friends as they rounded the corner and the children ran ahead to the next house on the left. "There's some activity at the mall, and I've pulled an extra security guard shift. I didn't really want to do it, but the few extra dollars will come in handy."

"Of course," the others responded.

"Thanks. I'll tell Dan that you're bringing them home. He'll either be snoring away on the couch or watching sports, maybe both. I'll see you tomorrow," Janice added as she headed to the second house on the right.

Thirty minutes later Janice was in her security guard uniform and entered through the employee entrance at a local mall. To counter the typically slow traffic on Halloween evening, mall management put on some special activities to attract customers, including a Halloween Costume Contest geared toward adults.

As she wandered along the main walkway, Janice smiled and said "Hello" to the shoppers, many of them in costumes. There were adult versions of the popular children's characters plus some from Star Wars and other series. Some responded in character while some said "Hello," and others just nodded or didn't respond at all. A mime rang a little bell, put it back into the shopping bag, and then the right hand came up and gave a big wide circular wave.

Many of the stores also held their own events. Judy's Bridal Shop was holding its "Fifth Anniversary Event," with its own wine and cheese party along with gown modeling. Janice watched as several people entered the store, including two in costume. One was dressed as Super Man, complete with bulging chest muscles and broad smile mask. The other was dressed as a mime, attired in black pants, a horizontally striped black and white long sleeve shirt, red suspenders, a white mask, black beret, and white gloves. Upon entering the shop, the mime reached into the large logoed shopping bag and pulled out a long flowing red scarf and waved it around in intricate-looking loops.

Janice watched from the outside of the shop as the mime's scarf movements caught the attention of several customers who smiled and politely clapped their hands. The mime's right hand came up, cupped behind its right ear. Those clapping clapped harder and louder.

"What a gig he's got," Janice said to one of the shoppers as she moved to the end of the shop's window and continued to watch.

"And next, ladies and gentlemen," the bridal shop owner announced into a microphone, "we'll see our three models in their stylish patriotic gowns." She turned and held out her right hand as the three beautiful models came into view.

All eyes were on the new arrivals. The first one's gown was brilliant velvet red; the second one's was shiny white satin, and the third one's was deep royal blue. Each one wore matching gloves and a veil.

Janice's eyes caught a flashing movement inside the shop. It was the mime's red scarf. The mime turned to look back, and then slowly stepped forward. Its right hand returned the scarf to the bag, and deftly pulled out an automatic machine pistol and dropped the bag to the floor. The mime placed its left hand on top of the pistol, holding it steady. The mime fired. The first shot hit the model in blue in the hip. The second struck the model in red in the chest, sending her to the floor. Blood spurted from the neck of the model in white as she slumped to the floor, falling to her left on top of the model in red.

The mime dropped the pistol, grabbed the bag, turned and ran from the shop.

Janice's vision of the bloodied models as they fell was blocked by the patrons inside the shop as they started to panic and back toward her, but she heard screams and saw the mime sprinting away and glimpsed it turning down the passageway away from her.

"Stop!" she yelled as she chased the mime. "Security! Stop!" she hollered again. As she ran, she dodged to avoid a stroller, but tripped on the wheel anyway and sprawled to the floor.

Ahead, she saw the mime slow to a walk and turn into the hallway for the restrooms.

She got up and ran that direction, but when she turned the corner, the hall was empty. "Where'd he go?"

She pulled out her walkie-talkie and pressed the call button. "10-31 at Judy's Bridal, a shooting. In pursuit of possible suspect in mime costume. Over."

"Roger," came the reply. "Backup on the way."

"Get everyone out and keep anyone from coming down this hall," Janice instructed one man as she headed down the restroom hallway. She turned right and stopped at the door to the Men's room. She pushed the door open slowly. "Female security coming in," she announced before entering. She stepped inside and saw no one. She got down on her knees and looked along the floor of the stalls. Nothing.

"Janice, where are you?" came the voice over her walkie-talkie.

"Men's room northwest," she replied. "It's empty."

"Get out now. Wait for back-up before proceeding further."

"Roger," she said as she looked into the mirror. *You've got a husband and kids at home,* she thought. *What are you doing chasing someone with a weapon when all you have is a radio?* She let out a deep breath, and exited the restroom. Several women, some in costume, were in the restroom hallway as she emerged. "Get out of here," she told them. "We have a potentially dangerous suspect at large."

A few women screamed and they all headed for the main hallway of the mall. One costumed woman ahead of the others was the first to exit the hallway and re-enter the mall's main passageway; she was an adult version of the Snow Queen Elsa Janice had seen earlier.

"Did you see a mime, or anyone running?" she asked one of the women closest to her.

"Nope," the woman replied, hurrying away.

Two security guards ran down the hallway toward Janice. "Anything?" one asked.

"Nothing," Janice replied as the other women emptied the hallway.

"We'll go inside," one of the men said as he a retrieved a pistol from its holster. "He could be standing on the toilet or could have broken into the service closet." The other guard also retrieved his pistol, and the two men entered the men's room.

Janice paced the area as she waited. She heard the faint announcement over the PA system. "Ladies and gentlemen, we've had a security incident in the mall. Security personnel and police will be escorting you to evacuation areas. Please meet them at the entrance nearest to where you are now."

"Nothing," one of the men said as he came back out of the men's room. "He was either really fast or he didn't come in here at all."

"Want to check the women's?" the other guard asked.

"Sure, why not," Janice replied as the three of them entered the women's room after announcing their presence. Paper towels were scattered on the floor by the sinks, but no one was there. The guards exited the women's room and re-entered the mall area where shoppers, some costumed, were meandering about.

"Lock the restrooms," one of the guards said. "And tape off the end of the hallway. No one goes in and out of here at all."

"This way," Janice said as she headed toward the bridal shop.

"Excuse me," she said as she approached the shop with its doors now closed.

A few of the people exiting the mall stopped to peer through the display windows. "Let's move on, please," said one of the male guards.

The crowd dispersed, murmuring as they went, and Judy knocked on the glass door.

The shopkeeper opened the door and let the guards in.

"Oh my god," said one of the guards as he approached the makeshift stage where bloodied sheets covered the three models. He bent over at the waist, brought a hand to his mouth and dry heaved. He slowly straightened back up and tried to speak. No words came out, just a dry guttural sound.

1
—————

ONE SMALL TOWN TO ANOTHER

Several Months Later

"Goodbye, river," Nick said as he crossed over the Missouri River for the last time. His navigation app showed the distance to Cheyenne, Wyoming to be four hundred twenty-four miles, but it looked to be fairly flat and open road. "It'll be a bit of a drive today, but getting one hour back will definitely help." He popped an audio book into the CD player, leaned back, and let the cool, Saturday morning air flow in through the vents.

Heading south on U.S. 83, Nick listened to the narration for about twenty minutes until he realized the moderator's voice was lulling him to sleep. He shook his head a few times and lowered a couple windows to let the fresh air keep him company on the empty and desolate highway. He made a turn onto Interstate 90 West and laughed when he saw a billboard to the right. "Nut Buster Grill & Lounge," the sign said. "I'm not hungry or thirsty," Nick said to himself, "but that name deserves a stop." He exited the freeway and pulled into the empty parking lot.

"Oh, well," he sighed as he looked at the "We Open at 4" sign. "It's just as well. I've still got about three seventy-five miles to go."

It was a quick return to the freeway. "So long, Draper," Nick said as he pressed down on the accelerator. "SPEED LIMIT 80" the sign said, and so Nick hit the Cruise Control button and set his speed accordingly. An Accounting major at Boston College, Nick had relied on spreadsheets and calculators to do his math. He remembered his dad telling him that it would take one minute to go one mile at sixty miles per hour. As the mile markers went by, he thought, *How long will it take to go a mile at 80?*

Nick pressed the top button on his watch when he saw the next mile marker. He missed the next marker, but when he pressed that button at the second mile, he glanced at his watch. "A minute and a half? That means forty-five seconds for each mile. Wow. That'll make this a quick trip."

And go by quickly they did. But only for about sixty miles as Nick turned onto State Highway 73 in Kadoka with what now seemed to be a tortoise pace limit of 55 miles per hour. He adjusted his Cruise Control, inching it up to 60, and turning on the radio for some company. Country and Western wasn't his preferred style, but it seemed to be the style in the area. He made his first rest stop in a small Nebraska town so small he didn't even pay attention to its name when he entered. Gasoline, bathroom, and a Burger King drive-through were the extent of his stay.

"Welcome to WYOMING," the road side sign said as Nick left Nebraska. "Entering Mountain time Zone" the next sign read. Knowing he was going to be going through several time zone changes along the way, Nick hadn't adjusted the car's clock since he left Boise, Idaho, also in the Mountain Time Zone.

About an hour later he joined Interstate 25 for the last few miles into Cheyenne. Having recently joined Marriott Bonvoy, the large chain's loyalty program, Nick had booked his stay in Cheyenne at the SpringHill Suites close to Interstate 80. When asked during check-in why he selected the hotel, Nick replied, "The hot tub is a must for me with my right knee. And the photos of your exercise room looked pretty good. I'm not a fitness fanatic, but I need to do some working out since I'm going to be on the road for a year."

Coming from Pierre with its population of about 14,000, Cheyenne seemed pretty big at 63,000.

"I've been to football games where there were more people than that in the stadium," Nick said as he went to his third-floor room. While he was still in the mood, he changed into his workout clothes and went downstairs to the exercise room. The pictures on the hotel's website definitely made the room look bigger than it was, but the machines were in good condition, and forty-five minutes later, Nick was sweating profusely. He went back upstairs, showered, got dressed, and went out for a bite to eat.

He'd munched on some gas station snacks on the drive, but the workout left him with a hearty appetite. He'd seen Chester's Chicken near the hotel. It was close, he was tired, and he was hungry. Nick ordered two fried chicken dinners, sat at a table near the front window, and consumed every morsel of food on the plates. His height, his hair, and his appetite drew stares from some of the staff and a couple other diners.

Nick cleared his table and went back to the hotel. He got into his pajamas, brushed his teeth, and was sound asleep in less than five minutes.

2

LAZY, LAZY SUNDAY

Waking from a most restful sleep, Nick stretched his long frame. "Nice bed," he said through a suppressed yawn. He got up, got dressed and went downstairs. "Good morning," he said to the reception clerk who looked up and smiled at him.

"Sleep well?" she asked.

"The best in a long time," Nick replied as he walked toward her. "It's funny how tired driving can make you. You're doing nothing but sitting there, making some turns, occasionally adjusting cruise control, and stopping every couple hours for gas and a pit stop. But at the end of the day, you're tired."

"Long drive yesterday?" she asked.

"From Pierre," he said as he bent his neck down to look her into her eyes. Bright blue eyes surrounded by pure white sclerae. His eyes stayed focused on hers. She blinked her eyes, blushed, and then cleared her throat.

"Uh," she started. "Pierre? Not much there, I hear."

"You're right," Nick said as he broke the stare. "I'm visiting each state capital to take photos of the capitol building and other interesting shots for a magazine. Been on the road for two months now, with about ten more to go."

"Oh," the clerk—Monica, her name tag revealed—said. "You're that guy who was in *USA Today*. Former basketball player and all that stuff."

"Former college basketball player," Nick replied. "A broken leg killed my chance of playing in the NBA." He instinctively reached down and rubbed his right knee. "In fact," he continued as he rose back up, "one of the reasons I chose this hotel was the exercise room and the hot tub. Used them both last night, and they were great. That and I just joined your rewards program. I figure by time I'm done with this assignment I'll have enough points for some nice getaways."

Monica smiled. "So you think you'll want to do more traveling after you've visited every state capital?"

Nick chuckled as he replied. "Well, maybe not right away." He paused. "Is the breakfast any good?" he asked as he looked toward the breakfast room.

"Actually it's pretty decent. We even have some locals who prefer to eat here in the morning over some of the nearby restaurants."

"I thought only hotel guests could eat here."

She leaned forward and whispered, "They're good friends with the manager."

"Never hurts to have connections," Nick replied. "Well, I better get in there before it closes."

"You're okay. Sunday morning is kind of slow. And if you want a local paper, I've got an extra one back here in case there's none left."

"Thanks," Nick added as he put his right hand out over the counter. "Nick O'Flannigan," he said.

She extended her hand and shook his. "Monica Ford," she said.

"Any relation?"

"To?"

"Harrison Ford."

Monica chuckled. "I wish," she said. "Rich, good looking. No such luck. Besides, his ranch in Jackson Hole is about as far away as your drive from Pierre yesterday."

"Too bad," Nick said as his lips tightened and he shook his head up and down. "If you don't mind, maybe I will take that paper just in case. I'll bring it back once I'm done."

"Sure," Monica said as she turned around and bent over to pick up the paper, the *Wyoming Tribune-Eagle*. Nick couldn't help but look as she bent over. "Here you go," she said as she turned back around and handed the paper to Nick.

"Thanks," he said. "By the way, any chance you could recommend a good place for dinner tonight? I went to Chester's Chicken last night. I think I'd like something, uh, a little higher end. Have you eaten at Chester's?"

"I don't eat out much, I've got a little one at home." The smile evaporated from her face. "I know, no ring," she said as she held her left hand. "Not married, never was. I'm able to go out for lunch occasionally, but most days I just sit in the break room and eat." Monica paused. "I know this might sound forward, and you can say 'No' if you want. Do you think we could go out for lunch one day?"

"I don't know what my schedule's going to be like, but sure," Nick replied.

The smile returned to Monica's face. "You're here all week, right?"

"Yeah, I plan to head out Saturday, Denver's the next stop." His eyes drifted upward as the mention of Denver brought the image of Sandra to mind. *I'll be seeing her soon.*

"Well, I'm here every day, so just let me know when's a good day for you."

"Will do," Nick said as he refocused and turned to leave. "Thanks again for the paper."

"No problem," she replied.

"Oh," Nick said as he stopped and turned back around. "That mall I passed coming in on I-25. Was that where there was a shooting there last year? Halloween, I think."

"That's the place," Monica replied. "We're not known for much here in town, but most visitors seem to know about that. Three people killed, and they still don't have a suspect."

"That's too bad. I saw a photograph online of one of the victims in a white dress covered in blood. It brought back some bad memories. My wife was drunk and spilled red wine all over her wedding dress during our reception. It didn't get a whole lot better from there. Two years and that was it." Nick paused. "Sorry to burden you with that."

"That's okay," Monica replied.

Nick tucked the paper under his left arm and walked into the breakfast room. *Kind of slow is an understatement*, he thought as he entered. He had his choice of tables, only one was occupied, and another still held remains from a previous occupant. He set the paper on a clean table and helped himself to coffee, orange juice, a cup of yogurt, and a plate of scrambled eggs, hash brown potatoes, and soggy bacon.

He drank the orange juice, and opened the paper. "Police Chief: He's a Hero!" read the headlines. *Every small town needs a hero,* Nick thought as he began turning the page before something in the front-page photograph caught his eye. He put the front page back down.

"Police Chief Williams on the left is handing a plaque to Officer Grady McVey," the caption read. "Grady McVey?" Nick said out loud as his eyes widened. He squinted and looked in tighter on the poor-resolution photograph. "Really?" Nick said with a laugh in his smile. "That son of a gun. From star guard to police hero in the middle of Wyoming. Huh," he grunted as he read the article.

Nick ate his breakfast, drank the coffee, and got one more cup of orange juice. He pulled out his phone, open the Facebook app, and searched for his former college basketball teammate. There was only one Grady McVey on Facebook, and it didn't look the Grady McVey he remembered. Nick sent him a Friend Request and then composed a short message: "Grady, Nick O'Flannigan from BC. Literally here in Cheyenne. Get together?" He hit the right arrow and SENT was displayed.

Nick cleared his table and took the paper back to the reception desk. He didn't see Monica so he set the paper down and returned to his room. He stepped toward the window where the brilliant morning sun was streaming through. He looked out the window and then back into the room. He saw his camera bag. "I know it's technically my day off, but I might as well go get some good photos while the sun's out." He brushed his teeth, grabbed the camera bag, and headed out.

HOW ABOUT LUNCH?

The next morning Nick looked at the photographs he'd taken of the capitol building the previous day. The sun bouncing of the gold leaf dome created a striking image of a spotlight bouncing off a mirror. "This will be a good batch. They should rock Emily for sure," he said as he shut down his computer and checked Yelp for a nearby breakfast location. Tortilla Factory looked the closest, and he headed there.

As he sat down to eat, his phone buzzed. He looked at it and saw he had a Facebook message. "Hi, Nick O'Flannigan. Don't know that I know you. What is BC?"

Nick typed in a message and sent it. "Boston College. Aren't you the Grady McVey who was on the basketball team with me?"

"Never been to Boston. Sorry." was the prompt reply.

"My apologies." Nick replied.

"No problem. Are you the photographer traveling from one state capital to the next, and also helping out on some murder cases?"

"Yes."

"You've been in the papers. Don't get many celebs here. Want to meet for lunch?"

Nick paused before replying. *What the heck*, he thought. "Sure" he replied.

"Meet me for lunch at 2 Doors Down, 118 E 17th Street. How about 11:45?"

Nick typed a quick reply, "See you 11:45. Nick."

Nick's Breakfast Burrito was just as good as the reviews had stated, and he tried both the green and the red salsas.

"Just the green next time," he said as a reminder to himself. The coffee, a blend of Colombian and Mexican beans, had a rich aroma that lured him into asking for a third cup. Nick drank the last of it, paid the bill, and left.

He didn't need any more morning shots of the capitol building, but he did want to visit the Wyoming State Museum across the street. He'd scouted out some free parking yesterday so he headed there only to find every spot taken. "Ah," he said, "probably workers at the capitol." But as he turned the corner he saw the parking lot for the museum, and pulled into the lot where a sign read PARKING FOR MUSEUM PATRONS ONLY.

As he wandered through the museum, he was busy with his camera taking pictures of the dinosaur and other exhibits. Even with his six-foot-six height, he had to walk around the life-size cast of a Camptosaurus skeleton, one of the first dinosaurs found in the state, several times before he was able to get the right perspective. He was headed toward the Museum store when he was approached by an official-looking gentleman. His name badge said, "Mark Brammer, Director."

"Excuse me, sir," the Director began as he leaned his head back. "You seem familiar, but yet I can't exactly place you."

Nick extended his right hand. "Hi, Nick O'Flannigan. You might have read the article in *USA Today* about me. I'm visiting each state capital and taking photographs for a magazine." Nick paused before changing subjects. "That's quite an exhibit you have on the dinosaurs. Is there anything special you'd like me to take photos of, not that I can guarantee that the magazine will use them in the book. They're primarily interested in photos of the capitol buildings."

"Mark Brammer," the Director responded. "Thanks for stopping in. Even though we're right across the street from the capitol, so many visitors to the area just skip us completely. Certainly the dinosaur exhibit, and the story about how Wyoming had the first National Park, the first National Forest, and the first National Monument make us pretty proud. That would be a nice highlight."

"I can do that," Nick said as his phone started to buzz. "Excuse me, sir," he added as he pulled out his phone. It was a message from Grady. "Can you make it 11:15? Have an urgent 1:00 Police staff mtg. Thx. Grady."

Nick looked at the time on the phone, 10:40. "At the Museum. I'll be there. Nick," was the short reply.

"Sorry. A fellow I'm having lunch with just pulled up our meeting time. Perhaps I can come back later in the week," Nick said as he put the phone in his pocket and pulled a card from his shirt pocket. "Here's my card if you want to set up a time for us to get together, just drop me an email."

"That would be great. Thank you."

"My pleasure, Mr. Brammer. Besides, I could use the excuse to visit your store." Nick turned and left the museum, entering the address for the 2 Doors Down restaurant into his navigation app. He arrived at the restaurant just as he saw a man get out of a police vehicle.

"Grady?" Nick hollered across the lot.

"Yes," the policeman replied. "I'd recognize you anywhere from the paper's description of you." The two men approached and shook hands. "Let's get in and place our orders as they'll get busy pretty quickly."

"Sure. I can always use a good meal," Nick replied as the two men walked toward the door. After they're seated, Nick asked, "So what's with this heroism thing?

"It's actually a little embarrassing," Grady began as the waitress came by with menus.

"Anything to drink, fellas?" she asked.

"Iced tea," Grady responded as he kept his eyes on the menu.

"Same for me, please," Nick said.

She turned and went toward the drinks dispenser.

"Before I get to that story, the burgers here are great," Grady said as he looked up from the menu.

"And I love a great burger."

"Any particular one you'd recommend?"

"I've never gone wrong with whatever they're serving for their Burger of the Month."

"Sounds good," Nick replied.

The waitress returned with two glasses of iced tea and set them on the table. "Have you had a chance to decide?"

"The Burger of the Month for me, please," Nick said.

"Same for me," Grady added.

"Sure thing, fellas," she replied as she wrote down their orders and left.

"Okay," Grady said, and then started his story. "I was coming home from work one afternoon, and saw this house on fire. People were outside, screaming and running around. I stopped, called 9-1-1, and then the man and I guess his wife yelled, 'Our babies are trapped inside!' 'Where are they?' I asked, and the woman shrieked, 'They were sleeping in the back bedroom.' I ran around back, and they were following me. I picked up a patio chair and broke the window. I was able to stand on the chair and climb into the bedroom and get them one at a time and hand the babies to them. I then climbed back out and I told them to get as far away from the building as possible.

"And then there was a big explosion that engulfed the entire house. It turns out that the gas water heater had overheated, starting the fire, and then they had some gasoline cans and propane tanks in the garage that completely destroyed the house."

"Wow," Nick said in awe after he took a sip of his tea. "That's fast thinking," he added as Grady's lips tightened and he shyly shook his head.

"So what's this photography trip you're on, and you've helped solve some murder cases?" Grady asked.

"Yeah," Nick said with a chuckle. "It's a one-year assignment where I spend one week in each state capital taking photographs of the capitol building and other interesting venues for a book that *Travel USA* magazine is putting together. One of my hobbies is macrophotography and so I sometimes notice small details that others might miss. I don't go looking for the cases, they just seem to fall in my lap."

"That's interesting, the photography thing," Grady said. "I think the article said you started in Washington State?"

"Yes, I'm living, or I was living in Seattle, so Olympia was the first capital city, and Cheyenne is number nine."

"Still got a ways to go, huh?"

"Yep, but it's been pretty good so far. I've met some really nice people." Nick took a drink of the tea. "Originally from Cheyenne?"

"Born and raised here, but went to Arizona for college."

"But you came back?"

"That wasn't the plan, but after graduation my dad was in an industrial accident, and was in pretty bad shape. Mom couldn't do it all by herself as she was still recovering from back surgery, so I came back to help her. A few weeks turned into months, and I knew I couldn't leave them alone. Cheyenne's not like Tucson, there's not a lot of jobs here if you're not into farming, and it's not a real high-tech boom place. Because of my ..."

"Here you go, fellas, two Burgers of the Month. More tea, anything besides the ketchup?" the waitress said as she set the platters in front of the men.

"No, thanks," Grady said as he reached for the salt shaker.

"Maybe some more tea," Nick replied. "For both," he added.

"Sure," she said as she turned, went to the server station, and then returned with a pitcher of tea, refilling both glasses.

"As I was saying," Grady continued, "there weren't a lot of jobs even though I had a background in Electrical Engineering and Computer Science. My dad was good friends with the Police Chief so he said I should talk with him. Anyway, I met with him and proposed setting up a Forensics Department. Well, not really a department, just me. And then we added Cold Cases since the two tie together fairly neatly. Some of the cases I'm working on now are getting colder all the time."

"You're right," Nick interrupted. "This is a great burger," he said with about a fourth of it in his mouth. He chewed it, swallowed, and then wiped his mouth with a napkin. "Such as?"

"Such as what?" Grady replied.

"The cold cases you're working on."

"So there's this one from last Halloween. Someone dressed up as a mime walks into this bridal salon at the mall as they're having a showing of new dresses. He pulls out an machine pistol, shoots the three models, drops the pistol and runs out. "

"Wow, that's creepy," Nick said as he continued to devour the burger and fries.

"Right," Grady added as the waitress returned.

"More fries?"

"Sure," Nick answered quickly.

"And tea?"

"Please," he added. "Grady?"

"Nothing more for me, I've got a staff meeting I have to stay awake in."

"Be right back," she said as she left the table.

"That's it?" Nick asked. "The mime just disappeared?"

"There is some surveillance video, and we did recover his outfit and mask in a shopping bag that was tossed into a dumpster outside There's some blood splatter on them, but we're fairly sure it's from the victims. Other than that, we haven't gotten any other clues or tips."

"Do you mind if I look at the surveillance footage or some of the photographs?" Nick asked. "I do notice details, like the case in Olympia where the police thought these two guys had overdosed on pills in the hospital. As I looked at one of the photos, I noticed that only one pill had been taken, so it wasn't an overdose. It turned out the pharmacist was lacing them with cyanide to get revenge on a nurse who'd spurned him."

"I'd have to ask the chief," Grady replied quickly. "I'll ask him at our meeting this afternoon. Do you think you could help us?"

"Can't guarantee it, of course, but maybe I can see something that you haven't because you're so close to the case."

"I'll ask the chief," Grady said as he looked down at his watch.

"Anything else, fellas?" the waitress asked as she returned with Nick's fries, tea, and the check.

"Nothing else, and I'll take it," Nick said as he reached for the check.

"Thanks, guys. Have a good day."

"Thanks. You too," Grady said to the waitress who then walked to another table. "And thanks for the lunch," he said to Nick. "I'll see what the boss says and let you know."

"Sounds good. Hey, if you need to run, go ahead while I finish the fries."

"If you don't mind," Grady offered.

"Not at all," Nick answered. "There was something else you said I want to ponder for a little bit anyway. Plus the fries are awesome!" Nick pulled a card out of shirt pocket and handed it to Grady.

"Okay," Grady replied as he slid out of the booth and left the restaurant.

"So Grady moved to this place because his parents needed him," Nick said to himself. "He's quite a guy. If I were still back in Seattle, I could take off a couple weeks and fly to Boston to help Mom and Dad. But the timeline is too tight on this assignment." He closed his eyes and let out a big sigh. "What will I do the next time something happens to Dad?"

4

WHERE'D THE MIME GO?

Nick returned to the hotel after lunch. He saw Monica at the reception desk as he passed through the lobby. "Hi," he said to her as he approached.

"Hey," she said with a broad smile on her face. "How was your morning?"

"Pretty good, went to the Tortilla Factory for breakfast, then the museum, and then lunch with a fellow with the Police Department who I confused with an old college teammate of mine. But the guy was receptive, and he wanted to ask me about the trip. We ate at 2 Doors Down. Good burger," he said as he rubbed his stomach. "But I probably shouldn't have had that second helping of fries. I think I'm ready for a nap."

Monica's smile stayed on her face, although it began to fade.

"How's your little one?" he asked.

"She's fine," she said as her voice turned flat. She squeezed her eyes shut, re-opened them and blinked a couple times. "Mom takes care of her while I'm at work, but that's my life now. I thought I was with someone who cared for me, but he only cared for himself. Once he found out I was pregnant, he was gone." Monica hesitated, sniffled, and then reached for a tissue.

"I'm sorry," Nick said in a quiet gentle voice.

Monica shook her head. "No, I'm sorry I mentioned it. It was all my fault. I know accidents happen, but I wouldn't trade her for anything now," she said in a soft quivering voice.

Nick reached into his back pocket and pulled out his handkerchief. "Here," he said as he put it into her hand. "Go compose yourself. I'll stand here and tell anyone who comes up that you're in the back looking for something for me."

"Thanks." she said as tears flowed down her cheeks. She turned and hurriedly went through an open doorway.

An older man in a business suit approached. "Is that girl here?" he asked in a brusque voice.

"You mean the young lady who is usually working here?"

"Yea. Where is she?"

"I'm afraid she's in the back looking for some things for me. It might be a couple more minutes." Nick reached over the counter, picked up a note pad and pen and put them on the counter. "You can write her a note and I'm sure she'll get in contact with you just as soon as she can."

"So you're playing receptionist now?"

"No, I'm just trying to be polite, something you apparently don't know about," Nick said, narrowing and focusing his eyes as he looked down at the man.

"You young punks think you're pretty smart, don't you?" the main responded.

"No, sir," Nick replied politely. "We just have manners, and we show respect for everyone, although I can imagine there are plenty of people who have a hard time showing that to you." Nick just stared at the man whose neck and face were flushed. He breathed in and out heavily.

"I'll-I'll," the man stammered, unable to complete his sentence.

"Should I have her call your room when she's available?" Nick asked as the man turned to leave.

There was no response as the man stomped his way toward the elevator and pounded on the Call button several times with his fist.

Nick watched as the elevator door opened, the man entered, and the door closed. A wry smile came across Nick's face.

"Thanks," came from the sweet voice behind Nick. He turned around and saw a refreshed Monica. "I'll wash your handkerchief at home tonight and bring it back tomorrow."

'Don't worry about it. I can rinse it out in the sink, like I usually do."

"I'm doing better, thanks for your concern."

"Glad I can help." Nick replied. "Oh, by the way, there was a man in a suit who wanted to see you, but I let him know he should show a little respect. He stormed out, and you or the manager will probably hear from him how rude I was. Let him complain, it appears to be his style."

"If it's the one I'm thinking of, I know who it is. Acts like he owns the place. And his name's not even Marriott."

"Well," Nick started, "you know my room number. Call me if you need to talk. Or," he paused as he pulled out a card, "call my cell if you need to."

"Thanks, Nick. You're so sweet."

"Don't make me blush now. It doesn't look good with this hair," he said as he raised his right hand toward his bushy head.

"I can't imagine anything not looking good on you," Monica replied.

"I think I'll go now," Nick responded. "I'll see you later," he added. He turned around and took the elevator up to his room.

Nick was in his room for about an hour when his cell phone rang. He looked but didn't recognize the number, a 3-0-7 area code.

"Hello, this is Nick."

"Hey, Nick. It's Grady down at the police station. Did you ever finish those fries?"

"I did, but I probably should've left a few. How'd the meeting go?"

"Good. I told the Chief about you and your offer to help. Can you come down here now?"

"Sure," Nick replied. "What's the address?"

Nick grabbed a pen and wrote down the address as Grady said it and then repeated it. "Give me about ten minutes?" Nick asked.

"We'll be here," Grady replied.

Nick ended the call, grabbed the paper with the address, and his phone and headed down the stairs. As he went through the lobby, he saw the man in the suit at the front desk.

"He was rude to me, he threatened me. He shouldn't be allowed to stay here, he's a menace to everyone using his size to intimidate people" the man yelled at Monica.

Nick smiled and waved to Monica as he went toward the front door.

"Yes, sir," Monica politely said to the angry man. "I'll be sure to tell the manager when he comes back in."

Nick pulled into the mostly parking lot at the Cheyenne Police Department, parked his car, and went into the lobby. Grady was waiting for him.

"Sign the log and show your driver's license," Grady began as he led Nick to the counter. "I've got your Visitor's badge right here."

Nick signed in, Grady handed him the badge and the guard buzzed them in through the locked door. They walked down the short hallway to an open door. Grady knocked on it.

"Come in."

"Chief, this is Nick O'Flannigan. He's that photographer I was telling you about. Nick this is Chief Kozak."

Kozak got up from behind the desk and stepped out to shake Nick's hand. "Brian Kozak," he said.

"It's a pleasure to meet you, sir," Nick said.

"Thanks, Nick. We're a small town and a small department. I appreciate your courtesy, but we don't use 'sir' much around here. It's 'Brian' or 'Chief.'"

"Got it," Nick replied.

"Grady said you're one amazing photographer and that you might be able to help us on the Halloween case that's been so baffling."

"No promises," Nick began, "but I've got an eye for minute details and I figure it's worth a shot. The worst thing is I don't find anything. But if I do, then you might be able to get a killer off the street."

"Close the door, Grady," Brian ordered and Grady closed the door. "Over here," Brian said as he turned and closed the blinds behind him.

Nick and Grady went to the other side of the chief's desk as he opened a folder on his computer and clicked on a video file. It showed the mime enter the bridal salon, wave the red scarf, look around, put the scarf in a shopping bag, and then pull out a semi-automatic pistol and shoot the models. The mime then dropped the weapon and ran out of the store.

The Chief explained. "So that's the video from the bridal salon. The only video from the mall itself showed the mime running down the hall and turning right toward the restrooms. Because of privacy reasons, we don't have any video of that hallway or inside the restrooms, so we don't know where he went. There is some video later showing some costumed characters being escorted out of the mall, but there wasn't a mime among them."

"Interesting," Nick began. "So why would a mime walk into a bridal salon and intentionally shoot three models? A divorce? Was he rejected by one of them? Certainly not all three. And he dropped the weapon before fleeing. Hmm." Nick paused. "Let's see that again from where the mime is in the shop."

The Chief played the video again. It got to the part where the mime was reaching into the shopping bag and pulling out the weapon.

"Stop!" Nick blurted. "What's that bag?"

The Chief zoomed in on the shopping bag. "JC Penney," he said. "Besides, Dillard's, it's the anchor department store."

"Now what about the video of people evacuating? Do any of them showing someone with a similar shopping bag?" Nick inquired.

"Good point," the Chief said. He played one of the mall videos, no bags seen. The he played another. There were some customers with shopping bags.

"Zoom in on those," Nick asked.

The Chief zoomed in on those people with bags. Several said JC Penney, and none of them seemed to be in a rush. He played one more video.

"There!" Nick said. "That woman in costume. She has a bag that looks similar. A JC Penney bag in her left hand just like the mime. Now you said you found a mime's outfit, so it could be the mime changed into this costume to throw people off and then just casually walked out of the mall."

"That's possible, of course," the Chief said. "But how does that help us to find him?"

"I don't have that answer right now," Nick replied. "But if you let me have a copy of those videos, I can study them lately in more detail, and maybe something will come to me."

"You'll need to sign some paperwork first," the chief said. "And I'll get you copies of the videos. If you find anything you think is evidence, you bring it to us and we process it here."

"I'm used to that," Nick said.

Grady went and got the necessary paper for Nick to sign, and he signed them and left with four videos on a flash drive.

GOLD OVER COPPER

Nick returned to the capitol building the next day and arrived in time to join one of the free guided tours. As he usually did, he stayed near the back since his height allowed him to see over the others and he typically also had a clear line for hearing the guide. Nick stood out from the crowd, not just because of his height, but his orangish-red bushy hair. The guide Alicia directed many of her questions his way, and it was a good technique as it made sure that everyone could hear them if Nick could hear them.

"When you're outside," Alicia said, "you will see the gold shine of the capitol's done. That's not the original color. The base of the dome is copper, but it had tarnished so badly by nineteen hundred that they began applying gold leaf to it."

"Is that real gold leaf?" one of the visitors asked.

"Yes," Alicia replied. "It's pure twenty-four karat gold leaf, and it has to be applied by a highly skilled craftsman because if it comes in contact with anyone's hands, it will disintegrate."

"How often does it have to be replaced?" another visitor asked.

"There isn't a specific timetable," Alicia replied. "The first time was in 1900, and the most recent was in 2010. So it's about, um, every twenty years or so."

"Twenty-seven and a half, actually," mouthed one person.

"Okay," Alicia muttered as she continued with the tour for another forty-five minutes.

The tour ended and some visitors hung around while most went off on their own. After the others finally left, Nick approached Alicia slowly, and a slight smile came across her face.

"Nice job," he said. "I'm on an assignment from a magazine to visit each state capital and take photographs. I'd like to learn a little more about the building if you have time. Buy you a coffee?"

"Sure," she said. "There's a coffee shop here or we can go a couple blocks to the Starbucks."

"I'm from Seattle, so your choice," he replied.

"Let's go to Starbucks. There are too many people listening in on every conversation everywhere around this building."

"Sounds good. The name's Nick," he said as he put out his right hand.

"Alicia," she replied as she shook his hand.

"Nice grip," he said in response to her strong hand shake.

"Training," she said.

Alicia led the way down Capitol Avenue to Twenty-second and then a left across Central. Nick immediately saw the familiar green and white sign for Starbucks. The went in, ordered, Nick paid, and they found a table near a corner.

"I might have missed what you said when the tour began. Did you say you were a student?" Nick asked.

"Yes, sir," Alicia replied. "I'm working on my MSW degree, and there's a volunteer requirement that I'm fulfilling by leading tours twice a week at the capitol." Her hands were busy as she talked. She was making three-sided pyramids with the sugar packets without looking down. The clinking sounds of her bracelets hitting the table as she moved her hands up and down and around each other in a rhythmical pattern he didn't understand.

"I got some great shots of the sun bouncing off the capitol's dome. You said they have to re-do the gold leaf on the dome every twenty-some years. Do you know roughly how long it takes to put the new gold leaf on?"

"The last time they did it took six or seven days," she replied.

"Interesting," Nick said as he watched as her hands moved around each other again in the twisting and compact movements. She stopped and he noticed her left hand. His eyes focused on the ring finger. There wasn't a ring there, but a tattoo where one would normally be. "That's an interesting tattoo," he said. "Boyfriend?"

"Nope," Alicia said as she smirked. "Girlfriend, or former girlfriend. We were going to get married and then cover this with a real ring. I went off for an Army Reserves weekend, and when I came back, she'd moved in with someone else."

"Oh, I'm sorry," Nick said genuinely. "Do you mind if I see what it says?"

Alicia held her left hand, spreading her fingers so Nick could read the tattoo.

"4ever," he said. "Sorry."

"I'm over it," Alicia said casually as she sipped her Mocha Latte.

The two talked about travel, Nicks' photography, and how she planned to help senior citizens once she got her MSW degree. An hour later, the coffees were empty, as was the conversation about the capitol building.

"Maybe I'll see you around the capitol again this week," Nick said as he got out of his chair. "Here's my card in case you want to see what some of the other capitol buildings look like."

"Thanks," Alicia said. "And thanks for the coffee," she added as she extended her right hand.

The two shook hands and went in their separate ways.

Nick was walking toward his car when his phone rang. "Hello, this is Nick."

"Hey, Nick. It's Mary in Bismarck."

"Oh, hi, Mary. How are you?"

"Fine. I know it's a long shot, but if you're ever back in Bismarck, let me show you parts of the town that most visitors never see."

"Thanks, Mary," Nick said. "I've learned to never say 'never,' so who knows, I just might be back there some day. Did Roberta ever find anyone to take photographs of the restaurant?"

"No," Mary said with a chuckle. "She was just trying to hustle you for some free photos."

"Okay. Well, speaking of photos, I've got to go upload some to the cloud for the magazine, but thanks for calling, Mary."

"Sure thing, Nick. Take care."

"Bye," he said as he ended the call. *Wonder why I haven't heard from Sandra yet about her flight plans*, Nick thought as he got into the car. He sent her a text message, "Hey, there. Have your flights to Denver yet?"

Back at the hotel, Nick uploaded to the magazine's cloud folder photos he'd taken the last few days, including some interesting ones from the State Museum.

He glanced at the flash drive on the desk, the one from the Police Department that had some videos from the massacre at the mall the previous Halloween. His mind wasn't on the shootings, however. He thought about what Grady had said and why he'd moved back to Cheyenne. To be near his parents who needed his help.

Nick sniffled, wiped his nose, and picked up his phone to call home. "Hi, Mom. It's Nick," he said as she answered in her typically loud, "Hello."

"No, Mom. Everything's fine. I just wanted to call and talk with you and Dad." And so the small talk went on for fifteen minutes.

6

MORE QUESTIONS THAN ANSWERS

Nick's mind raced all night with thoughts of the mime getting out of the costume and then leaving the mall. *How could he have changed clothes that quickly? And what was his motive?* Nick rewatched the videos the next morning as he wrote notes and questions.

- Mime entered bridal salon and got people's attention with wave of red scarf. *Why would he want to draw attention to himself if he was going to shoot people?*
- Looked around (*possibly looking for an escape route?*), put the scarf in bag, and pulled out semi-automatic pistol
- Put left hand on TOP of machine pistol while still holding bag. *Why on top?*
- Fired rapid burst at models, dropped weapon, and ran out of salon to hallway leading to restrooms. *Did he go in restroom or is there another exit from that hallway?*
- Mall videos showed several people with JC Penney bags, one of the two department stores in the mall
- Found the mime's outfit in a JC Penney bag outside in dumpster. Blood splatters on it but believed to be victims'

- *What did police find out about the mime's weapon that he dropped?*

He opened his phone and sent a text message to Grady: "Have questions about videos. When can we meet?"

Nick's stomach was growling, so he closed his laptop, grabbed his camera bag and phone and headed down to the lobby.

"Hi, Nick," a cheerful voice greeted him as he entered the lobby area. "I've got something for you," a smiling Monica said.

"Good morning," Nick said as he approached the reception area.

Monica held out her right hand, palm up. It held Nick's handkerchief, washed and folded.

"Thanks," Nick said as he gently took the handkerchief.

"Thank you," she replied as her sparkling blue eyes focused on Nick's.

"I know you've got a good breakfast here, but any restaurants out there that you would recommend?"

"The only one I've been to is Tortilla Factory, but you've already been there. Honestly, I don't get out for breakfast very often. Sorry," Monica said as her exuberance began to fade.

"That's okay. Just thought I'd ask rather than always relying on Yelp," Nick responded.

"Wait a second," Monica replied. "A couple of weeks ago some business guests said they'd been to the Luxury Diner for a breakfast meeting, and the food was really good. It's not far from here, a little bit west. And," she hesitated before continuing, "if the lunch option is still open, today would be a good day for me."

"Of course," Nick responded quickly. "What time?"

"Twelve thirty?"

"I'll be here, and on my best behavior," he said with a smile.

"I can't believe you're never on your best behavior," Monica replied.

"Well, ... back in college."

"Don't go there. Go eat breakfast," she added.

"Okay," Nick said as he headed out to his car and to the Luxury Diner.

The blueberry syrup drizzled down the side of the pancake stack as Nick picked up his knife and fork and cut into the pancakes, allowing steam to escape. The fork and its contents were just about in his mouth when his phone rang. "Rats," he said as he set the fork down.

He looked at the phone and answered it. "Hi, Sandra," he said in a soft but cheerful voice.

"Hey, Nick. Is this an okay time?"

"Sure. I'm at a restaurant so I don't want to be too loud," he replied.

"I've got my flight plans to Denver next week, and I just sent the email to you."

"That's great," Nick said. "It should be one of the easiest weekend trips for me, about a hundred miles due south and straight on the freeway."

"That sounds good," Sandra said. "Did you get the hotel?"

"Yes. We're at the Sheraton, and I got a suite for us."

"A suite?"

"Yea, I figured since I was going to be staying in hotels every night that I might as well join Bonvoy, the Marriott rewards program. When I called and told them it was a special week, they saw my account and upgraded me to a suite at no extra cost."

"Awesome. How's it going in Cheyenne?"

"Good. There was an article in the paper about a guy on the police department here. I thought it was one of my old college team-mates, but it's a different guy that has the same name."

"Uh oh," she replied.

"What do you mean by 'uh oh'?" Nick asked.

"You and police in the same sentence usually means you've gotten involved in some case."

"Well," he said hesitatingly.

"Well what?"

"One of the areas he works is cold cases, and there's this case from last Halloween that--" and Nick stopped mid-sentence.

"What?"

"I really shouldn't be talking about it while I'm here in the restaurant. I'll tell you all about it next week in Denver."

"Okay," she said following a pause. "Just be careful, and don't let it interfere with your main job."

"I won't, and I appreciate your worrying about me."

Well, I do care about you, Nick. A lot in fact," she said as her voice cracked.

"And I care a lot about you, Sandra. I can't wait until next week." Nick's lips tightened together as he closed his eyes and nodded his head.

Sandra broke the brief silence. "Well, I'll let you eat breakfast since I'm sure that's why you're at a restaurant. I'll see you next week."

"Thanks for calling. See you soon."

"Bye," she said.

"Bye," Nick answered as he ended the call.

The syrup had completely run off the pancakes so Nick put more on and then systematically ate the now-cool pancakes, the sausages, and the syrupy bacon. He lifted his coffee cup as he saw the waitress walking his direction.

"More coffee, sir?" she asked as she stopped at his table.

"I'm afraid I left this get cold. Could I bother you for a fresh cup?"

"No problem at all," she said as she poured coffee into a cup on her tray and set the new cup in front of Nick, while taking his old cup away.

"Thank you," he said as he looked her in the eyes.

"You're welcome," she said as she glanced down at his empty plate, empty except for the small puddle of blueberry syrup. "Everything okay?"

"Pretty good," Nick replied with a grin as he also looked down at his plate. "I'm glad the hotel recommended this place."

"Oh, where are you staying?"

"SpringHill Suites."

"My friend Monica works there, that's a great place."

"What a coincidence. She's the one who recommended I come here."

"That's so sweet of her, but then she's always sweet."

"Yeah," Nick replied.

"Anything else?"

Nick shook his head. "No, just the check, but no rush now that I have some hot coffee."

"Sure thing," she said as she went on her rounds.

Nick was enjoying the coffee when his phone buzzed. It was a text message from Grady: "Swamped today. Tomorrow afternoon?"

Nick replied: "2 PM Thursday, the station."

Nick left a tip on the table, paid the bill at the register, and went back to the hotel.

"How was breakfast?" Monica asked as he walked toward the registration counter.

"Great, and the waitress there said she knew you when I told her that you recommend the place."

"Oh, that must be Joyce. One of my high school friends. She's a sweetie."

"That's exactly what she said about you."

Monica chuckled.

"Anything more from Mr. Grumpy?"

"He checked out early this morning before I got here."

"That's good."

"Yep."

"Okay, I'll be back down at twelve thirty for lunch, right?"

"I'm counting on it," Monica replied.

"Me, too," Nick said as he went up to his room.

He started to do some research on the area when his phone buzzed. *Grady again?* he wondered. He looked at the phone, it was a 3-0-7 number but not one he recognized. He read the message: "Interested in seeing more of Cheyenne or learning some secrets of the capitol building? Alicia."

7

WHAT'S AFTER GRAD SCHOOL?

"Whaat's your afternoon like? Say after 2:30?" Nick replied to Alicia's message.

"Open for you. Your hotel or?" she replied immediately.

Whoa! he thought. "Capitol rotunda." he replied.

"CU then. :-)" was her reply.

Nick looked at her messages and let out a big sigh. "It'll be good to get some more intimate shots of the capitol building as well as some afternoon outside shots to complement the morning ones. He looked at the notes he'd written down about the Halloween videos. "Too bad Grady can't meet until tomorrow," he murmured.

He opened the laptop, got into mail, and looked at Sandra's flight schedule. "Nice," he said as he looked at her schedule. "Great flight Portland to Denver on Saturday afternoon, and then back home on Saturday. A full week together. That'll be good."

"I hope," he added.

Nick put the "Do Not Disturb" sign on the outside of the door, closed the curtains, and lay down for a rest. As he was drifting off, he started to think *I wonder why Monica wanted to go to lunch today all of a sudden?* Several thoughts came into his brain, and then quickly evaporated as he went into a deep sleep.

He awoke ninety minutes later to the buzzing and beeping of his phone. He shook his head sideways, rubbed his eyes, and slowly sat up on the bed. He got up, picked up his phone. There were three text messages from his friend Gerry who'd helped him get his current assignment with *Travel USA* magazine.

"Hey, there. We're getting excited about Denver. RU?"

"Where are you staying in Denver?"

"OK if we stay at same hotel (if we can afford to)? LOL"

Nick laughed at Gerry's messages. He was looking forward to seeing her since he hadn't seen her since he left Seattle nine weeks earlier.

"Hey, you," he started his reply. "Definitely looking forward to Denver next week with Sandra and you two. We're at the Sheraton Downtown, super location. Great if all four of us are in same hotel. I'm actually going to have to work some, you know. CU!"

"You call it work? ROTFL" Gerry texted.

"Yes," Nick replied. "When do you arrive?" he added.

"Sending you email," she texted.

"Thanks," he replied.

Nick looked at his watch. 11:45. *I've got time for another shower,* he thought as he put the phone down and went into the bathroom to shower.

While getting dressed, Nick thought about the people he'd already interacted with today, and it was just barely past noon. *There's Monica downstairs who's going to lunch with me soon. And Grady who somehow pulled me into a cold case investigation. Or did I invite myself in? Sandra who's meeting me in Denver on Saturday. The restaurant waitress who's good friends with Monica. Tour guide Alicia who reached out to show me more of Cheyenne. Is that the real reason? And my buddy Gerry. I'm looking forward to meeting her girlfriend.* "That's probably why I was so tired," he mumbled as he looked into the mirror, grabbed his keys and phone, and headed for the elevator.

Monica was sitting in one of the cushioned lobby chairs as Nick exited the elevator. The corners of her lips turned up as he approached. Her right foot was tapping the throw rug, keeping time to some inaudible song.

"Hungry?" he said as he reached out his rand hand to help her get out of the overly comfortable chair.

"You bet," she said as she grabbed his hand and pulled herself to a standing position. "What about you?"

"This body can always use food," he replied. "How was the rest of your morning?" he asked as he let her hand go.

"Good. Wednesday is usually slow."

"That's good. Let's go," Nick added. "We can talk on the way."

The two walked out the sliding glass doors and got into Nick's car.

"Where to?" Nick asked.

"Pizza okay?"

"Love it."

"Turn left out of the lot and I'll get you there," Monica said as Nick followed her instructions. The parking lot was half-empty as they arrived at Bella Fuoco Wood Fired Pizza. Nick parked, got out of the car, and went around and opened her door.

Monica just sat there, seatbelt undone, eyelashes raised as she looked up at Nick. "It's been a long time since someone did that."

"They don't know what they're missing," Nick replied as he held out a hand for her.

She took his hand, got out, and the two walked to the door. "The service isn't the fastest here, so we should order right away," Monica said as they entered.

"Okay," Nick said.

"Sit anywhere you want," the hostess said as she handed them two menus.

Nick's height allowed him to scan the room easily. "Let's go," he said as he led her to an empty booth. Heads turned as the two went by.

They sat down and opened the menus.

"The Garlic chicken is really good if you like garlic and don't mind the odor."

"Love garlic," Nick said.

"They also have a great selection of microbrews, but I'm not supposed to drink since I'm still working today."

"Not a problem."

The hostess returned with a pad in her left hand and a pen in the right. "Anything to drink?"

"Yes," Nick said. "We'll each have an iced tea and we'd like a Large Chicken Garlic Pizza with extra garlic, please."

"Sure thing," she said as she turned and headed toward the kitchen window.

A slight smile came across Monica's face as she looked at Nick. "So what's it like being on the road each week. A new girl in each city?"

"That's what a lot of people think," Nick said and then let out a big sigh. *But I will be with Sandra all of next week.* His eyes darted first to the left, and then to the right. "I'm sure a movie version would make it look that way, kind of like a James Bond flick. But I'm not that type. Believe it or not, I'm actually shy. I don't have a problem meeting or talking with people, but I'm not a love 'em and leave 'em guy. I can be friends with you, but I'm leaving in a few days, and probably never coming back to Cheyenne. At least not in the next forty-one weeks while I'm visiting the rest of the state capitals."

Monica reached over and put her left hand on his right thigh. "I shouldn't have said that. I'm sorry." She pulled her hand back, bit her upper lip and looked down.

"Hey," Nick said. "It's okay."

She smiled.

"Here's your iced teas," the hostess/waitress said as she set them on the table. "Sugar's right there," she added. "Need any lemon?"

"No, thanks," Nick replied.

"I told the kitchen to put a rush on your pizza, so it shouldn't be much longer."

"Thanks," Nick said as she left.

Nick turned back to Monica. "I've found that most of the people I've run into are very nice. They want to help without looking for anything in return. It kind of restores my faith in humanity. And I've met such wonderful hotel and restaurant employees that really care about others."

"That's good to hear in today's world," she said.

"Tell me about your little one, if you don't mind," Nick said turning the conversation away from himself.

"She's adorable," Monica began as her eyes brightened. "She deserves such a good life, I just hope I can give it to her"

"What's her name?"

Monica smiled. "Angelina."

"Beautiful name. I bet she is a little angel."

"She is."

"Here's your pizza," the hostess/waitress said as she delivered the large pizza to the table.

"Are you sure the extra garlic is okay?" Nick asked.

Monica nodded. "I've got a toothbrush and mouthwash at work."

They continued with small talk as they devoured the pizza. Nick ate most of it, of course, but Monica also displayed a healthy appetite.

Nick asked for the bill, paid it, with a tip, and the two left the restaurant. Nick unlocked the car and opened the door for Monica. Nick got in his side and put the key in the ignition.

"Thanks. The pizza. The conversation. For listening. For caring." She paused. "God, you're going to make some gal out there the happiest person alive."

"You're going to find your right guy. And in the meantime, you and Angelina are going to be just fine." Nick put on the seatbelt, and started the car. "I better get you back to work so you can brush those teeth."

Monica leaned her head back and closed her eyes as a smile engulfed her face.

Nick pulled into the hotel parking lot and parked in a spot out of view from the reception area. "Thanks for lunch."

"Thank you," she replied.

He got out of the car as Monica waited for him. She took in a big breath and let it out. There was definitely a garlic aroma in the car. Nick opened her door, held his hand out for her, and she got out. He let her hand go and the two walked into the hotel chatting as friends would do.

She went to the reception area and Nick went to the elevator.

He looked at his watch as the elevator door closed: 1:40.

Back in his room, Nick brushed his teeth twice.

He checked email, but there was nothing he had to attend to right away, so he shut the computer down. He sat on the bed and closed his eyes. *How does a girl like Monica find the right guy in this small town?* He went to the window and looked at the capitol building's dome, clearly visible from almost everywhere in town.

Nick grabbed his camera bag, and headed out. He had time before meeting up with Alicia, so he could get some photographs with the sun at different angles from previous shots. He spent fifteen minutes on the outside and then went into the Rotunda. Alicia was waiting for him there.

"Hi, there," he said as the two approached each other.

"Hey," she said as she extended her right hand, and Nick shook it.

"How's school?"

"It's okay. Fortunately, it's ending soon and maybe I can move to a real-sized town with a whole lot more opportunities."

"What about your Reserves work?"

"I can do that anywhere there's a facility, and believe me, if this town has one, any other place I go to will also."

"That's nice," Nick said. He paused before continuing. "I don't intend for this to sound sexist because I've always thought that women can do almost anything they make up their minds to do. What is it that you do in the Army Reserves?"

"Infantry Division, RPGs, almost any hand-held weapon you can think of. M-4, M-110, anything you can fire. We also train with enemy weapons at one school I attended. Everything from the Uzi to the AK-47. I didn't get the nickname 'Bad Ass Alicia' for nothing."

"Makes sense to me, but I don't know that much about guns," Nick said. "Do you get extra credit for giving me this private tour?"

"No, but I thought maybe we could also talk about photography."

"Sure," he said. "Show me some stuff that I can get great photos of. Places that most visitors don't see or can't get to."

Alicia and Nick wandered around various hallways and stairways of the capitol building for the next hour and a half as Nick explained how he determined the camera settings for specific shots. The tour ended up where it began, in the first floor Rotunda.

"Thanks so much," Nick said.

"My pleasure, Nick," replied Alicia who once again extended her right hand.

Nick grimaced ever so slightly as they shook hands.

The two headed off in opposite directions, and Nick returned to the hotel to download the day's photos.

"GREAT GOVERNOR STORY"

The room alarm and his phone alarm started within a minute of each other. Nick slowly opened his eyes. The glow of the room's clock and the flashing of his phone were the only things visible, not counting the red dot on the TV and the two detectors on the ceiling. He looked toward the window. No light there, the curtains were sealed shut thanks to his binder clips keeping them pleated together.

He wanted some sunrise shots for the magazine and also for his own portfolio. Plus he we occasionally surprised at the photos he was able to get. One of his favorites, and his online following loved it too, was the one of a formation of geese flying against the backdrop of a bright pink cloud set against the brilliant morning sky. Those were money shots, and they were never predictable.

Nick got out of bed, stretched his muscles, and yawned. He turned on the bedside lamp, used the bathroom, and got dressed. He took his phone off the charger, grabbed a light jacket, his keys, his camera bag, and he headed out for the capitol building.

He had his choice of parking spots as his was the only car within two blocks of the capitol. He went to the west side of the building so he could get the emerging light as it arose behind the capitol. He adjusted the camera settings so the building was a mere blind spot and the focus was on the sunlight coming from behind. "Brilliant!" he exclaimed as he looked at the image in the camera's display

Nick spent the next hour walking around the building capturing photos that the sun, the light, the shadows, and what the building itself gave to him. *As Ansel Adams once said,* he reminded himself, *a great photograph is more of a gift from God than it is because of the photographer's skill.* He'd taken enough photographs, including a few of birds in formation, and he went to his car and headed back to the hotel.

The coffee urns were in the lobby. Nick filled two cups with Dark Roast, secured them with lids, and went up to his room. After setting his camera bag on the desk he drained one of the cups, took off his shoes, and lay on the bed. *Just for a few minutes,* he told himself.

His pocket started vibrating an hour later. He opened his eyes as he tried to make sense of what was happening. The buzzing continued.

"My phone," he said as he fished it out of his pocket. "Hello," he said without looking at the display.

"Did I catch you at a bad time, Nick?"

Nick shook his head in an attempt to be coherent. "Um," he muttered as he then looked at the display. "Oh, hi, Emily. Sorry. I was up early and out taking photos, when I came back to the room and apparently fell dead asleep."

"Sorry I woke you," his magazine editor said. "I just wanted to call and tell you what a great story that was with the Governor of South Dakota. Nice job. That is definitely going to play well with the P.R. Department and with our readers."

"Oh, good," Nick said with some excitement. He went to the desk to get the second cup of coffee. He removed the lid and took a sip. Cold, but it was coffee. "And I've been getting some really interesting shots here in Cheyenne. I went with one of the volunteer guides at the capitol who took me on a private tour to some of the places most people don't see. Even though it's much bigger than Pierre, Cheyenne is still a fairly small town."

"Well, you're doing a great job, Nick. I know you have a long way to go, but I'm really proud of what you've done so far."

"Thanks, Emily. It's a challenge at times, certainly a bit more than I thought it was going to be. But I am having fun, meeting some really nice people. And maybe that's a side story there on how friendly people are all over the U.S. I'll definitely keep trying to do my best for you."

"I know you will, Nick. Get some more sleep if you need to.

"Yea, thanks, Emily. I'll get more photos uploaded soon."

"Okay. Take care, Nick. Bye."

"Bye, Emily. Thanks for the call."

"My pleasure, Nick."

QUESTIONS ABOUT THE VIDEOS

Nick ended the call with Emily, looked at the clock, and realized he should head downstairs if he was going to eat breakfast at the hotel. He removed the binder clips from the curtains and pulled them open. The sunlight bouncing of the capitol dome was once again light a spotlight in the sky.

Nick grabbed his phone and headed downstairs. Monica gave him a polite wave as he passed through the reception area. "Good morning," he said as he looked her way, nodded, and kept going. The aromas that hit him as he entered the breakfast room were delightful. *Either I'm really hungry or the cook has done something different today,* he thought as he went first for the glass of orange juice and a steaming cup of coffee.

He took them to an open table, sat down, and sipped on the coffee. He then drank some of the orange juice, back to the coffee, the juice, and repeated until the juice was gone. Nick refilled his coffee and then got a plate of scrambled eggs, bacon, hash browns, and a cup of yogurt.

Nick finished the pieces of bacon, the yogurt, and everything else on his plate between sips of coffee. He got up, cleared the items from his table, got a coffee refill, put a lid on it, and headed back to his room. He looked over toward Monica as he went through the reception area, but she was busy with another guest.

Back in his room, Nick opened his computer and downloaded the photos from his morning shoot to the computer. He went through them, deleting some, and then sorting the remaining ones into the "Magazine" folder and his "Personal" folder. Nick started to upload the "Magazine" photos to the cloud, but he stopped. He'd made mistakes before, and he really didn't want to do that again. He opened the "Magazine" folder," and looked at each photograph, one by one. *They're all okay,* he thought to himself, so he sent them to the cloud.

He looked at his calendar. "Nothing until meeting with Grady at two," he said. "Okay, Cheyenne, I've got a few hours. What's fun to do here?" He went to TripAdvisor and found the Top Ten things to do in Cheyenne. As he looked through the list, he remembered that he wanted to get back to the State Museum where he'd taken photos at the dinosaur exhibit. But then something caught his eye.

"The Big Boy Steam Engine" was something he'd not heard of, so he looked at the description. "I've got to go there," he said as he wrote down the address. He grabbed his notes from watching the videos in case he didn't return to the hotel before his meeting at the Police Department with Grady. The museum and the locomotive—and lunch—should fill up his time before two o'clock, he reasoned.

Nick grabbed his camera bag, his notes, his phone, and headed out. His first stop was the Wyoming State Museum. He parked his car, went inside and asked for Mark Brammer, the Museum Director. "We spoke a couple a days ago," Nick added.

"I'm sorry, sir, the Director is not in the office today," the volunteer said.

"Shoot," Nick replied. He took out a card and said, "Well, give him my card, please, and tell him that I was here, and that I'm hoping to get an article published about the museum."

"Of course, Mr. O', um, O'Flannigan," the volunteer said as she stumbled through his name.

"Don't worry, Miss. It happens all the time," Nick said. "What's your favorite part of the museum? Something you'd like to share with others?" he asked as he engaged with the young volunteer.

"The dinosaurs, for sure," she said. "It's, like, totally my favorite."

"Agreed. Thanks," Nick said as he smiled, nodded, and headed toward the Dinosaur Exhibit. He snapped a few more photos, went to the Museum Store, and then decided he'd seen enough. He got into his car and went to the Big Boy Steam Engine display.

"Wow," Nick said as he got to Holliday Park and got out of his car. He pulled out his camera and began snapping photos as he approached the locomotive. He read the sign:

"Even in retirement, ol' Number 4004 remains an imposing sight. The world's largest steam locomotive, this powerful coal-fired engine was designed to pull a 3600-ton train over steep grades between Cheyenne, WY, and Ogden, Utah. The 4004 is one of the eight remaining Big Boys throughout the country."

"To think that steam could create that kind of energy, that power. That's amazing," Nick said as he walked round the engine, snapping some high-detail photos for his macrophotography website. He wandered around the park, getting photos of various things before leaving. He went to lunch, and then headed to the Police Department for his two o'clock meeting.

Nick entered the police station and the clerk stood up. "I'll get Mr. McVey for you."

"Thanks, but don't stand for me. Please," Nick said as he moved to the side of the room.

Grady appeared shortly. "Hey, Nick. How's it going?"

"Awesome steam engine down there in the park," Nick replied as he stepped forward to shake Grady's hand.

"You've got to sign in again," Grady said.

"Yep, forgot about that," Nick replied as he went to the desk and signed in.

"This way," Grady said after Nick clipped on the Visitor badge and followed him through the doorway.

They went to Grady's office, an inside office that appeared to have been used as some storage area before. "It's not much, but at least I have a desk and a phone," Grady said apologetically.

"So, what do you have," Grady said matter-of-factly."

"A bunch of questions," Nick replied as he pulled out his notebook. "Can we go through those videos again?"

"Sure," Grady said as he clicked a few icons on his computer. The video from inside the bridal salon began.

"Stop," Nick said. "There," Nick said. "Why would the mime pull out that red scarf and intentionally draw attention to himself? Would you do that if you were planning to shoot a bunch of people?"

"We've asked that question lots of times already. We have no answer," Grady replied.

"Just a little more and stop," Nick said. "So now," Nick begins again, "he looks around. Do you think he's looking for an escape route?"

"That's our conclusion," Grady answers. "Keep going?"

"Up to the point where he pulls the pistol out and starts shooting," Nick replied.

"Look at that," Nick said. "He put his hand on top of the weapon. Most people would put their hand on the bottom to support it. But he put his hand on top. Why?"

"That's interesting," Grady began. "We talked with some weapons experts and what they told us is that this type of fully automatic machine pistol needs support from the top for a right-handed shooter. Without any other support, the natural kick will take the weapon up and to the left. So by putting his hand on the top, the shooter was probably attempting to control the piece and his aim for the short burst of fire."

"Wow," Nick said. "So perhaps this guy knew what the weapon would do, and was trying to keep it focused more on the abdomen areas of the models."

Grady let out a sigh. "We call it 'aiming center mass', but yeah, that's what we've thought."

"Nick continued. "So then he drops the weapon and runs out. Did you find anything on it?"

"Nope. It was clean. It's an extremely common machine pistol, and even though they are technically illegal, they're easy to get. The serial numbers had been filed off, pretty expertly. There were no prints, nothing," Grady replied. "Ballistics were useless. We already knew this was the weapon that fired the shots."

"And nothing was found in the bathrooms?"

"Clean. This dude had it planned out. He knew what he was doing and how to get away with it."

"Wow," Nick exclaimed. "Any other exits down that restroom hallway?"

"None."

"Let's look at the mall videos," Nick said. "There's got to be something there. The guy runs down the hallway toward the restrooms. There's no exit. So where'd he go? It's got to be in the videos."

The two men watched the videos over and over again. Grady chimed in, "The shopping bag with his costume was found outside in a dumpster, and there are a lot of shoppers with JC Penney shopping bags, including some in costume. Could he have had a costume on under the mime outfit?"

"But how quickly could he have gotten it off, whether it was another costume or not?" Nick asked. "Restart that one," he said as he saw more people with shopping bags. "How common is it for people to shop in costume on Halloween?"

"Pretty common here in Cheyenne. And the banks, they're always concerned, but there's never been a problem. People here really get into the Halloween thing."

"If there's no other way out, the shooter just walked out of the mall," Nick said calmly. "And that means there should be some video of him. We just don't know who or what we're looking for."

"Yep," Grady said.

10

WHAT'S YOUR TALENT?

Nick left the police station meeting with Grady with even more questions than he arrived with. "The mime clearly had this all planned out, including the timing when the models would appear, how to control the weapon, an escape route, and even the ability to get out of the costume quickly," he mumbled to himself as he walked down the main hallway of the mall.. He stopped in front the directory.

Nick used his right index finger and pointed to Judy's Bridal Salon. He moved his finger as he talked to himself. "He runs out and goes this way and down toward the restrooms. There's no exit down there, so he had to come back out this way. But then where'd he go?"

"Is there something I can help you find, sir?" the security guard asked.

Nick turned and looked at her. The badge on her uniform said, "Janice." "I was just trying to re-trace where that mime could have gone last Halloween after shooting those bridal models."

"Well," she began, "I was here and started chasing him down the hallway, but I tripped over a baby stroller, and he went down this way. Toward the restrooms. But no one saw him come out."

"That's the puzzling part, isn't it?" Nick asked.

"So how do you know this? I don't recall seeing you around here before."

"Just passing through," Nick replied. "And I got chatting with someone at the Police Department, and I've been trying to help him solve the cold case."

"Oh, you mean Grady?"

"That's him."

"I told him everything I know. I've watched the mall videos over and over many times. I just don't see anything."

"Yes, he's said everyone has been helpful," Nick said as he turned back to the directory. He pointed as he counted off the exits. "There are three mall entrances and exits, plus the ones in both Dillard's and JC Penney."

"Lots of possibilities," Janice said. "And we were evacuating the mall through all of them."

"Thank you," Nick said as he stuck out his right hand.

Janice shook his hand and that triggered a thought in Nick's mind. *A strong handshake, just like Alicia.* Nick headed down to Judy's, JC Penney, and then to Dillard's before heading back to the hotel.

Nick headed inside and grabbed a bag of snacks and a Coca-Cola at the small shop next to the reception area. "Charge it to my room please?" Nick said to the young man.

"Certainly," was the reply.

"Three twelve. Nick O'Flannigan," Nick said as the young man's fingers typed away on the keyboard.

"Thank you, sir," the young man said and Nick took his snacks to his room.

He turned on the TV and watched an ESPN re-run of a Michigan-Ohio State football game, munching on the snacks and drinking the Coke. "Not my favorite, but that's all that's on," he said as he zoned out to the drone of the announcers.

After watching enough of the game, Nick headed out to Applebee's Grill and Bar The hotel room snacks were just that, snacks, and his stomach wanted more. He ordered a Quesadilla Burger and "whatever dark beer you have on tap," he said.

Most of the televisions were tuned to sports stations. The one that was directly in front of him had a talent show on called *What's Your Talent?* Nick was entranced as he saw a mime walk onstage and perform a standard mime act. The white-gloved hands began "walking" up an invisible wall, and then feeling the top. "I wonder what's up there?" one of the judges said to the one next to him.

"Perhaps we'll find out," the other judge replied.

The mime brought his cupped hands together, making motions like packing a snowball. He brought his hands down, still together, and then threw his hands in the air and a dove flew out.

"Wow," the judges said in unison. The audience applauded and stood.

The mime expressed "Thank you" in sign language, bowed, and used his index fingers to imitate turning up the edges of his mouth.

"That was incredible," the lead judge. "Are you allowed to talk to us now?"

The mime shook his head up and down.

"Well," the judge began. "What's your first name?"

"My first name is Beverly," the mime said as she removed her mask.

"You're a woman," the second judge exclaimed. "And while you were performing, we thought you were a man. That was excellent."

"A woman," Nick said as his mouth stayed wide open. "The mime's a woman. Everyone's been thinking that the Halloween mime was a man, but what if it were a woman instead? Well that changes everything!"

Nick took out his phone and sent a text to Grady: "URGENT revelation about mime. When can we meet tomorrow?"

Nick devoured the huge burger and the two dark beers. He dipped the huge mound of fries, one at a time, into the cup of ketchup. After wiping the ketchup from his mouth, he asked for the check.

He paid the bill and returned to the hotel. *I want to look at those videos again, but this time with the mindset that the mime was female.*

11

WHAT DID I MISS??

Back in his room, Nick opened the computer and opened the first video. It was inside the bridal salon. He focused on the mime. *Is there anything to indicate a female instead of a male?* he thought. He wrote some notes after watching and re-watching the same video.

- No specific movements or gestures to indicate gender
- Swift and deft retrieval of weapon from JC Penney shopping bag might have biased thinking toward male
- Aim and control could mean weapons training, male or female
- Rapid escape and running means good physical fitness
- No one saw entry into restroom, but there's nothing else down that hallway
- Quick change of clothes, or into different costume
- Mime outfit found later outside in JC Penney shopping bag

Nick put his left elbow on the desk and then put his chin in the opened hand. "Hmm. Since thinking the mime was male hasn't produced any results, the assumption needs to switch to the mime being a female. So let's see what we can find in the other videos. Who's carrying a similar shopping bag?"

He opened one of the videos from the mall cameras. He saw several women carrying JC Penney shopping bags. Only one of them was alone, and she was coming from the opposite direction the mime ran. "I think we can eliminate the women who were with other people, unless there was an accomplice, which seems unlikely in a lone shooting. And an accomplice to murder is pretty risky. Nothing on this one."

Nick ran two more videos, numbers two and three. "What's that?" he exclaimed. He re-ran number two as he wrote more notes.

- Someone in costume leaving restroom hallway and carrying JC Penney shopping bag in left hand
- Same person turned left in direction of the bridal shop.

He noted the video time. "Okay," he said. "Now let's see number three again." He wrote down a few notes from the video

- Similar costume with shopping bag walking on opposite side of hallway past bridal shop
- Person glances to left, possibly at or into bridal shop

He noted the time on the video and watched the remaining videos.

"Come on. Grady," he said as he looked at his phone. But he didn't have any text messages. Nick sorted the remaining photos and uploaded those for the magazine to the Cloud before shutting down the computer and calling it a night.

12

COINCIDENCE OR ???

The buzzing phone woke Nick out of a deep sleep. "Did I set the alarm?" he wondered aloud as he sat up and reached for the phone. He started to silence the phone when he saw "Grady calling." He pressed "Answer."

"It's Nick."

"Yea, Nick. Grady here. What's so urgent about the mime?"

"Oh, yea," Nick said as he shook his head to awaken. "You know how all along we've been referring to the mime as a male? Well, I saw a show last night that had a mime, and the judges also thought it was a male. It turned out it was a female. What if your mime is actually female? I've watched the videos again, and I think I might have found a suspect."

"Really? Really?" Grady repeated himself, the second time with more emphasis.

"What time is it?" Nick asked.

"Six thirty Friday morning."

"Damn it's early," Nick replied.

"Hey, buddy. Your text said it was urgent, and urgent was in all caps."

"I know. Yesterday was a long day and night."

"So what time can you get down to the station?"

"Are you serious? Man, I need some breakfast."

"Well, get out of bed, grab some food, and be here by eight."

"Okay," Nick said as he stood up. "See ya," he said as he ended the call, took a quick shower, and got dressed. "Another hotel breakfast," he muttered as he rode the elevator down to the lobby. Nick grabbed a paper on the way into the breakfast room, ate the same stuff as before, *not much variety,* he thought, and went back upstairs.

He grabbed his camera bag and notes from the videos, and left.

Grady was waiting for him when Nick walked into the police station. "You're all signed in. Here's your badge," Grady said as he led him through the door and to his office.

Nick pulled out his notes. "The video in the bridal shop shows the mime is good with weapons, and her escape proves she's in good shape. What if the mime is female has both things going for her? She'd know how to handle that pistol-thing, and if she's athletic, she could run down the hallway quickly. Right?"

"Can't argue with any of that," Grady replied.

Nick continued. "Now on mall video number two, there's a person in a costume exiting the restroom hallway, carrying a JC Penney shopping bag in her left hand, just as the mime had done. It's a female costume, I looked it up, and it's the Snow Queen Elsa from the movie *Frozen*. So Elsa turns left back in the direction of the bridal shop."

"Okay," Grady said in a skeptical voice.

Nick went on. "On mall video three we see Elsa again. This time she's on the opposite side of the hallway as she walks past the bridal shop and looks over at it, slows down but keeps walking. Can you zoom in on her?"

"Sure," Grady replied and he typed a few commands.

"The mask is hiding her face," Nick said. "Pan down to see if there's anything visible in the bag."

Grady moved the image down past her left hand to the top of the open bag. "Looks like something striped in there. The mime's shirt?" Grady asked.

"Maybe," Nick responded. "Move back up slowly."

"Stop!" Nick yelled as the left hand came into view. "She's holding the shopping bag with the tips of her fingers. And look at her hand, the ring finger. Is it a ring or what?"

Grady zoomed in even tighter. "Looks like a tattoo," he said.

"Indeed it does," Nick said. "It says '4ever,' and I've seen that tattoo before. The tour guide at the capitol had '4ever' tattooed on her left ring finger."

"That rings a bell," Grady said. "Hang on a minute. Let me pull up the coroner reports," he said excitedly as he switched displays and brought up the coroner reports of the killed models. "Yes, I thought that sounded familiar. The model in the red gown, the one in the middle, she also had a '4ever' tattoo on her left ring finger."

"That tour guide, her name's Alicia," Nick began. "I asked her about that tattoo on her left ring finger. She said that she and her girl-friend had matching ones and they were going to get married and then cover the tats with rings. But one weekend while Alicia was away for Army Reserves training her girlfriend moved out and moved in with another girl. When I asked her about her training, she said it was with weapons, M4s and some other letters and numbers related to guns. She said she also trained with enemy weapons, anything you could shoot."

"Like an Uzi," Grady said. "Did she mention that?"

"She did," Nick said. "And her handshake was strong."

"So it sounds as if she had the means with her Army background training in weapons. She was familiar with the machine pistol used, but she still had the means, the knowledge and capability, to pull it off." Grady was writing while he talked.

"And she clearly had the motive," Nick said, "with her girlfriend leaving her and moving in with someone else. And then the oppor-tunity came when her former girlfriend was modeling those bridal gowns. I wonder which of the other models was the new girlfriend."

"Yea," Grady replied. "And the third victim was just collateral damage. A military mind could possibly justify that. Wow. Let me take this to the Chief and see about bringing her in for questioning. You said her name was Alicia. Know the last name?"

"She sent me a text, let me look." Nick scrolled back through his text messages. "Just Alicia, but I have her phone number."

"We'll find her then," Grady said as he looked at Nick's phone and wrote down the number.

"Thanks for your help, Nick. You know you're pretty good at this detective stuff."

"Maybe too good," Nick replied. "I'm actually starting to enjoy it."

"Where to next?"

"I'm off to Denver in the morning. I'll pick up a good friend at the airport later in the day, and then we'll have a full week together. I'm hoping to see if there really is a spark there between us. It feels good, but we haven't had much time together."

"I hope it works out for you, Nick."

"Thanks, Grady. Let me know how this turns out."

"I will," Grady replied. "Let me walk you out," and the two men walked out to the front lobby. Grady was going back toward his office, when Nick said, "Oh, and keep my name out of this, will you?"

"Sure thing."

THE END

SOME FACTS ABOUT CHEYENNE AND
THE STATE OF WYOMING

- The 24-carat gold leaf dome on the Wyoming state capitol building is visible from all roads entering the city.
- At an elevation of 6,062 feet, Cheyenne is the second-highest elevation of U.S. state capital cities. Santa Fe, New Mexico, is the highest with an elevation of 7,260 feet. After Cheyenne, the next highest is Denver, the "Mile High City," at 5,280 feet.
- Wyoming is one of only three states (along with Colorado and Utah) to have borders along only straight latitudinal and longitudinal lines, rather than being defined by natural landmarks. Its 7-degree distance from West to East and its 4-degree distance from South to North were chosen by U.S. Congress. However, due to surveying inaccuracies during the 19th century, Wyoming's legal border deviates from the true latitude and longitude lines by up to half of a mile in some spots.
- With a population of about 64,000 residents, Cheyenne is the 35th largest U.S. state capital. Conversely, the entire state of Wyoming has the smallest population (about

580,000) of any state in the U.S. (not counting territories), while it is the 10th largest in area.

- Another oddity is that Cheyenne is one of the least centrally located capital cities. As states were forming governments, it made sense to have the capital city in a location that was easiest to get to by all people. Thus, most U.S. capital cities are located in what was the most central city (population-wise) of the state at that time. Cheyenne is about 8 miles west of its border with Nebraska, and about 40 miles north of its border with Colorado.
- The city was named for the Cheyenne Tribe. Today, the Cheyennes are divided into two groups: the Northern Cheyenne, which has a reservation in Montana, and the Southern Cheyenne, which has a reservation in Oklahoma.
- Wyoming is popular with visitors as it has two National Parks on its eastern edge: Yellowstone (the first park in the National Park System) and Grand Teton. Wyoming is also home to the first National Forest (Shoshone) and the first National Monument (Devils Tower) in the United States.
- One of Cheyenne's sister cities is Bismarck, the capital city of North Dakota.
- In addition to tourism, Wyoming's economy is fueled by the extraction of coil, oil, natural gas, and the world's largest deposit of trona (the primary source of sodium carbonate). Livestock, hay, and other agricultural products are also big businesses in Wyoming's semi-arid climate.
- Wyoming state coin: Sacagawea Dollar
- Wyoming state emblem: Bucking Horse and Rider
- Wyoming state motto: "Equal Rights"
- Wyoming state fish: Cutthroat Trout (same as the state of Idaho)
- Wyoming state tree: Plains Cottonwood
- Wyoming state insect: Sheridan's Green Hairstreak Butterfly

DEFENESTRATION DENVER

BOOK #10 IN THE CAPITAL CITY MURDERS SERIES

1
____

THE FALLEN

Defenestration: (definition) The action of throwing someone out of a window. From the Latin *de* meaning 'from', and *fenestra*, meaning 'window'.

"The window, the window,
They threw them out the window;
Wearied by a war of words,
They threw them out the window."

-Michael Collings

Nick exited the freeway, took a right, and headed to the Sheraton where he had booked a room, close to the capitol and downtown. He knew from his research that parking in downtown Denver could be a nightmare, and that there were a lot of restaurants close by. With Sandra, Gerry, and Catherine coming too, he knew walking would be the best mode of transportation for all of them.

That was as soon as he got them from the airport, forty minutes from the hotel. At least the drive from Cheyenne had been a quick one, under two hours.

As he stopped at the hotel office and got out of the car, stretching every inch of his six-six frame, he cocked his head.

He heard something. Loud shouts, coming from nearby. It sounded like a crowd.

Odd, he thought.

He shrugged and went inside. The desk clerk looked up, and then up some more. He saw a dark-haired woman, brown eyes, and not too tall. She wore what he now clearly recognized as a pretty standard desk clerk attire: a white shirt covered by a dark blazer. Her name tag read, "Cheryl."

"Can I help you?" she asked.

"Hi there," he told her. "I have a reservation for tonight, and I am a bit early, but I have friends to pick up at the airport. Would it be okay if I checked in early?"

"Sure," she said. "Let me check and see if your room is ready. What's your name?"

"Nick O'Flannigan. Thanks."

She took a moment to type, and he glanced over her shoulder at a television tuned to the news. "Climate Change Protests in Denver" read the text under a photo of a crowd, armed with signs, walking in the streets.

"Is that close to here?" he asked.

"Yes," she said. "It is actually only a few blocks away. We've actually had some protesters staying here, and earlier there was a march right out front, heading to the capitol I assume."

"Why would they have been coming by here?"

"I have no idea. I'm really not into that kind of thing."

"Well, hopefully I won't run into any trouble getting to the airport."

"You shouldn't. You'll be going the opposite way of the capitol building."

"Great. I've got to get some good photos of the building this week."

"Oh, you're that guy. I thought I recognized your name. The photographer traveling around the country."

"You've heard of me?"

"I follow you on Instagram. I also have a sister in Pierre, and I saw an article about your visit there."

"Awesome," Nick said. *Great. No anonymity even in a big city like Denver.*

"Here's your key," she said. "New locks. You don't insert it. Just tap it on the panel outside the door. If you want, you can download our app, and open the door with Bluetooth and your phone."

"Very cool. I'll probably use the card for now but set up my phone later."

"Oh, yeah. Your friends at the airport."

Nick nodded and tapped the keycard on the counter. "Thanks. I'll see you around."

He headed up and put his things in his room, and then grabbed his camera bag. He was anxious to see Sandra especially.

If he was honest with himself, he wasn't certain why. She was a great gal, and he thought there was something there, but although they had been in touch, he'd hadn't seen her for over a month now. There had been other interesting girls along the way, too. Helen in Helena, he still giggled over that one, although he seemed to be hearing less from her, was probably chief among them.

This week would mean a lot. Perhaps they would figure out if they were in a relationship or not. More than anything else, Nick just craved in-person, real-time conversation with people he knew and liked.

Traveling was great, but new cities all the time meant developing new, but short-term friendships, and loneliness. That was the hardest part by far, even though he enjoyed being alone much of the time.

With camera bag in hand, he headed out past the desk, waving to Cheryl as he headed out the door.

Once in his car, he input the drive to the airport, and saw that it would only take a little over half an hour to get there.

"I've got some time," he said to himself. "Maybe I'll just do a quick drive by of the capitol." He put his camera bag on the passenger seat, and took the camera out, setting it next to the bag.

"Just in case I can snap some drive by photos," he said to no one.

He shifted into gear, and hit 15th Street, turning left and then taking a right on Cherokee. He then took a left on 14th Street, which jogged to the right and turned into Bannock.

He kept the navigation app open on the screen in his car but didn't hit the button for directions to the airport yet. He didn't want the talking voice to confuse him with directions he didn't want to follow.

Even though it was chilly, he rolled the window down, enjoying the crisp air in the Mile-High City, and taking in the sounds. It sounded like Seattle, like home.

Then he heard the sound of the crowd again, and it sounded like someone was shouting through a bullhorn. He wanted to turn on Colfax, but the street was blocked by a police barrier.

He kept going and ended up taking a left onto 14th Avenue. That would take him near the back of the capitol building as well as he could figure. Traffic was moving slowly, and he could see why walking would work better than driving. Pedestrians were making faster progress than he was.

He could hear the protestors chanting now, although the words were overlapping and not really clear. He saw the crowd on the sidewalk ahead and knew they must be filling the area by the capitol building there.

There must be a lot of them. The building must be surrounded.

Nick moved into the left lane, knowing that if he got stopped at a light or in traffic, he might get a clear shot or two of the building, even if there were protesters in the way, which clearly there were.

It was a good idea. So far, he'd looked for "pure" shots, with no people, focusing on macro and detail, but maybe a few human-interest shots would work for Emily this time by shaking things up. If nothing else, they would boost his social media and his own website.

He checked the time. He still had about an hour to get to the airport, so as long as it didn't take too long to get through this traffic, he'd make it.

Up ahead, he saw the light for Sherman Street. It was green, but they were moving slowly toward it. As he watched, it turned yellow, and then red. Three cars back, he still had a pretty cool angle shot of the capitol building.

He rolled his window down all the way and framed a shot of the building over the crowd, construction paper signs of green and pink with messages of "Climate Action Now" and "Earth is Our Home" were raised in the foreground.

He snapped several photos, taking a moment between each to keep an eye on the light.

Something caught his eye, and he turned to the right. On the sidewalk next to a building labeled the Colorado Department of Revenue, he saw some additional protestors. They filled the crosswalk on Sherman, stopping traffic. He looked ahead, and even though the light turned green, the street was filled with people crossing from the other side.

Traffic wasn't moving.

He heard a crash from the right, and turned his head to look, camera still raised. Must be a car accident, he thought at first. Not surprising with this congestion.

Then he saw it. There was a body on the hood of the car directly across from him. The driver stared ahead, face white with shock.

Nick put his car in park and exited, standing to his full height. He raised his camera and caught a photo.

He heard shouts from above.

He looked at the sixth story window they were coming from. The glass had broken outward, and there was another man wearing a suit struggling with two others wearing red hoodies.

Without thinking, he aimed his camera and took photos of all of them. A second later, the two men overpowered the other one. He flew from the window, his body striking another car. Nick followed the falling body, taking photos without stopping. He raised his attention back to the window above, and saw another struggle going on.

"No," he whispered. "Don't do it."

But a second later, another body fell.

People on the street screamed.

Several policemen ran toward the building.

The red-hoodie clad men disappeared from the window.

Nick ducked in his car and grabbed his phone, dialing 9-1-1, and got a busy signal.

What are you doing, Nick? The police are already here.

Then he felt a hand on his arm and turned to see an officer dressed in all black, a silver badge over his left breast pocket.

"Are you a member of the media, sir?" the officer asked. He was nearly eye to eye with Nick.

"No. I mean, yes. I'm a freelance photographer."

"Did you see what happened?"

"I-I did. I took some photos," Nick stammered.

"We're going to need to see those," the officer told him. "Come with me."

"But my car..." Nick said.

The officer whistled and waved to another officer.

"Secure this vehicle," he told him. "As soon as possible, park it securely, and bring the keys to me."

"Yes, sir," the clearly younger officer answered.

"Come with me," the first officer said, and steered Nick through the crowd toward the capitol building.

Other officers in riot gear cleared them a path, but the previously worked up crowd seemed subdued now. Some were even leaving, heads hung low.

Nick felt the adrenaline of the moment wearing off and started shaking.

"It's okay," the officer said. "We won't keep you long."

His phone dinged in his pocket, indicating a text message, but he ignored it.

What did I just see? he thought to himself, and at the thought of the three men he'd seen thrown from the window, a tear stung the corner of his eye.

His surroundings were a blur as he was ushered into a small room with a steel table and a hard metal chair.

"Stay here," the officer said, and left. The door clanged shut behind him.

Nick was alone, surrounded by cream colored walls lit by unforgiving fluorescents, and completely unsure of what had just happened.

2

SHAKEN AND STIRRED

Nick sat perfectly still, trying to keep himself from shaking any more than he already was. The next five minutes before the officer came back with a laptop seemed to last an eternity.

"Sorry about that," the officer said. "Sergeant Adams. Wish we were meeting under better circumstances."

"Me, too," Nick said. "Can we make this quick? I was on my way to the airport to pick up a friend, and I'm sure I'm going to be late."

"Do you have your phone with you?"

"I do."

Nick pulled it out and saw a message there from Sandra. "Landed a little early and taxiing."

"Shit," he said.

"Sorry?" the officer said.

"My friend landed early. Do you mind if I text her?"

"Go ahead."

Nick sent a quick message. "Got held up. I'll explain later. Can you take an Uber?"

"Sure." The reply came back, followed by a sad emoji.

"Sorry," he texted back with a sad emoji of his own.

Fortunately, it wasn't far, and Nick would simply pay her back for it, but it wasn't that he was concerned with.

He set the phone down. "Ready."

Sergeant Adams spun the laptop around. "If you can transfer all of your photos from this afternoon to this laptop, that would be greatly appreciated. Meantime, can I ask you some questions?"

"Sure."

"Full name?"

"Nick O'Flannigan."

"Where are you from?"

"Boston, by way of Seattle."

"What are you doing in Denver today?"

"I'm on assignment traveling around the country photographing every state capitol building for *Travel USA* magazine and a book they are putting together. I just arrived and hoped to get a few shots of the protest before I picked up my friend from the airport. I got stuck in traffic."

"I see. What did you see, exactly?"

Nick paused while he inserted the SD card in the reader attached to the laptop. He highlighted all of the photos, hit 'copy', and went to the indicated folder on the laptop and clicked on 'paste'.

He was keeping a copy of these, just in case. Plus, some of them were of the capitol and the protest and had nothing to do with the men thrown from the window.

"I heard a crash and saw the first body hit the car." He shuddered involuntarily. "I got out of my car and started taking photos, just to document what I saw," he said.

"That's when I saw the second man struggling, and then saw him fall. The third came right after that. I don't know what I was thinking, but I just kept taking photos one after the other. There are probably a lot of duplicates in here."

There were 160 photos being transferred.

The drummed his fingers on the table nervously as he watched the progress bar.

"Okay. Look, we're going to want to ask you more questions.

Maybe a more formal interview. But we're also going to be busy for a while. Keep in touch, stay in town, and all that."

"Sure thing," Nick said. The photos were done transferring. It must be a fast laptop. He took the memory card and put it back in his camera.

"Here's my card," he said, handing the sergeant one from his pocket. "I'm staying downtown, so call me any time."

"Thanks. Here's mine," the officer said. "If you think of anything, give me a call. Let me get your car for you. Follow me."

Nick stood, put his camera in the bag, and followed the officer down a marble lined hallway and out a small side door.

The officer spoke into a radio, and motioned Nick to follow him, taking a right and walking toward one of the side streets. Nick was a little disoriented but knew the maps in his car would get him back on track.

Right now, he just wanted to get out of here. The air was cool, and that didn't help his shivering.

Nick was shaken and he felt nauseous. Sure, he'd seen a dead body in Carson City, but today he'd seen people die.

No, he hadn't seen them die. He'd seen them purposely killed. Maliciously.

That was different. Until now, murder had been a close, but distant friend. Not something he witnessed.

He didn't look around like he usually did. He knew there was a crowd around, he could hear them. Feel them. Smell them.

His car was ahead, at the He shook hands with both men, then slipped behind the wheel.

The maps were clear. The road ahead was clear, too. The way back to his hotel was easy from here. It was just a few blocks.

He gripped the wheel tightly. Nick kept both windows rolled up completely and locked the doors. He glanced in his mirror, saw an opening, and eased into traffic.

A few moments later, he was at his hotel. He parked in the designated lot and walked toward the front door. As he did, he saw an Uber approaching.

It had hardly stopped when Sandra got out and ran up to him.

"I'm so happy to see you," she said. "What happened?"

She stepped back. "My god. You look like you've seen a ghost. Nick, are you okay?"

Nick fought his rising anxiety the best he could.

"Something happened. I saw something. Get your bags, and we can go up to the room. I'll tell you more there."

Sandra turned and walked back, grabbing a small bag from the driver, and Nick saw her hand him a tip.

He walked over to her and offered to take her bag. He did, shifting it to his left hand. She took his right in hers.

"Nick, seriously. Are you okay?"

"I think so," he said. The warmth of her hand and the feeling of her hug earlier really were relaxing him. The tension was leaving his shoulders and his vision seemed a bit more normal, not so heightened and focused. "I will be. There was a protest downtown."

"I know. I saw it on the news at the airport."

He pushed the button for the elevator and a second later, the doors slid open. Once they stepped inside, Sandra stepped close to him, guided his hand around her shoulder, and leaned her head on his chest.

Nick felt a warmth inside, something he hadn't felt for a long time. Too soon, they arrived on their floor and stepped out into the hallway. In silence, but not an awkward one, they made their way to their room.

"I really do hope this is okay," Nick said before opening the door.

"Don't be silly," Sandra said, and stepped inside ahead of him. She squealed with delight, and Nick followed, putting her bag on the luggage holder.

She danced around the suite area with a small loveseat and a recliner. With the same enthusiasm, she went into the next room, looking at the two beds there. Nick followed her.

"It's wonderful, Nick. This is going to be a great week. It will turn around, you'll see," she said, turning and sitting on the bed.

Nick nodded and smiled, hopeful. Sandra gave him hope even as still, in the back of his mind, he was haunted by what he had seen today.

Sandra stood and bounced back over to him, giving him a hug. "Thank you, Nick, for inviting me and getting the room. I really appreciate it."

"Anytime," he answered. "Can I just—," he looked right and left. "I need to take a shower. And I don't want things to be weird or anything."

Sandra laughed. "Go ahead, silly."

Nick gathered his clothes and took them into the bathroom with him. He stood in the shower for far too long but felt like he needed it. The hot water helped wash the cares of earlier from him.

Once he got out, he dried and dressed quickly, and opened the door.

"Surprise!" he heard.

Then Gerry jumped around the corner followed by a woman he'd never met.

Gerry was just as he remembered her, slim, dark haired, glasses of the hipster variety. Her hair was cut in a short bob, but not too short, trimmed to follow her jawline. It was a great look for her. She also looked happy.

The stranger was quite the opposite of what he expected. She was shorter than Gerry, not as thin, and she wore her hair long. It was dark like Gerry's, but more of a dark brown than black. She tilted her head back to look up at him.

"You must be Nick. I'm Catherine. I've heard all about you."

"I've heard about you, too," he said. He moved to shake her hand, but she stepped in and hugged him. He hugged her back.

Once they parted, Gerry took a hugging turn. It was the most physical contact Nick had in a several weeks.

It made him happy.

"I assume you've all met?" Nick indicated Sandra.

"Oh, yes," Sandra said. "We introduced ourselves while you were in the shower."

"We came to surprise you," Gerry said.

"Well, you succeeded."

"Sandra tells us you had an eventful afternoon, one you have yet to share."

"I did."

"Tell us, before we go to supper," Gerry said.

"It might ruin your appetite," Nick warned.

"I'll chance it," Catherine said. "Spill it."

"Well, you all better sit down," Nick said. He collapsed into the love seat and Sandra sat close to him. "Because I'm going to."

He proceeded to recount the story of what he'd seen.

"That's horrible," Sandra said when he finished.

"Yes. The police will be wanting to talk to me over the next couple of days. I'm hoping this is as involved as I get with any mysteries in Denver."

"We can hope so," Gerry agreed.

"You've had a lot of adventures, I hear," Catherine said.

"I have."

"Tell them about Helena," Sandra said.

"At supper maybe," he said. "I'm starving."

"Agreed," Gerry said. "Where should we go?"

3

RECOGNIZED

Nick opened his phone and did a quick search of restaurants in the area. There were a couple that looked interesting, but reservations were required. Around the corner was Yard House, a place with great American food and other choices, and a fantastic bar.

Nick felt like he needed the bar, if nothing else than to calm his nerves. The week had started in a way he'd hoped it wouldn't. All he wanted was a simple visit with his friends and some time with Sandra to figure out their relationship if possible.

Bodies falling from buildings was not something he'd ever wanted to see, let alone be part of. Yet he wondered as they walked around the block to the restaurant who would have done such a thing and why.

The protests were about climate change, he was sure. But the bodies had been pushed from the tax building. Was there a connection, and what was it?

The police are working on it, he told himself. *Leave it alone and enjoy your friends.*

Sandra took his hand, interrupting his thoughts, and he looked at her. Her forehead wrinkled with concern.

"Where were you, Nick?"

"Just thinking about today," he said. "Sorry. Some dinner will help."

She nodded, and he squeezed her hand back. *Don't blow this, Nick,* he told himself.

"So how did the two of you meet?" he asked Catherine who was walking just ahead of them.

"Now that is a funny story," she said.

"We can tell that one at dinner, too," Gerry said. "It's not a long one, but it is good."

A light blue bike-powered rickshaw sat on the corner as they approached, and Nick smiled. "A little more bike riding, and I could get a job," he said to Sandra, pointing.

"You have to tell us about your new hobby, too," Gerry said. "There is so much to catch up on."

"There is indeed," Nick answered.

They went inside. There was a short wait for a booth, and they were given a little pager that would let them know when their table was ready. They headed for the bar in the meantime. The girls all ordered Cosmos, and Nick ordered a porter while looking over their liquor selection. Perhaps a cocktail would be in order once he ate something, but one of those on an empty stomach might make him much more chatty than normal.

"So where are you from?" he asked Catherine.

"Originally from Georgia, but I moved to Seattle about ten years ago, fell in love, and stayed."

"Ten years ago? You must have been a teenager." She looked younger than the rest of the group and had an air of innocence about her that Nick liked right away.

"Well, I'm not as young as you might think. I was a freshman in college, at University of Washington, studying journalism and photography, dreaming of a career in New York or L.A."

"Photography?"

She laughed. "Yep. I never did much with that end of things, but I graduated, went to work for the Seattle Times, bounced around a bit after that, and now I'm freelance. The only thing I use photography for is to take photos to enhance my articles."

"Three photographers walk into a bar," Sandra said.

"Sounds like the start of a good joke," the bartender said as he walked by.

Everyone laughed. The beeper buzzed, and a second later the hostess showed up, showing them to a booth toward the back of the restaurant.

Sandra slid in first, and Nick followed on one side, and Catherine and Gerry took the other side of the booth.

They set their drinks down, ordered a tower of onion rings and a plate of Brussels sprouts, and looked over the menu, debating choices. One the appetizers arrived, they ordered.

"So do you have a photography background, too, Gerry?" Sandra asked.

"That's a good question and a good route to answer your question of how we met," she answered. "No, I don't. I was a journalism and creative writing major. You know the story. I was going to work as a reporter and write the great American novel in my spare time. The second one never happened, although it is still a dream of mine. I bounced around jobs for a bit too, and then started doing writing for SEO and social media management. Next thing I knew, I applied at *Travel USA* magazine, and the rest is history."

"How did the two of you meet, though?"

"I was actually working for a company doing some web content, and I needed some photos. The owner of the company told me they had a copywriter doing some other freelance work for them who had some photography experience. They introduced us."

"Turns out we were at WSU at the same time," Catherine added. "Even had classes together at the same time. I wasn't out yet, but I do remember meeting Gerry at least once back then. We hit it off, but lost touch for a bit. I took a trip to South America, decided to write about it, and submitted to *Travel USA*. Someone recognized my name in a meeting, pushed my story to the top of the list, and then promoted it hard on social media. It went viral."

"We got together for drinks to celebrate," Gerry said, taking over the story. "I may or may not have orchestrated some of those things just to see her again."

Catherine giggled. "I'm glad you did."

"Tell her about the two of you," Gerry said.

Nick started, explaining about meeting Sandra his last night in Salem and regretting he couldn't stay longer to get to know her better.

"Then my camera was stolen in Sacramento," he said. "Her card fell out of my laptop, and she'd told me to call if I ever needed help. So I did."

"It was an incredible week," Sandra said. "And we've been in touch ever since."

"But that isn't the only mystery story Nick has," Gerry said.

"Tell them about Helena," Sandra said. "You said you would."

Nick recounted the story of Harry as everyone ate. He talked about how the killer became an acquaintance, although not really a friend, long before Nick knew his history. "I'd love to know the rest of his story," Nick told them. "That should be your book, Catherine. Fill in the blanks we don't know about him."

"I could just write your story," she said. "The one of your trip. It sounds fascinating and filled with conflict and drama so far."

"No one would believe it," Nick said. "I hardly do, and I've lived it."

They laughed. The waiter cleared their now-empty plates, and they ordered one more round of drinks. Nick opted for an old-fashioned, and the gals stuck with their Cosmos.

As the drinks came, Nick raised his glass. "To friends. And a week with no more drama,"

"Cheers!" they said, clinking glasses.

Then a flash went off. Nick turned to see the source, and another one assaulted his eyes.

"What are you doing?" he asked the photographer standing there. Then a reporter shouldered him aside. She held a mic in her hand.

"You witnessed the events earlier today, the men pushed from the windows?"

"What—how do you—?"

"Nick," Sandra said, and pointed at the television over the bar.

He looked, and there he was, camera around his neck, talking to the police officer as they walked into the capitol building, his face clearly visible.

"No comment," he told her.

"You are Nick O'Flannigan, right? The photographer?"

"He said no comment," Gerry said. She was standing now, putting herself between Nick and the reporter.

"Let's go," Sandra said, pushing against him.

Nick stood to his full height. The reporter and the cameraman looked up at him.

"Wow, you're tall," she said under her breath.

"Leave me alone," he said. "I'll make any statements to the police."

"Just give us something. Did you get photos? Do the police have them?"

"I said no comment," Nick said. "I meant it."

The reporter signaled the photographer to put his camera down. "Look, this is national," she said, dropping her mic to her side. "Off the record, we'd pay you good money for those photos."

"I never said they were for sale."

"Either way," she said. "If you get an offer from someone else, call me first. We'll beat pretty much anything. But there is a clock on this story for sure. So don't wait."

Handing the microphone off, she took out a pen and wrote on the back of a business card. "That's our starting offer," she said. "Those photos belong to you, not the police or anyone else. You should make something from them."

Nick took the card without looking at it. "If I decide to sell them, I'll let you know."

"Sure you don't want to give me something in the meantime? Something you might have seen that no one else did?"

"Nope," he said. "But if I change my mind, I'll let you know."

The reporter left, but everyone in the restaurant around them was staring at the small group. A few pointed at him, whispered behind their hands, and pointed to the television, where the news had moved on to another story, but where his face had been just a few moments before.

As they paid the check, his phone rang at the same time Gerry's did. It was a three-way call from Emily, his editor.

"So much for staying under the radar," he said as he answered. "Hey Emily, we're just leaving dinner. Can we call you when we get to the hotel?"

"You better," she said. "Have you seen the news?"

"Just a few moments ago, yes."

"Damn, Nick. Why can't you keep a lower profile?"

"I told you in Pierre. It's my sparkling personality."

"Not funny, Nick," she said, but he could see Gerry, also on her phone, suppressing laughter.

"Gerry," Emily said. "Help him get this under control."

"Of course," Gerry said, hiding the chuckle in her voice exceptionally well.

"And call me in the morning. I want to know what's going on out there."

"We will," Nick and Gerry answers win unison.

The call ended.

"Let's get out of here," Sandra said. "Nick, try to duck or something until we get back to the hotel, okay?"

They made it around the block and even up to Nick and Sandra's room with only a couple of curious stares, including one from a young man who had replaced Cheryl at the front desk for the night shift.

They agreed to meet up early for breakfast even though the next day was Sunday, and Gerry and Catherine said goodnight and headed to their room.

4

SUMMONED

After Gerry and Catherine left, Nick and Sandra stayed up for a while and talked, catching up on the last few weeks, work, and family. Nick shared his worries about his mom and dad with her.

Both of them were tired. Sandra went to take a shower, and Nick laid back on the pillow.

I'll just rest my eyes for a moment, he told himself.

The next thing he knew, he woke up to find his arm tingling in an odd way.

He tried to move but couldn't. Something rested on his arm.

He looked to his right and saw Sandra laying there next to him. Soft snores escaped her lips. Nick was still in his shirt and the jeans he'd been wearing the day before. She was wearing a t-shirt and tiny shorts. Her leg was over his.

He moved his fingers, trying to wake his hand without disturbing her, but the muscles in his arm worked at the same time, and she mumbled and shifted. Instead of pulling his arm free, Nick touched her shoulder and pulled her closer to him, the pressure easing when she laid her head on his chest.

He smiled down at her, a gesture she could not see through her closed eyes. Beyond her curled body, her bed had not been touched.

They hadn't really made a decision together, but she'd apparently come back from her shower to find him asleep and chosen to cuddle up next to him.

He was glad she had.

Of all the women he'd met on his trip, Sandra held the greatest appeal for him. A fellow photographer, talented, pretty, and easy to talk to, she was in a way his dream girl.

The clock said 6:30, and Nick tried to lay in bed for a bit longer, letting her sleep in his arms. Pretty quickly his mind seemed to wander to random thoughts.

I wonder if the gym is open here. It's probably better than the last couple.

The police will want to talk to me today probably. I wonder when they'll call. Wait, they have my photos. It's Sunday. Maybe they won't call until Monday.

If these protests continue, how will I get some clean shots of the capitol building outside?

I wonder who they threw off the building, and why. I should check the news. No, maybe the morning paper at breakfast.

Breakfast. Why am I so hungry this early?

His stomach growled, and Sandra stirred in his arms. She mumbled, and then half sat up.

"Was that your stomach?" she asked, looking up at him.

"It was," he said. "I'm not sure why I'm hungry so early."

"Well, you did fall asleep early last night."

"I know. And I'm sorry."

"It's understandable. You were exhausted after a long day." She smiled up at him, then got up on her hands and knees. She kissed him on the cheek.

"I'd kiss you more properly, but morning breath," she said. "I'll be back."

Nick nodded, then sat in awe. "I'd kiss you more properly," she'd said.

The way he felt about her seemed to be mirrored in her feelings.

He ran his tongue over his teeth. He needed to brush his, too, or at least swish with some mouthwash. Running his hand up his cheek, he realized that he also needed a shave, something he didn't have to do every day, but needed to do more often with her around.

It had been a while since he'd had a woman around all the time.

He'd been married once, to a gal named Susie, a college cheerleader and a sweet woman. Neither of them had been secure enough or ready for marriage, and they divorced after Nick's twenty-fifth birthday, just before he moved to Seattle. That was the last time he'd lived with anyone really. He hadn't taken on roommates: his business had been enough that he didn't need to.

When he thought about it, he really hadn't had any commitments other than his work, and those were ones that he owned. This assignment was one of the longest he'd taken on, and while most were short term and lucrative, they didn't require him to interact for long with coworkers. He'd become a loner.

That had been amplified by this trip. His interactions with people, while not always his choice, were pretty much under his own control.

So was his involvement with mysteries, kind of.

At least to this point.

Maybe that's what my obsession is about, he thought. *Control. With Sandra around more, I'll have to let some of that go.*

His phone chimed with a text message from Gerry. "You guys up?"

"Sort of," he typed back. "I still need to get cleaned up."

"You hungry?"

"Definitely," he said. "Or always, I should say. Where do you guys want to eat?"

A large part of his marriage had been deciding what to cook for supper, or where to go if they ate out. Now it was true again, this time with not just Sandra, but his visiting friends too.

Although if he was honest, he hadn't even looked for breakfast places yet. He did a lot of eating on the fly on these trips.

"Let's go to Ellyngton's. I hear they have a killer Sunday brunch."

"You bet," he said, trusting Gerry to have similar taste to his own and having picked well.

"Half an hour?" she asked.

"Sure," he said, as Sandra poked her head out of the bathroom.

"You need in here?" she asked.

"Yep," he said. "Seems we're headed to breakfast shortly."

"Oh really? Where?"

"A place Gerry picked nearby called Ellyngton's."

"Sounds elegant."

"It does." As they traded places, she pecked him on the cheek, and he could smell the minty-ness of her breath.

Nick stepped in the bathroom intent on his morning routine. He brushed his teeth and shaved first, and then stepped into the shower. When he was covered in soap and applying the shampoo to his hair, he stopped mid-scalp scrub.

His clothes were in the room, and he didn't have anything but his clothes from the day before. His shirt clearly stunk, although he could get away with wearing his jeans again.

But underwear? No way.

There were two choices. Wander out in a towel, not something he was really comfortable with yet, or ask Sandra to hand him some clothes, not much better when that included underwear.

Neither was good, but he had to make a call about which bad choice was better, or worse.

"Just be yourself," he said out loud. He finished rinsing, grabbed a towel and dried off, and then wrapped it around his waist.

He cracked the door a little and could hear the television tuned to the news. "Hey Sandra," he said.

"Yes?" she answered.

"Can I ask a favor? Can you hand me some clothes?"

"Sure!" she said. "What do you need?"

"I-uh-some underwear and a shirt," he said. "Any of the ones from my suitcase."

She giggled. "Sure. Hang on."

A few seconds later, he had both items in his outstretched hand, and closed the door. He dressed quickly, combed his hair, and opened the door, taking his dirty clothes with him.

Sandra was sitting on the edge of the bed. She wore a simple blouse and a pair of jeans, but to Nick she looked amazing. He stopped for a second, just looking at her.

Then she stood and walked toward him. He tossed his dirty clothes at his suitcase and missed.

"I think I owe you a kiss," she said.

She moved into his arms, looking up at him, and he lowered his face toward hers. Their lips met, gently at first, and then the kiss developed into a more passionate one.

Nick closed his eyes, relishing the feel of her against him, the feelings the kiss stirred inside him. Beautiful and a great kisser, too.

She pulled away, and they looked in each other's eyes for a moment.

"That's better," she said. "I've been waiting for our first real kiss for a while."

Nick felt warm and weak, a feeling he hadn't had for a really long time. "Me, too," he said.

Their lips met again, but only for a second when a knock came at the door.

"There's our breakfast companions," Sandra said, disentangling herself and smoothing her shirt. "We'll have to continue this discussion later."

"Definitely," Nick said, not sure what they had been doing was a discussion exactly, but anxious to pick it up again nonetheless.

He opened the door to find Gerry and Catherine waiting for them. "Let's go, you two," Gerry said.

Catherine just smiled at them, and Nick blushed as if they could have seen them through the door.

The restaurant was a short walk, and in just a few moments they were seated at a table and presented with menus of amazing choices.

The friends ate and talked, catching up on their lives and getting to know each other. The brunch, what was really breakfast for them, turned out to be buffet style, and Nick restrained himself from going back after two heaping plates of pancakes, French toast, scrambled eggs, and the obligatory sausage and bacon. The discussion didn't turn to Nick and his mystery solving along the way, and he was perfectly happy with that.

From time to time, Sandra would put her hand on his arm or even his thigh and hold his hand. He loved it. It felt both familiar and brand new, comfortable and disconcerting. The unexpected comfort made him smile.

They finished, everyone clearly as full as they were going to get of both coffee and breakfast foods.

The check came, and Nick grabbed it for all four of them over everyone's objections.

As they stood, Nick's phone rang, and he answered. "This is Nick."

"This is Sergeant Adams. We have a few questions for you. Can you come down to the station today?"

"I have some friends in town," Nick said. "I was hoping that tomorrow— "

"We like to get this information as soon as possible while the scene is fresh," the officer said. "If you could make time this morning, that would be ideal. Then we'll be out of your hair."

"Okay," Nick said, looking at the puzzled faces of the others. "I'll stop by soon."

"I'll text you the address of the police station where I'd like you to meet me," the officer said.

"Sounds good," Nick said. He ended the call, and a second later his phone chimed with a text message from an unfamiliar number. It contained an address and nothing else.

"I guess I need to make a stop today before we do anything else," he said.

"It's fine," Sandra said. "We'll go with you and just hang out while you are taking care of whatever you need to take care of."

"Thanks," he said. "Let's stop at the hotel so I can get my camera."

"Me, too," Catherine said. "We can take photos while you talk to the police."

For the rest of the walk back to the hotel, Nick stayed ahead of the others while they chatted about photography, Denver, and plans for the day.

His stomach churned, but he was sure that had nothing to do with his large breakfast.

He didn't like the way he'd been summoned. Not one little bit.

"There's that control thing again, Nick," he said to himself.

"What was that?" Sandra asked.

"Nothing," he said. "Just talking to myself."

They walked into the hotel and took the elevator to their rooms, each of them grabbing their camera bags and heading back down to the lobby.

Nick wished they could just stay in the room and recreate the kiss they'd enjoyed earlier.

5

PHOTOS AND ART

The address Nick had been given was not far and was just beyond the capitol building from where they were. They decided to walk, as parking seemed to be at a premium anywhere they went.

Things started out well. Nick's leg had been bothering him less since he'd started riding a bike when he could and working on the stationary bike when not. As they went along though, it began to ache, and he limped a little.

"Are you okay?" Sandra asked.

"I'm fine," he said, and tried to conceal the limp as much as possible. It really wasn't that bad, but he didn't want to look weak or incapable, especially of something simple like walking. He was irritated with himself.

As they walked, they chatted idly, Catherine and Gerry pointing at various buildings and stopping to take photos from time to time. Nick watched but didn't participate. He just wanted to get this interview over and get on with his trip. They heard protestors as the passed the Civic Center Park, but they seemed subdued and there was a much larger police presence than there had been.

As they passed 14th Avenue, Nick saw a parking lot filled with State Police cars on their left. Up ahead, on the right, was the Public Safety building and the downtown branch of the police department.

"You guys can wait out here if you want, or wander around," he told them. "I won't be long."

"I'm going with you," Sandra told him.

"I appreciate that," he said.

"We'll keep walking," Gerry said. "Text us when you are done, and we'll meet up again for lunch and maybe a tour or something?"

"Sounds good," Nick told them, turned and squared his shoulders, then went inside.

The interior was sparkling white, and there were a lot of windows in the walls that let him see pretty much everything. He walked up to the front desk and greeted the officer there.

"Hi. I have a meeting with Sergeant Adams."

"Sure. Have a seat and he'll be right out."

Sandra grabbed his hand, and they went to the seating area where they'd been directed. A second later, the Sergeant appeared.

"Mr. O'Flannigan," he said, offering his hand to shake. "Welcome in. I'll try not to take up too much of your time."

"Just Nick is fine," he answered, taking the offered hand. "This is my—friend, Sandra."

"Ah yes," the Sergeant answered. "The one you were going to meet at the airport?"

"Yes," Nick said.

"Sorry for delaying him, ma'am, but I'm sure you understand. Right this way, sir. You can wait here," he said, pointing to Sandra.

"She can't come along?" Nick asked.

"I suppose so," the sergeant said. "But we have some images to show you that might be disturbing. Since she wasn't a witness, she certainly doesn't have to see them."

"I'll be fine," Sandra said.

"Okay," the officer shrugged. "Let's go."

He led them through a door and down a short hallway to a room with white walls where the top half was made of glass.

On a table was a laptop and a file folder.

"Did you see any of the men who were pushed?" the officer asked once Nick was seated.

"No," he answered. "At least not their faces. The first one I didn't even see fall. I only saw the second body falling and didn't get a good look at the third man before he was pushed."

The sergeant pushed a few photos his way. "These are yours. They were taken from where your car was stopped in traffic?"

Nick looked and saw one of the second man in mid-air. His face was visible, mouth wide in an "O" but not easily recognizable. Sandra gasped and looked away for a moment. When she looked back, her face was red, and a small tear dangled at the corner of her eye. She put her hand on his arm, and Nick put his hand over hers.

Next there was a shot of the third man balanced at the edge of the window, one of the figures wearing a red hoodie about to push him. His face was visible as well, and although Nick had no idea who he was, if he knew him, he was sure he would recognize him.

"Who were they?" he asked.

"All of them were local executives. Large companies. They were in the building for a seminar on some new taxation changes for companies who haven't embraced green initiatives yet."

"Thus the reason they were chosen by the protestors?"

"We think so." The sergeant opened the laptop and spun it around. "This is also your photo. Do you remember anything about any of these men, or anything that would distinguish them?"

The photo had been enlarged, but Nick could see nothing behind the man's mask. He was sure he hadn't seen him before. There was a gold glint visible through a small tear in the hoodie, but he couldn't see what it was at this angle. He certainly wasn't going to zoom in on the photo here.

Especially with Sandra next to him. He felt her hand tighten on his arm.

He wasn't worried. He wanted to look at the photos closer, but he could do it later, away from this officer and his inquisitive eyes. He still had copies of all of them on his camera.

Which reminded him that he should transfer them tonight.

But he'd have to be careful. He was so used to being alone that when Sandra had been with him in Sacramento, he'd totally lost track of time, and of her presence, looking at photos.

This time she wouldn't be retreating to her own room. She was staying with him.

Leave it be, Nick. This time leave it alone.

But there was something there. The gold glint meant something. He'd only look at that one photo, and not for a long time.

I promise, I won't blow this over a case that isn't even mine, he told himself.

"Do you see something?" Sergeant Adams asked.

"Maybe," Nick said. "That gold glint might mean something. It's the only thing I see that seems out of place."

The officer spun the laptop back around and looked at the photo for a moment. "Probably just the way the light is hitting him," he said. "But I'll have our guys take a look."

There. You've pointed it out. You've done your duty.

But it wasn't just the way the light was hitting him. There was something there. Nick knew it.

"Of course. Let me know if I can be of more help," Nick said. "Is there anything else?"

"Not at the moment. How long will you be in town, Mr. O'Flannigan?"

"A week."

"Okay. We'll be in touch."

Nick stood and shook his hand.

"Ma'am," Adams said, turning to Sandra. "Have a good time and stay safe out there."

She simply nodded, slipping her hand from Nick's forearm down to his hand, and gripping it tightly.

They walked out of the department into the sunlight. Even though it was chilly, it wasn't any worse than Seattle or for that matter, Salem.

At least it wasn't raining.

That reminded Nick of Carson City, and the unusual rain there. He'd been able to use a special software to help solve that crime, an app that removed layers of a photo to reveal what was underneath.

The app wasn't available to the public yet. But just maybe, he could get in touch with the professor who'd been showcasing it.

He wasn't even sure it would help in this case, but he thought it was definitely worth trying.

"Nick, you were so calm in there," Sandra said.

"I guess so," he said. "I've kind of gotten used to this type of thing. Seeing those men pushed really got to me, but the photos weren't too hard to look at."

"Wow," she said. "I don't know if I could ever get used to that."

Nick turned to face her. "It's not that I don't feel anything about seeing things like that. It's just I don't let my emotions override my need to be analytical and look at them objectively. I'm not sure yet if that is a gift or a curse, but I do find some satisfaction in helping catch the bad guys."

"I do understand, Nick. What you've done on this trip, and the people you've helped is amazing considering you've also managed to stay on track with your assignment, too. I have a lot of respect for you. You're amazing."

"Thanks," he said, leaning down to kiss her.

"Ohhh, caught!" he heard Gerry's voice say as their lips met. "I thought you were going to text us."

"We just got out," Nick said still staring into Sandra's eyes. "I was just about to."

"It doesn't look like that's what you were about to do," Catherine joked.

Nick smiled at Sandra and winked at her. "We'll continue this discussion later," he joked.

She smiled back. "Yes, we will."

Both turned to face their friends. "What's next?"

"Well, we found a walking tour of Denver, but we figured that might not work with your leg. We did some scouting. How do you feel about museums?"

"I love them," Nick said.

"Well, the Clifford Still Museum is close by and open until 5. They are closed tomorrow so we should hit that one today. The Denver Art Museum is around the corner if we have time."

"That one will take the entire afternoon by itself."

After a brief discussion, they headed for the Clifford Still Museum. After they spent a little over an hour and a half there, they headed to lunch.

They chose the Cap City Tavern across the street. Nick had a burger, Sandra and Catherine had salads, and Gerry chose a Rueben that looked amazing.

After that, they headed for the Denver Art Museum where they spent the better part of the afternoon looking over the exhibits.

The Denver Art Museum allowed photography, sans flashes, of much of their artwork, and they were all able to get some great shots, careful to follow the rules set by the museum. There were a couple of exhibits and some individual works that were off limits as well.

One of them was one of Sandra's favorites of the day. "Why can't we take photos of this painting?" she asked a staff member who was walking by.

"Some paintings we have on loan from collectors and others, and we don't own the copyright to those pieces. We can't let you take photos without the owner's permission."

"That's too bad," Nick said.

"This piece, however, is available as a print from the artist. I'll get you his contact information."

The employee disappeared and returned a moment later holding a card. "You can also order on his website I believe," she said. "I hope that helps."

"Thanks," Nick said, already wondering if he could afford a print, and preferably a framed one.

"That would be wonderful," Sandra said, looking at the card.

"We'll look when we get back to the hotel tonight," Nick said. "I'm sure we can have it shipped to your place in Salem."

'Sounds good," Sandra said. They moved on through the rest of the museum.

Once their tour was complete, they left the building and stopped outside.

"What are we eating tonight?" Gerry asked.

"Let's head to Pints Pub. It's a British style place just a block over," Nick said. Even though they hadn't walked around town, Nick's leg was sore from touring the various floors of the Denver Art Museum.

They headed that way, where they had a great dinner and a few drinks. They mostly talked art, and Sandra told Gerry and Catherine about the print she wanted to order.

"That sounds amazing," Catherine said. "I can't wait to see it."

They finished dinner then and headed to the hotel. Nick waved to Cheryl, the clerk who'd been there when he checked in, and she waved back.

When they got out of the elevator, each couple headed for their own room. Nick opened the door, and he and Sandra squeezed inside.

Nick opened his laptop, took his camera out of the bag, and set it near the computer.

He then excused himself and went to the bathroom. When he came out after washing his hands, Sandra was standing near the bed they'd slept in the night before. Soft jazz came from a music station on the television.

She'd changed into a light t-shirt and shorts similar to what she'd worn to bed the night before.

"Hey," Nick said. "You changed clothes."

"We weren't going out again, were we?" she said.

"Nope," he said. "But—"

Sandra stepped toward him and put her finger on his lips. "Shhh," she said. "I thought we had a discussion to finish."

Nick moved his lips toward hers, and she looked up at him. Their lips met, and Nick closed his eyes, letting all the cares of the day and the weeks before fade from his mind.

Their lips parted for a moment. "Does your leg hurt?" Sandra asked him.

"A little," Nick answered. "Why?"

"Because if it does, maybe you should lie down."

She took his hand and led him toward the bed, and Nick followed.

INSIDE TRACK

Nick woke early the next morning with Sandra cuddled against his back. He managed to slip out of the bed and to the bathroom without rousing her, where he stared at himself in the mirror. He turned the water on cold, splashed some on his face, and then brushed his teeth.

He'd never gotten around to looking over any photos the night before. They'd made love, talked, watched a little television, shows not normally in Nick's wheelhouse, but fun ones. Then they'd fallen asleep in each other's arms.

It was perfect.

This morning though, he knew he needed to get some work done before everyone else got up. He would need to take more photos today and needed to have his camera memory card clear and the photos he'd created so far in their own folders.

He slipped out of the bathroom as quietly as possible and opened his laptop. The first thing he did was create a new set of folders. One was titled "Denver Personal." The second was titled "Denver Capitol." He hesitated before creating the third.

In Pierre, he'd accidentally uploaded the wrong files to the magazine cloud folder. He didn't want to make the same mistake again. He thought back to his college days. What did they call it when you shoved someone out of a window? Didn't it come from some historical reference?

He opened a browser and searched for "What is it called when someone is killed by being shoved out of a window?" The first listing had the word he was looking for. "Defenestrated."

He highlighted the word, copied it, and then pasted it in the name of the folder.

Perfect.

He then opened the files in the SD card on his computer, sorting them by date. The ones from Saturday he put in the Defenestrated file. The ones from Sunday he put in the personal file. He left those alone for the moment.

Nick paused, listening, He heard rustling from the next room, and followed by tiny snores. Sandra was still sleeping. Good.

He opened up the Defenestration file and went through the photos, starting with the first one and working his way from there.

The first several photos were of protestors and the capitol building in the background. There were actually a few good shots in that set, and he copied them to the capitol files he would send to the magazine.

The first shot of the actual crime showed the man lying, apparently lifeless, on top of a car. The windshield was broken out, the roof slightly caved in, and the driver sat, horrified, behind the wheel. Her face was pale with fear.

The next shot showed two men pushing another out of the window above. Their faces were hidden, and the shot was wide. The next several showed his progress through the air until he reached the car behind the one the other man had landed on. The next shots focused on the men in the window and they were closer up. It was one of the ones the officer had shown him.

He could see a glint of gold, and he zoomed in on it. It looked almost like the edge of a badge. Under the clothing, he could almost see a similar shape to a badge.

He flipped forward through several photos to one that showed a

Denver police officer. His badge was silver, not gold, and it seemed to be a different shape.

Maybe they were fake badges, and not very good ones? Maybe they belonged to a security company?

The way to tell would be to enhance at least that photo and maybe some others as well. Nick thought of the software he'd used in Carson City, the one that eventually led to the capture of the murderer.

But that had been the removal of a photo layer, like rain, to make it clearer. It probably could not remove clothing.

But maybe there was an impression of the badge against the red hoodie in this or another photo. If he could enhance it, he could share what he found with the authorities.

Quietly, of course. This trip, Sandra and Gerry were here watching him. If he took too much interest, they would know, and Emily would find out. That would not be a good thing.

He opened his email, typing the first part of the professor's name in the "To" line. The email came up right away.

He wrote a quick note, asking for his expertise and help again, and asking if he could perhaps even get a copy of the app for his own use.

He then went back to the crime scene photos, choosing the ones that had close ups of the men in the window, and saving them to a sub-folder labeled "Close Ups." He then swiped through the others of the men falling, and of their landings.

He was just about to close the folder when he heard a voice behind him.

"What are you doing, Nick?"

He turned to see Sandra standing there, wearing nothing but a t-shirt that reached her mid-thighs. On the front it said "Not that Salem! The One in Oregon." A cartoon of a witch was woven through the letters.

"Just looking through the photos I have of the crime scene," he said. "Putting them in their own folder."

"You talked to the police already. You're not going to get involved or investigate more, are you?"

"No, no," he said. "I'm focused on the assignment this week. Well, and you."

"Okay," she said. Nick had the distinct impression she didn't believe him, and he totally got that. "Let's see the ones you took at the museum. I'll go get mine and we can compare."

"Sure," Nick said, opening that folder. "I had to clear out my memory card before today anyway. If the protests are still going on, we'll work on interior photos today."

"That sounds fun. I loved taking shots in Sacramento."

"I know," he said. "Let's get your camera ready, too."

Sandra brought her laptop and her camera to the desk. She took out the memory card and transferred her pictures to her computer.

For the next half hour or so, they compared photos and the things they had taken at the museum the day before.

Then Nick's phone dinged with a text from Gerry. "Breakfast?" it said.

He looked at the time, and realized it was just past eight thirty. The hotel breakfast would be closed soon, but he was sure there were other places around.

A quick search found Sassafras American Eatery, down by the capitol. It wouldn't be a long walk, and they would be close to where they needed to be anyway.

Nick texted her the link to the restaurant. "Head here in half an hour?" he typed.

"Meet you in the lobby!" the text came back.

"Shoot," Nick said. "I know I need a shower."

"Me too," Sandra said.

"You go first," Nick said. "I'll be quick, and I don't have to dry my hair or anything."

"We could save water, and take one together," she suggested.

"That sounds wonderful," he said.

Thirty-five minutes later they were headed downstairs, both clean and refreshed. Nick smiled to himself. It was the first time he'd showered with anyone since his marriage failed, but it felt incredibly natural.

"Hey, you two," Gerry called out. "It's about time!"

Nick detoured to the front counter. "Hey, Cheryl," he said to the clerk who'd been there when he arrived. "Is the American Sassafras place down by the capitol any good?"

"It's amazing," she said. "You guys will love it."

"This is Sandra," he said. "My friend, and a fellow photographer. This is Gerry and Catherine, friends from Seattle."

"Sandra helped you in Sacramento, didn't she?"

"Yep."

"Pleased to meet you," Cheryl said. "I follow you on Instagram, too."

"Pleased to meet you, too," Sandra said. "And thanks for the heads up with the restaurant."

"My pleasure," the clerk answered. "Enjoy your day."

They left, talking along the short walk to the restaurant. There were no signs of protestors, at least in the streets. Once they were inside, seated, and had ordered, Nick told them his plan for the day.

"Sandra and I plan to take interior photos of the capitol. If there are no protestors, we will take some of the exterior, too. You guys are welcome to come along or do your own thing."

"We'll probably take the walking tour of Denver," Catherine replied. "Then we'll meet you back at the capitol building."

"Sounds good," Nick said. "We can grab lunch, if we're hungry by then, and go from there."

Just then the food arrived. The portions were huge, and they all dug in, eating in silence except for the occasional "please pass the—" and answering yes to the server's inquiries of "More coffee?"

When they were done, they walked toward the capitol building. The streets were busy with commuters and pedestrians, and there was a small group of protestors by one capitol door. The rest had apparently gone back to their work week.

Nick and Sandra went inside, and Gerry and Catherine headed for the other side of the building where the walking tour kiosk was.

A white and gray tiled floor stretched over the first floor of the building, and after walking through a narrow doorway, the building opened up into the capitol dome. Around the base of it were several murals, and then a wide staircase led to the next level.

They took photos of the art and the staircase itself, trying to avoid the standard stock shots other people took, and putting a spin of their own on them.

They worked together, Nick taking a shot from one angle while she took one from another. They communicated easily, sometimes simply pointing at each other and various angles, making sure each knew what the other was doing.

The did similar things on the second level, getting the obligatory shot down at the floor looking from above, and the ones looking up into the dome.

After a few hours, still on the second level, they found themselves at the top of the stairs.

"We can come back and get the rest of the inside later," Nick told her. "We have all week."

"Sounds good. We can do some shots outside today, or we can do them tomorrow."

"Yep," he replied. "Let's see what Gerry and Catherine are up to."

He pulled out his phone, but before he could text the others, it rang.

"Hi, Professor," he said, answering. "How are you?"

"Great," the professor said. "Do you have a few minutes?"

"Sure," Nick said. Sandra looked at him with a puzzled expression on her face.

"Who is it?" she mouthed.

Nick waved his hand at her and mouthed back, "I'll tell you in a few minutes."

"We have a beta version of the app you tested in Carson City," the professor said. "We're letting a few photographers test it. We would love for you to be one of them."

"I would love that, too," Nick said. "I've got a photo it may or may not work for."

"Okay. I'll email you a secure link and password. Be sure to change it once you get access. If you have any questions, let me know. I am curious to know what you're using it for."

"I'll email you later," Nick said. "Thank you."

The call ended. "That sounded interesting," Sandra said.

"Yep. I get to beta test a new photo editing app," Nick said, not wanting to explain which app and what it was for. "It's going to be exciting."

"I can't wait to see it," she said.

"You'll love it," Nick said. He then texted Gerry. "Lunch?"

"We're still full from breakfast," came the reply. "We're exploring. See you at dinner?"

"Sounds good," Nick texted back.

"Sounds like it is just us for the afternoon," Nick told Sandra. "We can keep working here after we grab a bite. Unless there's something else you'd like to do."

"Let's stick around town this afternoon," she said. "I have a surprise for you tomorrow, so we may not get as much work done."

"Alright," he said. "We'll get some more interior shots this afternoon, but won't work too long," he said. "We do have the rest of the week."

"And we can play with that app you're testing," she said.

"Of course," Nick said. He'd have to think of how to show her how it worked and to tell her his plan without upsetting her.

She'd been a part of the mystery in Sacramento. He'd have to make her a part of it here, too if he was still going to explore it.

They walked hand in hand toward the Shish Kabob grill, planning a light lunch.

Her hand was warm in his. The sun added heat to the skin on his face, making him happy for the decent weather.

It was going to be a great week.

7

A SIMPLE PLAN

After an afternoon of fun that included interior shots of the capitol on the upper floors and a few portraits of each other on the lower floors, they headed to dinner with Gerry and Catherine, who had finished their tour. They shared photos at the dinner table at a place Calle Maggiano's Little Italy. A casual place with big booths, the table had plenty of room for them to spread out and pass around cameras where photos were viewed on tiny screens.

"Oh, this one is good," Catherine said, pointing to one of Nick standing beside the steps up to the second level of the capitol. Nick took Sandra's camera and looked. It was a great shot and cropped the right way could be his new social media profile picture. Even better, it looked like a professional headshot.

"That's amazing," he said. "You make even me look good."

Sandra smiled. "It wasn't that hard."

Nick laughed. "Seriously, I'll have to put on a nice shirt and tie and have you get some other new shots for me while you are here. This is amazing."

She blushed. "Sure, I'd love to."

"You two are too much," Gerry said. "Get a room already. Oh, wait—"

Nick blushed, sure his face was as red as his hair.

The rest of them giggled, even Sandra.

He gave in and laughed, too. Once they finished eating, they headed back to the hotel and split up again, promising to meet again the next morning for breakfast.

Once they were in the room, Nick opened his laptop to see an email from the professor. It contained a link and a temporary password.

"Is that it?" Sandra asked.

"Yep," he said, clicking through to the university's website. Clearly, he'd been given an internal portal, and he signed in as instructed. The software started to download, a progress bar slowly marking how many minutes remained.

"That must be some file," she said. "Remind me what this does?"

"This is what I used in Carson City," he told her. "It removes layers of a photo that it can remove and clarifies the image."

"Oh yes. The rain that obscured your view of the tree trimmer. I think you told me something about it."

"That's right. Until this point, it hasn't been available anywhere outside the university. I think I may be the first one to have a private copy."

"Do you know how it works?"

"Sort of, but just what a saw at a demonstration. I'll probably have to play with it a bit to get all the tricks working for me."

"And what photos are you going to use to play around with it?"

Nick sighed. "Look, I know you and Emily don't want me to get involved, but I think it might help see who the men were that threw those men from the window."

"You just can't leave it alone, can you?" A smile tugged at the corner of her mouth, and Nick wondered what she was thinking.

"I could. I'm just not comfortable. I tend to notice things others don't. And I was there. I'm already involved. The police didn't ask for my help specifically, but they did say if I thought of anything to give them a call."

"And this is what you thought of?"

"It is."

Sandra took his hand. "Hey, Nick. I want to tell you something. I know I got irritated in Sacramento when you got too deep into the mystery, and literally forgot I was there."

"I'm sor—"

"I'm not bringing it up for another apology, or to hurt your feelings. I'm saying while that was frustrating, I did admire how determined you are. That applies both to getting great photos for your assignment and to helping solve mysteries. It's one of the qualities that attracted me to you."

"Okay," Nick said, not knowing how to respond.

"But there is one qualification," she said.

"What's that?"

"You have to include me. Don't forget I'm here. Let me work with you and help you. Don't shut me out. That isn't fair, not after what we went through in Sacramento."

"Deal," he said, holding his hand out for her to shake it.

"Now, let's see this thing in action."

Nick first opened the original file from Carson City and showed her that by manipulating the photo with the app, they'd removed the rain and clarified the image.

"That's cool!" she said. "But what are you thinking with these photos?"

"I'm not sure," Nick said. "I know the app can't remove clothing, so seeing under the sweatshirt or the mask won't be possible. It can't show anything the camera didn't capture, just clarify what is there."

"Makes sense," she said.

"But maybe I can remove layers to make the cloth thin enough that the badge impression underneath the cloth is clearer, and I'll be able to read it or at least tell the shape more. Maybe the same with the face. Maybe if we can "thin" the cloth, a sketch artist can make out features better?"

"Has that ever been tried with this software before?"

"Not that I know of," Nick said. "I guess we'll be the first."

"Let's get to work then."

The pulled up the first photo, the one where Nick had seen the glint of what he thought was a badge under the fabric. He played with the settings of the program, and Sandra did too, but whatever was under the cloth didn't really show up any clearer.

"I think it's the angle," she finally said. "This is looking kind of sideways and from a distance. Do we have one with them facing your camera more directly?"

"I think so," he said, and scrolled through the pictures until he found one he hadn't looked as closely at before. One of the figures in the red hoodie faced him straight on, arms outstretched toward the camera. The other man stood next to him, arms down at his sides. The third victim hung in mid-air, feet off the window ledge, hands outstretched and grasping for a hold. A hold on anything.

"Oh my god," Sandra said. "That shot is terrifying and amazing."

"It is," Nick said, importing it into his new application and zooming in again.

"You could sell it, I'm sure."

Nick shrugged. "Maybe I will, once I get what I want from it."

"Seriously. You can do that on this trip, right? You aren't forbidden from selling other photos not related to your assignment?"

"Of course not," Nick said. "I can sell other pictures to whoever I want."

"Well, you should."

Nick went silent, zooming in on first the man with outstretched arms. His position made his hoodie too baggy and loose, and he couldn't make out the shape of his badge at all.

He moved his cursor to the second man and zoomed in. With his hands down by his side, Nick could clearly see two things. He could see the shape of the badge under the hoodie, and he could see, at least slightly, the outline of his face under the mask he wore.

He concentrated on the badge first, clearing what the app called 'layers' until the badge was clearer at least. He could only see the bottom half of it well, but with a single wrinkle obscuring it, he could see the word on the bottom read SE—RITY, "Security," he said, filling in the blanks.

"That's amazing," Sandra said. "Too bad you can't see the rest."

Nick realized for the last few moments, he'd been in the zone and broken his promise to her. He'd actually forgotten she was there.

"Yes, too bad," he said. "And I'm sorry."

"No worries," she said, kissing the top of his head. "I was busy sending an email anyway."

"To who?" Nick asked.

As he said it, her phone dinged. "Yes, we'd be very interested," she read, turning it toward him. The reply was from one of the local newspapers. As he watched her screen, two more responses popped up, both from different papers.

"A freelance photographer's favorite two words," she said. "Bidding war."

"What did you do?" Nick asked.

"I didn't even send them a photo yet. Just said that you had a great set of shots of the defenestration on Saturday, and these are the answers I got. Wait until they see that!" She pointed at the screen and smiled.

"Wow," Nick said. He was a little irritated, because he hadn't really given her a green light to sell his stuff, but secretly he was pleased, too. It would be a great payday, and a way to get another fantastic byline. He'd have to give Emily a 'heads up', though.

"Your wheels are spinning, huh?"

"They are. Now we can't show them any of the ones modified by the app. Those are for the police only. You know that, right?"

"Why is that again?"

"The app is still under development. We can't make it public yet."

"Okay. Well, the photos themselves, especially that one, even not modified, speak for themselves."

Nick yawned. "Okay, I'm done for the night. Let's call it for now. I'll take this to the police tomorrow, and we'll sell that one photo, maybe a couple of others, to a local paper. Whoever pays the highest price."

Sandra squealed. As she did, Nick's phone rang. It was his mom. "I have to take this," he said, and then answered.

Sandra turned on the television, muted, and then headed for the bathroom.

"Hi, Mom," he said. "How are things?"

"They are wonderful. How's Denver?"

Sandra sneezed.

"Who's that? Is there someone with you? Are you in your hotel room?"

"Yes, mom. A friend came from Salem to visit this week."

"A girl?"

"Yes, Mom, and my friend from Seattle, Gerry, came too. It's quite the reunion."

"How are things going in that area?"

"What area, mom?"

"Your romantic life, Nick. Are you two official or anything?"

"Mom, how's Dad?"

"Don't try to redirect me, Nicholas. I'm your mother. I have a right to know."

"You'll be the first person I update if anything changes."

"You better."

"Seriously, Mom. How's Dad?"

"He's fine, Nick. I won't keep you from your friend. I just wanted to check in and make sure you're okay."

"I am, Mom. I'll call again later in the week."

"Okay. Bye, Nick."

The call ended, and he looked up. Sandra was coming from the bathroom in her now familiar t-shirt and shorts she wore to bed. He smiled, but she looked at the TV and her mouth dropped open in a giant "O."

"Look," she said, and pointed. Nick grabbed the remote and stabbed at the volume button.

There on the screen was a photo of the crime scene with a reporter standing out front.

"—person of interest has been detained. Police are not yet calling the person a suspect, but say he has valuable information about the events of Saturday afternoon."

The shot cut to a police vehicle entering a basement parking garage with lights on. "Once he was taken to the police station, one other man has also been picked up, but the police won't identify either man yet, or comment on the investigation."

The shot cut back to the reporter. "Of course, this is a developing story, and we'll get back to you with any details as they become available."

"Thanks, Stephanie," the studio anchor said.

"Damn," Nick said.

"No wonder the newspapers are so hot for your photos. Are you sure you don't want to sell them tonight?"

She showed him her phone, and there were three emails marked urgent.

"As long as you don't mind getting dressed again," he said.

"Not at all," she replied. "Who should we call back first?"

8

TRAINING

"I can't believe they paid so much for that photo!" Sandra said.

"Me either," Nick replied. The two of them sat together in the Novo Coffee shop, holding hands across the table. The aroma from the local roast was amazing, and the pastries were delicious.

"So, I told you I have a surprise for you today," Sandra said. "You weren't the only one researching things to do while in Denver before we arrived. I know you need to get that photo we enhanced to the police, but this is pretty much an all-day excursion."

"All day?" Nick asked. Then he thought about it. They had a great start on capitol building photos. They could certainly get some night shots when they got back from whatever Sandra had planned.

He was here, he might as well see what Colorado and Denver had to offer.

"What about Gerry and Catherine?"

"They already know what I'm up to. They have their own plans for the day."

"You thought of everything. How about this? I'll send an email with the enhanced photo. I'm sure the officer will see the photos and my byline in the paper today with the suspects story. If he has questions, he can call or email, and I'll talk to him about it later tonight.

I'm not a cop after all, or an official part of the investigation. It can wait, right?"

"That's just what I wanted to hear," she said, leaning over and giving him a kiss. "You may want to call Emily, too, and let her know about your byline."

"Oh, yes. It would be better that she isn't surprised."

Nick opened his phone and dialed her cell. She didn't answer, so he left a message about the paper buying the photos and told her he would be gone for most of the day.

"Let's get back to the hotel and I'll send off that email," he said. "Then we can go."

"We better hurry," she said. "We need to get on the road. We have a tiny little drive to do."

They hustled back to the hotel and Nick quickly sent an email to the police detective he'd been working with. He attached the enhanced photos and promised to be in touch later in the day.

The couple made their way downstairs, waving to Cheryl on the way out, and then got into Nick's car.

"Where to?" he asked.

"Leadville," she said. "It's just a couple of hours away. Usually it would be pretty full of snow even this early in the fall, but it's been unseasonably warm this year."

'What's there?" Nick asked.

"A surprise. If I told you, that would ruin it."

Nick set his navigation, and then followed the directions out of town. The road quickly started to rise through the mountains around Denver and Nick smiled. They chatted as they went. A few places Nick wanted to stop and take photos, but she told him to keep going.

"There will be plenty of time for that," she said. "Trust me."

Sandra reached over and turned on his radio. She tuned into a jazz station and put her hand on his thigh. Nick dropped one hand from the wheel for a moment and squeezed hers.

The drive seemed to fly by, and before he knew it, they were in downtown Leadville, a quaint little town perched on the side of a mountain. As they pulled in, Nick saw an old train puffing up a hill, steam coming from the engine.

"Gorgeous," he said as they parked. "What are we doing here?"

"Going for a train ride," she said. "Follow me."

They headed for the ticket window nearby, and Sandra gave them her name.

"Here you go. Two tickets for the zip line and train ride. Enjoy!"

"Zip line?" Nick said. He loved this adventurous side of her.

"Yep," she said. "I hope you're not afraid of heights."

"I hope not either," he said. He had never tried anything quite like this before, but he was hoping it was as fun as it looked.

They set out on the train, each with their cameras. The views were gorgeous, and they snapped landscape shots all along the way. Nick got some close ups of the train and the tracks as they were moving, and when they stopped, he took more.

Then, they arrived at the zip line area. They secured their camera bags in a locker on the train, and a small four-wheel drive took them close to the starting platform, but they had to hike the rest of the way. By the time they arrived, Nick's leg was a bit achy, and both of them were out of breath due to the high altitude.

"What's the elevation here?" Nick asked their Zipline guide when they got to the platform.

"Just over ten thousand feet," he said. "You come up from Denver?"

"Yes," Nick panted.

"You'll be alright then. Just take your time. Your muscles and old injuries may be a bit achier, but once you head back down, you'll be fine."

"Thanks," he said. By this time, Sandra had caught her breath too, and there were a few others from the train lined up for the zip line adventure.

The guide explained the harnesses, helmets, and how to brake if they wanted to slow down. Everyone struggled with the harnesses at first, but after a bit, they were all situated.

"We call you 'ducks,'" he told them. "That's because you're all wearing yellow helmets. When I say, 'next duck' and it's your turn, step on up. Follow my instructions for locking in your harness, and then you'll be on your way. You'll notice we have two zip lines right next to each other, so if you are a couple and you want to race, or you just see someone you want to compete against, let me know."

There were a few teens in the group, and a brother and sister immediately volunteered to race and started jeering at one another.

"Let's race, too," Sandra said. "Just for fun."

"One thing to know about racing," the guide said. "Usually, the heaviest person wins. Because gravity. But if you are lighter, I might share some strategy with you once you step up here."

"I'm going for strategy," Sandra said, looking up at his large frame.

"I'm only looking to have fun," Nick said. "But you know what the most fun is?"

"What's that?"

"Winning," he said.

They were the second pair to race. The view from the platform was amazing, and the feeling of hanging in mid-air thrilled him. Nick pushed off and flattened his body, trying to be as aerodynamic as possible. At first, he shot ahead of Sandra, looking down and seeing the trees whiz by, the train tracks far below, winding down the mountain.

Then he looked over and saw Sandra caught up, feet straight out in front of her, moving like an arrow shot from a bow. She waved.

Nick followed her lead, positioning himself as well as he could, but still she stayed even with him. He groaned with effort and passed her just as they crossed over where their train was parked. It seemed they were only a few feet above it. It was thrilling.

Then they came toward the platform. As they approached, there was a red flag they were supposed to grab to help stop themselves. Nick nailed it first try, and his descent slowed. In a few seconds more, he was standing on the platform.

Sandra was next to him a second later. Employees helped them unclip, and then they moved off the platform to get out of the harnesses and return the helmets.

"Let's get a selfie," Sandra said. Nick took her phone and held it out, snapping a quick photo.

Another one of the 'ducks' offered to take one for them, and they posed with their helmets on before giving them back again.

"Thanks," Nick said.

"I'll post that later. We pretty much have no service up here," Sandra told him.

"I'd love that," he said.

"So, posting our first photo together. Does that mean we're official?"

"Official?" he asked. "Yes, I think you could say we're officially in a relationship."

"The great Nick O'Flannigan is off the market?"

"Of course," Nick said. "I haven't really been on the market, per se."

Sandra hugged him, and they walked back down to the train, hand in hand. There were a few snacks available, and they ate a few of them and drank some water.

The train headed back down the hill, and everyone seemed quiet and tired after the zip line rides. They took more photos and chatted idly. Nick felt amazingly comfortable.

Sandra was a good person, and he was glad they were connected. It would be a long nine months, but they would find ways to see each other. Nick felt happier than he had in a really long time.

As they got close to Leadville, Nick's phone started buzzing, and took almost a full minute to stop.

There were eight new text messages, a missed call, two voice-mails, and several emails.

He started with the text messages. One was from Gerry, and read, "I hope you two are having a great time." Under that was a photo of her and Catherine next to what appeared to be a ski lift.

The next was from Emily. There were three. "Glad you could sell your photos," was the first. Then it was followed by two more. "Nick you need to call me as soon as you can." That was followed by, "Call ASAP."

He scrolled down to find a new number, one he did not recognize but that had a Denver area code.

"Sergeant Adams. Call me. I have some questions about your photos."

"I know you said you would be out for the day but call me."

"Call me ASAP."

Nick looked from one message set to the other, and then looked at the voicemail. It was from a different Denver number.

"Hi, we're trying to reach Nick O'Flannigan about the photos you took the other day. You need to call us back as soon as possible." A number followed that, one digit off the one that had called him.

"What in the world?" he said. He and Sandra made their way to his car, and he leaned against the trunk. She leaned next to him.

"What is it?"

"My phone literally blew up," he said. "It seems I have some calls to make."

He decided to call Emily first, and get that out of the way. She was his priority after all.

"Nick, where have you been?" she asked.

"On a train ride. We didn't have cell service, but I got some great—"

"You need to get somewhere fast where you can watch the news," she said. "You're all over it, but it's not good."

"Okay," he said. He looked over at Sandra, who was close enough to have heard the conversation. She had the browser on her phone open and was performing a search for Denver news.

His image came up on the screen in the first story. The headline was, "Traveling photographer cashes in with sickening photos."

"Shit," he said. "Thanks for the 'heads up'. Let me see if I can do some damage control here."

"You better, Nick. This isn't good at all."

"Understood," he said. He decided to dial the police sergeant next.

9

THE BAD NEWS

Nick dialed the number for the police sergeant, and he picked up on the first ring.

"What the hell are you doing, O'Flannigan?"

"I'm sorry, sir. I just sold the photos because I figured they would be compelling and maybe help your investigation. I didn't sell or release the enhanced photos."

"Great. Good news. Where the hell did you get the enhanced photos?" Sergeant Adams demanded.

"I have access to an app that's still in development. I can't share it publicly—"

"Who says you're not just good with Photoshop and trying to earn a name for yourself?"

"I'm sorry you got that impression. That just isn't me."

"I looked you up, O'Flannigan. Made some calls. You and your capitol photos always seem to involve law enforcement and some kind of mystery. The other cops may not have been on to you, but I am. It's not a coincidence that trouble follows you around."

"Sergeant, I—"

"Shut up, O'Flannigan. I hear from you on this case again, one peep, and I'll arrest you for obstruction. Good luck cleaning up the mess you made of your name. Leave me and my department out of it."

"But—"

The line went dead, and Nick turned to Sandra. "Well, that didn't go well."

"I assumed not. What did he tell you?"

"Basically, to bug off, and not contact them again."

"Sounds like a good idea, Nick. Honestly."

Nick grunted. "I'm calling the news next. I'll start with the website who bought the photos."

Nick opened his email on his phone, thankful for decent Wi-Fi. The train would be boarding soon, and he didn't have much time. There wouldn't be great coverage again until they got down off the mountain and closer to Denver once they left Leadville.

There was a phone number in the signature on the email, the one that had confirmed his PayPal payment.

He dialed it and waited. "The number you have reached is no longer in service," a mechanical voice told him. "Please check the number and try again."

Nick double checked. The number he'd entered was correct. He tried again and got the same recording.

He looked at the email, and the website associated with it. *The Denver Daily Guardian.* He typed in the URL to his search engine.

It came up, and there were his photos next to a story about the events of the previous Saturday. The story said the police had "persons of interest" in custody. It looked pretty normal until he scrolled down to some of the other stories.

They all looked like click bait titles.

He then searched for 'Denver Newspapers'. He found several listed, including the *Denver Daily*, but no *Denver Daily Guardian.* Instead of typing in the website this time, he searched for 'Denver Daily Guardian'.

The first headline that came up startled him. "Fake News Sites Make Thousands a Month in Ad Revenue." In the text underneath, the name '*Denver Daily Guardian*' was highlighted in bold text.

"Damn!"

"Nick, I've never heard you cuss so much," she said. "What is going on?"

He silently showed her the search results. "Their number is out of service, or at least the one they gave me."

"I discovered that already, Nick. Read the news article."

The article simply stated that he, Nick O'Flannigan, had sold photos to a fake news site that was using them to generate clicks. "It turns out that Mr. O'Flannigan is a professional freelancer on assignment from *Travel USA* magazine to photograph state capitol buildings all over the country. But it seems nearly everywhere he goes, mystery and death follow. He's been an undercover part of several investigations throughout his trip. It seems he was in the right place at the right time to take advantage of the events in Denver, too.

"*Travel USA* and the Denver Police Department both refused to comment for this story, and the number for the click-bait site, the *Denver Daily Guardian*, is no longer in service. Our emails went unanswered. Mr. O'Flannigan himself could not be reached."

Nick handed her phone back. "What a mess."

"Nick, I think you better call the real newspaper, and set the record straight."

"I agree."

"The problem is you may have to show the other photos you have to do so. How much trouble will that get you into?"

"I don't know, but if I don't fix this, *Travel USA* could recall me and assign the rest of the country to another photographer. One big thing in this whole contract was no negative publicity. They picked me in part because I am squeaky clean. Some would say even dull. The only thing I do is work, and now travel."

"Except the mysteries."

"I didn't get involved in any of those on purpose." As he said it, Nick thought back. That was not entirely true.

He liked being a part of mysteries and solving them, even if just in a small way. It made him happy and helped him feel like he was making a difference. If he was honest, it also helped with the loneliness and potential boredom on this trip. It had the potential to be dull, going from one city to another, taking the same type of photos of very similar buildings with few exceptions.

The people made the places different, and the mysteries had added just enough spice to keep him on his toes. Nick honestly felt his photography was better when he had more than one thing to occupy his mind.

If he wanted this trip and this assignment to keep going, he needed to fix this, and fix it soon.

"All aboard," the "conductor," complete with train man uniform, called.

"I'll email on the train, and set something up for this afternoon," he told her. "I better email the professor, too, and warn him about potential publicity so he's ready."

"I hope you can make this right," Sandra said.

They boarded the train and settled into their seats for the ride back to Leadville. As Nick typed out emails, Sandra laid her head against his shoulder, and fell asleep.

Nick envied her. He wished he could do the same, but as they travelled, his mind raced.

This couldn't be it, couldn't be the end of the line for his trip.

When they got back to Leadville, Nick checked his phone before the two hour drive down to Denver. There was an email from the editor of the real paper.

"We'd love to have your comment on this story," it read simply. "Call us when you're back in town."

Sandra walked hand in hand with him to the car, and they got in.

"It's probably going to be a busy afternoon and evening," he told her. "I'm sorry."

"It's okay, Nick," she said. She kissed him on the cheek and then sat back in her seat, making herself comfortable.

Nick shifted the car into gear and turned on music through his phone. The mild playlist let his mind wander as he drove, as much as the winding roads would allow.

By the time he got to town, he knew what he needed to do. He turned the music down.

"I know what do to," he told Sandra. "I just need to get to the hotel first."

"What are your thoughts?" she asked.

He outlined his plan to her and finished just as they reached the parking lot.

"That should work, or at least it should help," she said.

"Let's go," he said. "We have work to do."

10

GLINT AND GLIMMER

Once in the hotel room, Nick called the professor in Carson City.

"So," he said once they exchanged pleasantries. "I have a situation here in Denver."

"Oh?"

"Yep. I sold some photos to what I thought was a local paper and turned out to be a fake news site. The local real paper picked up on it and ran a negative story about me."

"Oh man. That is rough. What can I do to help?"

"I took one of the photos I took of the events as they were happening and used your app to enhance it a little bit. It shows the badge of a security company, I think. If I offer them some real news, maybe they will retract the story, or at least shift their focus to the good I am trying to do."

"I see," the professor said. "But if they ask how you enhanced the photo, you want to be able to tell them. And that means they would know about my app."

"Yep. And probably a lot more people too, unless I can convince them to keep it under wraps."

The professor sighed. "Try to convince them. If you can't, please have them contact me before they print their story."

"Will do. Thanks, Professor."

Nick hung up. "One down," he told Sandra. "Now to contact the paper."

Nick found the number on the email the paper had sent him, the real paper, and punched it in.

The phone rang twice, and a female voice answered. "Crime section, Nancy speaking, can I help you?"

"Hi, Nancy. Nick O'Flannigan here."

"Hi, Nick. Good to hear from you."

"I'd like to come in for an interview and to clear the air."

"That would probably be good for you, this paper, and your assignment."

"Okay," Nick said. "That sounds kind of ominous."

"It doesn't have to be. How soon can you get here?"

Nick looked at Sandra, who had been listening and had searched the address. She held up two fingers in a "V" and then a fist with no fingers.

"Twenty minutes," he said.

"Looking forward to it." The call ended.

"Now what?" Sandra said.

"We take my laptop, I turn on my charm, and I hope for the best."

"What about the fake news site?"

"Oh, I've got an idea for them, too."

"I can't wait to hear about that," she said. They kissed, briefly, and then headed down for the car.

Nick walked into the front of the newspaper office and found himself in a reception area. The walls were stark white, decorated with cheap art. Equally cheap furniture, including a lime green couch, a banana yellow chair, and a small table decorated with maga-zines, completed the style-less room.

A reception desk was backed by glass windows. Through them he could see a few apparently bored reporters wearing headphones, typing on computers. A few walked around, but several desks were empty.

"Hi, I'm Nick, I'm here to see—"

"Nancy. I know. She's been expecting you."

"Thanks," he said, but the woman was no longer looking at him. Nick glanced at Sandra, and then, sans instructions, simply stood there, waiting.

He looked to the right and saw a security guard standing stock-still in one corner. He eyed Nick, nodded, and went back to watching the door. Nick noted there were several cameras in the lobby.

A moment later a door opened to his left and a woman walked out. Tall, blonde, in six-inch heels and a maroon business suit, she extended a hand. "I'm Nancy. I wish I could say it's a pleasure to meet you, but that remains to be seen."

"I hope you'll change your mind," Nick said. "This is my—girl-friend—Sandra."

Sandra blushed and then the two women shook hands.

"Follow me," Nancy said.

She led them through the door, and to their right they saw the bank of reporters and all of the empty desks. At the end of the open area they entered a short hallway, and then went straight into an office labeled "Crime Editor" on the door.

"Have a seat," Nancy told them.

They did, and she just stared at the pair.

"Well?" she finally said.

Nick cleared his throat. "First, I want to apologize. I had no idea that site was a click-bait and fake news site. I got all kinds of offers from the media, and they were the highest bidder."

"There's a reason for that, and we will get to it. We were second."

"Again, I'm sorry, and I hope I can make it right. May I show you something?" Nick asked.

"Sure," she said.

Nick slipped his laptop from the case and opened it. He typed in his password, and then turned the computer toward her. On it was the close up, enhanced photo of the badge under the red hoodie one of the perpetrators had been wearing.

"What's this?"

"It's a photo I took of the crime. I zoomed in and enhanced this one with a special program. As you can see, there's a badge, and it says, "Security." I'm not sure what else it says, but I am betting it is a clue."

"Why are you giving this to me?"

"Because this was one of the photos I didn't—couldn't sell. But I did show it to the police first."

"Again, why me?"

"Well, thanks to your story, they don't trust me anymore."

"Imagine that."

"Hey," Sandra said. "He's trying to help. Seriously. Let him explain."

"They, of course, think I am really good with Photoshop or something and looking for credit and publicity. But I'm not. Believe me, I get enough attention."

"Convince me."

"I got an app from a professor in Carson City. He and his students have developed a tool that helps photographers remove certain layers in photos to make them clearer. I used it there to help catch a murderer and it could work here, too. They are still in the patent and development process, but I got an advanced beta version."

"And that's how you enhanced this photo?"

"Yes."

"So, basically, you have tech the cops don't have access to yet. You enhanced the photo to help them. Why?"

"I saw the glint of something gold through a rip in this guy's hoodie, and I had to check it out. What I saw sickened me. But sometimes I see things others miss, and I can help the authorities figure out who did this."

Nancy sat back. Her chair looked comfortable, one of those mesh ones with a headrest and what Nick imagined would be great back support. He immediately missed his own chair and desk back home in his apartment, and he hoped Ben, the guy who was subletting it from him while he was gone, was putting it to good use.

The chairs hotels, even the good ones, provided at the desks in the rooms just didn't compare.

He and Sandra, on the other hand, were sitting in the typical wire and plastic chairs that you found in libraries and conference rooms. It didn't matter to him. He sat on the edge, waiting for Nancy to say something.

She sighed. "May I?" she gestured at the laptop.

"Sure," he said.

She pulled it further onto her desk and put it next to her own screen. She stared at it, and then used the trackpad to zoom in even further.

"Can this professor verify the capability of this app, and that you used it properly to enhance this photo?"

"Yes," Nick said. "In fact, he asked that you call him before you publish anything related to the app."

"Hmmfff." Nancy studied the screen again.

Nick glanced at Sandra and mouthed, "It's working." She smiled back at him and nodded.

"Okay," she said. "Send this to me. And the professor's contact information. I'll check it out. If it is legit, I will let the police know, and I will run a story about what you're really doing. Now, what about the photos you did sell?"

"I tried to contact the site, but the phone number they gave me is no longer working."

"Damn virtual numbers."

"What?"

"You can get a virtual number through a Voice Over Internet Protocol system, called VoIP from pretty much anywhere, and make it seem like a local number. It is a real help for some businesses, but it does give scammers a great tool too. Sometimes they get caught. Other times, they don't."

"It has to be registered somewhere, right?"

"It does, but it may not be worth tracking down."

"Okay. What do you want from me to make this right?"

"What do you want to do?"

"I'll give you the photos," Nick said. "And I'll take the money I got for them and donate it to the victim's families to help them recover."

"That's quite generous of you."

"It's the least I could do."

"And I can run a story to that effect?"

"Of course."

"Okay. Now tell me about your experience. Where were you that you got these photos and why? Tell me your side of the story."

Nick explained for several minutes and answered Nancy's questions. She typed furiously on her keyboard as he spoke.

"Okay, Mr. O'Flannigan," she said. "Provided all this checks out, we'll run a new story tomorrow if I can get confirmation fast enough. I hope so. What are you going to do next?"

"Track down the fake news people and have a chat with them. Maybe I'll have another story for you."

"That sounds interesting. I'll be in touch. You know the way out?"

"We'll be fine," Nick said. "Let me transfer these files to a thumb drive for you." He took back his laptop and did just that. As he did, Nancy turned to Sandra.

"And you, Miss," Nancy said. "Sorry to bring your boyfriend in on this. We just had to make this right somehow."

"I understand," Sandra said. "I do have a question, though."

"Shoot."

"Why all the empty desks out there?" She indicated the area where the writers were working.

"Layoffs. The news biz isn't the best at the moment, and that's why when these fake sites steal stories and engage in sensationalist headlines it hurts us so much. They steal our traffic, a lot of it."

"Why?"

"Money. Ad revenue. NPR had investigated it themselves. Search it out on the web."

"I may just do that. And I'm sorry about the sale of the photos. I may have encouraged Nick to sell them, and we should have checked on the buyer more thoroughly."

"Water under the bridge," Nancy said. "Thanks for coming in. I need to get to work if we're going to get this out tomorrow."

"I understand," Sandra said. "Nice meeting you."

The two of them stood, and after Nick placed the thumb drive on the desk, he took Sandra's hand and they left the room together headed for the front of the building.

"On to the fake news site?"

"I think I need some food and rest first," Nick said. "Let's see if Gerry and Catherine want to meet for dinner."

11

TRUE LIES

The next morning, Nick woke to his phone ringing. Sandra lay sprawled across his chest, and he moved carefully to take the call, trying not to wake her.

After dinner and sharing their eventful day with Gerry and Catherine, they'd been up too late the night before, first talking, then making love again, and then talking some more.

Nick felt a bit nervous. He felt like he was falling in love, and he wasn't sure what to do with that.

"Hello," he said, his voice sounding raspy in his own ears.

"Hi, Nick, did I wake you?" Emily said.

"Sort of," he said. "But I'm up now."

As he spoke, Sandra woke, and rolled off of him and the bed, headed for the bathroom.

"I can probably guess you haven't seen the paper yet this morning?"

"Not yet."

"That reporter, Nancy, reached out to me late last night. I gave her a quote about you. Whatever you did yesterday afternoon, good job."

"Thanks."

"Are we going to get some more capitol building photos today? Some with a little less drama attached?"

"Of course."

"Is Sandra there with you?"

"Yep. Gerry and Catherine, too."

"I'm jealous. Wish I could be there with you all. Stay focused the rest of the week, Nick. I don't want to see your name in the paper again for a while, good or bad."

"Of course," Nick said, knowing if his plan worked, he might not be able to keep that promise.

"Take care, Nick. Talk soon. Check out the paper. Again, good job."

Nick smiled. "Thanks. I appreciate your trust in me."

"I wouldn't go that far. Just keep up the good work and stay out of trouble."

"Of course," Nick said, and the call ended.

Sandra emerged from the bathroom. "What did Emily have to say?"

"We need to go look at a paper. I guess whatever I did worked."

"So, we have to get dressed and head to breakfast then?"

"Yep."

"Don't you need a shower first?" she asked, moving into his arms.

"I guess I should get cleaned up," he said.

"I'm happy to help," she said, and he followed her into the bathroom.

Half an hour later, he texted Gerry as Sandra was blow drying her hair.

"Breakfast?" he said simply.

"Absolutely," came the reply. "We have just the spot."

"Lobby in ten minutes?"

"Give us fifteen," the answer came.

Nick shrugged, opened his laptop, and put the name of the newspaper in his browser. He wanted to look at a physical copy, but he could scan the digital version before breakfast.

"Photographer Vows to Make Things Right," the headline read, and Nick smiled to himself. Front and center were two photos he had taken, an enhanced one of the suspected badge and one pulled back that showed the covered face of the perpetrator. The article briefly explained how the photos had been enhanced and credited the professor.

"Police have two persons of interest in custody, and are seeking two more," the paper said. Below that statement were photos of the two men, both mugshots. "Impersonating employees of a local security company, the men were able to gain access to the building. Both men deny having any knowledge of the crime, although both have extensive criminal records."

Nick clicked away from the article and checked his email. Something ticked away at the back of his mind though.

Something was off. The men in the mug shots didn't seem to match the ones in the photos he had taken. He wasn't sure why.

"Maybe it's just the angle of the photo, or the distance," he said. "I'll look later."

Sandra finished blow drying her hair and dressed in a simple sweater and jeans. She came out of the bathroom.

"Hump day," she said. "We're halfway through the week, and you still like me."

He smiled up at her, ready to shut his laptop, and she came over and kissed him. As their lips met, his computer dinged with a new email.

It was from the *Denver Daily Guardian*. The subject line read, "Photos."

"Those photos were supposed to be exclusive to us. You owe us money," the text said. "Call me as soon as you can."

The signature said "Daniel Webster," and listed a number that was two digits off the one in the previous email from them.

"Whoa!" Sandra whistled. "These guys are brave."

"I'm counting on it," Nick said.

"Let's go to breakfast. We've got to get some capitol building photos today, or Emily will have my head. We'll let those guys stew awhile."

"Do you think this will work?"

"I'm almost positive."

"Almost?"

"My dad says the only sure things in life are death and taxes."

"That and the need for coffee," she said.

They headed down the elevator and met Gerry and Catherine already waiting. The women all exchanged hugs.

"Where are we going?" Nick asked.

"To Dozens down on 13ᵗʰ Avenue."

"Hey!" Nick heard from the front desk. He turned to see Cheryl who had been there when he checked in. "I saw you in the paper the last couple of days."

Nick groaned but walked over. "Yeah, I never intended to be news," he said. "Especially this week."

"I know," she said. "But I saw in the story how you are trying to make things right, and I just wanted to tell you I admire what you are doing."

"Thanks," he said. "I appreciate you telling me."

He walked back over to the group. As he did, a couple walked in the front door, looked up at him, and whispered to each other.

"Seems I've become a public figure here," he said. "Let's get going."

They headed out the door, walking again. Nick limped slightly, his leg a little sore. He silently wished for a bike.

Then he saw it. A Denver B-cycle station, right across the street. "Hey, isn't that one of those bike sharing things?" he said.

"Oh, we could ride to the restaurant." Sandra seemed enthused.

Catherine looked decidedly uncomfortable. "I haven't ridden a bike since high school."

"You never forget how," Nick said. "It's like—"

"Riding a bike?" Gerry said sarcastically.

"Yes! I took it up again in Helena, and it really helps my leg."

"Okay. Maybe we'll try it later. Can we just walk for now?" a nervous Catherine said.

"Sure," Nick said. "I'll be fine. But it is definitely something you should do." The streets were busy with pedestrians and he had to admit, bicycles. This wasn't the best time of the day for Catherine to learn again.

"Maybe while you two are working taking photos of the capitol, we will ride around and practice," she said.

"Sounds good," Sandra said. "Let's go. I'm hungry."

The walk made them all ravenous, and they ordered and devoured big breakfast plates. Then they split up. Nick and Sandra headed to the capitol building. They started outside and worked their way inside.

Sandra took some wide shots, and Nick focused on unusual macro photos, wanting to get something entirely different for Emily this time. He really wanted the photos to pop, and he wanted her to remember why she'd hired him, not someone else.

This afternoon, they would set his trap for the fake news guy and turn him into news. After that, Nick resolved, he would stay out of mysteries. He could focus on Sandra, even though a long-distance relationship would be hard, and he would focus on the assignment and his parents.

It wasn't like he didn't have enough to do without police investigations. He should've stayed in his car and minded his own business.

But that was the problem. He couldn't do that. And still, even when they'd looked at the newspaper at breakfast, he sensed something wrong. The suspects didn't fit, and not just to the enhanced photos, but all of them. The two men didn't seem like any of the four in the various photos.

You can look later, he told himself. *Right now, it doesn't matter. Just do your job.*

Sandra bumped his elbow. "Where were you just now? You seemed like you were far away for a minute."

"Just thinking," he said. "Got some good stuff?"

She showed him her camera, and he showed her some of his.

"We'll need to come back and get some sunset shots if we can. The sun is a bit to the south and west when it sets this time of year, but my bet is we can get some good light. That means an early dinner."

"I'm good with that."

She gave him a quick kiss, and they held hands and headed outside again.

As they passed, one of the security guards looked at both of them, smiled, and waved.

When they came into the sunlight, Nick's phone rang.

"Nick," he said.

"Sergeant Adams here. What's going on, O'Flannigan?"

"What do you mean?"

"The photos in the paper today. You leaked them."

"No. I gave them to the paper to get them out there. You weren't communicating with me, and I understand why, but I also needed to make things right."

"Those photos helped us find the suspects we have in custody. We plan to charge them later today."

"Glad I could be of help."

"I hope leaking those photos didn't contaminate our jury pool."

"I didn't leak them. And I would say that is something for the DA to worry about."

"You may be right, O'Flannigan. But you didn't do the right thing here." The call ended.

"Who was that?" Sandra asked.

"Sergeant Adams. Seems like in his eyes, I can do no right," Nick said.

"Don't worry about it. Are you hungry?"

"Sure," he said. "Should we text Gerry and Catherine?"

"Sure," she said. Then his phone rang again.

The number was unfamiliar again, but Nick answered. "This is Nick."

"Daniel Webster, *Denver Daily Guardian*," the person on the other end said. "We need to talk."

"We should," Nick said. "We were about to head to a light lunch. You're welcome to join us."

"Us?"

"Me and my girlfriend, Sandra."

"Okay. Where?"

"We're down by the capitol building. Somewhere close."

"Meet you at the Shish Kabob grill, ten minutes."

"Ten minutes," he told Sandra after hanging up. "I hope Gerry and Catherine are close."

Nick called Gerry's phone. "Hey, where are you guys?"

"Just about to the capitol. Are you two down for some lunch? Something light. That breakfast was huge."

"Actually, we need you. Bring your cameras to the Shish Kabob grill. Don't join us, we'll be meeting a Mr. Daniel Webster from the *Denver Daily Guardian*."

"Hmmff," she said. "Do you think that's his real name?"

"We're going to find out. You guys take photos while we talk. We're going to make this guy headline news."

"Good," she said. "We'll be there, but we'll stay out of the way until he leaves. We'll try to get as good of photos as possible without letting on to what we're doing."

"See you soon," Nick said, and hung up. It was time for the final step in making things right.

Then he would be out of the mystery solving business.

12

———

JUST THE FACTS

They walked in and a mountain of a man waved them over. He was just under Nick's height, with broad shoulders and a narrow waist. He wore a black and brown flannel shirt. He wore a red ball cap over a round, bearded face with a nose that looked small compared to the rest of his features. Next to him stood another man, slightly smaller in both stature and build, wearing a security guard's uniform.

"Daniel Webster," he said.

Nick chuckled. "Nick O'Flannigan. This is my girlfriend, Sandra."

"Nice to meet you."

"Is this your bodyguard?"

"Just a friend." Mr. Webster didn't introduce him.

Nick tried really hard not to glance over his shoulder and look for Gerry and Catherine. He had to trust that they were here, and trust they were doing as instructed.

"Shall we sit?" Sandra said.

"Sure, but we won't be long," Webster answered.

He stood next to an empty table with four chairs, and they all sat.

"You owe me money," he said simply. "Those photos were supposed to be an exclusive for me."

"Well," Nick said. "Those photos caused a lot of trouble for me."

"That's not exactly my fault."

"You're right. I should have done my research."

Daniel smirked. "But you didn't. You still signed a contract."

"Is Daniel Webster your real name?" Sandra blurted out.

"Yes, it is." He pulled a wallet from his back pocket and laid it on the table, flipping it open. Opposite his driver's license was the badge of a security company, the same badge his un-introduced friend wore.

"Are you a security guard?" Nick asked.

"Are you going to pay me what you owe?"

"On one condition. You take all the photos and the story you wrote down. Now. Before I pay."

"No."

"Then, no."

"I could sue you."

"Then do it. I'd love to come back to Denver, talk about your 'news organization' in open court, and then when I win, expense you for my trip and my lost work on this assignment. I'm sure that will be worth more than anything you made from running that story."

Daniel shook his head. "You think you're pretty smart, huh?"

"Nope, I think I'm dumb for ever trusting you, but I am trying to make it right."

"Fine," Daniel said, standing. "We'll see what my lawyers think of this."

"I look forward to hearing from you," Nick said.

"Bye," Sandra told them as they turned. She waved at their backs. "Well, that didn't go well."

"Sure it did," Nick said. "What I really wanted was photos of them. And this." He pulled a recorder out of his pocket. "Let's grab Gerry and Catherine, and head back to the hotel. We can get some evening shots of the capitol later on."

The girls were waiting outside. "That was short," Catherine said.

"I fully expected it to be," Nick told her. "Did you get some clear photos of the two of them?"

"Of course I did," she said, and then Nick looked at her camera.

There was a long lens attached. "I started as a sports photographer in high-school. I never lost the touch."

Gerry looked at her, and then pecked her on the cheek. "Isn't she adorable and talented?"

Nick laughed. "The two of you make quite a pair. Okay, let's get something to eat, and then see what we've got."

"Are you ever not hungry?" Gerry asked.

"Hey, it's been hours since breakfast."

They all laughed, and then went back inside. Shish Kabobs sounded just about perfect.

About an hour later, they all exited the restaurant. Nick felt full, but not too full. Having Sandra and his friends around curbed his inner glutton, at least a little bit, and all of this walking, while hard on his leg at times, was good for him in the long run.

"Let's head back to the hotel," he said. "I'll get those photos from you, and we can look them over. Then I'll decide what to do next."

When they arrived back at the hotel and in Sandra and Nick's room, Catherine handed over the memory card from her camera. Nick knew one of the keys to his success and to figuring this out was his ability to keep all these photos organized.

He found early on that he was taking hundreds of them a week, between the ones for his personal sites and social media, and those for his assignment. A couple of times, he'd uploaded the wrong photos to the magazine cloud folder, luckily with no disastrous results yet. Since then, he'd taken to labeling folders much more carefully.

He labeled these "C-Denver Daily Guardian_" followed by the date.

The photos were actually amazing. She'd gotten amazingly close and clear shots without being detected at all by the subjects. There were close ups of their faces, of the mystery man's badge, and wider ones of the group talking.

"These are great," he told Catherine while flipping through them. "Perfect in fact."

"Thanks," she said. "What are your plans for the rest of the evening?"

"I'll look these over, and probably send them to the paper I imagine, with a little story background and the recording file. They can run with the story however they want. Then Sandra and I will head back to the capitol for some sunset shots."

"That sounds great. Mind if we go get some rest? Then maybe we will meet you for a late dessert after you finish with photos tonight."

"Sounds good," he said.

"Nick, you're such a hard worker and an amazing guy. You're handling this really well. Emily will be very reassured," Gerry said.

"Thanks," Nick said, blushing a little. "I appreciate you, too."

"Sandra, you're so good for this guy," she said. "You better hang on to her, Nick."

"I plan on it," he said.

The two women left through the door, and as it closed behind them, Sandra wrapped her arms around him from behind. Her head came only to the middle of his back. "Alone at last," she said. "Have I told you how attractive you are when you're confronting bad guys?"

"Not yet," Nick said, turning to face her. And looking down into her eyes. "But do tell me more."

Half an hour later they were back at the computer looking through photos. Nick was now in just his t-shirt and a pair of gym shorts. Sandra wore one of his t-shirts too, slipped on over a pair of her own tiny shorts.

Instead of sitting at the desk, Nick had the laptop balanced on his legs, and Sandra sat next to him on the couch.

As they looked through them, Nick saw that Catherine was pretty talented. She'd gotten some great closeups of both men, even from a distance. There was a close photo of "Daniel" followed right after by one of his sidekicks.

Nick paused.

"What is it?" Sandra asked.

"There's something about that guy. He looks familiar for some reason, but I would swear I never met him before."

"Zoom in closer," Sandra said, snuggling up to him. It was distracting, but a good kind of distracting.

"Hmm," Nick said. "Hang on a second."

He put the photo, zoomed in, on one side of the screen. On the other, he opened the enhanced photo he had sent the police. First, he looked closely at the badge the man wore, and then zoomed in on the enhanced version from the day of the defenestration.

"See it?" he said, pointing.

"The badges. They do look similar. I wonder why that is?"

"Well, I know what it isn't," Nick said. "It isn't enough for the police to change their mind about me. If there's one thing I've learned on this trip, it's that once you've broken trust, it's hard to earn back, especially with law enforcement. They want just the facts."

"That's understandable," Sandra said. "You really think they are involved in staging this whole thing?"

"Well, they do make a lot of money from the news they print, even if it is fake. But this was something real. Maybe it was designed to make them seem legitimate."

"Why do it themselves? Why not just report on what is happening? And they really didn't have blockbuster traffic until they got your photos."

"True," Nick said. "What else could their motive be besides news and money?"

"And think about how many security personnel actually work at that company. There could be dozens of them, more. What ties this guy or Daniel to them, or whoever pushed those men?"

Nick zoomed in on the man's face. He pointed at the screen. "There. That's why he looks familiar."

The man had unusually colored eyes, a steel gray that certainly wasn't common. But that wasn't what Nick noticed first. He pointed it out to Sandra.

Look at his eyelid. There's a scar, and a small skin tag on it that's really close to his nose. How common can that be?"

"That and the eye color," she said. "That's striking. Seems like he was one of the guys who pushed those men from the window."

Nick nodded. "It looks like it, and also like we can prove it. But one more thing."

He pulled up the newspaper article online and looked closely at the mug shots the police had taken.

"Neither suspect has this color of eyes. In fact…"

He exited from the enhanced photo and quickly looked through all the others showing the perpetrators of the crime. In each, he zoomed in on their eyes.

"None of the eyes match the suspects in the mug shots," he said. "Not one."

"They sure don't," Sandra said. "What now?"

Nick thought for a second. There was really nothing they could do. They didn't have a name, just a couple of photos.

"I can send them to the police," he said. "And wait for them to take action."

"I guess so," she said.

"I could also turn them over to the newspaper, but that might be even worse." Nick stared at the screen. "They would have to share the photos anyway with the police, and if they printed them first, it might turn into another P.R. disaster. I don't think I can afford another one of those this trip."

"I don't think Emily would appreciate that," Sandra said, laying her hand on his forearm. "What do you think?"

"I think I need to think about it while we take photos, and maybe over that dessert Gerry and Catherine mentioned."

"Sounds like a plan."

They both dressed, gathered their cameras and headed out into the late afternoon sun. They should be just in time to get some great late-light and sunset photos.

Nick's mind worked, even as he watched Sandra work and took photos of his own. The capitol sat so the dome pretty much faced north, but that meant as they faced south, the sun was behind the building and to their right. Nick started by taking photos straight on, and then moved to the northeast corner of the lawn area to get some more shots.

There was a light cloud cover, and the setting sun turned those clouds pink where the coming night had not turned them a dark purple. One shot looked like pink streaks in the sky, and the lights in the building had just come on, some apparently on a timer or activated by someone.

It was framed perfectly, the dome seemingly touching the sky. Nick took several shots in a row as the sun rapidly sank and the sky changed minute by minute.

He was so focused he didn't even hear Sandra come up beside him.

"Beautiful, isn't it?"

He looked down at her and saw the evening sky reflected in her eyes. He smiled and leaned in to kiss her. As their lips met, he heard someone say:

"I knew we'd find you two lovebirds here." Gerry walked up, hand in hand with Catherine.

"Oh yeah?" Nick said, reluctantly releasing Sandra and then reaching down to hold her hand. "Come to see the sunset yourselves?"

"Yes, and it's gorgeous, Catherine said. "I don't want this trip to end. It's all been so amazing."

"It has, hasn't it?" Gerry said. The two of them kissed, and Nick cleared his throat.

"Not to break up your happiness there. But what about that dessert you promised me?"

"Gee, Nick, is it always about food with you?" Catherine asked.

"Not always," Sandra said. "Where are we headed?"

Nick blushed.

"We thought we'd try 5280 Ice Cream. It's right around the corner from the hotel," Gerry said.

"Alright, let's go," Nick said.

He and Sandra followed as the other couple led the way.

13

THE EYES HAVE IT

"What do you think?" Nick asked the group while scraping the last bit of hot fudge from his plate and licking it off the spoon.

"You want me to be honest?" Gerry said.

"Of course," Nick told her.

"I think anything you do other than giving this stuff to the police, you're likely to step in it and get yourself in trouble. I don't think you want or need that at this point."

"You do have another choice," Catherine said quietly.

Nick looked at her - really looked at her and smiled. Gerry had done well, and although Catherine hadn't talked much, she'd been a pleasant little addition to their group.

"What might that be?" Nick asked.

"When I was in college, there was a group of guys harassing the girls in the photography department. We would be taking photos, and they would jump into the frame, and would make fun of us constantly. It was awful."

"Sounds like it. What did you do?"

"Well, one of them started to be a bit obscene. Instead of just jumping into the frame of photos, he would flash us. While it seems funny now, it was pretty traumatic. He was a football player, and no one wanted to believe us at first."

"I've never heard this story before," Gerry said.

"I usually don't tell it, but it applies here. He should have known better than to mess with photographers. We took the photos we had of him streaking and put them together in a short video. We even zoomed in on "key parts" in various shots. She made air quotes with her fingers.

"What did you do with it?"

"We confronted him. We told him to stop, and to turn himself in, or we would show the video to everyone and turn him in ourselves."

"What did he do?"

"He turned himself in. Apparently in some of those shots, it was cold outside."

Sandra giggled and Nick blushed. Gerry's mouth hung open for a second, and then she joined Sandra in laughing.

"You think I should confront them?"

"It's an option. I don't know what risks that holds, beyond the possible publicity."

"Hang on," Sandra said. "As much as I respect what you did, Catherine, these men are criminals. Killers. They shoved a couple of guys from windows. We have no idea what they are capable of."

"Maybe," Nick said. "But that actually might be an idea. We don't really have enough to convict them, but if we can get them to confess—"

He stopped and stared into space.

"What are you thinking?" Sandra asked.

"I need to sleep on the idea," he said. "It's late, and I'm full. Let's go get some sleep and meet up in the morning."

"Sounds good," Gerry said.

"Sorry my idea was a little out there," Catherine said.

"No, it's not, "Nick said. "In fact, it might be the best idea I've heard this week."

They walked back to the hotel and split up in the hallway.

"What did you mean by that being a good idea?" Sandra asked when they were alone.

"In this case, I think it matters where and how we confront them. These guys are always looking for another story, right?"

"Of course," she said.

"Then let's give them one."

"They know you. They won't trust you again."

"But they don't know Catherine or Gerry."

"Nick!"

"It's just an idea. Let me think it over."

"You want to go to sleep already? It isn't that late."

"Maybe it's too early for sleep. But not too early to head to bed."

"Now you have my attention," Sandra said.

Nick woke early the next morning and slipped from the bed. He went to his laptop and created a slide show with some of the photos from the ones he'd taken at the scene of the crime and the ones Catherine had taken at the meeting.

He concentrated on eyes and the badges. He mixed in some of the mug shots and put some clever subtitles in the captions.

Sandra woke just as he was finishing up. "What do you have there?" she said, yawning.

"A slideshow, similar to what Catherine talked about."

"Nick, you're not going to try to confront these men yourself?"

"No. I'm going to offer them a story, but not through my email. Through Catherine's or Gerry's. Someone they won't recognize. Then I'm going to tip the police, but through the newspaper."

"What makes you think they will cooperate?"

"Because I'm given them a story for real."

"Do you think it will work?"

Nick shrugged. "I don't know. But if it doesn't, at least I will know I did all I could. And it should keep my name out of the papers if they follow my instructions."

"That would be good. Remember what Emily said."

"Believe me, I won't forget. Look, Sandra, can I tell you something?"

"Of course," she said. "You can tell me anything."

"I love this assignment. But in my travels I have discovered a couple of things. First, the variety I find is in the people I meet. These cities are all great, and I'm really looking forward to having visited and photographed every state capitol building."

"That's a definite plus. This is a dream job."

He shook his head. "Yes, it is. But I love looking for details in photographs, even photographing crime scenes. A part of me was sickened by what happened on Saturday, and witnessing those men thrown from the window. But another part of me found it exciting."

"What are you saying?"

"I'm saying after this assignment, I may choose another career path, or at least do more of this as part of my overall business."

"You mean like crime scene photography and even detective work?"

Nick shrugged. "I'm sure I can find a way to work it in."

"Um, okay," she said. "That would be quite a change."

"I'm just considering it," he said. "I have no idea yet how such things would work."

"I thought you loved being a freelancer?"

"I do. But maybe there is a way I can do both. Look, I'm only ten weeks in, and I have a lot of time to think this over. I just wanted to talk it out with someone."

"I'll think about that, too, Nick. I'm not even sure what to say right now."

"That's okay," he said. "For now, let's just get past Denver." He grabbed his phone, and texted Gerry. "Can you bring Catherine and your laptops, and meet us in our room?"

"Breakfast?" her reply came.

"After we do some things. My treat."

"Okay. Ten minutes."

When they arrived, Nick explained his plan. Catherine agreed, and sent an email to the *Denver Daily Guardian*. He sent an email to the editor at the actual newspaper that helped clear his name with a copy of the video he had created and his idea to catch the real criminals, or at least one of them.

He then packed his laptop and his camera.

"What now?" Catherine said.

"We wait," Nick said. "And we might as well eat while we do."

They followed him downstairs, and out into the sunlight, headed for the Delectable Egg.

"What better place for a Denver omelet than in Denver?" Nick said. Everyone groaned, but no one disagreed. As they walked, he realized his leg ached, worse than it had in a long time. He kept a smile on his face and joined the small talk, but he couldn't walk without limping. Usually this kind of ache signaled something like a weather change, but he truly felt it was something else this time.

About halfway through breakfast, Catherine's phone dinged.

She looked at it, and her face went pale.

"It's them," she said. "That Daniel guy wants to meet and take a look at what I have."

"Let me see." Nick looked over the email, and saw the offer to pay, just as they had offered him.

"Interesting," he said. "They want to meet in an hour. Let me call the paper and alert them."

He excused himself and stepped outside so he would not disturb the other diners and dialed the direct extension for Nancy, the crime editor.

"Hi, Nick," she answered. "I just got your email. Interesting idea."

"It is. And the *Denver Daily Guardian* took the bait."

"When's the meet?"

"An hour." Nick gave her the name of the place.

"Got it. I'll be there with a cameraman, and I'll alert the cops. You want me to send them the video you created?"

"Yes," Nick said. "Just leave my name out of it. Tell them you have an anonymous source."

"They'll know from the enhanced photos in here."

"Maybe. But they probably don't want my name involved at this point. And neither do I."

"Suit yourself. We'll be there either way."

"Thanks," Nick said, and ended the call.

He walked back into the restaurant. "We're all set," he said, sitting down.

"What do you think got them to agree to this?" Gerry asked.

"Honestly," Nick said. "I think the eyes have it."

Everyone but Sandra giggled, breaking the tension for a moment. But she simply remained quiet, and Nick could feel her staring at him.

14

PRESS IN

The meeting place was a new business, a tiny Chinese tea house. Red paper lanterns, not currently lit, hung from entrance supports, each carved with a different set of images, but both containing a large dragon.

Nick watched the situation unfold. He was in his car with Sandra, and Gerry about half a block away. Catherine had joined the press, but at a distance. She and a newspaper photographer were on the roof of a nearby building with long lenses trained on the entrance to the tea house and what little they could see through the windows.

The police had agreed to work with the reporters in exchange for their information but had kept them at a distance on the other side of the entrance. They were promised an exclusive if things panned out and an arrest was made.

First, a female officer dressed in plain clothes entered the tea house, followed a few moments later by a male officer dressed the same way, like an American tourist.

After a few moments, he saw half a dozen officers in uniform head toward the building. Three stayed in the front, and three went around back.

A moment later, Nick heard two loud pops that sounded like gunshots.

"What was that?" Gerry asked.

Two more pops followed in quick succession. Nick reached for the door handle, and Sandra put a hand on his arm.

"Don't," she said. "Just let the police handle it."

"I will," he said. "I just want a closer look."

Sandra withdrew her hand and folded her arms across her chest.

"I'll be right back," he reassured her, but she turned and looked out the passenger window in the opposite direction.

Nick rose to his full height and could see over the rest of the cars on the street. Now only one officer was outside the front door of the tea house. The door itself was open.

Distantly, a siren wailed. Probably an ambulance.

Then Nick saw a man, crouching on his side of the street, just ahead of him. The man wore a red hoodie, but it had pulled up over his belt due to his position. A gun belt was visible around his waist. On one side rested a can of mace in a leather sheath. A holster was on the other side, empty.

"Look out!" Nick shouted to get the officer's attention. "Gun!"

The officer turned, but slowly.

Red Hood stood and started to turn towards Nick.

Time slowed down. Nick looked for cover, seeing a gap between his car and a truck parked in front of it.

He stepped toward the potential hiding place.

The gun was visible now, a revolver with a long barrel. As the figure in the hoodie kept turning, Nick tried to accelerate. His weak right leg failed him, and he slipped off the curb.

He felt himself falling, saw the bumper of the truck rushing up at him, and then heard a shot from behind him. At the same time, he heard a woman scream.

His chest struck the bumper, and the breath went out of him. He spun and landed on his back on the street. To his right he saw the rear tire of the truck, and oddly took note of the fact that a small white stone was stuck in the tread.

He tried for breath, and after a moment got it. Sandra's face appeared, upside down in his vision, and he heard, "Nick, are you alright?"

He tried to sit up. She kneeled beside him and put her hand on his chest.

"Don't move yet, Nick. Let's get you checked out."

This time when she commanded him to stop, he did.

As he lay there, he did a mental evaluation of his body. His leg ached, but only slightly more than normal, except at the ankle.

May have twisted it, he thought.

A spot in the center of his chest was the source of some sharp pain. That would probably bruise.

Sandra held his face between her hands. As far as he could tell, there was nothing wrong with his head.

His right elbow felt skinned, like in a childhood bike accident.

Other than that, he felt okay.

"What happened?" he asked once his breath had slowed.

"The police officer got him, before he got you."

"Red Hood, you mean?"

"Who?"

"Never mind," he said, closing his eyes. "As long as everyone is safe."

"They are," she told him, stroking his cheek.

Just then his phone rang. Sandra slipped it from his pocket, but not before he saw the name on the screen. "Mom."

"Hello?" Sandra answered.

"He'll have to call you back. He's a little busy." There was a short pause. "I'm Sandra. No, I'm not sure. Yes, we are dating. We're just focusing on right now and figuring it out."

There was a longer pause.

"I'm sorry about your husband. Nick told me. I am glad he's feeling better though."

"No, I don't know if that's possible, but we will see."

"To Boston? Um, maybe. That is still a long way away."

She ended the call.

"What was that about?" Nick asked.

"She wanted to know about grandchildren."

"What?" Nick tried to sit up.

"Relax," Sandra said. "She's fine."

Gerry appeared then, Catherine by her side with a camera hanging from her neck.

"You okay?" Gerry asked.

"Yes," Nick said. "But Sandra won't let me up yet."

Sandra sighed. "Okay, you can try to stand, but if you feel anything wrong, you get right back down, deal?"

Nick stood, finding his ankle tender, but it would hold his weight. He stepped toward the sidewalk and saw two men placing a sheet over the body lying there. A red-sleeved arm poked out from underneath it.

The two EMTs looked up. "You okay?" they asked.

"I'm fine."

"Let us check you anyway."

One man took each side of him and they walked him to an ambulance. Sandra smirked and followed.

As he sat down, a uniformed officer headed over. "Hey, thanks man. You saved my life."

"I think you may have saved mine, too," Nick said.

"Well, I appreciate it," the officer said. "You were a big help."

Behind him, Sergeant Adams appeared. After the two men shook hands and the other officer left, he stepped forward.

"I was wrong about you, O'Flannigan. Thanks for the video and the heads up. We have one sort-of confession, and since both men ran, we have cause to arrest and hold them for now. Until we find more evidence, but you pointed us in the right direction."

"I tried. What about him?" Nick nodded toward the body.

"We'll know more in a couple of days. I'm going to bet he was one of the pushers."

"Let me know?"

The sergeant smirked. "Read about it in the papers, Photo Boy. Good luck with your assignment and your trip."

The officer left. The EMTs gave him the all clear, and Nick and Sandra walked back toward his car, his limp more pronounced than before.

"What's next?" Sandra asked.

"Well, I was going to suggest the botanical gardens, but—" he pointed at his leg.

"Understood," she said. "Why don't we get you some rest?"

As they reached the car, Nancy walked up to them. "Thanks, Nick. For making this right, and for helping to catch the bad guys."

"It's the least I could do," Nick told her.

"We'll do our best to keep your name and photo out of this if that's what you still want."

"It is," Nick said. "I appreciate it."

"See you around?"

"I hope not. I'm only here for another day and then a few hours on Saturday. Hopefully, I can stay out of the news that entire time."

Nancy laughed. "Take care."

Gerry and Catherine walked up to the car. "Where to?" Gerry asked.

"We're going back to the hotel so Nick can rest, at least for a little bit. Dinner tonight?"

"Sure," both said. "We'll stay downtown and walk back from there if you don't mind dropping us."

"No problem," Nick said. He went to get in the driver's seat.

"Let me," Sandra said. "Rest your ankle."

He got in the passenger seat, and she quickly adjusted the seat and mirrors and drove them back to the hotel, dropping Gerry and Catherine downtown on the way.

Once they got to their room, Nick collapsed on the bed, and in a matter of moments he was asleep. He didn't dream at all.

A FINAL NOTE

Nick woke up hungry, and to the sound of Sandra's voice, talking on the phone apparently.

"No, he's fine, just sleeping. Oh, wait, he's awake."

She walked over and handed him the phone, mouthing, "Your mom."

He answered. "Hi, Mom."

"Are you okay, Nick?"

"Yes, Mom. I just had a wild morning."

"Yes, Sandra told me about it. You should leave catching criminals to the police."

"I know, Mom, I—"

"Sandra seems nice. Doesn't she seem nice?" She shouted the last part of her sentence.

"Yes, she seems nice!" Nick heard his dad yell in the background.

"You're going to have to settle down somewhere after your assignment. No girl wants to be traveling around the country taking photos all the time."

"Actually, Mom—"

"No girl, Nick."

"I'm planning to go back to Seattle, at least that's the plan now."

"You should think about Boston."

"I will, Mom. I still have a long way to go."

"Okay, Nick. We love you."

"I'm glad Dad is feeling better."

"Me, too," she said. "But don't tell him I said that."

Nick laughed. "Love you, Mom. Bye."

He sat up and looked at Sandra. "You talked to my parents."

"They're very nice."

"My mom will have all her friends believing we are getting married."

"I know."

"On our way to the altar."

"I know."

"Settling down and giving her grandchildren."

"Well, she'll have to slow that thought train down."

"We'll see," Nick said. "But I'm glad they seem to like you."

"I like them, too. I like you, Nick."

"I like you, too."

"Are we going to try to make this work then?"

"Even long distance? Yeah, we are. Or at least, I want to."

"I want to," Sandra said. "I think we need to give it a shot. But one thing, Nick."

"What's that?"

"At least for now, try to cut back on the mysteries, okay?"

Nick smiled. "Sure, I'll try."

"You up for some dinner, or you want to eat in?"

Nick glanced at his phone. "I slept all day?"

"Pretty much. I took a nap, too. You've been through a lot today."

"Thanks for letting me sleep."

"Anytime."

Nick stood, favoring his ankle, and made his way to the bathroom. While he was in there, he splashed some water on his face, and brushed his teeth. Feeling a little more human, he came back out again.

"I'm up for dinner," he told her. "I'm starving. But let's pick somewhere close or take an Uber or something."

"Sure," she said.

She sent a text message, and a soft ding indicated she got one back right away.

"Gerry and Catherine are right around the corner. Let's just go to Yard House again."

So, they did. Everyone ate their fill, and Catherine told them about selling her photos from today's events to the paper. When the check came, she paid the bill.

They walked back, everyone moving slowly so Nick could keep up.

"Let's do the botanical gardens tomorrow," Nick said. "I want to get up early and get some sunrise shots for my assignment."

"What about your ankle?" Gerry asked.

"It feels better already," Nick said. It did feel better, but certainly not great. Still, he didn't want to sleep another day away. He'd already missed an entire day in the limited time he had with his friends.

He didn't think he'd be able to sleep, but he and Sandra watched an old James Bond movie on the hotel television while lying in bed. Toward the end, they kissed, lightly at first, and then more passionately. Sandra moved against him carefully, trying not to hurt his chest or his ankle.

"Is this okay?" she asked, straddling his lap as he sat propped up against some pillows.

"Yes," he said, swallowing a lump in his throat. "You're gorgeous."

"Thank you," she said. She leaned forward and wrapped her arms around his neck. "I've fallen for you, Nick. You better not break my heart."

"I won't," he said, hoping he could keep his word.

They made love again, and afterward, Nick found himself able to sleep after all.

The next morning, they woke, and Nick and Sandra rose early to get some sunrise photos. There was just enough light cloud cover for them to get some pink skies over the southeast end of the building, and once again, Nick was pleased to have someone else taking photos as well. After about an hour, they made their way back to the hotel. By then, Nick was limping pretty badly, even though he tried to hide it.

They made it inside, and once they showered, Gerry sent Nick a text. "We'll be there in five with breakfast."

"Okay," he texted back.

Two minutes later there was a knock at the door. Nick finished pulling his shirt on and opened the door. Catherine stood there, holding a box of Krispy Kreme donuts. Gerry was behind her with a tray of four coffees in to-go cups. He took the box from her, and they both came in.

Sandra joined them a moment later. No one mentioned the day before, as if in some unspoken pact, and Nick put away a maple bar and three of the traditional donuts.

"Catherine had an idea," Gerry said. "Go ahead, Hon."

"They have those little scooters here," she said. "You now, the ones you rent. Your ankle might not be up for riding a bike, but we could rent those and tour the botanical gardens and get around that way."

"I'm game to try," Nick said.

He managed to get his shoes on, even though is ankle was still a little swollen. They found four scooters, and made their way over to the botanical gardens, a little farther than Nick originally thought it was. The scooter was easier on his leg, but it was still a bit tender by the time they arrived.

They wandered, all taking photos in the different sections of the gardens. Nick watched Sandra and Catherine, marveling at how talented they both were. Gerry took some photos, but clearly, she enjoyed just looking around and watching the others.

They grabbed a quick lunch, and then went by the capitol building again. They passed much of the afternoon taking photos and walking around, Nick resting when he needed to.

Finally, Nick settled on a bench.

"You done walking?" Sandra asked.

Nick nodded. "Yeah, for now."

As he sat there, Sandra took photos of him. At first, he protested, and then allowed it.

When she was done, he took a turn. He captured her profile, told a few jokes and made her smile. He then went and sat down next to her, putting his hand on her thigh.

"Those are the best photos I have taken all week," he said.

"Doubtful, but thanks," she said.

They sat holding hands for a bit, until Gerry and Catherine came around the corner, holding hands as well.

'Hey you two," Gerry said. "How are you feeling, Nick?"

"Better," he said. "But sore."

"Scooch over," she said. He did, moving closer to Sandra, and the two ladies sat down.

"Our last night in Denver," Catherine said. "We all fly out tomorrow."

"I know," Nick said.

"I guess there is only one question left," she said.

"Where do we eat?" they all said in chorus, and then laughed.

"How about Guard and Grace?" Nick said.

"Oh, high end. Good taste," Catherine said. "We're in."

"Good," he said. "I already made reservations last week. You have to plan ahead for this place on Friday night."

Gerry rolled her eyes. "Boy Scout."

"Hardly," he said. "Can we take an Uber?"

Sandra used the app, and in a few moments, they got picked up and were on the way.

Dinner went smoothly, and toward the end, Nick's phone rang with a Denver number.

"Hey, Nick, it's Nancy. Hope I'm not interrupting."

"Just dinner," he said. "What's up?"

"Are you sure you don't want your name shared? You're kind of a hero to the police after they were pretty upset with you."

"I'd rather not," he said.

"It's your call," she said. "I just thought I would check. We're running a special story tomorrow. A lot has happened in one week."

"Indeed, it has," Nick said. "All the same, I'd like to remain anonymous."

"Okay," she said. "You're leaving town tomorrow?"

"Yep," he said.

"Well, good luck."

"Thanks," he said, and hung up.

"What was that?" Sandra asked.

"Nothing important," he said.

She smiled and grabbed his hand.

They ordered dessert. Sandra, Gerry, and Catherine split the white espresso mud pie.

Nick ate an entire piece of the sticky toffee cake all by himself.

They headed back to the hotel one last time. Nick looked around as they walked, him a little behind the others, limping noticeably.

He was going to miss this, not the place necessarily, but being surrounded by friends.

SEE YOU LATER

The next morning, they all got up early and packed. Nick put his stuff in the trunk first so he could get the other's things out first. He and Sandra hugged before she got in the passenger seat. His leg was better this morning, a good thing since he had a long drive ahead after dropping everyone.

The ride to the airport went fast, with talk of the week's events passing the time.

When they arrived, Nick pulled to the curbside drop off.

Gerry hugged him first. "See you later, Nick. Stay safe on your trip."

"I love you," he told her. "Thanks for getting me this assignment. I do appreciate it, and it has been great so far."

Catherine came next. She hugged him tightly, too. "It was great to meet you," she said. "Gerry talks about you all the time."

"She talks about you all the time, too. I wish you guys all the best," he said. "I can't wait to spend more time with you both."

Sandra hugged both of them, and they said their goodbyes.

Nick lifted her bag from the trunk.

"I have an idea," he said.

"What's that?" she said, moving into his arms.

"Stay with me. Just travel with me for the next nine months or so. It will be fun."

"Um, yeah. That won't work right now."

"I know," he said. "But a guy can dream."

"So can a girl," she said. "We'll do this again, Nick. I promise. Maybe in another month. Until then, call me? Text me?"

"Every day," he said.

"Well, you don't have to be extreme," she said. "But often."

"I will," he said. "I miss you already."

"See you later, Nick," she said.

They kissed and hugged one last time, and then Nick watched her walk through the airport doors. He waved one more time, even though he knew she couldn't see him.

Then he got into his car and shifted into gear. Just then, his phone rang. It was Emily.

"Hey Nick," she said. "Great job. Did everyone get to the airport?"

"Just now," he said.

"Well, nice recovery this week. And great photos."

"I've got some more from yesterday to upload. I'll do that in Salt Lake."

"Speaking of Salt Lake," she said. "Try to stay out of trouble there, alright?"

"For sure," he said. "I promised Sandra no more mystery stuff."

"Good," she said. "I like this girl, and I've never even met her. Talk to you later, Nick."

He pulled onto the freeway and hit the cruise control. He almost dialed Sandra's number, but he didn't want to seem foolish. But he had to admit to himself that he was crazy in love with her and would miss having her around.

Just as he had the thought, his phone rang.

"Nick," he said, hitting the green answer button without looking.

"Hi, handsome," Sandra's voice said. "I'm through security already. Can we talk while you drive, and I wait to board?"

"Sure," Nick said, with a smile on his face. And for the next twenty minutes, they talked about nothing specific he could remember. He just relished the sound of her voice.

"They're going to start boarding soon, and I need to use the bathroom first," she said finally.

"Okay," Nick said. "Sandra?"

"Yes?"

"I love you."

"I love you, too," she said. "See you later."

AUTHOR'S NOTE: DEFENESTRATION

Defenestration: The action of throwing someone out of a window. From the Latin *de* meaning 'from', and *fenestra*, meaning 'window'.

The term is thought to have originated from the Defenestration of Prague, an incident that took place in 1419, when the Hussites marched on the new city hall, demanding the release of several Hussite prisoners. The council refused, and someone threw a stone at their leader. So, the protestors stormed the hall and tossed the council members out the window. The crowd below held up spears for them to land on, and those who were not impaled in the fall were quickly killed.

Oddly enough, the same thing happened again in the same city, two hundred years later. This time the combatants were the Bohemians and the Hapsburgs. The Bohemians threw two men from the windows seventy feet up from the ground in Wenceslaus Hall in Prague. The men survived.

Supporters claimed the Virgin Mary had intervened. The real story is that they landed on a convenient pile of dung in the castle moat, which cushioned their fall.

When writing this, a fellow writer and poet, a friend's father, actually shared this poem with me, and graciously let me share it with you. Here it is, with all my thanks to Michael Collings:

> *Four centuries ago this year,*
> *The politicians rose;*
> *Wearied by a war of words*
> *They faced off with their foes.*
>
> *The window, the window,*
> *They threw them out the window;*
> *Wearied by a war of words,*
> *They threw them out the window.*
>
> *As one, they grabbed the Deputies,*
> *Each well-known men of note;*
> *And they, regardless of their pleas,*
> *Were tossed into the moat.*
>
> *The window, the window,*
> *They threw them out the window;*
> *All three, regardless of their pleas,*
> *Were thrown right out the window.*
>
> *The record states they were not harmed*
> *By their precipitous fall—*
> *But with the filth those moats contained,*
> *They must have been appalled.*
>
> *The window, the window,*
> *They threw them out the window;*
> *Into the filth the moat contained,*
> *They threw them out the window.*
>
> *For Thirty Years a war raged on*
> *In nation after nation,*

Triggered in an instant by
A brash defenestration.

The window, the window,
They threw them out the window;
War triggered in an instant when
They threw them out the window.

Thanks for reading! I hope you enjoyed this book as much as I enjoyed writing it.

FACTS ABOUT DENVER

From Troy: The city of Denver is actually a pretty amazing place, as is the state of Colorado. When I was a young man, somewhere around 10-12 years old, I spend a good part of the summer there. My grandfather was in the VA hospital there for some pretty serious surgery, and while my mother and grandmother tended to him, we spent many days in the lobby of that hospital.

Various residents of the city, friends of my grandparents, took us around various places nearby, and I grew to love Colorado.

We also witnessed some pretty traumatic events in and around that hospital, ones that stick with me until this day, including a fall from a window that fortunately the individual survived, in part due to the huge amount of drugs in his system.

My grandfather made it through those surgeries, sans his right leg, lost due to diabetes and blood clots, and I never visited Denver again until I was an adult, and much older.

The city sits a mile above sea level, at 5,280'. This is, oddly, nearly the same elevation as the town I grew up in located in the southeastern portion of Idaho. Nestled in the Rocky Mountains, Denver is surrounded by great skiing and some fabulous activities, like the trains in Leadville, named for the mining that took place in the area.

The Colorado State Capitol, the official name of the building, was created in the 1890'a from Colorado white granite by designer Elijah Meyers, and opened for business in 1894. It became a part of the National Register for Historic Places in 1974, along with other parts of the Denver Civic Center Area. The building sits only slightly higher than the rest of the Denver downtown area, and 15th step bears a sign that declares it is exactly 5,280 feet above sea level.

The interior of the building contains huge amounts of a rare marble found in Colorado known as Rose Onyx. In fact, the marble work in the building consumed the entire known supply, making it invaluable. A major safety upgrade project, like those conducted at many other capitol buildings Nick will visit, started in 2001 and ended in 2009.

The building is on many of the historical and architectural tours given in downtown Denver area, and would certainly have been on the tour Catherine and Gerry took.

Many of the restaurants and places mentioned in the book actually exist, but the names and even locations of some have been changed to fit the story.

All the persons in this book are fictional, but we would like to thank Cheryl for volunteering to be in our story. She's the hotel clerk you see from time to time.

If you want to ever be a part of one of our stories in your hometown or another capital city, feel free to contact us at authors@capitalcitymurders.com.

ABOUT THE AUTHORS

Troy Lambert and Stuart Gustafson are each successful authors in their own rights. As residents of the Great State of Idaho (Troy lives in Meridian, and Stuart is in the capital city of Boise), they have teamed up to bring to you, the reader, this new and exciting series of novelettes **set in each capital city** of the United States of America!

And yes, a total of fifty states means a total of fifty novelettes. Are you ready?

Troy Lambert is a full-time writer and author. Having written over two dozen mysteries and other novels, Troy is well-versed in story creation, and he knows what it takes to make a fictional story real! Troy's hobbies and pastimes (when he's able to break away from the computer) include hiking into the mountains of Southwest Idaho, fishing in a fast-rushing stream, and going for a drive where his mind can work on creating that perfect twist to the book he's currently writing. A native of Idaho Falls, Idaho, Troy and his wife live in Meridian, Idaho. You can find his other works, including his latest book, *Harvested*, at fictionupdates.troylambertwrites.com.

Stuart Gustafson took early retirement in 2007 to spend more time traveling (he's been to 55 countries and 155 cruise ports) and writing (four novels, nine non-fiction books, lots of travel articles). Speaking on cruise ships in many parts of the world has been a great "post-retirement gig," as some have put it. He has leveraged some of the experiences from those travels to insert reality into a few of his mystery novels set in exciting locations around the globe. A native of Southern California, Stuart and his wife live in Boise, Idaho. The majority of his books are available at stuartgustafson.com/books.

THE "CAPITAL CITY MURDERS" SERIES

"Introduction to Nick"

    Book # 1 "Overdoses in Olympia"

    Book #2 "Slaying in Salem"

    Book #3 "Strangled in Sacramento"

    Book #4 "deCapitated in Carson City"

    Book #5 "Buried in Boise"

    "The Wicked West"—a compilation of books 1-5, available in both e-books and print

    Book #6 "Hanging in Helena"

    Book #7 "Branded in Bismarck"

    Book #8 "Parricide in Pierre"

    Book #9 "Carnage in Cheyenne"

    Book #10 "Defenestrated in Denver

All the books in the "Capital City Murders" series are available at www.CapitalCityMurders.com and your favorite e-book seller.

ON TO BEING SILENCED IN SALT LAKE CITY
PROLOGUE — NOT YOUR NORMAL DENTAL VISIT

Elizabeth Gordon, DDS, "Liz" to her friends, stepped out of her rock and glass rainfall shower and looked in the full-length mirror. She twisted her body slightly to the left and then slightly to the right, nodding her head up and down. "Maybe not as slim and tight as in my twenties, but not bad for mid-forties," she said, admiring her fit body. She pulled a plush towel off the bar and quickly dried herself from the warm refreshing shower.

She strolled into her walk-in closet, pulled open a drawer, and pulled out a matching bra and panty set, put them on, and glanced at her reflection in one of the two mirrors in the closet, once again admiring her body. *No slip needed tonight*, she thought as she selected a tight-fitting red dress and slipped it over her head. She wiggled into it as she pulled it down and noted how well it accentuated her curves. She padded back into the bathroom to dry and brush her hair, apply some makeup, and then headed back to the closet for accessories.

Lis opened her watch drawer. She paused for a moment before she selected the slim gold Rolex Datejust watch. She looked at the time. "Almost seven. Kerry should be here soon," she muttered, then picked out a pair of long hammered gold hoop earrings. She looked in the mirror and smiled. "Perfect, just perfect," she said as she tidied up the bathroom and headed for the kitchen.

She lit a couple scented candles, turned on some soft music, and thought about her plans for the evening. *Dinner before or after? Will he even have a clue? No, this will be so easy.*

Liz heard two honks of the horn, and she went to the garage and opened the roll up door closest to the house. Her silver Lexus was normally parked on the far side, but it wasn't there this evening. Kerry Lewis pulled his red Mustang into the familiar spot where he'd parked several times before. He stopped the car, turned off the engine, and got out. Liz pushed the button again and the garage door slid shut. He walked toward her, holding a bottle of wine.

"Hi," she said as she smiled at him.

"Hi," he responded. "Your dress matches my car."

"Two hot, fast machines," she replied as she propped her left hand on her hip.

"Vroom," Kerry replied. "Thanks for the invite," he said as he approached her.

"My pleasure," Liz replied. "All my pleasure," she repeated. "Mmmm, a Pinot Noir," she said as she looked at the wine bottle. "I love Pinot Noir," she said as she leaned forward and kissed him

"I remember," he replied.

Liz smiled, turned around and went in the house, holding the door open for him.

He followed her in and set the wine bottle on the kitchen counter. He looked around and didn't see any sign of dinner preparations. "Was I supposed to get something on the way?"

"Oh, no," she replied. "It's, uh, being delivered later. How about if we have some wine? I'll get the opener," she said as she opened a kitchen drawer, pulled out a cork screw, and handed it to him. Two wine glasses sat ready on the counter.

"Thanks," he said as he sliced off the bottle's foil and uncorked it.

"Love that sound," she said as the cork sounded a sharp "Pop" upon being extracted from the bottle.

"Me, too," he said as he poured wine into each glass. Some

droplets splashed onto the tile counter. "Sorry," he said as he picked up a sponge and wiped them up.

"Oh, that's okay, Kerry. I know it's a little different being here as a dinner guest rather than as a patient. Cheers," she offered as she lifted her glass.

"Ch-cheers," he stuttered as he picked up the other glass and touched it to hers.

"Come on," she said as she led the way to the couch in the living room. "It's more comfortable in here. She held out her left hand for his wine glass as they approached the couch.

He handed his glass to her and sat down as she set both glasses on the long table in front of them.

"Now, let's enjoy this nice wine," she said as she handed him his glass and picked up her own. She took a slow sip. "Mmmm, very good."

"I've had it before," Kerry said as he then took a swallow of his, more of a gulp than a sip.

Their glasses were soon empty. "I'll go get us a refill. You just sit and make yourself comfortable here," Liz said as she got up and took the glasses back into the kitchen.

"Okay," he said as he wiped his sweaty palms on his pants.

Liz grabbed both wine glasses and went back to the kitchen where she re-filled each. She returned to the living room, set the glasses on the table, ran her hands down the sides of her dress, and looked at her watch. "We've got time before dinner gets here. Want to make love?"

"More than an hour?" he asked. "You always booked me for an extra one when I was here for a filling or a checkup."

"That was because I always gave you that shot for extra strength and performance. I have a new shot that works just as well, but we won't need as much time."

Kerry reached forward, picked up his wine glass, and took a big gulp. "How can I refuse an offer like that?" he said as he stood.

Liz led the way down the hallway to her bedroom. It wasn't the first time that he'd been there. She took both wine glasses, set them on the dresser, and stood in front of him. She let her hands drop from his neck to start unbuttoning his shirt as he stood motionless. She finished, and removed it. "You'll like this one better than the ones you've had before," she said as she opened a dresser drawer and pulled out a syringe. She looked at the cloudy substance, phenylethyl benzylglyceride. *It's supposed to numb his senses without inhibiting anything physical. At least that's what I read,* she thought to herself. She poked the needle into his arm and slowly pressed in the plunger.

A few minutes later they were both between the polka dot sheets making love.

When they were done, Liz got out of bed first, dressed and headed for the kitchen with the wine glasses.

Kerry got out of bed, pulled the sheets up to the pillows and dressed. He left the bedroom and walked down the hall to the kitchen where Liz had just finished emptying the wine bottle into the two glasses. "Wow," he said as he approached her.

"You were great; thanks," she said with a sly smile.

"Thank you," he replied. "I'm getting hungry, what about you?" He picked up a wine glass and took a sip.

"We have a little more time before dinner gets here. Would you like to see what I've done in the basement?"

"Why not?"

She led him to the basement door, opened it, flipped on the switch and walked down the stairs.

He followed her down to the patient area where she'd taken him several times.

"Have a seat," she commanded as she pointed to the dental chair.

"A new game?" he asked with a smile on his face as he got into the reclining chair.

"Sort of," she replied as she fastened the leather straps around his ankles first, then around the thighs, followed by his chest, and then individual straps around each arm.

"You're really into this stuff, aren't you?"

Liz pursed her lips. "Shhh, don't talk. Silence is much better."

"You want me to be shilent?" he responded, struggling to form the words.

"Yes, I want you to be silent. Let me help you with that." She then brought two straps around to the front of his forehead and latched them tightly, immobilizing him. She turned around and picked up two clamps from the table tray behind her. "Open wide," she said as she turned back around and inserted the clamps into his opened mouth.

"Ow," he murmured.

"I'm sorry dear," she said sarcastically. "Let me ease that pain for you." She turned back around, picked up the opioid-filled syringe and inserted it into his right shoulder. "You won't feel any pain in a couple minutes." She twisted the clamps to force his mouth open even wider, causing cracks to form where his upper and lower lips met.

Kerry's breathing got heavier as his throat opened wide from the clamps, and she grabbed his tongue with a cold metallic object and raised it toward the roof of his mouth. With one quick snip, she snipped the piece of flesh connecting his tongue to the bottom of his mouth. He tried to resist. *Probably because of the slight jerk he felt,* she thought.

Liz then forced a red PVC pipe cutter into his mouth and put it around his now-free tongue. She squeezed the pipe cutter until it met resistance on his tongue. He tried to jerk his head, but the straps she'd used kept it in firmly in place.

Liz pumped the handle until the sharpened blade sliced its way completely through his tongue. She removed it, and blood flowed out of his mouth and down his chin. She immediately gave him a shot of Keratonin, a clotting agent, where the remnant of Kerry's tongue connected with the back of his mouth. She swabbed the laceration with Alum, dramatically reducing the amount of blood flow. She looked at the pipe cutter and then at his crotch. "Too easy," she muttered. She removed the clamps and straps, got him out of chair, put on gloves, and walked him back upstairs.

Liz picked up her extra garage door opener, put it into her purse, got the keys from his pocket, put him into his car, and drove him to a nearby park. She turned off the lights, put the car in park, and turned off the engine. She pulled his cell phone from his shirt pocket and dialed 9-1-1. "Medical emergency," was all she said as she opened the car door, put the phone on the seat, and left.

"What kind of emergency?" was faintly heard from Kerry's phone as Liz briskly walked to her car parked around the block. She drove home, went downstairs, and cleaned the area back to its spotless state. She put everything, including the gloves she used to drive his car, into a trash bag and took it out to the garbage can.

Back in the kitchen, Liz dialed the local Thai restaurant. "Yes, I'd like to place an order for delivery," she said.

www.ingramcontent.com/pod-product-compliance
Lightning Source LLC
Chambersburg PA
CBHW050856130726
47900CB00013B/62